Mary Balogh is a *New York Times* bestselling author. A former teacher, she grew up in Wales and now lives in London.

Also by Mary Balogh

SIMPLY LOVE

Simply Unforgettable

Mary Balogh

PIATKUS

PIATKUS

First published in Great Britain in 2006 by Piatkus Books
This paperback edition published in 2006 by Piatkus Books
First published in the United States in 2005 by
Bantam Dell, a division of Random House Inc.

A CIP catalogue record for this book
is available from the British Library

ISBN 978-0-7499-3688-4

Printed and bound in Great Britain by
Clays Ltd, St Ives plc

Piatkus Books
An imprint of
Little, Brown Book Group
100 Victoria Embankment
London EC4Y 0DY

An Hachette Livre UK Company
www.hachettelivre.co.uk

www.piatkus.co.uk

Simply Unforgettable

It never snowed for Christmas. It always snowed—if it snowed at all—before Christmas, when people were trying to travel to family gatherings or house parties, or long after Christmas, when it was a mere nuisance to people trying to go about the business of their everyday lives. It never snowed actually *on* Christmas, when it would have added a picturesque quality and some magic to the celebrations.

Such was the sad reality of living in England.

This year had been no exception. The skies had remained stubbornly gray and heavy with the promise of something dire all over the holiday, and the weather had been chilly and blustery and really not very pleasant at all. But the ground had remained obstinately bare and as drab as the sky.

It had been a rather dreary Christmas, if the truth were told.

Frances Allard, who had made the long day's journey from Bath, where she taught at Miss Martin's School for Girls on Sutton and Daniel streets, in order to spend the holiday with her two great-aunts near the village of Mickledean in Somersetshire, had looked forward to being in rural surroundings. She had dreamed of taking long walks in the crisp winter countryside, blue skies overhead, or else of wading to church and the Assembly Rooms through a soft white fall of snow.

But the wind and the cold devoid of sunshine had forced her to curtail the few walks she had undertaken, and the Assembly Rooms had remained firmly closed, everyone having been content, it seemed, to spend Christmas with family and friends this year rather than with all their neighbors at a communal party or ball.

Frances would have been lying to herself if she had not admitted to feeling just a little disappointment.

Miss Gertrude Driscoll and her widowed sister, Mrs. Martha Melford, Frances's great-aunts, who lived at the dower house in the park of Wimford Grange, had been invited to join Baron Clifton's family at the big house on Christmas Day, the baron being their great-nephew and therefore a cousin of some remove to Frances. Frances had been invited too, of course. They had also all been invited to a few other private parties in the neighborhood. But the great-aunts had sent back polite refusals to them all, declaring themselves too cozy in their own house to venture outdoors in such inclement weather and too contented with the coveted company of their great-niece to bother with any invitations. They could, after all, visit their great-nephew and his family and their neighbors any day of the year. Besides, Great-Aunt Gertrude had fancied that she was coming down with something, though she had displayed no clearly discernible symptoms, and dared not stray too far from the fireside of her own home.

Frances's wishes had not been consulted.

Only when the holiday was over and they were hugging her and shedding a few tears over her and kissing her good-bye before she stepped up into their rather rickety private carriage, which they had insisted upon sending with her though it did not usually venture beyond a five-mile radius around the village, did it occur to her great-aunts that maybe they had been selfish in remaining at home all over the holiday and ought to have remembered that dear Frances was only three-and-twenty and would perhaps have enjoyed a party or two and the company of other young people to enliven the tedium of a Christmas spent entirely with two old ladies.

She had hugged them in return and shed a few tears of her own and assured them—almost truthfully—that they were all she had needed to make Christmas a wondrously happy occasion after a long term at school, though actually it had been more than one term. She had remained at the school all through last summer, since Miss Martin took in charity girls and it was always necessary to provide for their care and entertainment through the various holidays—and Frances had had nowhere particular to go at the time.

Christmas had, then, been a disappointingly dull holiday. But she really had enjoyed the quiet after the constantly busy bustle of school life. And she was extremely fond of her great-aunts, who had opened their arms and their hearts to her from the moment of her arrival in England as a motherless baby with a French émigré father who had been fleeing the Reign of Terror. She had no memory of that time, of course, but she knew that the aunts would have brought her into the country to live with them if Papa had chosen to let her go. But he had not. He had kept her with him in London, surrounding her with nurses and governesses and singing masters, and lavishing upon her all that money could buy for her comfort and pleasure—and oceans of love besides. She had had a happy, privileged, secure childhood and girlhood—until her father's sudden death when she was only eighteen.

But her aunts had had some role to play in her growing years. They had brought her into the country for holidays and had occasionally gone to London to take her about and buy her gifts and feed her ices and other treats. And ever since she had learned to read and write she had exchanged monthly letters with them. She was inordinately fond of them. It really had been lovely to spend Christmas in their company.

There had been no snow to enliven her Christmas, then.

There *was* snow, however—and plenty of it—soon after.

It began when the carriage was no more than eight or ten miles from Mickledean, and Frances did consider knocking on the roof panel and suggesting to the elderly coachman that they turn around and go back. But it was not a heavy snow, and she did not really want to delay her journey. It looked more like a white rain for all of the hour after it began. But inevitably—when it really was too late to turn back—the flakes became larger and thicker, and in an alarmingly short time the countryside, which had been looking as if it were rimed with heavy frost rather than with snow itself, began to disappear under a thickening blanket of white.

The carriage moved steadily onward, and Frances assured herself that it was foolish to be nervous, that the road was probably perfectly safe for travel, especially at the plodding speed to which Thomas was keeping the horses. Soon the snow would stop falling and begin to melt, as was always the way with snow in England.

She concentrated her thoughts on the term ahead, planning which pieces of music she would choose for the senior madrigal choir to sing. Something bright and brilliant and Elizabethan, she thought. She wondered if she dared choose something in five parts. The girls had mastered three-part singing and were doing rather well at four-part pieces, though they did sometimes break off in the middle of a phrase to collapse in laughter as they got hopelessly entangled in complex harmonies.

Frances smiled at the thought. She usually laughed with them. It was better—and ultimately more productive—than weeping.

Maybe they would *try* five parts.

Within another half hour, it was no longer possible to see anything but unrelieved white in any direction—and no longer possible to concentrate upon thoughts of school or anything else. And the snow was still falling so thickly that it dazzled the eyes and made it hard to see any great distance from the windows even if there had been anything to see. When she pressed the side of her face against the glass in order to look ahead, she could not even distinguish the road from the ditches or the fields beyond. And there did not even seem to be any hedgerows on this particular stretch that might have provided some sort of dark border to signify where the road was.

Panic clawed at her stomach.

Could Thomas see the road from his higher perch on the box? But the snow must be blowing into his eyes and half blinding him. And he must be twice as cold as she was. She pressed her hands deeper into the fur muff that Great-Aunt Martha had given her for Christmas. She would pay a fortune for a hot cup of tea, she thought.

So much for wishing for snow. What sage was it who had once said that one should beware of what one wished for lest the wish be granted?

She sat back in her seat, determined to trust Thomas to find the way. After all, he had been her great-aunts' coachman forever and ever, or at least for as far back as she could remember, and she had never heard of his being involved in any sort of accident. But she thought wistfully of the cozy dower house she had left behind and of the bustling school that was her destination. Claudia Martin would be expecting her today. Anne Jewell and Susanna Osbourne, the other resident teachers, would be watching for her arrival. They would all spend the evening together in Claudia's private sitting room, seated cozily about the fire, drinking tea and exchanging reminiscences of Christmas. She would be able to give them a graphic account of the snowstorm through which she had traveled. She would embellish it and exaggerate the danger and her fears and have them all laughing.

But she was not laughing yet.

And suddenly laughter was as far from her thoughts as flying to the moon would be. The carriage slowed and rocked and slithered, and Frances jerked one hand free of her muff and grabbed for the worn leather strap above her head, convinced that they were about to tip right over at any moment. She waited to see her life flash before her eyes, and mumbled the opening words of the Lord's Prayer rather than scream and startle Thomas into losing the last vestiges of his control. The sound of the horses' hooves seemed deafening even though they were moving over snow and should have been silent. Thomas was shouting enough for ten men.

And then, looking out through the window nearest her rather than clench her eyes tightly shut and not even see the end approaching, she actually *saw* the horses, and instead of being up ahead pulling the carriage, they were drawing alongside her window and then forging ahead.

She gripped the strap even more tightly and leaned forward. Those were not *her* horses. Gracious heaven, someone was *overtaking* them—in *these* weather conditions.

The box of the overtaking carriage came into view with its coachman looking rather like a hunchbacked snowman bent over the ribbons and spewing hot abuse from his mouth—presumably at poor Thomas.

And then the carriage passed in a flash of blue, and Frances had the merest glimpse of a gentleman with many capes to his greatcoat and a tall beaver hat on his head. He looked back at her with one eyebrow cocked and an expression of supercilious contempt on his face.

He dared to be contemptuous of *her*?

Within moments the blue carriage was past, her own rocked and slithered some more, and then it appeared to right itself before continuing on its slow, plodding way.

Frances's fears were replaced by a hot fury. She seethed with it. Of all the reckless, inconsiderate, suicidal, homicidal, dangerous, *stupid* things to do! Goodness gracious, even if she pressed her nose to the window she could not see more than five yards distant, and the falling snow hampered vision even within that five yards. Yet that hunchbacked, foul-mouthed coachman and that contemptuous gentleman with his arrogant eyebrow were in such a hurry that they would endanger life and limb—her own and Thomas's as well as their own—in order to *overtake*?

But now that the excitement was over, she was suddenly aware again of being all alone in an ocean of whiteness. She felt panic contract her stomach muscles once more and sat back, deliberately letting go of the strap and folding her hands neatly inside her muff again. Panic would get her nowhere. It was altogether more probable that Thomas would get her somewhere.

Poor Thomas. He would be ready for something hot to drink—or more probably something strong *and* hot—when they arrived at that somewhere. He was by no means a young man.

With the fingers of her right hand she picked out the melody of a William Byrd madrigal on the back of her left hand, as if it were the keyboard of a pianoforte. She hummed the tune aloud.

And then she could feel the carriage rocking and slithering again and grasped for the strap once more. She looked out and ahead, not really expecting to see anything, but actually she could see a dark shape, which appeared to be blocking the way ahead. In one glimpse of near-clarity between snowflakes she saw that it was a carriage and horses. She even thought it might be a blue carriage.

But though the horses pulling her own had drawn to a halt, the carriage itself did not immediately follow suit. It swayed slightly to the left, righted itself, and then slithered more than slightly to the right—and this time it kept going until it reached what must have been the edge of the road, where one wheel caught on something. The conveyance performed a neat half-pirouette and slid gently backward and downward until its back wheels were nestled deep in a snowbank.

Frances, tipped backward and staring at the opposite seat, which was suddenly half above her, could see nothing but solid snow out of the windows on both sides.

And if this was not the outside of enough, she thought with ominous calm, then she did not know what was.

She was aware of a great clamor from somewhere—horses snorting and whinnying, men shouting.

Before she could collect herself sufficiently to extricate herself from her snowy cocoon, the door opened from the outside—not without some considerable assistance from male muscles and shocking male profanities—and an arm and hand clad in a thick and expensive greatcoat and a fine leather glove reached inside to assist her. It was obvious to her that the arm did not belong to Thomas. Neither did the face at the end of it—hazel-eyed, square-jawed, irritated, and frowning.

It was a face Frances had seen briefly less than ten minutes ago.

It was a face—and a person—against whom she had conceived a considerable hostility.

She slapped her hand onto his without a word, intending to use it to assist herself to alight with as much dignity as she could muster. But he hoisted her out from her awkward position as if she were a sack of meal and deposited her on the road, where her half-boots immediately sank out of sight beneath several inches of snow. She could feel all the ferocity of the cold wind and the full onslaught of the snow falling from the sky.

One was supposed to see red when one was furious. But she saw only white.

"You, sir," she said above the noise of the horses and of Thomas and the hunchbacked snowman exchanging vigorous and colorful abuse of each other, "deserve to be hanged, drawn, and quartered. You deserve to be flayed alive. You deserve to be boiled in oil."

The eyebrow that had already offended her once rose again. So did the other.

"And you, ma'am," he said in clipped tones that matched the expression on his face, "deserve to be locked up in a dark dungeon as a public nuisance for venturing out onto the king's highway in such an old boat. It is a veritable fossil. Any museum would reject it as far too ancient a vehicle to be of any interest to its clientele."

"And its age and the caution of my driver give you the right to endanger several lives by overtaking it in such appalling conditions?" she asked rhetorically, toe to toe with him though none of their toes were visible above the snow. "Perhaps, sir, someone ought to relate to you the story of the tortoise and the hare."

"Meaning?" He dropped both eyebrows and then cocked just the original one.

"Your reckless speed has brought you to grief," she said, jabbing a finger in the direction of the blue carriage, which completely blocked the road ahead—though it did appear to be *on* the road, she saw when she looked directly at it. "You are no farther ahead after all."

"If you will use your eyes for looking instead of just flashing fire and brimstone, ma'am," he said, "you will see that we have come to a bend in the road, and that my coachman—and I too until I was interrupted by your coachman's ineptitude in drawing from a crawl to a complete halt—is clearing a drift of snow so that my hare may proceed on its way. Your tortoise, on the other hand, is deep in a snowdrift and will be going nowhere for some time to come. Certainly not today."

She looked over her shoulder. It was suddenly, sickeningly obvious that he was right. Only the front part of the carriage was even visible, and that was pointing half at the sky.

"And so who is likely to win the race?" he asked her.

What on earth was she going to *do*? Her feet were wet, her cloak was matted with snow about the hem, she was being heavily snowed upon, she was cold, and she was miserable. She was also frightened.

And furious.

"And whose fault is all this?" she asked him. "If *you* had not been springing your horses, *we* would not now be in a snowbank."

"Springing the horses." He looked at her with incredulity mingled with contempt and called over his shoulder. "Peters! I have it on expert authority that you were springing the horses when we overtook this ancient relic. I have told and told you not to spring the horses during a snowstorm. You are dismissed."

"Give me a moment to finish digging through this drift, guv, and I'll walk off into the sunset," the coachman called back. "If someone will just tell me which direction that is."

"You had better not do it anyway," the gentleman said. "I would have to drive the carriage myself. You are rehired."

"I'll think about it, guv," the coachman called. "There! That about does it."

Thomas meanwhile was busy releasing the horses from their useless burden.

"If your carriage had been moving at any speed above an almost imperceptible crawl, ma'am," the gentleman said, turning his attention back to Frances, "it would not have posed a reckless endangerment to serious, responsible travelers who would really prefer to get somewhere by the end of a day instead of spending eternity on one stretch of road."

Frances glared at him. She would bet a month's salary that not one whisper of cold could penetrate that greatcoat he wore, with its dozen capes, or that one speck of snow had found its way down inside his top boots.

"Ready to move on, then, guv," his coachman called, "unless you prefer to stand admiring the scenery for the next hour or so."

"Where is your maid?" The gentleman's eyes narrowed.

"I have none," she said. "That should be perfectly obvious. I am alone."

She was aware of his eyes sweeping over her from head to foot— or to just below the knee anyway. She was dressed in clothes that were perfectly good and serviceable for her return to school, though it would be quite obvious to such a fashionable gentleman, of course, that they were neither expensive nor modish. She glared back at him.

"You are going to have to come along with me," he said ungraciously.

"I most certainly will not!"

"Very well, then," he said, turning away, "you may remain here in virtuous isolation."

She looked about her, and this time panic assaulted her knees as well as her stomach, and she almost sank into the snow never to be heard from again.

"Where are we?" she asked. "Do you have any idea?"

"Somewhere in Somersetshire," he said. "Apart from that I have not the foggiest notion, but most roads, I have learned from past experience, lead *somewhere* eventually. This is your last chance, ma'am. Do you wish to explore the great unknown in my fiendish company, or would you prefer to perish alone here?"

It irked her beyond words that really she had no choice.

The two coachmen were exchanging words again, she was aware—none too gentle words either.

"Take an hour or two in which to decide," the gentleman said with heavy irony, cocking that eyebrow again. "I am in no hurry."

"What about Thomas?" she asked.

"Thomas being the man in the moon?" he asked. "Or your coachman, perhaps? He will bring the horses and follow us."

"Very well, then," she said, glowering at him and then pressing her lips together.

He strode ahead of her to the blue carriage, sending up showers of snow as he went. Frances picked her way more cautiously after him, trying to set her feet in the ruts made by the wheels.

What a coil this was!

He offered his hand again to help her up into the carriage. It was a wonderfully new carriage, she saw resentfully, with plush upholstered seats. As soon as she sat on one of them she sank into it and realized that it would offer marvelous comfort even through a long journey. It also felt almost warm in contrast with the raw elements outside.

"There are two bricks on the floor, both of them still somewhat warm," the gentleman told her from the doorway. "Set your feet on one of them and cover yourself with one of the lap robes. I will see about having your belongings transferred from your carriage to mine."

The words themselves might have seemed both kind and considerate. But his clipped tone belied that possible impression, as did the firmness with which he slammed the door shut. Frances nevertheless did as he had suggested. Her teeth were literally chattering. Her fingers might have felt as if they were about to fall off if she could just feel them at all—she had abandoned her muff inside her own carriage.

How long was she going to have to endure this insufferable situation? she wondered. She was not in the habit of hating or even disliking people on sight. But the thought of spending even half an hour in close company with that arrogant, bad-tempered, sneering, contemptuous gentleman was singularly unappealing. Just the thought of him made her bristle.

Would she be able to find some other mode of travel from the first village they came to? A stagecoach, perhaps? But even as the thought flashed through her mind, she realized the absurdity of it. They would be fortunate to reach any village. Was she expecting that if they did, there would be no trace of snow there?

She was going to be stranded somewhere overnight—without any female companion and without a great deal of money since she had refused what her great-aunts had tried to press upon her. She would be fortunate if that somewhere did not turn out to be this carriage.

The very thought was enough to make her gasp for air.

But it was a distinct possibility. It had seemed to her eyes just a couple of minutes ago that the road was all but invisible.

She countered panic this time by setting her feet neatly side by side on the slightly warm brick and clasping her hands loosely in her lap.

She would trust to the skills of the strange, impertinent Peters, who had turned out not to be hunchbacked after all.

Now *this* would be an adventure with which to regale her friends when she finally reached Bath, she thought. Perhaps if she looked more closely at him, the gentleman would even turn out to be describable as tall, dark, and handsome—the proverbial knight in shining armor, in fact. *That* would have Susanna's eyes popping out of her head and Anne's eyes softening with a romantic glow. And it would have Claudia pursing her lips and looking suspicious.

But, oh, dear, it was going to be hard to find any humor or any romance in this situation, even when she looked back on it from the safety of the school.

2

His mother had warned him that it would snow before the day was out. So had his sisters. So had his grandfather.

So indeed had his own common sense.

But since he rarely listened to advice—especially when offered by his family—and rarely heeded the dictates of common sense, here he was in the midst of a snowfall to end snowfalls and looking forward with less than eager zeal to spending the night at some obscure country inn in the middle of nowhere. At least he *hoped* he would spend it at some inn rather than in a hovel or—worse yet—inside his carriage.

And he had been in a black mood even before this journey began!

He looked hard at his woman passenger after he had climbed inside the carriage with her, everything that needed tending to having been accomplished. She was huddled beneath one of the woolen lap robes, the muff he had rescued from the other carriage and tossed in a couple of minutes ago under there with her, and he could see that her feet were resting on one of the bricks. *Huddled* was perhaps the wrong word to describe her posture, though. She was straight-backed and rigid with hostility and determined dignity and injured virtue. She did not even turn her head to look at him.

Just like a dried-up prune, he thought. All he could see of her face around the brim of her hideous brown bonnet was the reddened tip of her nose. It was only surprising that it was not quivering with indignation—as if the predicament in which she found herself were *his* fault.

"Lucius Marshall at your service," he said none too graciously.

He thought for a moment that she was not going to return the compliment, and he seriously considered knocking on the roof panel for the carriage to stop again so that he could join Peters up on the box. Better to be attacked by snow outside than frozen by an icicle inside.

"Frances Allard," she said.

"It is to be hoped, Miss Allard," he said, purely for the sake of making conversation, "that the landlord of the next inn we come to will have a full larder. I do believe I am going to be able to do justice to a beef pie and potatoes and vegetables and a tankard of ale, not to mention a good suet pudding and custard with which to finish off the meal. Make that several tankards of ale. How about you?"

"A cup of tea is all I crave," she said.

He might have guessed it. But, good Lord—a cup of tea! And doubtless her knitting with which to occupy her hands between sips.

"What is your destination?" he asked.

"Bath," she said. "And yours?"

"Hampshire," he said. "I expected to spend a night on the road, but I had hoped it would be somewhat closer to my destination than this. No matter, though. I would not have had the pleasure of making your acquaintance or you mine if the unexpected had not happened."

She turned her head then and looked steadily at him. It was quite obvious to him even before she spoke that she could recognize irony when she heard it.

"I believe, Mr. Marshall," she said, "I could have lived quite happily without any of the three of those experiences."

Tit for tat. Touché.

Now that he had more leisure to look at her, he was surprised to realize that she was a great deal younger than he had thought earlier. His impression when his carriage passed hers and again on the road outside had been of a thin, dark lady of middle years. But he had been mistaken. Now that she had stopped frowning and grimacing and squinting against the glare of the snow, he could see that she was only perhaps in her middle twenties. She was almost certainly younger than his own twenty-eight years.

She was a shrew, nevertheless.

And she *was* thin. Or perhaps she was only very slender—it was hard to tell through her shapeless winter cloak. But her wrists were narrow and her fingers long and slim—he had noticed them when she took the muff from his hand. Her face was narrow too, with high cheekbones, her complexion slightly olive-hued, apart from the red-tipped nose. Put together with her very dark eyes, lashes, and hair, her face invited the conclusion that she had some foreign blood flowing through her veins—Italian, perhaps, Mediterranean certainly. That fact would account for her temper. Beneath her bonnet he could see the beginnings of a severe center part with smooth bands of hair combed to either side and disappearing beneath the bonnet brim.

She looked like someone's governess. Heaven help her poor pupil.

"I suppose," he said, "you were warned not to travel today?"

"I was not," she said. "I hoped for snow all over Christmas and was convinced it would come. By today I had stopped looking for it. So of course it came."

She was not, it seemed, in the mood for further conversation. She turned her face firmly to the front again, leaving him no more than the tip of her nose to admire, and he felt no obligation—or inclination—to continue talking himself.

At least if all this had had to happen fate might have provided him with a blond, blue-eyed, dimpled, wilting damsel in distress! Life sometimes seemed quite unfair. It had been seeming that way a great deal lately.

He turned his attention back to the cause of the black mood that had hung over him like a dark cloud all over Christmas.

His grandfather was dying. Oh, he was not exactly at his last gasp or even languishing on his deathbed, and he had made light of the verdict his army of London physicians had passed on him when he had gone to consult them in early December. But the fact of the matter was that they had told him his heart was fast failing, that there was nothing any of them could do to heal it.

"It is old and ready to be turned in for a new one," his grandfather had said with a gruff laugh after the news had been forced out of him and his daughter-in-law and granddaughters were sniffling and look-ing tragic and Lucius was standing deliberately in the shadows of the drawing room, frowning ferociously lest he show an emotion that would have embarrassed himself and everyone else in the room. "Like the rest of me."

No one had been amused except the old man himself.

"What the old sawbones meant," he had added irreverently, "was that I had better get my affairs in order and prepare to meet my maker any day now."

Lucius had not had a great deal to do with his grandfather or the rest of his family during the past ten years, having been too busy living the life of an idle man about town. He even rented rooms on St. James's Street in London rather than live at Marshall House, the fam-ily home on Cavendish Square, where his mother and sisters usually took up residence during the London Season.

But the shocking news had made him realize how much he actu-ally loved his grandfather—the Earl of Edgecombe of Barclay Court in Somersetshire. And with the realization had come the knowledge that he loved all this family, but that it had taken something like this to make him aware of how he had neglected them.

Even his guilt and grief would have been quite sufficient to cast a deep gloom over his Christmas. But there had been more than that.

He just happened to be the earl's heir. He was Lucius Marshall, Viscount Sinclair.

Not that that in itself was a gloomy fact. He would not have been quite normal if he had hated the thought of inheriting Barclay, where he had grown up, and Cleve Abbey in Hampshire, where he now lived—when he was not in London or somewhere else with his friends—and the other properties and the vast fortune that went with them, even though they must come at the expense of his grandfather's life. And he did not mind the political obligations that a seat in the House of Lords would place upon his shoulders when the time came. After all, ever since the death of his father years ago he had known that if life followed its natural course he would one day inherit, and he had educated and prepared himself. Besides, even an idle life of pleasure could pall after a time. Being actually engaged in politics would give his life a more positive, active direction.

No, what he *really* minded was that, in the opinion of his mother, his married sister and possibly her husband too—though one could never be quite sure with Tait—his three unmarried sisters, and his grandfather, a man who was soon to become an earl also needed even sooner to become a married man. In other words, an earl needed a countess.

Lucius needed a bride.

It had been as plain as the noses on all their faces, it seemed, except his. Though even that was questionable. He knew all about duty even if he had spent a large part of his life ignoring and even running from it. But up until now he had been free to do as he pleased. No one had even objected too loudly to his way of life. Normal young men were expected to sow wild oats, provided they did not descend too deeply into vice, and he had done what was expected of him.

But now everything was to change. And if one was to be philosophical about it, one would have to admit that duty caught up with most young men sooner or later—it was the nature of life. It had caught up with him now.

His relatives had all separately expostulated on the theme throughout the holiday whenever one, or sometimes two, of them could maneuver him into what they were all pleased to describe as a comfortable coze.

He had enjoyed more comfortable cozes over Christmas than ever in his life before—or in his life to come, he sincerely hoped.

The consensus was, of course, that he needed a bride without delay.

A perfect bride, if there were such a paragon available—and apparently there was.

Portia Hunt was far and away the most favored candidate, since it was next to impossible to find any imperfection in her.

She had remained single to the advanced age of twenty-three, his mother explained, because she fully expected to be his viscountess one day—and his countess eventually, of course. And the mother of a future earl.

She would make him an admirable wife, Margaret, Lady Tait, Lucius's older sister, assured him, because she was mature and steady and had all the accomplishments a future countess would need.

She was still a diamond of the first water, Caroline and Emily, his younger sisters, pointed out—quite correctly, as it happened, even if they did choose to express themselves in clichés. There was no one more beautiful, more elegant, more refined, more accomplished, than Portia.

Miss Portia Hunt was the daughter of Baron and Lady Balderston and the granddaughter of the Marquess of Godsworthy, his grandfather reminded him—Godsworthy was one of his oldest and closest friends. It would be an eligible and highly desirable alliance—*not* that he was trying to put undue pressure on his grandson.

"Your choice of bride must be yours alone, Lucius," he had said. "But if there is no one else you fancy, you might seriously consider Miss Hunt. It would do my heart good to see you wed to her before I die."

No undue pressure, indeed!

Only Amy, his youngest sister, had spoken up with a dissenting voice, though only on the question of the candidate for perfect bride, not on the necessity of his finding such a creature somewhere within the next few months.

"Don't do it, Luce," she had said when they were out riding alone together one day. "Miss Hunt is so very *tedious*. She advised Mama just last summer not to bring me out this year even though I will be eighteen in June, just because Emily's broken arm prevented *her* from coming out last year and so her turn was delayed. Miss Hunt might have spoken up for me since she intends to marry you and become my sister-in-law, but she did not, and then she smiled that very patronizing smile of hers and assured me that I would be glad next year when the focus of family attention will be on me alone."

The trouble was that he had known Portia forever—her family had frequently come to stay at Barclay Court, and sometimes, when his grandparents had gone to visit the Marquess of Godsworthy, they had taken Lucius with them, and as like as not the Balderstons would be there too with their daughter. The desire of both families that they would eventually make a match of it had always been quite evident. And while he had never actively encouraged Portia after her come-out to sacrifice all other offers in favor of waiting for him to come to the point, he had never actively discouraged her, either. Since he was not of a romantical turn of mind and had always known that he was going to have to marry one day, he had assumed that probably he would end up married to her. But knowing that as a vague sort of future probability was altogether different from being confronted now with the expectation that it was actually to happen—and soon.

Indeed, a vague sort of panic had assailed him at frequent intervals all over the holiday. It happened particularly when he tried to picture himself in bed with Portia. Good Lord! She would doubtless expect him to watch his manners.

And yet another small fact that had darkened his mood even further was that he had distinctly heard himself promise his grandfather—it had happened when they were sitting together in the library on Christmas evening after everyone else had retired for the night, and a few glasses from the wassail bowl had mellowed his senses and made him really quite maudlin—that he would look seriously about him this coming spring during the Season and choose a bride and marry her before the summer was out.

He had not exactly promised to marry Portia Hunt, but her name had inevitably come up.

"Miss Hunt will be happy to see you in town this year," his grandfather had said—which was a strange thing really as Lucius was *always* in town. But what the old man had meant, of course, was that Portia would be happy to see him dancing attendance on her at all the balls and routs and other faradiddle of social events that he normally avoided as he would the plague.

He was a doomed man. There was no point in even trying to deny it. His days as a free—as a *carefree*—man about town were numbered. Ever since just before Christmas he had felt the noose tightening ever more firmly about his neck.

"That coachman of yours deserves to be led in front of a firing squad," Miss Frances Allard, that charmingly gentle lady, said suddenly and sharply, and at the same moment her hand clamped like a vise about Lucius's sleeve. "He is going *too fast* again."

The carriage was indeed slithering and sliding as it plowed its way through the heavy snow. Peters, Lucius thought, was probably enjoying himself more than he had in many a long day.

"I daresay you *would* say that," he said, "since you have your own coachman trained to proceed at about half the walking speed of a gouty octogenarian. But what have we here?"

He peered out through the window and saw that the slithering had been occasioned by the fact that the carriage was being drawn to a halt. They had arrived at what appeared to be an inn, though it was a decidedly poor specimen of its type if this first glimpse of it was anything to judge by. It looked more as if it might be a community center for the drinkers of the village that must be close by than a stopping place for respectable travelers, but, as the old adage went, beggars could not be choosers.

The inn also looked somewhat deserted. No one had cleared any snow away from the door. The stables to the back of the building were shut up. No light flickered behind any of the windows. No reassuring plume of smoke was billowing from the chimney.

It was something of a relief, then, when the door opened a crack after Peters had yelled something unintelligible, and a head complete with unshaven jaws and chin and a voluminous nightcap—in the middle of the afternoon—peered out and bellowed something back.

"Time to wade into the fray, I believe," Lucius muttered, opening the door and jumping out into the knee-deep snow. "What is the problem, fellow?"

He interrupted Peters, who was in the process of informing the man of his startling and quite uncomplimentary pedigree from his perch on the box of the carriage.

"Parker and his missus has gone away and not come back yet," the man shouted. "You can't stop here."

Peters began to give his unbidden opinion on the absent Parkers and on unshaven, bad-mannered yokels, but Lucius held up a staying hand.

"Tell me that there is another inn within five hundred yards of this one," he said.

"Well, there ain't, but that ain't my problem," the man said, making as if to shut the door again.

"Then I am afraid," Lucius said, "that you have guests for the night, my fine fellow. I suggest that you get dressed and pull your boots on unless you prefer to do some work as you are. There is baggage to carry inside and horses to attend with more on the way. Look lively now."

He turned back to hand down Miss Allard.

"It is a relief at least," she said, "to see your ill humor turned upon someone else."

"Do not try me, ma'am," he warned. "And you had better set your arm about my shoulders. I'll carry you inside since you did not have sense enough this morning to don proper boots."

She favored him with one of her shrewish glares, and it seemed to him that this time the reddened tip of her nose did indeed quiver.

"Thank you, Mr. Marshall," she said, "but I shall walk inside on my own two feet."

"Suit yourself," he told her with a shrug and had the great satisfaction of watching her jump down from the carriage without waiting for the steps to be set down and sinking almost to her knees in snow.

It was very hard, he observed with pursed lips, to stalk with dignity from a carriage to a building several yards distant through a foot or more of snow, though she did attempt it. She ended up having to wade, though, and flail her arms in order to avoid falling after one inelegant skid just before she reached the door, which the nightcapped occupant of the inn had left open.

Lucius grinned with grim amusement at her back.

"We picked up a right one there, guv," Peters commented.

"You will keep a civil tongue in your head when referring to any lady in my hearing," Lucius said, bending a stern gaze on him.

"Right you are, guv." Peters jumped down into the snow, looking quite uncowed by the reproof.

"It looks as if I may indeed have my ale," Mr. Marshall said. "And it looks as if you may have your tea if we can get a fire going and if there is tea hidden away somewhere in the kitchen. But I despair of my beef pie—and my suet pudding."

They were standing in the middle of a shabby, cheerless taproom, which felt no warmer than the carriage, since there was no fire burning in the hearth. The servant who had opened the door to them and then not wanted to allow them inside despite the inclement weather came lumbering in with Frances's portmanteau and deposited it on the floor just inside the door together with large clumps of snow.

"I don't know what Parker and the missus will have to say when they hears about this," he muttered darkly.

"Doubtless they will hail you as a hero for hauling in extra business and double your wages," Mr. Marshall told him. "You have been left here all alone over the holiday?"

"I have," the man said, "though they didn't leave till the day after Boxing Day and they are supposed to be back tomorrow. They give me strict orders not to let no one in here while they was gone. I don't know about no double wages, but I do know about missus's tongue. You can't stay here the night and that's flat."

"Your name?" Mr. Marshall asked.

"Wally."

"Wally, *sir*," Mr. Marshall said.

"Wally, *sir*," the man repeated sullenly. "You can't stay here, sir. The rooms ain't ready and there ain't no fires and there ain't no cook here to cook no victuals."

All that was painfully apparent to Frances, who was about as deeply sunk into misery as it was possible to be. Her only consolation—the *only* one—was that she was at least alive and had solid ground beneath her feet.

"I see that a fire is ready laid in the hearth here," Mr. Marshall said. "You may light it while I go outside to bring in the rest of the baggage. Though first you will provide the lady with a shawl or blanket so that she may remain moderately warm until the fire catches. And then you will see about getting two rooms ready. As for food—"

"I will step into the kitchen myself to reconnoiter," Frances said. "I do not need to be treated like a delicate burden. I am no such thing. When you have finished lighting the fire in here, Wally, you may come and help me find what I will need to produce some sort of meal that will satisfy five people, yourself included."

Mr. Marshall looked at her with both eyebrows raised.

"You can cook?" he asked.

"I do need food and utensils and a stove if I am to succeed," she told him. "But I have been known to boil a kettle without causing the water to turn lumpy."

For the merest moment she thought that the gleam in his eyes might be amusement.

"That was *beef pie* in case you did not hear it the first time," he said, "with plenty of onions and gravy—without lumps."

"You may have to settle for a poached egg," she said, "*if* there are any eggs."

"At the moment," he said, "that sounds like a worthy substitute."

"There are eggs," Wally said, his voice still sullen as he knelt to his task of lighting the fire in the taproom hearth. "They are supposed to be for me, but I don't know what to do with them."

"One would hope, then," Mr. Marshall said, "that Miss Allard does know and is not merely indulging in idle boasting when she promises poached eggs."

Frances did not bother to reply. She pushed open the door that she guessed led to the kitchen while he went back out into the snow to help his coachman unload the carriage.

The building was chilly and cheerless. The windows were small and let in very little light even though there was so much whiteness outside. Her feet inside her boots were wet and cold. The inn was not dirty, but neither was it sparkling clean. She dared not take off either her cloak or her bonnet lest she freeze. There was no one to see to her needs except for one slovenly, lazy serving man. There was no one to prepare a hot meal—or even a cold one for that matter. And she was alone here with one bad-tempered, ill-mannered gentleman and three crotchety menservants.

The situation was decidedly grim.

She was expected back at the school today. The girls would be returning for the new term the day after tomorrow. There was much work to do before then if she was to have her classes all ready for the following morning—she had deliberately not worked over Christmas. There was a pile of French essays by the senior class waiting to be marked and an even larger pile of stories—in English—from the junior girls.

This whole turn of events with its resulting delay was more than grim. It was a total disaster.

But as Frances first looked about the kitchen and then explored tentatively and then more boldly in drawers and cupboards and pantry, and finally went in search of Wally and ordered him into the kitchen to clean out the ashes in the large grate and build another fire and light it, she decided that practicality was the only sane way of dealing with the situation.

And perhaps looking back on this day from the safety of school once she finally got there, she would see it after all more in the light of an adventure than a disaster. She might even find something funny in the memories. It was hard to imagine such an outcome now, but she supposed this might well be considered an adventure of the first order.

Now if only she were stranded here with a handsome, smiling, charming knight in shining armor . . .

Though this man was certainly one of the three, she was forced to admit. Her first impression of him had been wrong in one detail. He was exceedingly large, but he did have a handsome face, even though he liked to ruin it by frowning and sneering and cocking one eyebrow.

He doubted she could poach an egg. He had spoken of beef pie as if it might be something she had never even heard of. Ha! How she would love to deal him his comeuppance. And she would too. She had amused her father and everyone else in his household by spending hours in the kitchen, watching their cook and helping her whenever she had been allowed to. It had always seemed to her a marvelously relaxing way of using her spare time.

She examined a loaf of bread that she found in the pantry and discovered that though it was not fresh enough to be eaten as it was, it would be appetizing enough if toasted. And there was a wedge of cheese that someone had had the forethought to cover, with the result that it looked perfectly edible. There was a slab of butter on another covered dish.

She sent Wally outside to the pump to fetch some water, filled the kettle, and set it to boil. It would take some time, she estimated, since the fire was only now crackling to life, but it would be worth waiting for. In the meanwhile, there was probably enough ale in the inn to slake the thirsts of four men. Indeed, it was her guess that Wally had consumed little else in the time since he had been left alone at the inn. Certainly there was no sign of any dishes having been used or any food handled. And he had probably done nothing else but stay warm in his bed, too lazy even to light a fire for comfort.

Mr. Marshall was in the taproom when Frances went back in there. A fire now burned in the hearth, making the room look altogether more cheerful, though nothing could save it from ugliness, and he was in the process of moving a table and chairs closer to the fire. He straightened up to look at her.

He had removed his greatcoat and hat since she last saw him, and she almost stood and gaped. That he was a large gentleman she had seen from the first. She had also thought of him as a heavyset gentleman. But she could see, now that he stood before her, clad in an expertly tailored coat of dark green superfine with fawn waistcoat and pantaloons and dry Hessian boots with white shirt and neatly tied cravat, that he was not heavyset at all but merely broad with muscles in all the right places. His powerful thighs suggested that he was a man who spent a great deal of time in the saddle. And his hair without the beaver hat looked thicker and curlier than she had imagined. It hugged his head in a short, neat style.

He was a veritable Corinthian, in fact.

Indeed he was nothing short of devastatingly gorgeous, Frances thought resentfully, remembering fleetingly all the amusement she felt every time she overheard the girls at school giggling and sighing soulfully over some young buck who had taken their fancy.

Yet here she stood, gawking.

Nasty gentlemen, she thought, deserved to be ugly.

She moved forward to set the tray down on the table.

"It is only teatime," she said, "though I suppose you missed luncheon as I did. The kitchen fire will be hot enough for me to make a cooked meal for dinner, but in the meanwhile toast and cheese and some pickles will have to suffice. I have set some out on the kitchen table for the men too and have sent Wally running to the stables to fetch Thomas and your coachman."

"If Wally is capable of running," he said, rubbing his hands together and eyeing the tray hungrily, "I will eat my hat as well as the toast and cheese."

Frances had dithered in the kitchen about whether to join Mr. Marshall in the taproom or stay there for her own tea. Her inclination was very much to stay in the kitchen, but her pride told her that if she did that she would be setting a precedent and putting herself firmly in the servant class. He would doubtless be content to treat her accordingly. She might be a schoolteacher, but she was no one's servant—certainly not his.

And so here she was, alone in an inn taproom with Mr. Lucius Marshall, bad-tempered and arrogant and handsome and very male. It was enough to give any gently reared young lady the vapors.

She finally removed her cloak and bonnet and set them down on a wooden settle. She would have liked to comb her hair, but her portmanteau and reticule had disappeared from inside the door, she could see. She smoothed her hands over her hair instead and seated herself at the table that had been pulled forward.

"Ah, warmth," she said, feeling the heat of the fire as she had not yet done in the kitchen, where the fireplace was much larger and slower to heat. "How positively delicious."

He had seated himself opposite her and was regarding her with narrowed eyes.

"Let me guess," he said. "You are Spanish? Italian? Greek?"

"English," she said firmly. "But I did have an Italian mother. Unfortunately I never knew her. She died when I was a baby. But I daresay I do resemble her. My father always said I did."

"Past tense?" he said.

"Yes."

He was still looking at her. She found his gaze disconcerting, but she was certainly not going to show him that. She set some food on her plate and took a bite out of a slice of toast.

"The tea will be a while yet," she said. "But I daresay you would prefer ale anyway. Perhaps you can find some in here without having to disturb poor Wally again. He has had a busy afternoon."

"But if there is one thing he is good at and even enthusiastic over," he said, "it is the liquor. He has already given me a guided tour of the shelves behind the counter over there."

"Ah," she said.

"And I have already sampled some of the offerings," he added.

She did not deign to reply. She ate more toast.

"There are four rooms upstairs," he said, "or five if one counts the large empty room, which I assume is the village Assembly Room. One of the smaller rooms apparently belongs to the absent Parker and his missus of the formidable tongue, and one is a mere box room with a single piece of furniture that may or may not be a bed. I did not sit or lie on it to find out. The other two rooms may be described in loose terms as guest chambers. I purloined sheets and other bedding from the large chest outside the landlady's room and made up the two beds. I have put your things in the larger of the rooms. Later this evening, if Wally can keep awake so long, I will have him light the fire in there so that you may retire in some comfort."

"You have *made the beds*?" It was Frances's turn to raise her eyebrows. "That would have been something to behold."

"You have a wicked tongue, Miss Allard," he said. "I might have seen a mouse or two setting up house beneath your bed, but doubtless you will contrive to sleep the sleep of the just tonight anyway."

And then suddenly, looking across the table at him, trying to think of some suitably tart rejoinder, she was assaulted, just as if someone had planted a fist into her stomach, with a strong dose of reality. Unless the absent landlord—and, more to the point, the land*lady*—arrived home within the next few hours, she was going to be sleeping here tonight quite unchaperoned in a room close to that of Mr. Lucius Marshall, who was horribly attractive even if he was also just plain horrible.

She lowered her head and got to her feet, pushing out her chair with the backs of her knees as she did so.

"I will go and see if the kettle is boiling yet," she said.

"What, Miss Allard?" he said. "You are allowing me the final word?"

She was indeed.

As she hurried off into the kitchen, her cheeks felt suddenly hot enough to boil a kettle apiece.

It was the damnedest thing, Lucius thought when he was left alone, getting to his feet and going in pursuit of more ale.

She was clad quite hideously in a brown dress a few shades lighter than her cloak. It was high-waisted, high-necked, and long-sleeved and about as sexless as dresses came. It draped a tall figure that was slender almost to the point of thinness. It was a figure that was as un-voluptuous as figures came. Her hair was much as he had expected it would look when she still wore her bonnet. It was dressed in a purely no-nonsense style, parted ruthlessly down the middle, drawn smoothly back at the sides, and coiled in a simple knot at the nape of her neck. Even allowing for the flattening effect of a bonnet, he did not believe she had even tried this morning to soften the style with any little curls or ringlets to tease the masculine imagination. The hair was dark brown, even possibly black. Her face was long and narrow, with high cheekbones, a straight nose, and a nondescript mouth. Her eyes were dark and thick-lashed.

She looked prim and dowdy. She looked—and behaved—like the quintessential governess.

But he had been dead wrong about her, nevertheless.

For some reason that he had not yet fathomed—and it had to be the sum of the whole rather than any of the individual parts them-selves—Miss Frances Allard was plain gorgeous.

Gorgeous, but without anything in her manner that he found

remotely appealing. Yet here he was, stuck with her until sometime tomorrow.

He ought to have been happy to leave her alone in the kitchen, since she seemed content to be there. Certainly she did not put in any further appearance after drinking her tea and then clearing the table. Fortunately, she appeared to have taken just as strong an aversion to him as he had to her and was keeping out of his way.

But after half an hour he was bored. He could go out to the stables, he supposed, to discover if Peters and the other coachman had come to blows yet. But if they had, he would be obliged to intervene. He wandered into the kitchen instead—and stopped abruptly just inside the door, assaulted by sights and smells that were totally unexpected.

"Good Lord!" he said. "You are not attempting a beef pie, are you?"

She was standing at the great wooden table that filled the center of the kitchen, her sleeves rolled up to her elbows, a voluminous apron wrapped about her, rolling out what looked suspiciously like pastry.

"I am," she said as he breathed in the aroma of cooking meat and herbs. "Did you think I was incapable of producing such a simple meal? I shall even contrive not to give you indigestion."

"I am overwhelmed," he said dryly, though really he was. Poached eggs had never been high on his list of favorite dinnertime fare.

There was a smudge of flour on one of her cheeks—and both the cheeks were flushed. The apron—presumably belonging to a very buxom Mrs. Parker—half drowned her. But somehow she looked more appealing than she had before—more human.

He reached out and picked up a stray remnant of pastry from the table and popped it into his mouth a moment after she slapped at his hand—and missed it.

"If all you are going to do is *eat* the pastry when I have gone to the trouble of making it," she said sharply, "I shall be sorry I bothered."

"Indeed, ma'am?" He raised his eyebrows. He had not had his fingers slapped for at least the past twenty years. "I shall pay you the compliment of returning the beef pie untouched after dinner, then, shall I?"

She glared at him for a moment and then ... dissolved into laughter.

Lord, oh, Lord! Oh, devil take it! She suddenly looked very human indeed, and more than a little attractive.

"It *was* a foolish thing to say," she admitted, humor still lighting her eyes and curving the corners of her lips upward so that he could see they were not nondescript at all. "Did you come in here to help? You may peel the potatoes."

He was still gawking at her like a smitten schoolboy. Then he heard the echo of her words.

"Peel the *potatoes*?" He frowned. "How is that done?"

She wiped her hands on her apron, disappeared into what he assumed was a pantry, and emerged with a pail of potatoes, which she set at his feet. She took a knife from a drawer and held it out, handle facing him.

"Perhaps," she said, "you are intelligent enough to work it out for yourself."

It was not nearly as easy as it looked. If he cut the peel too thickly so as to obtain a smooth, clean potato, he was also ending up with very small potatoes and a great mound of peelings. If he cut it too thinly, he had to waste another minute or so on each, digging out eyes and other assorted blemishes.

His cook and all his kitchen staff would have an apoplexy apiece if they could see him now, he thought. So would his mother and sisters. His friends would not have an apoplexy, but they *would* be under the table by now, rolling around under there with mirth and holding their sides. Behold Viscount Sinclair, the consummate Corinthian, singing for his supper—or at least peeling potatoes for his dinner, which was even worse!

At the same time he kept more than half an eye on Miss Frances Allard, who was lining a deep dish with the pastry, her slim hands and long fingers working deftly, and then filling the shell with the fragrant meat, vegetable, and gravy concoction that had been simmering over the fire, and finally covering the whole with a pastry lid, which she pressed into place all about the rim with the pad of her thumb and then pierced in several places with a fork.

"Why are you doing that?" he asked her, digging an eye out of a potato before pointing the knife at the pie. "Will the filling not all boil out?"

"If there were no outlet for the steam," she explained, bending to put the pie into the oven, "the pastry lid would quite possibly blow off and we would be scraping half of both it and the pie's contents off the roof of the oven and onto our plates. Onto *your* plate, I should say. I would have whatever was left in the dish."

And speaking of lids blowing off . . .

She probably had no idea what an enticing picture she presented as she bent over the oven, her derriere nicely rounded against the fabric of her dress—proof positive that she was certainly not unshapely. She certainly had not gone out of her way to entice him since they had met. Indeed, her very first words to him, if he remembered correctly, were that he deserved to be subjected to any number of ghastly terminal tortures.

But there—he had just been proved wrong again. First she had seemed shrewish and prunish. Then she had appeared gorgeous but unappealing. Now he was feeling as if the top of his head might blow off at any moment.

"Have I peeled enough potatoes to please you?" he asked irritably.

She straightened up and looked, her head cocked a little to one side.

"Unless each of you men eats enough for a whole regiment instead of just half, yes," she said. "This is the first time you have done this, I suppose?"

"Strangely, Miss Allard," he said, "I do not feel unmanned in admitting that, yes, indeed it is—and the last time too, I fervently hope. Who is going to wash all those dishes?"

A stupid question if ever he had asked one.

"I am," she said, "unless I have a volunteer helper. I doubt it is even worth asking Thomas. And I sent Wally away to shave. I daresay that task will occupy him for the next hour or so. That leaves your coachman or . . ." She raised her eyebrows.

How the devil had he got himself into this ridiculous situation? She was not seriously expecting . . . But of course she was not. There was undisguised ridicule in her eyes.

"Do you want me to wash or dry?" he asked curtly.

"You had better dry," she said. "You might ruin your gentleman's hands if you had to keep them submerged in water for too long."

"My valet would weep," he admitted. "He went home ahead of me yesterday. He would refuse to leave my side ever again."

This was turning into a stranger day by the moment, he thought as they proceeded to wash and dry the dishes while the potatoes bubbled merrily in their pot and the smell wafting from the oven caused his stomach to groan in protest at being kept waiting for its dinner. It was a day unlike anything else in his previous experience.

He never ever stopped at any inn but the very best. He rarely traveled without his valet, but Jeffreys had had a cold and Lucius had not been able to bear the thought of listening to his self-pitying sniffs all the way home in the carriage. He had not set foot inside a kitchen since he was a child, when he had visited frequently and clandestinely in order to beg tasty morsels. He liked his creature comforts, or, if he did give them up, in order to go out riding on a rainy day, for example, he liked to do so voluntarily and in pursuit of an activity he enjoyed or considered worthwhile.

This day had been a disaster ever since Peters had overtaken a carriage so ancient that Lucius had wondered if the snowstorm had somehow catapulted him back in time. And the day was not getting any better.

It was strange, then, that he was beginning almost to enjoy it.

"You do realize, do you not," she said as he tossed down the wet towel on top of the final dish after drying it, "that there will be this to do all over again after dinner?"

He looked at her with incredulity.

"Miss Allard," he said before making his escape back into the taproom, "has no one ever explained to you what servants are for?"

By the time they had dined and Mr. Marshall had assigned Wally and the two grooms the task of washing the dishes, Frances was feeling tired. It had been a long, more than strange day, and the darkness of the winter evening made it seem later than it was. The wind that rattled the window of the taproom and moaned in the chimney, and the heat and crackling sounds coming from the fire were lulling. So was the hot tea she was sipping.

She sat gazing into the fire, drinking her tea and watching with her peripheral vision the supple, highly polished leather of Mr. Marshall's Hessian boots crossed at the ankle and resting on the hearth in an informal, relaxed pose that somehow made him seem twice as male as he had seemed before.

Dangerously male, in fact.

She dared not excuse herself and go up to bed. She would actually have to get to her feet and announce that she was going up there, to the room next to his. There was not even a lock on the door, she had discovered. Not that she suspected him of fancying her. But even so . . .

He sighed with apparent contentment.

"There was only one thing wrong with that beef pie, Miss Allard," he said. "It has spoiled me for all others."

It *had* turned out rather well considering the fact that she had never before cooked unsupervised and had not cooked at all for several years. But the compliment surprised her. He did not seem like the sort of man who handed out a great deal of praise.

"The potatoes were rather good too," she said, provoking an unexpected bark of laughter from him.

Their acquaintance had started very badly, of course. But there was no point in keeping up an open hostility just for the sake of being nasty and provoking nastiness, was there? Somehow, by unspoken consent, they had laid down their weapons and made a sort of grudging peace.

But how strange it was to be sitting thus, alone with a very handsome, masculine gentleman, who was slouched in his chair, totally at his ease. And to know that they would spend the night within a few feet of each other, alone together on the upper floor of the inn. This was the stuff of fantasy and daydreams. But such fantasies were not quite as comfortable when they became reality.

Good heavens, for the past three years she had lived and consorted with none but females, if one discounted Mr. Keeble, the elderly porter at Miss Martin's school.

"Your home is in Bath, is it?" Mr. Marshall asked her.

"Yes," she said. "I live at the school where I teach."

"Ah," he said, "so you *are* a teacher."

He had guessed it, had he? But it was not surprising. She was obviously not a fashionable lady any longer, was she? Even the private carriage in which she had been traveling was shabby despite the wealth of her great-aunts.

"At a girls' school," she said. "A very good one. Miss Martin opened it nine years ago with a few pupils and a very small budget. But her reputation as a good teacher and the help of a benefactor whose identity she does not even know enabled her to expand into the house next door and to take in charity girls as well as paying ones. She was also able to employ more teachers. I have been there for three years."

He sipped from his glass of port.

"And what does such a school teach girls?" he asked her. "What do *you* teach?"

"Music and French and writing," she said. "Creative writing, not penmanship—Susanna Osbourne teaches that. The school instructs girls in all the accomplishments they are expected to acquire as young ladies, like dancing and painting and singing as well as etiquette and deportment. But it also teaches academics. Miss Martin has always insisted upon that, since she firmly believes that the female mind is in no way inferior to the male."

"Ah," he said. "Admirable."

She turned her head sharply to look at him, but it was unclear to her whether that judgment had been spoken ironically or not. His head was resting against the high back of his chair. He looked sleepy. His short curly hair looked somewhat rumpled. She felt a strange little fluttering in her lower abdomen.

"I like teaching there," she said. "I feel that I am doing something useful with my life."

"And you were not doing anything useful with it before three years ago?" He rolled his head around to look at her.

Her mind touched upon the two years following her father's death, and for a moment she felt that she could weep. But her tears for those distressing, bungled years had all been shed long ago. And she had never been sorry for the choice she had then made to teach instead of running off abjectly to the sanctuary of her great-aunts' house and support. If she could go back, she would do the same thing all over again.

Independence was a marvelous thing for a lady.

"I was not happy three years ago," she said. "Now I am."

"Are you?" he asked, his eyes moving lazily and disconcertingly over her face and neck and shoulders and even down to her bosom. "You are fortunate to be able to say so, ma'am."

"Are you not happy, then?" she asked him.

"*Happiness.*" His eyebrows rose in obvious scorn. "It is a foolish word. There are enjoyment and sensual gratification, and there are their opposites. I cultivate the former and avoid the latter whenever I may. It is, you may say, my philosophy of life—and of most people's lives if they are honest with themselves."

"I spoke unadvisedly," she said. "I used the wrong word. I ought to have said that I am *content* with my life. I avoid either of the extremes you named for the sake of greater peace. It is *my* philosophy of life, and I believe many people have discovered that it is a wise way of living."

"And also dashed boring," he said.

And then he did something that caused far more than flutterings within her. It took her breath away for a moment and left her almost panting.

He grinned at her—and revealed himself as a very handsome man indeed.

She reached for a reply, failed to find one, and ended up gazing silently into his eyes and feeling heat rise in her cheeks.

He gazed back, equally silent, his grin fading.

"I think," she said, finding her voice at last, "it is time for bed."

If ever she had wished to recall words after they were spoken, this was the occasion. And if ever she had wished for a black hole to open at her feet and swallow her up whole, this was the time.

For a few ghastly moments she could not look away from him, and he did not look away from her. The air between them seemed to sizzle. And then he spoke.

"I presume," he said, "that you mean alone, Miss Allard. And you are quite right—it *is* time for bed. If we were to sit here much longer, I daresay we would both nod off only to be awoken later when the fire had burned down, with cricked necks and frozen toes. You go on up, and I will see to banking the fire and putting the guard across it. I'll check the kitchen fire too, though I daresay Peters and your Thomas will be playing cards in there and grumbling darkly at each other for some time to come."

He got to his feet and bent over the fire even as he spoke.

She wondered as she rose from her chair if her knees would support her. What a ghastly slip of the tongue! She should have made her home in the kitchen after all.

"Good night, Mr. Marshall," she said to his back.

He straightened up and turned to her, one mocking eyebrow cocked.

"Are you still there?" he said. "Good night, Miss Allard."

She fled, stopping only long enough to take up one of the candles from the counter. She hurried upstairs to her room, where she was surprised to see a fire burning. Although Mr. Marshall had said earlier that he would get Wally to light one, she had not heard him give the order. She undressed and made her other preparations for bed quickly even though the room was not cold, and dived beneath the covers, pulling them up over her head as if to shut off her thoughts.

There were feelings, though, as well as thoughts—and they were definitely not the feelings of one who cultivated calm contentment in her life. Her breasts felt uncomfortably tight. Her lower abdomen throbbed. Her inner thighs ached. And she was not such an innocent that she did not recognize the symptoms for what they were.

She desired a man she did not even know—and probably would not like if she did. She had even despised him for a few hours. How mortifying!

She waited tensely beneath the covers for the sound of his footsteps coming up the stairs and entering his room.

But though she did not fall asleep for a long time, she did not hear him come.

The snow had stopped falling by the time Lucius got up the next morning and peered out through a small circle he cleared with his warm breath on the window of his bedchamber. But a great deal had come down and the wind had blown it into massive drifts. In addition, the sky had still not cleared off, and if the temperature of his room was anything to judge by, there was not going to be much melting for a while.

Although it was still dark and impossible to see any distance with perfect clarity, nevertheless it was painfully obvious that no one was going to be doing any traveling today.

He waited for gloom and ill-humor to descend upon his spirits again and was surprised to discover that instead he was feeling more cheerful than he had since before Christmas. None of the new conditions of his life had changed, of course, but fate had provided him with this slight respite from them. There was going to be nothing he could do today that would in any way further his plans to reform his life and be the model grandson, son, brother, and bridegroom, and so he might as well enjoy what the day might offer.

It was a strange thought when he was stranded at a sorry apology of a country inn without his valet—and without most of the other comforts he usually took for granted.

He shaved in the cold water that had been sitting in the pitcher on the washstand since the night before, got dressed, and pulled on his top boots, his greatcoat, and his hat. He held his gloves in one hand as he descended the stairs. All was in darkness. As he had fully expected, Wally was still in his bed—and maybe the coachmen were still in theirs. They had still been playing cards and voicing dark suspicions about each other's honesty when he had finally felt it safe to go up to bed well after midnight—safe for his own peace of mind, that was. When she had said that it was time for bed, he had felt for a few moments—again!—that the top of his head might well blow off.

He had an excess of energy this morning despite the fact that he had not slept much. And since he could not go riding—his favorite early morning exercise—or boxing or fencing, which would have been worthy alternatives, he would clear some of the snow away from before the door, he decided, pulling on his gloves, letting himself out into the dusk of approaching daylight, and wading back to the stables in search of a shovel and broom. With the help of Peters, who was already out there tending the horses, he found what he was looking for.

"I'll do it myself after I've finished in 'ere, guv, if you like," Peters said. "I'd rather that than wash bloomin' dishes again. But I can see you are fair to bustin' with wanting something to do yourself. So you go ahead."

"Much obliged to you," Lucius said dryly.

He took the shovel and set to work with it.

In the gathering light he could see that the inn was at some remove from a village, which he had suspected must be there, but that the road connecting them was so completely submerged beneath the snowfall that it was impossible to know exactly where it was. There were unlikely to be visitors today even if would-be imbibers of ale knew that the landlord was due home. It was even more unlikely that the Parkers would be able to return.

He rather suspected that he might prefer Miss Allard's cooking anyway, unless beef pie was her pièce de résistance and she was incapable of preparing anything else. She could make it again, though, as far as he was concerned.

After an hour he had shoveled a path from the door to the stables and another from the door to what he estimated to be the road. He felt breathless and warm and invigorated. While he had been working, the sun had come up. At least, he presumed it had—the sky was still cloudy and a few snowflakes still sifted down from the heavens now and then. But at least the world was light.

He leaned on the shovel and drew in a deep breath of fresh air. He still had more energy than he was going to be able to use up stranded inside a small country inn for a whole day.

He shoveled along beside the inn, past what he realized was the kitchen window. He straightened up and glanced inside.

Frances Allard was up already and busily employed close to the fire. Whether she had built it and lit it herself he did not know, but it looked as if it had been going for some time.

She was wearing a similar dress to yesterday's except that this one was cream in color and suited her better. Her hair was neatly, sleekly dressed. She was wrapped again in a large apron. He could see steam curling from the spout of the kettle. There was something cooking on the range top. On the table was a bowl of what looked like whipped eggs.

He was, he realized suddenly, ravenously hungry.

He was also curiously charmed by the domesticity of the scene— and more than a little aroused by it. There was something almost erotic about the sight of a woman bending and turning and absorbed in the task of cooking a meal.

It was a thought that he must definitely not pursue any further. She was a schoolteacher and doubtless virtuous to a fault.

She was, in other words, strictly off-limits.

She turned from the fire as if she felt his eyes on her and saw him looking in on her. And then—*damnation!*—she actually smiled and looked dazzling even this early in the morning. That smile of hers was a lethal weapon, and under present circumstances he would be just as happy if she did not use it on him.

She beckoned him and pointed at the cooking food.

When he entered the kitchen a few minutes later after shaking out his greatcoat and changing his boots, he could see that she had laid two places at the long kitchen table.

"I trust you do not mind eating in here," she said, turning her head to acknowledge his presence before returning her attention to the eggs, which she was now scrambling over the heat. "I roused Wally a while ago and sent him for water. Then he felt he had earned breakfast with Thomas and Peters. Only now has he been assigned the lighting of the fire in the taproom. The kitchen will be a cozier place for us to eat."

"The men have already eaten?" he asked, rubbing his hands together and breathing in the mingled smells of smoked bacon and fried potatoes and coffee.

"I could have called you in too," she said. "But you looked as if you were enjoying yourself."

"I was," he said.

She set a generous plateful of food before him and a more modest one at her place. She removed the apron and took her seat.

"I suppose," he said, getting up again to pour the coffee, "you made the fire in here yourself."

"I did," she said. "Is this not a strange adventure?"

He laughed, and she looked sharply at him before dipping her head to look down at her plate again.

"Have you ever been in charge of an inn kitchen before?" he asked her. "And the appetites of four grown men?"

"Never," she said. "Have you ever shoveled snow away from a country inn?"

"Good Lord! Never."

This time they both laughed.

"A strange adventure indeed," he agreed. "You told me yesterday that all over Christmas you longed for snow. What would you have done with it if it had come?"

"I would have gazed out on it in wonder and awe," she said. "Snow for Christmas is so very rare. And I pictured myself wading about the neighborhood through it with the village carolers—but there *were* no carolers this year. And wading through it to the Assembly Rooms for a Christmas ball. But there was none."

"A poor-spirited village if ever I heard of one," he said. "Everyone stayed at home and stuffed themselves with goose and pudding, I suppose?"

"I suppose so," she said. "And my great-aunts refused the invitations they received in favor of remaining home in order to enjoy the company of their great-niece."

"Who would have far preferred to be kicking up her heels at a village dance," he said. "A grim Christmas you had of it, ma'am. You have my heartfelt sympathies."

"Poor me," she agreed, though her eyes were now dancing with merriment.

"Those are the only uses you would have put the snow to?" he asked her. "It was hardly worth longing for, was it?"

"Well, you see," she said, setting one elbow on the table and resting her chin in her hand, against all the rules of etiquette, "my great-aunts would not have enjoyed engaging in a snowball fight and one can hardly fight with oneself. I probably would have built a snowman. When it snowed two winters ago, Miss Martin canceled afternoon classes and we took the girls out into the meadows beyond the school and had a snowman-building contest. It was great fun."

"Did you win?" he asked.

"I ought to have," she said, picking up her knife and fork again. "My snowman was far and away the best. But the teachers were declared ineligible for prizes. It was grossly unfair. I almost resigned on the spot. But when I threatened to do so, I was rolled in the snow by a dozen or more girls, and Miss Martin studiously looked the other way and made no attempt to exert her authority and come to my rescue."

It sounded, he thought, like a happy school. He could not somehow imagine rolling any of his own former teachers in the snow, especially with the headmaster looking on.

Miss Frances Allard was certainly not the bad-tempered, prunish woman he had taken her for yesterday. And he must admit that if their positions had been reversed, he would have been in an even more cantankerous mood than he had been anyway and would have been entertaining gruesome dreams of boiling someone in oil too. Not that either he or Peters would tolerate someone's overtaking them on any road under any circumstances, of course.

"Teachers are not ineligible for this morning's prizes," he said.

"Oh?" She looked at him with raised eyebrows.

"Out beside the inn," he said, pointing in the direction of the side facing away from the village. "As soon as I have helped you do the dishes. One problem, though. Do you have proper boots?"

"Yes, of course I do," she said. "Would I have longed for snow for Christmas if I did not? Am I being challenged to a snowman-building contest? You will lose."

"We will see," he said. "What did you put in these potatoes to make them so delicious?"

"My own secret combination of herbs," she said.

He finished his meal and gathered the dishes together to wash while she set about mixing a fresh batch of bread—it could rise while she was outside winning the competition, she told him.

Fresh bread! His mouth watered even though his stomach was full.

He even—horror of horrors!—*dried* the dishes.

If it had not snowed, he would now be on the final leg of his journey. He could have been home by this afternoon—to the quiet, familiar peace of Cleve Abbey and the prospect of an early return to London and its myriad pleasures—though only until the Season began, by Jove. But here he was instead, planning to alleviate the boredom of a useless day by building a snowman.

Except that he was no longer bored—had not been since he rose from his bed actually.

He tried to remember the last time he had built a snowman or otherwise frolicked in the snow, and failed.

4

He was making the mistake, Frances noticed with a furtive glance in his direction, of building his snowman too tall and thin—an error often made by novices. It looked much larger than hers, but he was going to have problems with the head. Even if he could lift a suitable one that high, it would not remain in place but would roll off and ruin all his efforts. She would be the undisputed winner.

Her snowman, on the other hand, was solid and squat. He was broader than he was tall. He was—

"Too fat to pass through any door," Mr. Marshall commented, diverted from his own efforts for a moment, "even if he were to turn sideways. Too fat to find a bed wide enough or sturdy enough to sleep on. Too fat to be allowed any bread or potatoes with his meals for the next year. He is disgustingly obese."

"He is cuddly," she said, tipping her head to one side to survey her unfinished creation, "and good-natured. He is not cadaverous like some snowmen I have seen. He does not look as if he will blow over in the first puff of wind. He is—"

"Headless," he said, "as is mine. Let us get back to work and resume the name-calling afterward."

Her poor snowman looked even more obese after she had fixed a nice round head on his shoulders. The head was too small. She tried to pack more snow about it, but it fell off in clumps about his shoulders, and she had to be content with picking out the two largest coals they had brought from the kitchen with them so that she could at least give him large, soulful eyes. She added a somewhat smaller coal nose and a fat carrot to act as his pipe and a few more small coals for coat buttons. With one forefinger she sculpted a wide and smiling mouth about the carrot.

"At least," she said, stepping back, "he has a sense of humor. And at least he *has* a head."

She looked down with a smirk at the massive one he had sculpted on the ground, complete with jug-handle ears and sausage curls.

"The contest is not over yet," he said. "There was no time limit, was there? It would be somewhat premature to start jeering yet. You might feel foolish afterward."

She saw then that he was not as ignorant of the laws of gravity as she had assumed. He spent some time on the shoulders of his snowman, scooping out a hollow to hold the head so that it would not roll off. Of course, he still had to get the head up there.

She watched smugly as he stooped to pick it up.

But she had reckoned without his superior height and the strength of those arm muscles. What would have been an impossibility for her looked like child's play for him. He even had the strength to hold the head suspended over the torso for a few moments so that he could get it at just the right angle before lowering it into place. He selected the coals and carrot he wanted and pressed them into place—though he used his carrot for a nose. And then he reached into one of the pockets of his greatcoat and drew out a long, narrow knitted scarf in a hideous combination of pink and orange stripes and wrapped it about the neck of his snowman.

"The vicar's wife in my grandfather's parish presented it to me for Christmas," he said. "General opinion in the village has it that she is color-blind. I think general opinion must have the right of it. It is kinder than saying she has no taste at all, anyway."

He stepped back and stood beside Frances. Together they contemplated their creations.

"The scarf and the curls and the lopsided mouth save yours from looking mean and humorless," she said generously. "Not to mention those ears. Oh, and those pockmarks are meant to be *freckles*. That is a nice touch, I must confess. I like him after all."

"And I must admit to a fondness for Friar Tuck with his black coat buttons," he said. "He looks like a jolly old soul, though I do not know what holds his pipe in his mouth if he is smiling so broadly."

"His teeth."

"Ah," he said. "Good point. We forgot to appoint a judge."

"And to have a trophy awaiting the winner," she said.

It was only then, when he turned his head to grin at her, that she realized he had one arm draped about her shoulders in a relaxed, comradely gesture. She guessed that he had only just realized it himself. The smiles froze on their faces, and Frances's knees felt suddenly weak.

He slipped his arm free, cleared his throat, and wandered closer to the snowmen.

"I suppose," he said, "we might as well declare the competition a draw. Agreed? If we do not, we will get into a scrap again and you will be devising some other hair-raising scheme for putting a period to my existence. Or are you going to insist upon declaring me the winner?"

"By no means," she said. "Mine is definitely sturdier than yours. It will withstand the forces of nature for much longer."

"Now that is a provocative statement when I have been magnanimous enough to suggest a draw," he said, and he stooped and turned and without warning hurled a snowball at her. It caught her in the chest and spattered up into her face.

"Oh!" she cried, outraged. "Unfair!"

And she scooped up a gloveful of snow and tossed it back at him. It hit the side of his hat, knocking it askew.

The battle was on.

It raged for several minutes until to a casual observer it might have looked as if four snowmen had been erected beside the inn. Except that two of them were moving and were helpless with laughter. And except that one of them, the taller and broader of the two, suddenly lunged for the other and bore her backward until she was lying on her back in a soft snowdrift with his weight pressing her deeper and his hands clamped to her wrists and holding them imprisoned on either side of her head.

"Enough!" he declared, still laughing. "That last one caught me in the eye."

He blinked flakes of snow off his eyelashes.

"You admit defeat, then?" She laughed up at him.

"Admit defeat?" His eyebrows rose. "Pardon me, but who is holding whom vanquished in the snow?"

"But who just declared that he had had enough?" She waggled her eyebrows at him.

"The same one who then ended the battle with a decisive annihilation of the enemy." He laughed back at her.

She suddenly became aware that he was actually on top of her. She could feel his weight bearing her down. She could feel his breath warm on her face. She looked into his hazel eyes, only inches away, and found them smoldering back into her own. She looked down at his mouth and was aware at the same moment that his eyes dropped to hers.

Her strange adventure moved perilously close to danger—and perhaps to something rather splendid.

His lips brushed across hers and she felt as if she were lying beneath a hot August sun rather than December snow clouds.

She had never known a man so very male—a thought that did not bear either pursuing or interpreting.

"I have just remembered the bread," she said in a voice that sounded shockingly normal to her ears. "I will be fortunate indeed if it has not risen to fill the kitchen to the ceiling. I will be fortunate if I can get through the door to rescue it."

His eyes smoldered into hers for perhaps a second longer, and then one corner of his mouth lifted in what might have been a smile or perhaps was simple mockery. He pushed himself to his feet, brushed himself off, and reached down a hand to help her up. She banged her gloved hands together and then shook her cloak, but there was as much snow down inside the collar of it as there was on the outside, she was sure.

"Oh, this was *such* fun," she said, not looking at him.

"It was indeed," he agreed. "But if I ever meet fortune face-to-face, I will demand to know why I had to be stranded here with a prudish schoolteacher. Go, Miss Allard. *Run.* If I can have no fresh bread with my soup after all, I shall be quite out of humor."

For the merest moment Frances thought of staying in order to protest his use of the word *prudish*. But if she were foolish enough to do that, she might find herself having to prove that it did not apply to her.

She fled, though for very pride's sake she did not run.

Part of her was feeling decidedly annoyed with herself. Why had she broken the tension of that moment? What harm would one full kiss have done? It was so long since she had been kissed, and the chance might never come again—she was all of twenty-three.

By the same token, she was *only* twenty-three.

What harm would a kiss have done?

But she was no green girl. She knew very well what harm it would have done. Neither of them, she suspected, would be content with just one kiss. And there was nothing in their circumstances to inhibit them from taking more.

And more . . .

Heavens above, even just the brush of his lips had half scrambled her brains and every bone and organ in her body.

She hurried into the kitchen after removing her outer garments and threw herself busily into baking the bread and making the soup.

The conversation at luncheon was rather strained and far too bright and superficial—on her part anyway. Lucius retreated into taciturnity. But though the bread was light and among the best he had ever tasted and the soup more than worthy of a second bowl, he found himself unable to concentrate upon the enjoyment of either quite as much as he might have liked.

He was distracted by unconsummated lust.

And he cursed his luck that while circumstances were ideal for a little sexual fling, the woman with whom he was stranded was not. If only she had been an actress or a merry widow or . . . Well, anyone but a schoolteacher, who might be gorgeous but who was also prim and virtuous—except when she was building snowmen and hurling snowballs and forgot herself for a while.

While she talked brightly on a variety of inane topics, he tried to think about Portia Hunt. He tried to bring her face into focus in his mind and succeeded all too well. She had that look in her eye that told him she despised all men and their animal appetites but would tolerate them in him provided she never had to know about them.

He was probably doing her an injustice. She was a perfect lady, it was true. It was also possible, he supposed, that there was an appealing woman beneath all the perfection. He was going to discover the answer soon.

And this adventure, as Frances Allard had called it, would soon be over. Already the sun had broken through the clouds, and water was dripping off the eaves outside the taproom window. There was only the rest of today to live through.

And tonight . . .

Tonight he would sleep in the taproom. He would not set even one toe beyond it in the direction of the stairs and the chambers above. When he died, his virtue would take him straight into heaven, where he could bore himself silly by playing on a harp for all eternity.

Damnation! Why could she not have continued to be the prunish shrew he had taken her for yesterday—less than twenty-four hours ago? Or else the laughing, eager woman she had been outside until his lips had touched hers? Why did she have to be such a frustrating mix?

He ordered Wally and Thomas to do the dishes—Peters was still busy with the carriage, though that fact did not stop Thomas from muttering something about favoritism as Peters disappeared through the back door. Lucius pulled his boots and his greatcoat back on and spent most of the afternoon outside, first in the carriage house feeling useless, and then chopping wood, since the pile that was already chopped looked seriously diminished. He could have hauled Wally outside to do the job, of course, and would have done so under normal circumstances. But he was glad of the excuse to remain outside. He was doubly glad of the chance to use up more energy. He chopped far more than would be needed tonight and tomorrow morning. This wood would be warming the toes of the Parkers for the next week or more.

She had tea ready when he went back inside—fresh bread with more of the cheese and pickles, and some currant cakes that were still warm from the oven. Who was it who had said that the way to a man's heart was through his stomach? Not that it was exactly his heart that was the affected organ, but she was certainly a good cook.

"I have decided," he said when they had finished eating, "not to offer you employment as my cook. I am large enough as I am—or as I was yesterday."

She smiled but did not say anything. And when he got to his feet to help her into the kitchen with the tray, she told him to stay where he was, that he had been busy enough all afternoon.

She had been reading, he could see. Her book was resting open and facedown on the settle beside the hearth. It was Voltaire's *Candide,* of all things. She was reading it in French, he saw when he picked it up. She had said that she taught French, had she not? French and music and writing.

She was a prim, staid schoolteacher. No doubt she was a dashed intelligent one too. If he repeated those facts to himself often enough, perhaps he would eventually accept them as hard reality and the knowledge would cool his blood.

Who the devil would want to bed an intelligent woman?

Wally came to make up the fire, and Lucius nodded off in his chair soon after. Frances Allard did not rejoin him until dinnertime, when she appeared with a roasted duckling and roast potatoes and other vegetables she had found in the root cellar.

"I did not even help with the potatoes tonight," he said. "I am surprised you will allow me to eat."

"I did not help chop the wood," she said, "but here I am sitting in front of the fire."

Lord, they could not even have a satisfactory quarrel any longer.

"*Candide,*" he said, nodding his head in the direction of the book. "Do you always read in French?"

"I like to when the original was written in that language," she said. "So much is lost in translation even when the translator is earnest and well educated. Something of the author's voice is lost."

Yes, there was no doubt about it. She was intelligent. He tried to feel his attraction to her wane as a result. He was attracted only because he was stranded here and she was the only woman within sight, he told himself. Under normal circumstances he would not afford her so much as a second glance.

They conversed without too much awkwardness or too many silences for the rest of the meal, but he found as it progressed and then as they washed and dried the dishes together that a certain melancholy had descended upon his spirits. It was not the black mood that had assailed him all over Christmas and even yesterday but a definite . . . melancholy nevertheless. Tomorrow they would part and never see each other again. By this time next week she would be simply a memory. By this time next month he would have forgotten all about her.

Good Lord! Next he would be growing his hair and wearing brightly colored cravats and spouting sentimental verse and sinking into a decline.

He set down a heavy pot he had just dried and cleared his throat. But when she looked up with raised eyebrows—and slightly flushed cheeks—he had nothing to say.

She led the way back into the taproom and sat on her usual chair. He stood before the fire, gazing into it, his hands clasped at his back. And he gave in to temptation. Not that he put up much of a fight, it was true. Perhaps he would do that later.

And perhaps not.

"And so," he said, "you never did get to dance over Christmas?"

"Alas, no." She chuckled softly. "And I was all prepared to impress the villagers with my prowess in the waltz. Mr. Huckerby, the dancing master at school, insisted upon teaching the steps to the girls, as he says it will almost certainly be all the rage within a few years.

And he chose me with whom to demonstrate. As if my days were not busy enough without that. But I stopped grumbling once I had learned the steps. It is a divine dance. However, I was given no chance to dazzle anyone with my performance of it over Christmas. How sad!"

Her voice was light with humor. And yet in her words, and in what she had said during the morning, he gathered an impression of a Christmas that had been dreary and disappointing. A lonely Christmas, with only two elderly ladies for company.

But he had already given in to temptation and could not now deny himself the pleasure of pressing onward.

He looked over his shoulder at her.

"Dazzle *me*."

"I beg your pardon?" She looked blankly up at him, though some color had crept into her cheeks.

"Dazzle *me*," he repeated. "Waltz with *me*. You do not even have to wade through snow to reach the Assembly Room. It awaits you abovestairs."

"What?" She laughed.

"Come and waltz with me," he said. "We can have the luxury of the room and the floor to ourselves."

"But there is no music," she protested.

"I thought you were a music teacher."

"I did not see either a pianoforte or a spinet up there," she said. "But even if there were either, I would not be able to play and dance at the same time, would I?"

"Do you not have a voice?" he asked her. "Can you not sing? Or hum?"

She laughed. "How absurd!" she said. "Besides, it is cold up there. There is no fire."

"Do you feel cold, then?" he asked her.

He suddenly felt as if the taproom fire were scorching him through to the marrow of his bones. And with his eyes intently holding hers, he knew that she felt the same way.

"No." The word came out on a breath of sound. She cleared her throat. "No."

"Well, then." He turned fully, made her an elegant leg, and reached out one hand, palm up. "May I have the pleasure of this set, ma'am?"

"How absurd!" she said again, but the color was high in both cheeks now, and her eyes were huge and bright, and he knew that she was his.

She set her hand in his, and his fingers closed about it.

Yes, they would waltz together at the very least.

At the very least!

And perhaps he would remember her even this time next year.

5

He carried two candles in tall holders up the stairs while she carried one, which she took into her room in order to find a shawl in her portmanteau. She wrapped it about her shoulders before going into the Assembly Room, taking her candle with her.

He had placed his at either end of the room, which was not really very large at all. He took hers from her hand and strode across to the fireplace opposite the door to set it on the mantel. He must have made a quick visit to his room too. He was wearing shoes in place of his Hessian boots.

This was terribly foolish, she thought. They were actually going to *dance* together? Without company, without music, without heat?

No, there was heat aplenty. And foolishness could sometimes feel marvelously exhilarating. She held the ends of her shawl and tried to steady her heartbeat as he came back across the room, his eyes intent on hers, looking distinctly dangerous. He repeated the elegant, marvelously theatrical bow he had made her downstairs, and cocked one eyebrow.

"Ma'am?" he said. "This is my dance, I believe."

"I believe it is, sir." She dipped into a low curtsy, set her hand in his, and felt the warmth of his fingers close strongly about hers again.

They spoke and behaved frivolously as if this were some amusing lark.

It felt anything but.

It felt downright sinful.

But, good heavens, they were only going to *dance* together.

He led her to the center of the floor and stood facing her.

"I confess," he said, "that my experience with the waltz is somewhat limited. Let me see. My right hand goes here, I believe."

Holding her eyes with his own, he slid it about her waist to come to rest against the small of her back. She could feel the heat of it through her wool dress and chemise—and there went her heartbeat again.

"And my left hand goes here." She set it on his broad shoulder, a few inches above the level of her own—and there went the bones in her knees.

"And—" He held up his left hand and raised his eyebrows.

"This." She placed her palm against his and curled her fingers in between his thumb and forefinger even as his own fingers closed over the back of her hand.

Her shawl, she suddenly felt, had been quite an unnecessary addition even though the air she was inhaling was chilly. She was terribly aware that his broad chest, encased behind his expertly tailored coat and the pristine shirt and elegantly tied neckcloth, was only inches away from her bosom. And that his face was close enough that she could feel the warmth of his breath.

Her eyes were locked with his.

It was no wonder some people still considered the waltz an improper dance. It had felt nothing like this at the school. And they had not even *started* it yet.

"The music, ma'am?" His voice was low, even husky.

"Oh, dear," she said. Was she going to have breath enough for this?

But she had had experience singing when she was nervous. Not *this* type of nervousness, it was true, but even so . . . It was a matter of breathing from deep in the diaphragm, where the air could be stored and released gradually, instead of from the throat, from which the nerves would expel it all in one breathy *whoosh*.

Now if she could just think of a waltz tune. If she could just think of *any* tune—other than a William Byrd madrigal, that was.

She closed her eyes, breaking at least some of the tension, and remembered the rhythm and the pleasure of waltzing with Mr. Huckerby, who was a very good dancer even if he *was* rather a fussy man and even if he *did* always smell strongly of lilies of the valley.

She hummed softly to herself for a few moments, and then she opened her eyes, smiled at Mr. Marshall, and hummed more loudly and firmly, emphasizing the first beat of each measure.

His right hand tapped the rhythm lightly against her back and then tightened slightly as he led her off into the steps of the waltz—small, tentative steps at first and then gaining in confidence, until after a minute or so they were moving with long, firm, rhythmic steps and twirling about until she could have sworn there were a dozen candles instead of just three.

She laughed.

So did he.

And then, of course, they came to grief because she had stopped humming for a moment.

She started again.

It soon became clear to her that when he had said he had limited experience with the waltz, he must have been talking in relative terms—or lying outright, which was more probable. He knew the dance very well indeed. More than that, he had a feel for the rhythm and the grace of it, his left hand holding hers high in a strong clasp, his right hand splayed against the arch of her back, leading her with such assured command into intricate little twirls and wider whirls that she felt as if her feet moved almost of their own volition, and as if they scarcely touched the wooden floor.

Their dance could not have been more exhilarating, she thought, even if it had been performed in a warmed, brightly lit Assembly Room full of people glittering in their evening array and with a full orchestra to provide the music.

By the time the tune came to an end, she was breathless. She was also fully aware that she was flushed and that she was smiling and happy and sorry the dance was over. His eyes glinted with a strange light and gazed very directly back into her own. His lips were pressed tightly together, making his jaw look very square and masterful.

She could feel his body heat and smell his very masculine cologne.

"Now," he said, "you may no longer say that you did not attend an assembly over the Christmas season or that you did not dance. Or waltz."

"What?" she said. "I may no longer wallow in self-pity?"

"Not," he said, "unless I did not measure up to the standard of the dancing master."

"Oh," she assured him, "you far surpass Mr. Huckerby."

"Flattery," he said, both eyebrows arching upward, "will get you everywhere, Miss Allard. Have you recovered your breath? A set, I believe, consists of more than just one dance. And I *did* reserve the whole set with you, if you will recall. Something a little slower this time, perhaps?"

She was assaulted suddenly with the realization that this adventure was almost at an end. They would not be here at the inn this time tomorrow. She would probably be back at the school, and he would be . . . wherever he was going. Somewhere in Hampshire, he had said.

She would never see him again.

But they were to waltz together one more time—one last time. She knew then with utter certainty that she would live on the memory of this day and this evening for a long time to come, perhaps even for the rest of her life. She rather believed it might be a painful memory for a time, though surely at some time farther in the future she would remember with pleasure.

She thought of another waltz tune, a slower one, which Mr. Huckerby had used to begin his instructions, though she had not realized until she began first to hum it and then to la-la-la it how poignantly beautiful it was, how haunting, how heartbreakingly romantic.

She was as foolish as any of the schoolgirls under her care, she thought. She was quite in love with him.

She kept her eyes closed as they waltzed this time, their steps slower and longer, their twirls more sweeping, until it felt altogether more natural to feel the fingers of his right hand slide farther up her back to bring her closer to him, to move her own hand farther into his shoulder and then behind his neck. It felt comforting to spread her right hand over the warm fabric of his coat above his heart and to have it held there by his palm and his fingers. It felt wonderful to rest her cheek against his, and to reduce the volume of the music to a soft humming.

Her bosom brushed against his chest and then pressed more firmly against it. With her abdomen she could feel his watch fob and his warmth. Her thighs touched his as they continued to dance.

And then they stopped dancing and she stopped humming.

It felt like the most natural thing in the world. As if yesterday had been meant to happen, as if this had been meant to be. Although she did not actually think such foolish thoughts, she *felt* them. She felt that she was where she belonged, where she had always belonged, where she always would belong. It did not matter that a saner, more practical part of herself was clamoring to be heard. She simply did not listen. The whole of the rest of her life was for sanity, but for now, for this moment she had found something deeper than sanity. She had found herself. She had found what all her life she had dreamed of and searched for and doubted really existed.

"Frances," he murmured, his voice low against her ear.

The intimacy of her name on his lips sent a thrill along her spine and warmed her all the way down to her toes.

"Yes." She drew back her head to smile at him, and she lifted her hand from behind his neck to twine her fingers in his short curly hair. She knew then what the strange, intense light in his eyes was. But of course, she had never *not* known. It was desire. Raw and naked desire.

And then he moved his head closer to hers and closed his eyes and kissed her.

She had been kissed before. She had been kissed by a man she thought she loved. But it had never been like this. Ah, surely it never had. His arms came about her, the fingers of one hand closing over the knot of hair at her neck, the other spread below her waist, drawing her intimately against him. His mouth opened over hers, teasing her lips apart, inviting further intimacy. When she opened her mouth, his tongue came inside, circled hers, and stroked the roof of her mouth.

She leaned into him, her arms about his hard-muscled frame, her body on fire from the topmost hair on her head to her toenails. If she could have drawn him closer, she would have. She knew beyond any doubt that he would be an expert and experienced lover. Curiously, that knowledge did not alarm her at all. It only thrilled her.

"Lucius."

He had lowered his head to nuzzle the hollow between her neck and her shoulder. His hands were cupping her breasts through the wool of her dress beneath her shawl, molding them, making them tender with need.

When he lifted his head, his hair looked slightly rumpled, his hazel eyes heavy with passion.

"I want you," he said against her lips. "I want you in bed. I want to get inside these clothes."

She was not so far gone into mindlessness that such plain speaking did not jolt her. It was the moment of ultimate decision. She knew that. He would not force her—she knew that too. There were all sorts of dangers and moral concerns to discourage her from proceeding. And he was, when all was said and done, little more than a stranger. She knew almost nothing about him. She would be sure to regret giving in to a temptation that she had been fighting valiantly since last evening.

But she knew too in the few seconds that elapsed before she answered him that she would also and always regret *not* being bold enough to carry her adventure to its ultimate conclusion. She could spend this one night with Lucius Marshall if she chose. Or she could spend the night virtuously tossing and turning in her own solitary bed and forever regret that she had said no.

Besides, saying no now would make her into a tease. She had come too far—much too far—to pretend that she thought they had been indulging in a mere kiss.

"Yes," she said, hearing the throaty catch in her voice as if it were someone else's. "It is what I want too."

It was a relief to have spoken the words, to have owned her own desire, her own freedom of choice.

Her own madness.

He drew her close again and parted his lips over hers.

"It will be good," he promised. "This will be a night to remember, Frances."

She did not doubt it for one moment.

They did not take a candle with them when they went to her room. But Wally must have taken the rare initiative of starting a fire in there unbidden. It burned warmly in the grate, and light from it flickered over the walls and ceiling—and over the bed. But it was only when they stepped inside the room and he shut the door behind them that he realized how very chilly the Assembly Room must have been.

She turned to face him, her very dark eyes heavy with desire, her teeth sinking into her lower lip. She lifted her arms to wrap about his neck, and he set his arms beneath hers and reached up to tackle the prim schoolteacher's knot at the back of her head. He dipped his head to touch his lips lightly to hers. She released her lower lip and thrust both softly, and parted, against his own.

This was *not* seduction, he told himself, or even half seduction. She was very willing. And it was not cynical amusement he was taking with a willing partner to while away an idle night. He burned for her, though, if he had been forced to put into words the powerful attraction he felt toward her, he would have been hard-pressed. He did not normally favor either dark women or tall women. He admired small women with blond curls. And he liked them well rounded and softly feminine. He liked English rose complexions. Frances Allard was none of those things.

But he burned for her as he had rarely burned for any other woman before her.

His fingers deftly removed hairpins, and her hair came cascading down over her shoulders, heavy and sleekly gleaming in the firelight and almost waist length. It framed her narrow face, and made her look like a Renaissance madonna. At that moment he could not imagine any woman more beautiful, more desirable. He ran his fingers through her hair, wrapping them in it in order to cup the back of her head and keep her face tilted toward his.

"It is glorious," he said. "And yet you keep it so ruthlessly confined. It is a crime against mankind."

"I *am* a schoolteacher," she said, feathering light kisses along his jaw to his chin.

"Not tonight," he told her, dipping his head to take her mouth with his again. "Tonight you are my woman." He sucked her full lower lip into his mouth.

She drew back her head and gazed into his eyes, her own heavy-lidded now with desire.

"And tonight," she said, "you are my man."

Well. He felt himself harden into arousal.

"Yes, tonight," he said, kissing her eyes closed, kissing her lips again, kissing the hollow at the base of her throat. "For tonight, Frances."

He took hold of her shawl and tossed it aside before opening her dress down the back. He felt her shiver against him as her fingers twined tightly in his hair, though he knew it was not with cold.

He slid first one hand inside the soft wool of her dress, and then the other. Her flesh was warm and smooth, with the slight stickiness of desire. He drew the garment off her shoulders and down her arms until of its own momentum it fell to the floor. She wore a chemise beneath but no stays—an explanation, perhaps, for the fact that he had thought her small-bosomed until he had cupped her breasts in his hands in the Assembly Room. They were not voluptuous, but they were enticingly feminine for all that. He held her a little away from him and looked down at her.

She was long-limbed, slender, beautifully shaped. With her thick, very dark hair about her, she looked younger.

He drew a slow breath.

"Sit down on the bed," he said, turning to it and drawing back the covers.

He set his hands on her bare shoulders as she did so, and bent his head to kiss one shoulder in the hollow where it met her neck. She smelled enticingly of soap and woman.

He went down on one knee before her and lifted one of her feet onto his raised knee before rolling the stocking down her leg and off her foot. He leaned forward and kissed the inside of her knee and trailed kisses down her shapely calf to her heel and her instep.

"Oh, yes," she said in the same low, throaty voice she had used earlier.

He looked up to smile at her. But she was supporting herself with both hands behind her on the bed, and her head was thrown back and her eyes closed. All her glorious hair trailed to the bed behind her and spread over the bottom white sheet.

He removed her other stocking in the same way.

She lay down when he got to his feet in order to remove his own clothes. But she did not close her eyes or turn her head away. She lay with her arms spread loosely to the sides, her head half turned toward him, one leg straight, the other slightly bent with her foot flat on the mattress. It was difficult not to tear off his clothes in order to join her there as quickly as he could. But with slow deliberation he shrugged out of his tight-fitting coat and dropped it to the floor, and then out of his waistcoat. He untied his neckcloth and dropped it to the pile. And then he drew his shirt off over his head and discarded that too.

Her bosom, he could see in the firelight, was rising and falling quite noticeably against her shift. Her lips had parted.

He smiled deliberately at her and crossed to the fire in order to throw on a few more coals before returning to the bed and removing his remaining garments.

He smiled again when she crossed her arms and stripped her shift off over her head before dropping it over the edge of the bed. That answered one question. He had been wondering whether he would allow her to keep that final barrier of modesty at least until both of them were beneath the covers.

It was strange how just yesterday he had thought her thin and un-appealing. Tonight her beauty was so perfect in every detail that it quite took his breath away. She reached up her arms to him.

"The bed is rather narrow," she said.

"But why would we want one that is any wider?" he asked her, lowering himself into her arms and sliding one of his own beneath her before kissing her. "Half of it would be wasted."

"To echo what you said earlier of the waltz," she said, threading the long fingers of one hand into his hair, "I must confess that my experience with this sort of activity is severely limited."

"Or perhaps nonexistent?" He kissed the tip of her nose and looked into her eyes.

"Something like that," she admitted.

"I had no experience in peeling potatoes," he said, nuzzling one earlobe.

He felt her shiver.

"But they ended up tasting delicious," she said.

"Exactly my point." He blew softly into her ear.

She drew his mouth to hers once more, and the passion that had ended their waltz prematurely and brought them to this moment was instantly rekindled and redoubled in force. He kissed her open-mouthed, reaching deep into the heat of her mouth with his tongue while his hand moved over her, fondling, teasing, arousing. And her slender, long-fingered hands touched him, lightly, tentatively at first, and then boldly, urgently, hungrily.

They made love to each other with hot, fierce, panting foreplay. When his mouth enclosed and suckled a nipple and one of his hands slid between her thighs to find the hot, moist core of her desire, his fingers probing, rubbing, scratching lightly, she rolled onto her back and he came over on top of her, pinning her to the bed with his not inconsiderable weight. She needed no coaxing to spread her legs. They came up, slim and strong-muscled, to hug his hips and twine about his own legs. He slid his hands beneath her, positioned himself, and entered her firmly and as slowly as he could contrive.

But she would not let him make any allowance for her virginity.

She pressed up against him so that he ruptured the barrier and embedded himself deeply in her far more forcefully than he had intended. Her hands pressed against his buttocks, straining him to her. She was gasping for air.

She was tight and hot and wet. The blood hammered through his body so that he heard his heart like a drum beating urgently in his ears. He held very still in her and fought for control.

"Easy," he murmured, lowering his mouth to hers. "Take it easy. I would give you pleasure, Frances, not go off like a schoolboy on his first outing."

Surprisingly—and delightfully—she laughed. He could feel the tremors of her amusement shivering through her body, and her inner muscles tightened about him.

"You *are* giving me pleasure," she said. "Oh, Lucius, you *are*."

He kissed her into silence. But some of the frenzy of their joining had been dissipated for the moment, and he was able to move in her with slow, deliberate strokes while she closed her eyes and tipped back her head and relaxed her muscles. He worked her through several minutes, her passage growing wetter and slicker until sound mingled with sensation and drove him closer and closer to his own limits.

But he would not change the rhythm yet. There was too much pleasure in anticipating pleasure, and she was a gorgeous, responsive, passionate bedmate. After the first minute she had begun to move with him, and her inner muscles had caught and complemented the rhythm of his thrusts. Her hips circled slowly, creating a pleasure so exquisite that it bordered on pain.

He had had experienced courtesans who were less skilled.

And then finally her control slipped, and she moaned softly to each stroke and contracted her muscles convulsively and off-rhythm. He could feel her increased body heat and the slickness of her sweat. He could hear the raggedness of her breathing. Her arms and thighs strained him closer.

He thrust faster and deeper.

It was impossible for a virgin to reach climax the first time. It was rare for a woman to reach climax at all. He had heard both pronouncements—from other men, of course. Frances Allard proved them all wrong.

She came to a sudden and shattering climax, every muscle in her body tensing before she cried out and shuddered in his arms while he stopped moving. It was a strangely wondrous gift, her cresting of the wave of passion, her shuddering descent down the other side. It had rarely happened to him before, though he had known many women who went to valiant lengths to pretend.

He waited until she was quiet and still beneath him, and then he completed his own pleasure, plunging into her over and over again until he reached the blessed moment of release.

He sighed against the side of her face and relaxed his weight down onto her warm, yielding body.

It had been and was, he thought as he rolled off her a few moments later and gathered her close in his arms, a fitting ending to an adventure—to use her word—that had been strange and unpredictable from the first moment.

Though his mind shied away from dwelling upon the realization that this was the end.

He would think about that tomorrow morning.

Frances was, she discovered, totally head over ears in love with Lucius Marshall. With yesterday's nasty, bad-tempered gentleman, of all men. She smiled against his shoulder. She almost chuckled aloud.

With her intellect, of course, she knew that she was not in love at all. Not really. Not in the way of those great, enduring romances one occasionally heard or read about anyway. She had only just met him, after all, and she really did not know him. Even though he had somehow managed to learn several details of her life, he had said remarkably little about his own. What they had shared and were sharing tonight was entirely physical. It was lust pure and simple. She was under no illusions about that. And she was not ashamed of the admission. Perhaps she would be later, but not now. For now she was quite happy to accept the situation for what it was.

As she lay in the narrow bed with him, their limbs all tangled together, and he slept while she tried hard not to, she did her thinking with her emotions rather than with her intellect.

And she tried—she desperately tried to cling to the moment, to revel in the sensation of being in love and of having been physically loved in a manner more glorious than anything she could possibly have imagined.

She had expected lovemaking to be painful. It *had* been when he first came inside her and for a minute or two after he had started moving in her. She had also expected it to be horribly embarrassing. How could it not be when one considered what actually happened? But ultimately it had been neither.

It had been by far the most wonderful experience of her life.

And it was still wonderful. She was warm and cozy. She could feel his strong arms about her and one powerful leg pushed between her own. She could feel his hard-muscled body against hers, her breasts pressed to his chest with its light dusting of hair. She could smell his cologne, his sweat, his maleness, and thought that no perfume could ever smell half so enticing.

Strange thought!

It was a good thing, she thought, nestling closer to him and butting her head into a warm spot beneath his chin, prompting a sleepy grunt of protest from him, that she would never have anyone with whom to compare him. Marriage opportunities—or even opportunities for casual amours, for that matter—did not come the way of lady schoolteachers with any great frequency. Once she had had chances to make a good marriage, even a happy one, but those days were long gone.

She was trying to stay awake, not because she was not tired but because tonight was something that was going to have to last her for all the rest of her life. Whenever her mind touched upon the thought that tomorrow she would be back in her own bed on Daniel Street in Bath, she felt twinges of panic somewhere in the region of the bottom of her stomach.

If she did not sleep, perhaps the night would never end.

What foolishness!

But tragedy—the certain knowledge of a dreadful, desolate pain to come—loomed just beneath the surface of her drowsy happiness.

She would think about it tomorrow when she would have no choice.

"Cold?" a low, sleepy voice asked her.

The fire had burned itself out sometime before, but she was as cozy as she could possibly be where she was.

"No," she said.

"Too bad," he said. "I might have thought of a way of warming you up if you were."

"I am *frozen*," she assured him, chuckling softly.

"You lie through your teeth, ma'am," he said, "but I like your spirit. Now, I suppose I need to think of some way of warming you— and myself. Doubtless you can tell that I am shivering too. Any suggestions?"

She drew her head back from its warm burrow and kissed him on the mouth. He had a lovely mouth, wide and firm, with the promise of all sorts of delights within.

"Mmm," he murmured. "Keep thinking."

It was not just his physical appeal, she thought, though there was tons and tons of that. But today she had discovered wit and humor and intelligence in him with the result that she had been able to rather like him as a person as well as to admire him as a man. They could perhaps be friends under different circumstances, if only there were more time. But time was something they did not have. Not much time anyway—only the rest of tonight.

She lifted herself on one elbow in order to kiss him more thoroughly, but suddenly two strong hands grasped her by the waist and lifted her bodily upward while he turned over onto his back and into the middle of the bed, and then deposited her right on top of him.

"That is better," he said. "You make a nice warm blanket." He pulled the rest of the covers right up over their heads and kissed her with lingering thoroughness, his tongue circling hers, exploring the inside of her mouth and then simulating the sexual act.

Ah, yes, there was still the rest of tonight.

She drew her head free and nuzzled the side of his neck with her lips and teeth and splayed her hands over his shoulders so that she could lift herself sufficiently to rub her breasts and nipples over his chest.

"Mmm," she said.

"You took the words right out of my mouth," he told her.

She spread her legs wide so that she could kneel astride his body and thus have greater freedom to move, to touch him, to caress him, to explore his body with palms and fingers and nails and lips and teeth and tongue. He lay still and let her do it, responding for a while only with low, appreciative little grunts. And then she felt him grow large and hard against her abdomen and rubbed against him until she felt that someone must have lit a dozen fires in the room.

It was marvelously exciting to feel her power over him, to know that they would make love again, that she led the way.

But finally he took charge, spreading his hands over her hips, drawing her into position over his hard erection, and pulling downward. Though that last was not necessary. She pressed down onto him until once more she was filled with him.

Gloriously, wondrously filled.

She leaned over him, her hair falling about them both, and gazed into his eyes, just visible in the faint light coming through the window. She lifted some of her weight onto her knees again, spread her hands over his chest once more, and moved, lifting and pressing, creating again the heady rhythm of love.

"Ah, yes," he murmured to her, "ride me, then, Frances."

It was a startling and erotic image. But she did indeed ride him over and over again until she could ride no more but only surrender to his hands that came back to her hips to hold her steady as he pressed up hard into her and held there while something at the core of her burst open and blossomed into perfect pleasure—and then perfect peace.

She knelt where she was until he had finished, and then she lay down on him, her legs stretched on either side of his, while he drew the covers warmly over her again and wrapped his arms about her.

They were still joined.

This, she thought drowsily, was what happiness felt like. Not contentment, but *happiness*.

And tomorrow . . .

But mercifully she slept.

6

*Peters and Thomas had both gone out by the time Lucius ap-*peared downstairs the following morning, even though it was still well before dawn. They returned soon after he had gone out to the stables himself, bringing with them the news that the snow had melted considerably and that the road was already passable, provided one proceeded with extreme caution. Miss Allard's carriage, though, was still firmly stuck in its snowbank. It would take assistance and the best part of the day to haul it out and dry it off and look it over to ensure that it was roadworthy.

"Though it might be said, guv, that it never was that anytime during the last thirty years or so," Peters could not resist adding.

Thomas muttered darkly to the effect that there would be nothing wrong with his carriage if a certain impudent young 'un, who would remain nameless for the sake of peace, had not passed it when he didn't ought and then stopped dead in front of it in the middle of the road. And in *his* day, he added, carriages were made to last.

If Thomas's coach had not been moving so slowly that it was almost going backward, Peters retorted, and if at that pace it could not stop behind another carriage without slithering into a snowbank, then it was high time a certain coachman who would remain nameless was put out to grass.

Lucius left them to it without attempting any mediation and went back inside the inn and into the kitchen. Frances was in there, busy getting breakfast.

Knowledge hit him like a fist to the stomach. He had been holding that slender body naked in his arms not so long ago.

"If you wish," he said after giving her the bad news about her own carriage, "we will both remain here another day. It will surely be rescued and roadworthy by tomorrow."

The suggestion certainly had its appeal—except that the world would find them sometime during the course of the day even if they stayed here. Villagers would come for their ale. The Parkers would return from their holiday. There was no way of recapturing the charm of yesterday's isolation—or the passion of last night's.

Time had moved on as it always and inevitably did.

She hesitated, but he could almost read her mind as it turned over the same thoughts and came to the same conclusions.

"No," she said. "I must get back to the school today somehow. The girls return today, and classes begin tomorrow. There is so much to do before then. I will see if a stagecoach stops somewhere in the village."

She was not quite looking into his eyes, he noticed. But her face was flushed, and her lips looked soft and slightly swollen, and there was something more than usually warm and feminine about her whole demeanor. She looked like a woman who had been well and thoroughly bedded the night before.

He felt partly aroused again by the sight of her. But last night was over and done with, alas. It ought not to have happened at all, he supposed, though of course he had gone to some pains to see that it *did* happen. And to say that he had enjoyed the outcome would be to understate the case.

It was simply time to move on.

"There is none," he said. "I have asked Wally. But if you are willing to leave Thomas here to take your carriage back where it came from tomorrow, you may come with me this morning. I'll take you to Bath."

She raised her eyes to his then, and her flush deepened.

"Oh, but I cannot ask that of you," she said. "Bath must be well out of your way."

It was. More than that, since yesterday could not be recaptured, he did not really want to prolong this encounter beyond its natural ending. It would have been best this morning if they could simply have kissed, bidden each other a cheerful farewell, and gone their separate ways. It would have all been over within an hour or so.

"Not very much out of the way," he said. "And you did not ask it of me, did you? I think I ought to see you safely delivered to your school, Frances."

"Because you feel responsible for what happened to my carriage?" she asked.

"Nonsense!" he said. "If Thomas were my servant, I would set him to digging about the flower beds in a remote corner of my park, where no one would notice if he pulled out the flowers and left the weeds. If he ever was competent at driving a carriage, it must have been at least twenty years ago."

"He is a loyal retainer to my great-aunts," she said. "You have no right to—"

He held up a staying hand and then strode toward her and kissed her hard on the mouth.

"I would love to have a good scrap with you again," he said. "I remember you as a worthy foe. But I would rather not waste good traveling time. I want to take you to Bath in person so that I do not have to worry about your getting there safely."

The roads might be passable, but there was no doubt that they would be dangerous. Snow, slush, mud—whichever they were fated to encounter, and it seemed probable that it would be all three before the journey was ended—the going would be difficult. He *would* worry about her if he knew she was alone with the elderly Thomas driving her more-than-elderly carriage. Even tomorrow the roads would not be at their best.

Good Lord! he thought suddenly. He had not gone and fallen in love with the woman, had he? That would be a deuced stupid thing to do.

He had just promised his grandfather that he would begin seriously courting a suitable bride—and a suitable bride in his world meant someone with connections to the aristocracy, someone who had been brought up from the cradle to fill just such a role as that of Countess of Edgecombe.

Someone perfect in every way.

Someone like Portia Hunt.

Not someone like a schoolteacher from Bath who taught music and French.

It was a harsh reality but a reality nonetheless. It was the way his world worked.

"I would be very grateful, then," she said, turning away to finish cooking their breakfast. "Thank you."

She was cool and aloof this morning—except for the flushed cheeks and swollen lips. He wondered if she regretted last night, but he would not ask her. There was no point in regretting what was done, was there? And she had certainly not been regretting it while it was happening. She had loved with hunger and enthusiasm—a thought he had better not pursue further.

He *wished* there were a stagecoach coming through the village. He needed to get away from her.

But less than an hour later, having eaten and washed the dishes and left money and instructions with Thomas and a generous payment with Wally for their stay at the inn, Lucius's carriage set out on its way to Bath with Frances Allard as a passenger.

There had been some argument, of course, over who should make the payments. He had prevailed, but he knew that giving in had been painful, even humiliating, to her. If his guess was correct—and he was almost certain it was—her reticule did not contain vast riches. Her pride was doubtless stung. She sat in stiff silence for the first mile or two, looking out through the window beside her.

Lucius found himself wishing again that they could relive yesterday—just exactly as it had been except perhaps for the afternoon, which they had wasted by spending apart in a vain attempt to avoid what had probably been inevitable from the moment of their meeting.

It must be years since he had frolicked as he had with her out in the snow just for the simple enjoyment of frolicking. It *was* years since he had danced voluntarily. Indeed, he did not believe he had ever done so before last evening. And he still felt relaxed and satiated after a night of good, vigorous sex.

Damnation, but he was not ready to say good-bye to her yet.

And why should he say it? The Season would not begin in any earnest until after Easter. There was not much he could do about fulfilling his promise until then. And despite what his mother and sisters seemed to believe, he had not yet committed himself to Portia Hunt. In fact, he had always been very careful in her presence and in that of Balderston, her father, and most especially in that of *Lady* Balderston *not* to commit himself in any way, not to say anything that might be construed as a marriage offer. He had not even promised his grandfather that she would be the one.

Honor was not at stake here, then. Not yet, anyway. He had not been unfaithful to anyone last night.

Why *should* he say good-bye?

He was rationalizing, of course. He knew that. There was no realistic future for him and Frances Allard. But he went on trying to devise one anyway.

He had little experience with not getting whatever he wanted.

Why could there not have been a stagecoach passing through the village?

Or why could she not simply have said that she would wait alone for her great-aunts' carriage to be ready tomorrow? But he would not, she was sure, have been willing to leave her alone at the inn. And, truth to tell, she could not have borne to be left alone there, to watch his carriage drive away from the inn and disappear to view. The emptiness of the inn, the silence, would have been unbearable.

It was what would happen in Bath, though. The thought caused a painful churning of her stomach that made her sorry she had eaten any breakfast.

The best solution, of course, would have been to say good-bye this morning after breakfast and to have both left in a different carriage—to go in the same direction for a while. His carriage would soon have outpaced hers, though. Anyway, that had not been an option.

Ah, there *was* no easy way to say good-bye.

What on earth had possessed her last night? She had never come close to giving in to such temptation before.

She had given herself to a stranger. She had made love with him and spent all night in bed with him. They had coupled three separate times, the third time hot and swift and wonderful just before he got up and left her room, wearing only his pantaloons and carrying the rest of his clothes.

And now she was going to have to suffer all the considerable emotional consequences. She was already suffering them even though she was still with him. She could feel his body close to hers on the carriage seat. She could feel his body heat down her right side. But it was the end. Soon—at the end of this slow, dreary journey past snow fields that looked gray rather than pristine white today—soon they would be saying good-bye, and she would never see him again.

And as if depression and grief were not enough, there was her nervousness every time the carriage wheels slithered on the slushy road surface—and they did so almost constantly during the first few miles until Lucius Marshall slid his hand beneath her lap robe, drew her right hand free of her muff, and held it firmly in his, lacing his fingers with hers.

She could have wept at his warm, assured touch.

"Peters is not the most subservient of retainers," he said, "but he is the finest driver of my acquaintance. I would, and do, trust him with my life."

"I think," she said, "that the feeling of slithering then sliding backward right off the road and finding myself submerged in a snowbank will live in my nightmares for a long time."

"But if it had not happened to you," he said, "you would not have met me."

He was looking down at her, she knew, but she would not turn her head to see his expression. He had said the same thing on that very first day—was it only the day before yesterday?—but he had been being nastily ironic on that occasion.

"No," she said. "I would not, would I? How dreadful that would have been."

"There, you see?" He chuckled. "You forgot your nervousness for a moment in order to be spiteful. Or do you mean it?"

She laughed too despite herself.

Her nervousness largely disappeared after that, and so did the tension there had been between them ever since he walked into the kitchen this morning. They continued to hold hands, and after a while she realized that her shoulder was resting against the heavy capes of his greatcoat. She could feel the warmth and strength of his arm beneath them.

She would have her classes write an essay—no, a story—within the next few days, she thought. Not the dull topic of how they spent Christmas that they might expect, but something more creative— "Imagine that as you returned alone to school after Christmas, you ran into a snowstorm and were stranded at a deserted inn with one other person. Write the story . . ."

Marjorie Phillips would dip her quill pen in the inkwell and bend over her paper without further ado and would not straighten up again until she had scribbled a dozen pages of closely packed writing. Joy Denton would do almost as well. Sarah Ponds would put up her hand and remind Miss Allard that she had not left the school before Christmas and therefore did not return to it after Christmas. The rest of the class would sit with furrowed brows and inactive or even nonexistent imaginations, wondering if she would notice if they wrote large, widely stretched words on widely spaced lines and made their stories one page long.

Frances smiled fondly at the thought. All the girls were very precious to her.

But her thoughts were not easily diverted during that long day of travel.

They stopped a few times for changes of horse, and once for

almost a full hour to dine, but for the rest of the time they sat together in the carriage, not talking a great deal, their hands clasped, their thighs and arms touching, her head sometimes tipped sideways to rest on his shoulder. Once she dozed off and, when she woke up again, she found that he had laid his cheek against the top of her head and was himself asleep.

Again she felt like weeping. Her chest was tight and sore from the necessity of holding back her tears.

It was sometime after that, when it seemed to her that they must surely not be very far from Bath, that he set one arm right about her shoulders, turned her to him, lifted her chin in the cleft between his thumb and forefinger, and kissed her.

His mouth felt shockingly warm in contrast to the chill of the air. She heard herself utter a low moan, and she wrapped her arm about his neck and kissed him back with all the yearning she felt.

"Frances," he murmured after a long, long while. "Frances, what the devil am I going to do about you?"

She drew away from him, sat back in her seat, and eyed him warily.

"I think," he said, "we ought to ask ourselves if it is really necessary to say good-bye to each other when we arrive in Bath."

His words were so exactly what she had been dreaming of hearing all day that her heart lurched with painful hope.

"I teach school there," she said. "You have your own life elsewhere."

"Forget about teaching," he said. "Come with me instead." There was a reckless intensity in his eyes.

"Come with you?" She frowned, and her heart raced enough to make her breathless. "Where?"

"Wherever we choose to go," he said. "The whole world is out there. Come with me."

She set her shoulders across the corner of the seat, trying to put a little more distance between them, trying to think clearly.

The whole world is out there.

It *was* reckless.

"I do not even know anything about you beyond your name," she said.

And yet a part of her, that equally reckless part of herself that had waltzed and then lain with him last night, heedless of the consequences, wanted to shout out yes, yes, *yes,* and go off with him wherever he chose to take her—to the ends of the earth if need be. Preferably there, in fact.

"You do not even know my name in its entirety." He made her a half-bow with a flourish of one hand. "Lucius Marshall, Viscount Sinclair, at your service, Frances. My home is Cleve Abbey in Hampshire, but I spend most of my time in London. Come there with me. I am vastly wealthy. I will clothe you in satin and deck you with jewels. You will never want for anything. You will never need to teach another class in your life."

Viscount Sinclair . . . Cleve Abbey . . . London . . . wealth . . . satin and jewels.

She sat staring at him aghast, while her initial euphoria drained away and with it the romantic dream that had fogged her mind since last night—or perhaps even before then.

He was not just an almost anonymous gentleman with whom she could perhaps have disappeared into the obscurity of a happily-ever-after—though even that was a childish and impossible dream. No one was anonymous or even *almost* so. Whoever he had turned out to be, he would have had a family and a history and a life somewhere. He was no fairy-tale prince. And there was no such thing as happily-ever-after.

But the reality was so much worse than anything she could have anticipated or guessed at. He was *Viscount Sinclair* of Cleve Abbey, and he was vastly wealthy . . .

"Viscount Sinclair," she said.

"But also Lucius Marshall," he said. "The two persons are one and the same."

Yes.

And no.

An impossible dream died and she saw him for what he was—an impulsive, reckless aristocrat, who was accustomed to having his own way regardless of cold reality—especially where women were concerned.

But perhaps reality had never been cold for him.

"Forget about having to work," he urged her. "Come with me to London."

"Perhaps," she said, "I enjoy teaching."

"And perhaps," he said, "convicts enjoy their prison cells."

His words angered her and she frowned. She was reminded that this was the same man as the one who had so angered her just two days ago with his arrogant, high-handed behavior.

"I find that comparison insulting," she said.

But he caught her hands in his and pressed his lips first to one palm and then to the other.

"I absolutely refuse to quarrel with you," he said. "Come with me. Why should we do what neither of us wishes to do? Why not do what we *want*? I cannot say good-bye to you yet, Frances. And I know you feel as I do."

"But you *will* be able to say it next week or next month or next year?" she asked him.

He looked sharply up into her face, his eyebrows raised.

"Is that why you hesitate?" he asked. "You think I would make you my mistress?"

She *knew* he would.

"Is it marriage you offer, then?" she asked, unable to keep the bitterness from her voice.

He stared at her for what seemed a long while, his expression fathomless.

"In truth," he said at last, "I do not know what it is I offer, Frances. I just cannot bear to say good-bye, that is all. Come to London with me and I will find you lodgings and a respectable woman to live with you as a companion. We may—"

She closed her eyes briefly and shut out the sound of his voice. It was clear he had not thought this through at all. But of course, he did not need to. He was not the one being asked to throw away all that had given anchor and meaning to life for three years. His own life would remain much the same as usual, she supposed, except that he would have a new mistress—and of course it *was* as a mistress that he wanted her. He had looked somewhat stunned when she had mentioned marriage, as if it were something he had never heard of.

"I will not come with you," she said.

Even as she spoke the words, though, she knew that she might still have been tempted if it were not for one fact—London was the one place on this earth she could never go back to. She had promised . . .

There was something else too. When he spoke of clothing her in satin and decking her in jewels, he sounded so much like other men she had once encountered that she could not avoid seeing with blinding clarity the sordidness of the future that would be awaiting her if she gave in to this longing to grasp at anything that would save her from having to say good-bye to him.

The thought of never seeing him again was almost unbearable.

He squeezed her hands painfully. "I will remain in Bath with you, then," he said.

For a moment her heart leaped with gladness at his willingness to be the one making the sacrifice—but only for a moment. It would not work. He was Viscount Sinclair of Cleve Abbey. He was a wealthy, fashionable aristocrat. He lived much of his life in London. What would Bath have to offer him that would keep him there indefinitely? If he stayed, they would be merely postponing the inevitable. Nothing could ever come of any relationship between them. And no relationship satisfying to him could exist between them in Bath. No sexual relationship anyway—and no other type would satisfy him. Good heavens, she was a teacher!

There simply *was* no future for them. Some realities were that stark, and all one could do was accept them.

She shook her head, her eyes on her hands still clasped in his.

"No," she said. "I would rather you did not stay."

"Why the devil not!" he exclaimed, his voice louder and more irritable—the voice of a man unaccustomed to being denied what he had set his heart on.

She tried to withdraw her hands, but he held on, squeezing her fingers and hurting them.

"The last couple of days were very pleasant," she said. "At least, yesterday was. But it is time to get back to normal life, Mr. Marshall—Viscount Sinclair. It is time for both of us. I will never be your mistress and you will never marry me—or I you for that matter. There would be no point, then, in trying to prolong what was merely a pleasant interlude in both our lives."

"*Pleasant,*" he said, sounding more than irritable now. He sounded downright thunderous. "We spent a day in close company with each other and a night in bed together, and it was *pleasant,* Frances?"

"Yes." She kept her voice steady. "It was. But it was not something that can ever be repeated. It is time to say good-bye."

He stared at her for a long time before releasing her hands. His eyes had flattened, she noticed, so that she could no longer read any of his thoughts or feelings in them. His expression had changed in other ways too. His mouth had lifted at the corners, but not really in a smile. One eyebrow had risen. He had retreated behind a mask of cynical mockery. It felt as if he had already gone away.

"Well, Miss Allard," he said, "it seems that I was right about you at the start. It is not often I am rejected by a woman. It is not often my lovemaking is damned with such faint praise as to be called *pleasant.* You have no wish for any continuation of our acquaintance, then? Very well. I shall grant your wish, ma'am."

In one short speech he had turned into a chilly, haughty aristocrat who bore little resemblance to the Lucius Marshall who had held her and loved her through the night.

She had expressed herself poorly, she realized.

But how else could she have expressed herself when she must have said essentially the same thing? There was no point now in telling him that his lovemaking had been earth-shattering, that her heart was breaking, that she might well mourn his loss for the rest of her life.

None of those things was true anyway in all probability. They were all true today, but tomorrow they would be a little less so and next week less so again. It was in the nature of strong emotion that it faded away over time. Her own previous experience had taught her that.

They sat silently side by side until finally—it seemed like forever, and it seemed far too soon—they were entering the outer limits of the city of Bath.

"You see?" he said, his voice so normal that her heart lurched again. "I told you I would deliver you safely to your school."

"And so you did." She smiled brightly, though he did not turn his head to see. "Thank you. I appreciate your coming out of your way more than I can tell you."

"Miss Martin will be relieved to find that she is not to be one teacher short for tomorrow," he said.

"Yes, indeed." She was still smiling. "This evening is going to be a very busy one, with classes to prepare for tomorrow and everyone clamoring to share their Christmas stories with me."

"And you will be happy to be back at work." It was not really a question.

"Oh, yes, indeed," she assured him. "Holidays are always welcome and always pleasant, but I enjoy teaching, and I have good friends at the school."

"Friends are always important," he said.

"Oh, yes, indeed," she agreed brightly.

And so their last few minutes together were frittered away in bright, stilted, meaningless chatter as they avoided touching or looking into each other's eyes.

The carriage turned onto Sydney Place and passed Sydney Gardens before turning onto Sutton Street and then onto Daniel Street, where Peters drew it in ahead of another carriage, which was disgorging a few passengers, including a young girl, and a mound of baggage outside the two tall, stately houses that together comprised Miss Martin's school.

"Hannah Swan," Frances murmured. "One of the junior girls." As if he might be interested.

He reached into one of his pockets and drew out a visiting card.

He folded it in two, pressed it into her palm, closed her fingers about it, and raised her hand to his lips.

"You may prefer it if I remain in here unseen," he said. "This is good-bye after all, then, Frances. But if you should have need of me, you will find me at the address in London written on that card. I will come immediately."

Her eyes had been fixed on the button that held his greatcoat closed at the neck. But now she raised them to gaze into his—hard, intense hazel eyes. There was no mistaking his meaning, of course. His jaw too looked hard and very square.

"Good-bye, Lucius," she said.

By that time Peters had the door open and was setting down the steps.

"If they had any more baggage in that there coach," he said conversationally, jerking his head in its direction, "the springs would be dragging on the road. You are staying in there, are you, then, guv? Too lazy to stretch your legs? Right you are, then. Give me your hand, miss, and mind this puddle."

She turned quickly and descended hastily to the pavement. Within a moment she was swallowed up in the bustle surrounding the other carriage as baggage was lifted down from the roof and sorted and carried inside.

She put her head down and hurried past without a backward glance.

Although there was a great deal of commotion in the hallway inside the school doors with Hannah Swan standing there and both her parents taking their farewell of her and admonishing her with all sorts of last-minute advice, Mr. Keeble, the elderly porter, found time to greet Frances with a bow and wink at her and inform her in a quiet aside that *some* teachers would go to any lengths to avoid returning to school one moment sooner than they must. And Claudia Martin patted her on the arm, welcomed her back, told her she was glad to see her safe, and promised that they would talk later.

But she was not to avoid a more effusive welcome, Frances found. Even before she reached the head of the stairs she met two more junior girls on their way down to claim Hannah, and they chattered and giggled at her for a whole minute without stopping, telling her something about Christmas that she could scarcely comprehend. And no sooner had she arrived upstairs in her room, shut the door behind her, undone the ribbons of her bonnet with her left hand and tossed it onto the bed, and blown out air from her puffed cheeks than the door burst open again after the merest tap of a knock and Susanna Osbourne came hurrying in to catch up Frances in an exuberant hug.

"Oh, you wretch!" she cried. "You have given Anne and me two sleepless nights, and even Miss Martin was worried, though she would insist that you are far too sensible to have risked putting yourself in any danger. We pictured you frozen into an icicle in some snowbank. It is *such* a relief to see you back safe."

Susanna was the youngest of the four resident teachers at the school. Small, auburn-haired, green-eyed, exquisitely pretty, and vivacious, she looked far too young to be a teacher—and in truth she was still only a *junior* teacher, promoted two years before after six years as a pupil at Miss Martin's school. But despite her small stature and youthful looks, she had succeeded at the difficult task of winning the respect and obedience of girls who had once been her fellow pupils.

Frances hugged her in return and laughed. But before she could say anything, she was caught up in another hug by Anne Jewell, one of the other teachers.

"I assured Susanna, just as Claudia did, that you are far too sensible to have left your great-aunts' house in such inclement weather," she said. "I am glad we were both right, Frances. Though of course I *did* worry."

Anne was loved by staff and pupils alike. Fair-haired, blue-eyed, and lovely, she was also even-tempered, approachable, and sympathetic to even the lowliest, least intelligent and well-favored pupils— especially to them, in fact. If she had favorites, they tended to be among the charity girls, who made up half the school's population. But there were always those few girls of more elevated social status who lost no opportunity to remark upon the fact that Miss Jewell— with a significant emphasis on the *Miss*—had a young son living with her at the school.

Even Frances and Susanna did not know the full story behind David Jewell's existence, though Claudia Martin doubtless did. They were firm friends, all four of them, but even friends were entitled to some secrets. And as for David, he had a nursemaid all to himself as well as several unofficial teachers and was adored by the girls and spoiled by the staff. He was a sweet child nonetheless, and he had great artistic talent and potential, according to Mr. Upton, the art master.

"Well," Frances said, "I am quite safe, as you see, though I am two days late and dread to think how much work will be facing me for the rest of today. I did, of course, remain with my great-aunts until early this morning and so you need not have worried at all. They sent me back here in their own carriage."

And friends were sometimes entitled to lie to one another.

She could not *bear* to tell the truth. She could not bear the look of sympathy she knew she would see in their eyes when she came to the end of her story.

"Work or no work," Anne said firmly, "you are going to have tea with us, Frances, and relax after what I am sure has been a trying day. I do not suppose the roads were at their best, and you would have had nothing but your own company to distract your mind from a contemplation of them. But no matter. You are safe now, and Claudia has ordered tea to be served in her sitting room in ten minutes' time. Susanna and I have decided to be utterly selfless and not fight you for the chair by the fire."

They both laughed, and Frances smiled brightly.

"I will certainly not argue that point," she said. "And tea will be very welcome. Give me ten minutes to comb my hair and wash my hands and face?"

Anne opened the door.

"All the girls have now arrived," she said. "Hannah Swan was last, as usual. Matron has them all firmly under her wing. So we can *relax* for a whole *hour*."

"We want to hear everything about your Christmas," Susanna said. "Every last detail. Including a description of every gentleman you met."

"No, only the handsome ones, Susanna," Anne said. "And the unmarried ones. We are not interested in the others."

"Ah. In that case an hour may be just long enough—if I talk fast," Frances said.

They went on their way, laughing merrily.

Frances sat down abruptly on the bed. Her legs would not have supported her if they had stayed one minute longer, she was sure. She shut her eyes tightly. She felt very close to hysteria, though she knew she had far too much pride to give in to it. What she wanted to do more than anything else on this earth was burrow beneath the covers of the bed and lie there, curled into a ball, for the rest of her life.

If she were to look out through her window, she knew, the street below would be empty.

He was gone.

Forever.

By her own choosing.

He would have taken her with him. Or he would have stayed in Bath.

She clenched both fists in her lap and fought panic, the foolish urge to rush back downstairs and outside in the hope of somehow catching up to his carriage before it disappeared forever.

It was hopeless—*hopeless*. He was not only Lucius Marshall, gentleman. He was also Viscount Sinclair. He lived most of the time in London. She could never return there, and she could never move in high circles again—even if he had ever asked her to. He would not have done so, of course. He would have made her his mistress for a while, until he tired of her. And that would have happened. What had been between them during the past couple of days was no grand romance, after all.

She was in no doubt that she had done the right thing.

But doing the right thing had never seemed bleaker.

This is good-bye after all, then, Frances.

She swallowed once, and then again.

And then she heard the echo of his final words.

But if you should have need of me, you will find me at the address in London written on that card. I will come immediately.

She opened her eyes, realizing that her right hand was still clenched about the card he had placed there. She opened her hand and looked down at it, still folded in two, the partially opened sides facing away from her.

It was over. They had said good-bye. He would come again with assistance if she should need it—if she discovered that she was with child, that was.

But it was over.

Very deliberately she folded the card once more, tore it across and across again, and as many more times as she could before dropping the pieces into the back of the fireplace. She recognized the rashness of what she did. But she had sent him away. She could never now appeal to him for aid.

"Good-bye, Lucius," she said softly before turning determinedly to the washstand and pouring cold water into the bowl.

Ten minutes, Anne and Susanna had said. She would look present-able by the time she arrived in Claudia Martin's sitting room. And she would be smiling.

And she would be armed to the teeth with amusing anecdotes about Christmas.

No one was going to know the truth.

No one was even going to suspect.

Lucius spent the following week at Cleve Abbey and then removed to London even earlier than he had planned, too restless to remain alone in the country with his own thoughts—or, more to the point, with his own emotions.

The latter consisted predominantly of anger, which manifested it-self in irritability. Being the rejected rather than the rejecter was a new experience for him in his dealings with women. It was also, he sup-posed, a humbling experience and therefore good for the soul. But the soul be damned! The very idea that anything good might come of his experience only added to his ill humor.

What could be good about losing a bedfellow one had only just begun to enjoy?

That Frances Allard had been quite right in ending their budding affair did nothing to alleviate his irritability either. When he had made his offer to take her to London with him, he had not stopped to con-sider in what capacity he would take her there. But it could not have been as a wife, could it? Devil take it, he had just promised to wed an eligible bride before the summer was out, and he did not imagine that either his grandfather or his mother would consider a schoolteacher from Bath in any way eligible.

He had always been impulsive, even reckless. But this time part of him realized that if she had taken him up on any of his suggestions, he would have found himself in an awkward position indeed. He had not only promised his grandfather, he had also pledged himself to turn over a new leaf, to become a responsible, respectable man, perish the thought. He was going to court a wife during the spring, not indulge his fancy with a new mistress.

And that was what Frances would have been if she had come with him. There was no point in denying it. He could not have kept her long. Part of turning over a new leaf involved committing himself to one woman for the rest of his life—the woman he would marry.

It was time to say good-bye, Frances had told him. They had enjoyed a pleasant day or two together, but it was time to get back to normal life.

Pleasant!

That particular choice of word still rankled for a while even after he had arrived in London and immersed himself in the familiar daily round of his clubs and other typically masculine pursuits with his numerous friends and acquaintances.

His lovemaking had been *pleasant*. It was almost enough to make a man weep and tear his hair and lose all confidence in himself as a lover.

She had done him a favor by saying no. She really had.

Which fact made ill humor cling to him like an unwanted headache.

But it was not in his nature to brood indefinitely. And there was plenty to occupy his mind, in addition to the familiar pleasures of town life.

There was the fact that he was now living at Marshall House on Cavendish Square, for example, and that soon his mother and sisters were there too. There was all the novelty of being part of a family again for an extended period of time and being involved in all their hopes and fears and anxieties over the coming Season—in which he was pledged to play an active role this year. Emily was to make her come-out and needed to be properly outfitted for it and her presentation to the queen. And he needed to court a bride.

And there was the fact that Portia Hunt was expected to arrive in town immediately after Easter. His mother reminded him—as if he could have forgotten—at breakfast one morning after reading a letter from Lady Balderston.

"I will write back to her this morning," his mother informed him, "and tell her that you are already in town too, Lucius, and living at Marshall House this year and planning to escort your sisters to a number of *ton* events."

In effect, his mother would be announcing to Portia's mama that he was poised to take a bride at last. Why would someone of Viscount Sinclair's reputation be planning to attend balls and routs and Venetian breakfasts and such like events, after all, if he were not seriously in search of a leg shackle?

The Balderstons and Portia—as well as the Marquess of Godsworthy, her grandfather—would come to London, then, fully expecting that a betrothal was imminent. Lucius did not doubt it. It was how society worked. A great deal could be said and arranged—especially by women—without a direct word ever being spoken. The direct word would come from him when he finally made his call on Balderston to discuss marriage settlements and then made his formal offer to Portia herself.

The mere thought of what awaited him was enough to make him break out in a cold sweat.

However, he might be pleasantly surprised when he saw Portia again. It struck him that it must be two years or so since he had actually held any sort of conversation with her. Perhaps seeing her again would help him focus his mind on duty and the inevitable future. After all, a man must eventually marry. And if he must, and if the time happened to be now, he might as well marry someone eminently eligible and someone he had known most of his life. Better the devil you know . . .

Not that he was making any comparison between Portia and the devil. Good Lord, she would be the quintessentially perfect bride. He could not do better if he hunted the length and breadth of the country for the next five years. He did not have five years, though. He had promised to be married long before this year was out.

He was *almost* looking forward to her arrival in town.

But something else was different about this spring too. He was anxious about his grandfather's health and pounced upon every letter that came from Barclay Court. And one of those letters, delivered a week or so before the Balderstons were expected, brought word that the earl had made arrangements to remove to Bath for a couple of weeks or so in order to take a course of the spa waters. They had always been beneficial to his health in the past, he explained, and he intended to see if they would have a similar effect again. He had taken a house on Brock Street rather than stay at a hotel.

Lady Sinclair, genuinely concerned though she was about her father-in-law's health, could not possibly leave London at that particular moment. Emily was soon to be presented at court and there were a thousand and one details to be attended to before the great day dawned. And Caroline, two years older than Emily, could not leave London, as she was entering her third Season, still unmarried, though it was fully expected that Sir Henry Cobham would come to the point within the month and apply for her hand. Amy was too young to go to Bath alone to care for her grandfather even though she expressed her willingness to do so.

That left Lucius. It was desirable that he stay in town, of course. But he was deeply concerned about his grandfather and felt the need to assure himself firsthand that his health had not seriously deteriorated since Christmas. It would not hurt to be away from London for a week or two, anyway. He would be back by the time the Season swung into full action.

There would be more than enough time to go courting after he returned.

By that time almost three months had passed since Christmas, and

he had more or less forgotten about Frances Allard except for the oc-
casional nostalgic memory of their one night together. Even so, he was
not quite insensible of the fact that in going to Bath he would also be
putting himself in close proximity to her again. He did not dwell upon
the thought, though. He was unlikely to see her, and he would certainly not make any active attempt to do so. She was firmly in his past
and would remain there. And indeed she had occupied a very tiny corner of his past.

He was somewhat disconcerted, then, when his traveling carriage
came within sight of Bath in the valley below the road from London,
all white and sparkling in the spring sunshine, by the power of the
memories that assaulted him. He remembered so plainly the pain he
had suffered the last time he had been on this road—being driven in
the opposite direction—that he felt the pang of it even now. He remembered the almost overwhelming urge he had felt to turn back and
beg her to come with him—on his knees if necessary.

The very thought that he might have done such an embarrassing
and humiliating thing was enough to give him the shudders. He certainly had no wish to set eyes again on the woman who had brought
him so abjectly low.

Amy, his youngest sister, was traveling with him. She was at the
awkward age of seventeen. She had been released from the school-
room after Christmas so that she could accompany the rest of the family to London in the early spring, but any excited expectations that
fact had aroused in her bosom had soon been dashed. Their mother
had been quite firm in her refusal to allow her to make her come-out
this year, since it was Emily's turn and Caroline was still unmarried
too. Poor Amy had been less than delighted at the prospect of being
excluded from almost all the dizzying array of activities that would
soon brighten her sisters' days and had jumped at the chance of accompanying her brother to Bath.

Listening to her exclamations of delight at the scene spread before
her and pointing out to her some of the more prominent landmarks of
Bath diverted Lucius's attention. In fact, her company had enlivened

the whole of the journey. He was rather enjoying his close contacts with his family again, if the truth were told, and was beginning to wonder why it had seemed important to him for so long to maintain a distance from them.

It was because he was no longer a thoughtless young man, he supposed. It was because he had finished sowing his wild oats and was beginning to realize the value of love connections.

He pulled a face in the carriage. Could he really have descended to such depths of dullness?

She had never written to him, though he had watched for a letter until well into February. *She* being Frances Allard. He was suddenly thinking about her again—quite unwillingly.

There was little possibility of seeing her, though, even accidentally. She lived at the school across the river, all the way down by Sydney Gardens, and would be busy with her teaching duties. He would be staying on upper-class Brock Street and would be mingling with other genteel guests and residents of the city. Their paths were very unlikely to cross.

He stopped thinking about her altogether after their arrival on Brock Street in order to focus the whole of his attention on his grandfather. He was looking frail, but he was his usual cheerful self and insisted that the Bath air and the Bath waters had already done him some good. He sat listening with twinkling eyes to Amy's enthusiastic account of their journey and the amusing anecdote she told of stopping at one posting inn and being mistaken for Lucius's wife. She had been addressed as *my lady*.

Lucius took Amy for a short walk to see the Royal Crescent at the other end of Brock Street after tea while their grandfather rested. He listened with amused indulgence while she exclaimed with delight and declared that the Crescent was the most magnificent architectural sight she had ever seen.

But later that same evening after dinner while his grandfather sat reading by the fire and Amy was seated at a small escritoire writing a letter to their mother and sisters, Lucius stood looking out the window of the sitting room at the stately architecture of the circular street known as the Circus not many yards distant. He found himself thinking that in all probability, if she was still at Miss Martin's school, Frances was no more than a mile or so away. The thought annoyed him—not so much that she was only a mile or so distant, but that he was thinking about it at all. And about *her*.

He turned firmly away from the window.

"Feeling maudlin, Lucius?" his grandfather asked, lowering his book to his lap.

"Me, sir?" Lucius rested a hand lightly on Amy's shoulder as she wrote. "Not at all. I am delighted to be here with you. I was glad to see you eat a good dinner and come to spend an hour with Amy and me in here."

"I thought," his grandfather said, regarding him with twinkling eyes from beneath his bushy white eyebrows, "that perhaps you were pining for the sight of a certain pair of fine eyes."

So brown they were almost black. Wide, expressive eyes that could spark with anger or dance with merriment or deepen with passion.

"Pining, sir?" he said, raising his eyebrows. "Me?"

"You are talking of Miss Hunt, Grandpapa, are you not?" Amy said while she dipped her quill pen in the silver ink holder. "She has the bluest eyes I have ever seen. Some people might call them fine, but *I* prefer eyes that can laugh even if they are the most nondescript shade of gray. And Miss Hunt never laughs—it is undignified and unladylike to do so, I daresay. I *do* hope Luce does not marry her."

"I daresay Lucius will make the right choice when the time comes," their grandfather said. "But it would be strange indeed if he did not admire Miss Hunt's blue eyes and blond hair and flawless complexion, Amy. And she *is* a refined lady. I would be proud to call her granddaughter."

Lucius squeezed his sister's shoulder and took the chair on the other side of the hearth. His grandfather was quite right. Portia was a beauty. She was also elegant and refined and perfect. Rumor had it—

in other words, his mother had informed him—that she had turned down numerous eligible suitors during the past few years.

She was waiting for him.

He concentrated his mind upon her considerable charms and felt the noose tighten about his neck again.

8

The following day was cold and blustery and not conducive to any prolonged outing, but the day after that was one of those perfect spring days that entice people to step outdoors to take the air and remind them that summer is coming in the not too distant future. The sun beamed down from a cloudless sky, the air was fresh and really quite warm, and there was the merest of gentle breezes.

After an early morning visit to the Pump Room to drink the waters and a rest afterward at home with the morning papers, the Earl of Edgecombe was quite ready for an afternoon airing with his grandchildren on the Royal Crescent. Fashionable people strolled there each day, weather permitting, to exchange any gossip that had accumulated since the morning, to see and to be seen. It served much the same function as Hyde Park in London at the fashionable hour, though admittedly on a smaller scale.

Strolling along the cobbled street of the widely curving Crescent and then down into the meadow below was not exactly vigorous exercise, and Lucius missed his clubs and activities and acquaintances in London, but really he was quite resigned to spending a week or so here with just a few early morning rides up into the hills as an outlet for his excess energy. It was good to see his grandfather in good spirits and slightly better health than he had enjoyed at Christmas. And Amy, now leaning upon Lucius's arm, positively sparkled with enjoyment at the change of scene, free as she was of the stricter social restrictions that London had imposed upon a young lady who was not yet out.

They were in conversation with Mrs. Reynolds and Mrs. Abbotsford when Lucius, half bored but politely smiling, looked up toward the Crescent and became idly aware of a crocodile of school-girls, all uniformly clad in dark blue, making its way along Brock Street, presumably having just admired the architecture of the Circus and coming to do the same for its companion piece, the Royal Crescent. A lady, probably a teacher, marched along at its head, setting a brisk pace and looking rather like a duck cleaving the waters for its two straight lines of ducklings following along behind.

. . . probably a teacher.

He squinted his eyes in order to look more closely at the woman. But the group was still too far away for him to clearly distinguish the features of any of its members. Besides, it would be just too much of a coincidence . . .

"And Mr. Reynolds has agreed to take a house there for the summer," Mrs. Reynolds was saying. "Our dear Betsy will be with us, of course. A month by the sea in July will be just the thing for all of us."

"Sea bathing is said to be excellent for the health, ma'am," the earl said.

Mrs. Reynolds uttered what sounded like a genteel shriek. "Sea *bathing,* my lord?" she cried. "Oh, never say so. One cannot imagine anything more shocking to tender sensibilities. I shall be very careful not to allow Betsy within half a mile of any bathing machines."

"But I could not agree with you more, Lord Edgecombe," Mrs. Abbotsford said. "When we spent a few days at Lyme Regis two summers ago, both Rose and Algernon—my daughter and my son, you will understand—bathed in the sea, and they were never more healthy than they were for the rest of that holiday. The ladies were kept quite separate from the gentlemen, Barbara, and so there was no impropriety."

Lucius exchanged an amused smirk with his grandfather.

"Now before I forget, Lord Edgecombe," Mrs. Reynolds said, "I must beg you . . ."

The crocodile had reached the corner of Brock Street and the

Crescent, and the teacher stopped it in order to point out the wide sweep of magnificent architecture before their eyes. One slim arm pointed. One slender hand gesticulated.

She had her back to Lucius. Over a fawn-colored dress she wore a short brown spencer. Her bonnet too was brown. It was impossible from where he stood to see either her face or her hair.

But his mouth nevertheless turned suddenly dry.

He was in no doubt at all of her identity.

Coincidences, it seemed, did happen.

"And you will come too, I trust, Lord Sinclair?" Mrs. Reynolds was saying.

"Oh, do say yes. Do say yes, Luce," Amy said, squeezing his arm and gazing up at him imploringly. "Then I can go too."

"I beg your pardon?" He started and looked from one to the other of the ladies, with blank eyes. What the devil were they talking about? "I do beg your pardon, ma'am. I fear I was wool-gathering."

"Lord Edgecombe has graciously agreed to attend my little soiree tomorrow evening," Mrs. Reynolds explained. "It will be nothing to compare with the London squeezes to which you are accustomed, of course, but the company will be genteel, and there will be musical entertainment of a superior quality in the drawing room, and there will be a card room for those who do not appreciate music—Mr. Reynolds always insists upon it. I do hope you will agree to join us and bring Miss Amy Marshall with you."

"I should be honored, ma'am," Lucius said, making her a bow. "So, it would seem, will Amy."

Good Lord! A soiree. In Bath. What was life coming to?

His sister was almost jumping up and down with excitement at his side. A soiree in Bath might not rate highly on most people's social calendar—and it would surely rate at the very bottom of his—but it was vastly enticing to a girl who was excluded from almost all the social events that her mother and sisters were preparing to attend in London all spring.

He might have smiled down at her with fond amusement if at least half of his attention had not been directed elsewhere—and if his heart had not started to pound in his chest just as if someone had taken a hammer to it.

Damnation, but he had not wanted this to happen. He had not wanted to set eyes on her again. He gazed upward again, nevertheless, for one more glance at the woman who had sent him away three months ago with the proverbial flea in his ear and had then proceeded to set up shop in his memory and refuse to go away for a good long while afterward.

The well-disciplined double line of girls was making its way along the Crescent and stopping again at the halfway point. Again the teacher spoke, facing the buildings and describing bold half circles with both arms as she explained something to her apparently attentive class.

She had not once turned to face the meadow. But she did not need to do so. Lucius *knew*. Some things did not need the full evidence of one's eyes.

"*Two* titled gentlemen among your guests," Mrs. Abbotsford was saying. "You will be the envy of every hostess in Bath, Barbara, and your party will be assured of success. Not that it would not have been anyway, of course."

"I quite agree with you, ma'am," the earl said. "Mrs. Reynolds already has a reputation as an excellent hostess. I always look forward to receiving one of her invitations whenever I am in Bath."

The teacher turned around. So did all her girls, and she proceeded to indicate with a wide sweep of her arm the splendid view down over the city and across to the hills beyond.

Frances!

He was still too far away to see her face clearly, but he was quite close enough to know that it was filled with warm animation. She was absorbed in her task of instructing the group of girls, and she was enjoying herself.

She was not, he noticed, looking either haggard or heartbroken.

Devil take it, had he expected that she would—no doubt as a result of having pined away over him to a shadow of her former self?

She was also, it seemed, quite unself-conscious about the presence of other persons in the vicinity. She did not glance at any of the fashionable people strolling on the Crescent or in the meadow below it. Even so, after one long look, Lucius tipped the brim of his hat lower, as if to ward off the bright rays of the sun and half turned as if to admire the view behind him.

"Bath never ceases to astonish me with its loveliness," he said stupidly.

Mrs. Reynolds and Mrs. Abbotsford, both of whom were residents of the city, were quite happy to take up the theme with voluble enthusiasm, and Amy told them how very much she had enjoyed shopping on Milsom Street the afternoon before, when her brother had bought her the bonnet she was now wearing.

The two ladies admired it with effusive compliments.

When Lucius next turned his head to look, the schoolgirls had completed their walk about the Crescent and were making their brisk way down the hill past the Marlborough Buildings.

Goddamn it, he thought profanely, had he actually been *hiding* from her? From a mere schoolteacher, who had wanted to boil him in oil one day, who had slept with him the next, and who had passed judgment on his lovemaking the day after that by calling it *pleasant* before saying a very firm and final good-bye to him?

Had he really been hiding behind his hat like a groveling coward?

He felt decidedly shaken, if the truth were known. He wondered what would have happened if he had been standing up on the street rather than down here in the meadow and they had come face-to-face. He wondered if he would have stuttered and stammered and otherwise made a prize ass of himself or if he would have gazed coolly at her, raised his eyebrows, and pretended to search for her name in his memory.

Lord, he *hoped* it would have been the latter.

And then, as the girls disappeared into Marlborough Lane, he found himself wondering how she would have behaved. Would she have blushed and lost her composure? Would *she* have raised *her* eyebrows and pretended to have half forgotten him?

Damnation! Perhaps she *had* forgotten him.

It was a very good thing they had not come face-to-face. His self-esteem might well have suffered a blow from which it would never recover. His grandfather and Amy and these two ladies would have witnessed his humiliation. So would the crocodile of schoolgirls, their eyes avidly drinking in the scene so that they could titter and giggle over it in their dormitory for the next week or month or so.

There would have been nothing left for him to do but find a gun somewhere and blow his brains out.

He felt suddenly irritated again and intensely annoyed with Miss Frances Allard, almost as if she *had* seen him and had *not* recognized him.

Perhaps, he thought, gritting his teeth, she had been brought into his life by a malevolent fate in order to keep him humble—this schoolteacher who had preferred her teaching job to him.

Mrs. Reynolds and Mrs. Abbotsford were taking their leave. Lucius touched the brim of his hat to them and looked closely at his grandfather.

"I think that is definitely enough for one afternoon, sir," he said. "It is time to go home for tea."

"Perhaps Amy would like to stay out longer," the earl suggested.

But Amy smiled cheerfully at him and took one of his arms while her other was still linked through Lucius's.

"I am very happy to go home for tea with you, Grandpapa," she said. "It has been a wonderfully exciting afternoon, has it not? We must have spoken with a dozen people or more. And we have been invited to a *soiree* tomorrow evening. I will have much to say when I write to Mama and Caroline and Emily tonight. I do not know *what* I am going to wear."

"I believe," Lucius said with an exaggerated sigh, "I can predict another shopping expedition to Milsom Street tomorrow."

"You may purchase a ready-made gown with my purse, child," the earl said. "And all the trimmings to go with it. But do trust to Lucius's good taste when you make your choices. It is impeccable."

As they walked, Lucius found himself grappling with a memory of Frances Allard sealing the edges of a beef pie with the pad of her thumb, pricking the lid so that the steam would not blow it off, and then bending over the hot oven to set it inside.

Why he should still feel rather like the beef filling lying beneath the unpricked lid in the middle of the hot oven was a mystery to him—not to mention a severe annoyance.

Why had she chosen today of all days to bring a class up onto the Crescent?

Or, perhaps more to the point, why the devil had he chosen today of all days to stroll there with his grandfather and sister?

It felt damnably unmanly to have had his composure shaken by a one-night lover three months after the event.

"Oh, Luce," Amy said, squeezing his arm, "is not Bath a wonderful place to be?"

"It is absolutely not fair," Susanna Osbourne declared, "that I spent only an hour outside playing games with the junior girls and have acquired lobster cheeks and a cherry nose and freckles to boot while Frances spent a whole afternoon walking with the middle class and looks bronze and beautiful. It is not even summer yet."

"Bronze is not considered any more becoming for a lady than lobster," Miss Martin said, looking up from the tatting with which she kept her hands busy. "You teach the girls that they must guard their complexions against the sunlight at all costs, do you not, Susanna? I have no sympathy, then, if you were too busy having fun with your class to guard your own—and I could see whenever I glanced out the window at you that you *were* having fun. You were actually participating in the games yourself. As for Frances—well, she is the exception to all rules as far as looks and complexions are concerned. It is her Italian heritage. We poor English mortals must simply endure the unfairness of it."

But despite the words themselves, her eyes twinkled as she looked across the room at her youngest teacher, who was sitting forward in her chair, her slippered feet propped on a stool, her slim arms clasped about her knees, her face bright and noticeably sunburned.

"Besides," Anne Jewell said as she mended a tear down the back of a small boy's shirt, "you do not look like any lobster I have ever seen, Susanna. You look rosy and youthful and healthy and prettier than ever. Though your nose *would* shine like a beacon in the dark, I suppose."

They all laughed at poor Susanna, who touched the offending organ gingerly and wrinkled it as she smiled and then joined in the laughter.

They were sitting, the four of them, in Miss Martin's sitting room as they often did in the evenings after the girls had been sent to their dormitories under Matron's care and David had been put to bed.

"Did your walk prove thoroughly educational, Frances?" Miss Martin asked, her eyes still twinkling. "Did the girls acquire as much material for writing assignments as you hoped?"

Frances chuckled. "They were marvelously attentive," she said. "I do wonder, though, how much detail their minds retained of the architecture of the Circus and the Crescent and the Upper Assembly Rooms. I do not doubt they could describe down to the minutest detail every person of fashion we passed—especially if that person happened to be male and below the age of one-and-twenty. I was very proud of them all when we were crossing the Pulteney Bridge on the way back here, though. There was a group of young bucks swaggering there and making a few pointed remarks. One of them was even impertinent enough to make use of a quizzing glass. The girls all stuck their noses in the air and walked on past as if the young men were invisible."

Anne and Susanna laughed with her.

"Oh, *good* girls," Miss Martin said approvingly, bending her head to her work again.

"Of course," Frances added, "they did rather spoil the effect after we had crossed Laura Place and were safely out of earshot by buzzing and giggling over those very young men the whole length of Great Pulteney Street. I suppose that is what they will remember most about the outing."

"But of course," Anne said. "Would you expect anything different, Frances? They are all either fourteen or fifteen years old. They were acting their age."

"Quite right, Anne," Miss Martin said. "Adults are very foolish when they admonish unruly children to act their age. In nine cases out of ten that is exactly what the children are doing."

"What are you going to wear tomorrow evening, Frances?" Anne asked.

"My ivory silk, I suppose," Frances said. "It is the best I have."

"Oh, but of course." Susanna grinned mischievously at her as she got to her feet to pour them all a second cup of tea. "Frances has a beau."

"Frances," Miss Martin said, looking up from her work once more, "has been invited to Mrs. Reynolds's soiree quite independently of Mr. Blake, Susanna. She was invited on account of her voice, which is like an angel's. Betsy Reynolds undoubtedly told her mother about it, and Mrs. Reynolds very wisely added Frances to the list of guests who will entertain the company with their superior talent."

But Susanna could not resist teasing further.

"It is Mr. Blake who is to escort her, though," she said. "I think Frances has a beau. What do *you* think, Anne?"

Anne smiled from one to the other of them, her needle suspended above her work.

"I believe Frances has an admirer and *would-be* beau," she said. "I also believe Frances has not yet decided if she will accept him in that latter capacity."

"I think she had better decide against it," Miss Martin added. "I have a strong objection to losing my French and music teacher. Though in a good—a *very* good cause—I suppose I could be persuaded to make the sacrifice."

Mr. Aubrey Blake was the physician who attended the pupils at Miss Martin's school whenever one of them needed his medical services. He was a serious, conscientious, handsome man in his middle thirties who had begun to show an interest in Frances during the past month or so. He had met her shopping on Milsom Street one Saturday afternoon and had insisted upon escorting her all the way back to the school and upon carrying her purchases himself, small and lightweight though they were.

Her three friends had collapsed in mirth afterward when Frances had told them how she had almost expired of embarrassment lest he somehow discover that that light bundle contained new stockings.

And then when she had taken one of the day pupils home early one day because the girl had a fever and waited until Mr. Blake had been summoned so that she could carry word of the girl's condition back with her, he had insisted upon walking her all the way to the school doors.

Now he had got word of the fact that she had been invited to sing at the Reynolds soiree, and since he was an invited guest himself, he had called at the school, had Keeble summon Frances to the visitors' sitting room after very correctly asking permission of Miss Martin, and asked to be allowed the honor of being her escort for the evening.

She would have had a hard time saying no if she had wished to do so. Actually, though, she had been relieved. Since the outing was to be in the evening, she knew that Claudia would have insisted upon sending one of the maids with her. It would have been a dreadful inconvenience. Besides, walking in on an evening party alone would have required a great deal of fortitude.

"I do not believe a teacher has *time* for a beau," she said now. "And even if this teacher did, I am not at all sure she would choose Mr. Blake. He is perhaps a trifle too earnest for her taste. However, he *is* handsome and he *is* a perfect gentleman and he has a perfectly respectable profession, and if she decides that she *does* want him as a beau, she will be sure to inform her dearest friends and warn her employer of her impending departure into the world of idle marital bliss."

She laughed as she lifted her cup to her lips.

"Well, *I* would not settle for a mere physician," Susanna said, sitting down again and clasping her knees as before. "He would have to be a duke or no one at all if he were to attract me. Except a prince, maybe."

Susanna had come to the school at the age of twelve as a charity pupil. She had lied about her age before that, saying she was fifteen in an attempt to acquire employment as a lady's maid, but two days after she had been rejected in that capacity she had been found by Mr. Hatchard, Miss Martin's London agent, and offered a position as pupil at the school. Two years ago Miss Martin had given her employment as a junior teacher. What her background was before the age of twelve Frances did not know.

"Oh, not a *duke*, Susanna," Miss Martin said firmly.

Frances and Anne exchanged amused glances. Susanna rested her forehead on her knees to hide her own smile. They all knew about Miss Martin's aversion to dukes. She had once been employed by the Duke of Bewcastle as governess to his sister, Lady Freyja Bedwyn. Like a string of governesses before her, Miss Martin had resigned after a very short time, having discovered that the job—or rather her pupil— was impossible. But unlike the others, she had refused to accept either the money payment the duke had offered or the recommendation to another post. Instead she had marched down the driveway of Lindsey Hall, taking her triumph and her personal possessions with her.

After she had opened the school and struggled to keep it going, she had been offered the financial assistance of an anonymous benefactor. But before she had accepted, Miss Martin had made Mr. Hatchard swear on a Bible that the benefactor was not the Duke of Bewcastle.

"He will have to be a prince," she added now. "I flatly refuse to attend your wedding if the groom is a duke."

Anne had finished her mending. She folded the shirt, picked up her scissors, needle, and thread, and got to her feet.

"It is time I looked in on David," she said, "to make sure he is still sleeping peacefully. He ought to sleep well, though, after all the running he did in the meadows this afternoon. Thank you for the tea, Claudia. Good night, all."

But the others had risen too. Days at the school began early and ran late and were extraordinarily busy between times. Very rarely did they talk late into the night.

Frances thought about the following evening as she got ready for bed. The singing was something she looked forward to with eager anticipation, though she had not done any public singing in three years. She would be nervous when the time came, of course, but that would be natural. She would not let it affect her performance.

She was, however, a little nervous about another aspect of the evening. Mr. Blake really would become her suitor with a little encouragement. He had not said so, but her woman's intuition told her she was not wrong. He was perfectly eligible even though he must be at least ten years older than she. He was also good-looking, intelligent, amiable, and well respected.

Her prospects of marrying were not bountiful. She would be foolish not to encourage him. She enjoyed teaching, and her salary was sufficient to cover all her most basic needs. The school provided her with a home and friendship. But she was only twenty-three years old, and her life had once been very different. She could not pretend to herself that she would be perfectly happy to remain as she was for the rest of her life.

She had needs, basic human needs that were very hard to ignore.

Mr. Blake might be her only chance of attracting a decent husband. Of course, matters were not quite that simple. There would be details from her past to explain to him, some of them not reflecting well on her. He might not be at all willing to pursue his interest in her once all had been told. On the other hand, perhaps he might. She would not know if she did not put the matter to the test.

She blew out her candle when she was ready for bed, drew back the curtains as she always did, and lay on her back, staring out into the darkness and picking out a few stars.

She had wept when she had learned that she was not with child. Tears of relief—of course!—and tears of sadness.

In three months she had not fully recovered her spirits. It was because she had lain with him, she told herself, because she had given him her virginity. *Of course* it was difficult to recover, to forget him. It would be strange if it were not.

But when she was being strictly truthful with herself, she knew that it was more than that. Most of the time when she remembered

Lucius Marshall, it was as much other things about him she recalled as it was *that*. She thought of him peeling potatoes and shoveling snow and drying dishes and lifting his jug-eared snowman's head onto the hollowed-out shoulders and waltzing and . . . Well, of course, her thoughts always did come back to what had followed that waltz.

She even remembered him angry and contemptuous and arrogant and standing toe-to-toe with her on a snowy road after hauling her unceremoniously out of her carriage.

Staring out at one particular star and wondering how many thousands or millions of miles away it was, she admitted to herself that if it were not for Lucius Marshall she would be able to see her way more clearly in this matter of Mr. Blake—and of course there would be less to confess. But she was all too painfully aware of the differences between the two men and—more to the point—the differences in her reactions to them.

With Mr. Blake there was no magic.

But then Mr. Blake was a steady, dependable man who could perhaps offer her a decent future. And she did not know for certain that there would never be any magic if he should choose to court her, did she?

She should encourage him, she decided, closing her eyes.

She *would* encourage him, in fact.

She was going to start being more sensible.

Her eyes opened again and focused on the star.

"Lucius," she whispered, "you might as well be as far away as that star for all the good pining for you has done me. But this is the end. I am not going to think about you ever again."

It was an eminently sensible decision.

Frances lay awake half the night contemplating it.

9

It was Miss Martin herself rather than Keeble who came to Frances's room the following evening five minutes before Mr. Blake was due, to inform her that he had already arrived.

"Fortunately," Frances said while Miss Martin looked her over, "I have so few chances to wear the ivory silk that not many people would know it is several years old."

"And it is of such a classic design," Miss Martin said, looking assessingly at its high waistline and short sleeves and modestly scooped neckline, "that it does not look out of fashion at all. It will do. So will your hair, though you have dressed it as severely as ever. There is no way, of course, that you can hide your great beauty. If I were given to personal vanity, I would be mortally envious. No, jealous."

Frances laughed and reached for her brown cloak.

"No, no," Miss Martin said, "you must wear my paisley shawl, Frances. That is why I am carrying it over my arm. And one more thing before you go. I was not serious last evening. Of course, I would hate to lose any of my teachers. We are a good team and I have grown inordinately fond of the three of you who live at the school with me. But if you should really develop an attachment to Mr. Blake—"

"Oh, Claudia," Frances said, laughing again and catching her up in a quick hug, "what a goose you are. He is accompanying me to a party at which I am not even a full-fledged guest. That is all."

"Hmm," Miss Martin said. "You have not yet seen the look in his eye this evening, Frances."

But Frances did see it a few minutes later when she went downstairs and found him pacing the hall while a darkly frowning Keeble stood guarding his domain with his habitual suspicion for the whole of the male world once it stepped over the threshold. Mr. Blake looked very distinguished indeed in his black evening cloak with his black silk hat in one hand. And when he looked up to watch her descend the stairs, there was a gleam of approval and something more in his eyes.

"As always, Miss Allard," he said, "you look remarkably elegant."

"Thank you," she said.

He had a carriage waiting at the door, and within a very short time they had arrived at the Reynolds house on Queen Anne Square. It felt strange to Frances after so long to be going to a party again. She was once more very thankful for the escort of Mr. Blake. The house seemed already to be filled with guests for all that Bath was reputed to be no longer the fashionable place to be. Mrs. Reynolds was very proudly letting each arriving guest know that the Earl of Edgecombe was in attendance with his two grandchildren.

They must be in the card room, Frances concluded after she had been in the drawing room for a short while. There seemed to be no one in here grand enough to invite bowing and scraping from the other guests. More to the point, there was no one she recognized apart from a few Bath acquaintances—and therefore no one to recognize her. She had felt a little anxiety lest she be seen and recognized by some of her former London acquaintances. She would far prefer that no one from that former life of hers ever discover where she had gone.

So far no one had.

The musical entertainment began soon after Frances's arrival, and she took her seat beside Mr. Blake to enjoy the other performances, though she did assist with the first item on the program, an étude on the pianoforte played by Betsy Reynolds, the thirteen-year-old daughter of the house, who was also a day pupil at Miss Martin's. Frances was her music teacher and helped her position her music and murmured encouragement to her until the girl's nerves were sufficiently under control that she could begin.

The recital went well, if not brilliantly, and Frances smiled warmly at Betsy when she had finished, and got to her feet to hug her before Betsy was sent off to bed.

Frances's own turn came almost an hour after that. She was, in fact, the final performer of the evening. Supper would be served after she had finished.

"I daresay, Miss Allard," Mr. Blake whispered, leaning closer to her as Mrs. Reynolds was getting to her feet to announce her, "you have been kept until last because it is expected that you will also be the best."

Mr. Blake had not heard her sing. Neither had anyone else in the room except Mr. Huckerby, the school's dancing master, who was to accompany her. But Frances smiled her gratitude anyway. The familiar butterflies were fluttering in her stomach.

She had chosen an ambitious and perhaps not quite appropriate piece for the occasion, but "I Know That My Redeemer Liveth" from Handel's *Messiah* had always been a great favorite of hers, and Mrs. Reynolds had given her free rein in her choice of music.

Frances stood to a polite smattering of applause and took her place in the middle of the drawing room beside the pianoforte. She took her time, preparing her breath with a number of slow inhalations and exhalations, closing her eyes for a few moments while she thought her way into the music.

Then she nodded to Mr. Huckerby, listened to the opening bars of music, and began to sing.

As soon as she did so, all her nervousness fled and along with it most of her awareness of her audience, her surroundings, and her very self.

The music took on an existence of its own.

Having settled Amy in the drawing room with Mrs. Abbotsford and her daughter, both of whom had welcomed her warmly into their midst, Lucius had spent most of the evening in the card room, though he had sat in for only a hand or two himself. For the rest of the time he had stood watching his grandfather play, conversing with fellow guests who had wandered in from the other room, and trying not to dwell upon how excruciatingly bored he was.

He would have gone into the drawing room when the musical entertainment began since he was partial to music even if that provided at a Bath soiree was sure to be insipid at best. But Mr. Reynolds managed to corner him first and launched into a lengthy, prosy discourse on the virtues of hunting as a thoroughly English and aristocratic sport and the evil natures of those who opposed it, whom Lucius gathered must be deemed unnatural traitors to their very country. He watched his grandfather for signs of weariness and half hoped that he would see some. Although his London self would be nothing short of horrified at the prospect of having to return home so early in the evening, his Bath self could only think longingly of sitting with his feet up in the sitting room on Brock Street, reading a book.

Reading a book, for the love of God!

Of course Amy would be bitterly disappointed if such a thing actually happened.

The Earl of Edgecombe, however, appeared to be happily absorbed in the play. His winnings and losses were about evenly balanced. Not that the stakes were high anyway. They rarely were in Bath, where the Masters of Ceremonies had always frowned upon heavy gambling.

The music was clearly audible. It began with a rather plodding étude on the pianoforte, which Reynolds explained was being performed by his daughter, though he made no move to go into the other room to play the role of proud parent—or even to stop talking in order to listen. There followed a violin sonata, a tenor solo, a string quartet, and another recital on the pianoforte, performed by someone with a surer and more skilled touch than Miss Reynolds had displayed.

Lucius gave the music as much of his attention as he could.

Fortunately, he realized within a couple of minutes that he needed to bend only half an ear to Reynolds without danger of missing anything significant in what the man had to say.

And then a soprano began to sing. At first—for just a very few moments—Lucius was prepared to turn much of his attention away from her performance. The female soprano voice was not his favorite, its tendency being all too often to shrillness. And this soprano had made the mistake of choosing a sacred piece for a very secular party.

However, in those same few moments he realized that this soprano was very far superior to the norm. And within a few moments more he had focused all of his attention on her and her song, leaving Reynolds to address the air about him.

"I know that my Redeemer liveth," she sang, "and that He shall stand at the latter day upon the earth."

Indeed, very soon a number of the other guests in the card room, and even a few of the players lifted their heads and listened. Conversation did not stop entirely, but it decreased considerably in volume.

But all this Lucius did not even notice. The voice had captured his whole being.

It was rich and powerful without being overbearing. It had the full quality of a contralto voice but could soar to the highest notes without effort or even a suggestion of shrillness or strain. It was a voice that was as pure as a bell, and yet it resonated with human passion.

"Yet in my flesh shall I see God."

It was without all doubt the most glorious voice he had ever heard.

He closed his eyes, a frown of almost pained concentration creasing his brow. And finally Reynolds, perhaps realizing that he had lost his audience, fell silent.

"For now is Christ risen from the dead," the voice sang on, joyful and triumphant now, carrying Lucius's soul with it.

He swallowed.

"The first fruits of them that sleep."

He felt a touch on his sleeve and opened his eyes to see his grand-father beside him. Without exchanging a word, they moved together toward the drawing room.

"For now is Christ risen." The voice gathered itself for the soaring climax. "For now is Christ ri-sen, from the dead."

They arrived in the doorway and stood side by side, looking in.

She stood in the middle of the room, tall and dark and slender and majestic, her arms at her sides, her head lifted, classically beautiful but using only her voice with which to captivate her audience.

"The first fruits—" she held the high note, let its sound and triumphant acclamation linger and begin to die away, "of th-em that sleep."

She stood with lifted head and closed eyes while the pianoforte played the closing measures, and not a person in the audience moved a muscle.

There was a brief silence.

And then enthusiastic applause.

"Dear God," the earl murmured, joining in.

But Lucius could only gaze as if transfixed.

My God! My God!

Frances Allard.

She opened her eyes, smiled, and inclined her head in acknowledgment of the applause, her cheeks flushed, her eyes glowing, her smooth, dark hair gleaming in the light cast down upon it from the chandelier overhead. Her eyes moved over the audience until they reached the doorway and . . .

And locked upon Lucius standing there gazing back.

Her smile did not falter. Rather, it froze in place.

In that fraction of a moment it seemed that the whole world must have stopped spinning.

And then her eyes moved onward until her smiling face had thanked the whole audience. She then made her way toward an empty chair on the far side of the room, close to where Amy sat with her hands clasped to her bosom. A gentleman rose as Frances approached, bowed to her, and repositioned the chair before she sat down on it. He bent his head close to hers to make some remark to her.

"That was quite, quite splendid, Miss Allard," Mrs. Reynolds was saying with hearty joviality. "I was well advised to position you last on the program. My dear Betsy was quite right when she said you sing superbly. But I am sure that after sitting for a whole hour everyone must be ready for supper. It will be served immediately in the dining room."

"Lucius," his grandfather said, setting a hand on his shoulder as everyone stirred and the room filled with the buzz of conversation, "I have rarely if ever heard a voice that so moved me. Whoever is she? If she is someone famous, I do not recognize the name. Miss Allen, is it?"

"Allard," Lucius said.

"Let us go and pay our compliments to Miss Allard," the earl said. "We must invite her to sit with us for supper."

She was on her feet again. Several of the other guests were crowding about her to speak with her. She had a bright, fixed smile on her face. She was determinedly not looking their way, Lucius saw. Mrs. Reynolds, smiling graciously, had made her way to her side and saw them coming.

"Ah, Lord Edgecombe," she said in the sort of voice that made everyone else stand back to give them room, "may I have the pleasure of presenting Miss Allard to you? Does she not sing divinely? She teaches music at Miss Martin's school. It is a very superior academy. We send Betsy there."

Frances fixed her eyes on the earl and curtsied.

"My lord," she murmured.

"I have the honor, Miss Allard," Mrs. Reynolds continued, clearly puffed up with the pride of having such illustrious guests in her own home, "of making known to you the Earl of Edgecombe and his grandson, Viscount Sinclair. And his granddaughter, Miss Amy Marshall."

Amy had stepped up beside him, Lucius realized, and taken his arm.

Frances turned to him then and her eyes met his once more.

"My lord," she said.

"Miss Allard." He bowed to her.

Her eyes moved on to Amy. "Miss Marshall?"

"You brought tears to my eyes, Miss Allard," Amy said. "I wish *I* could sing like that."

Lucius felt as if someone had dealt him a blow to the lower abdomen.

But one thing was perfectly clear. Whatever her feelings toward him might be, she certainly had not forgotten him.

"Miss Martin's may be a superior school," his grandfather was saying, "but what on earth are you doing teaching there, Miss Allard, when you should be enthralling the world with your singing voice?"

The color deepened in her cheeks as she turned back to him.

"It is very kind of you to say so, my lord," she said, "but teaching is my chosen profession. It gives me great satisfaction."

"It would give *me* great satisfaction," the earl said, smiling kindly at her, "if you would take supper with Amy and Sinclair and me, Miss Allard."

She hesitated for just a moment.

"Thank you," she said. "That is very obliging of you, but I have already agreed to sit with Mr. Blake and a few of his acquaintances."

"But, Miss Allard," Mrs. Reynolds protested, sounding horrified, "I am quite sure Mr. Blake would be more than willing to relinquish your company to the Earl of Edgecombe for half an hour. Would you not, sir?"

The gentleman she addressed frowned but inclined his head to his hostess in an obvious preliminary to agreeing with her demand. However, Frances spoke first.

"But *I* am unwilling to relinquish *his*," she said.

"And quite right too, my dear," the earl said with a low chuckle. "It has been a pleasure to make your acquaintance. Perhaps you would do me the honor of taking tea with me tomorrow in Brock Street. My grandson will be delighted to come and fetch you in the carriage, will you not, Lucius?"

Lucius, who had been standing there staring like a dumb block or a moonstruck halfling, inclined his head. It was, he realized, far too late for either him or Frances to do the sensible thing and admit to a previous acquaintance.

Deuce take it, but why could he not be simply surprised to see her or pleased to see her or *dis*pleased to see her? Why the devil had he been knocked so off balance that he still felt as if he were staggering around like a man who had no control over his own world or his own impulses?

But, Lord—*that voice*!

She drew breath as if to say something but apparently changed her mind.

"Thank you." She smiled without looking at Lucius. "I would like that, my lord."

The devil! Lucius frowned ferociously, but no one was paying him any attention.

"Oh, and I shall look forward to it of all things," Amy cried warmly, clapping her hands. "I shall be able to be hostess since only Grandpapa and Luce live there on Brock Street with me."

And then other people claimed Frances Allard's attention, and there was nothing left for Lucius to do but remark upon his grandfather's obvious tiredness, ignore Amy's look of disappointment, and have the carriage brought around without further delay.

It seemed an age before it came.

"I want to be able to listen to that voice again in my memory," the earl said as he settled in his carriage seat for the short drive to Brock Street. He set his head back against the cushions, sighed deeply, and made no further attempt at conversation.

Amy was either doing the same thing or else she was reliving the whole party, which she had obviously enjoyed enormously even though she had been deprived of the pleasure of partaking of supper before leaving. She sat in silence, looking out into the darkness, a dreamy smile on her lips.

Lucius sat in his corner, quietly seething. It was bad enough that he had sighed over the memory of her like a damned lovelorn poet for at least a month after Christmas. It was worse that after seeing her on the

Crescent yesterday he had suffered through a largely sleepless night, though he must have nodded off occasionally or he would not have had such vivid dreams about her. It was worst of all to have discovered her at a party he was attending tonight—and in such a manner.

That voice!

Deuce take it, what a voice it was. It added a whole new dimension to his knowledge of her character, of the talent and beauty of soul that lived within her beautiful body. It made him realize how much more of her there must be that was still unknown to him. It filled him with a yearning to know more.

He had a bad case of resurrected infatuation—there was no denying it. And he did not appreciate it one little bit. It had taken him long enough to forget her in the first place.

And to cap it all, she had looked even more beautiful tonight than he remembered her. Her naturally olive-hued complexion had looked darker, as if from exposure to the sun. Her eyes had looked a richer brown in contrast, and her teeth whiter. She still wore her hair the same way, but the style that had seemed merely severe after Christmas had looked elegant and richly shining tonight. She was as slender as he remembered her, but the simply styled ivory silk gown she had worn tonight and her almost regal bearing had made her look quite exquisitely feminine.

Was that fellow who had been with her a suitor? A fiancé? He was half bald, for the love of God. And he had been prepared to relinquish her company at supper, albeit reluctantly. If she had promised to sit with *him,* Lucius thought, and someone had tried to usurp his place, he would have offered fisticuffs or pistols at dawn, not meek compliance, by Jove.

"I have been royally entertained this evening, I must say," his grandfather said as the carriage rocked to a halt, "and should sleep soundly tonight. I can only wish that I had been sitting in the drawing room as you were, Amy, to watch the whole of that last performance. Miss Allard has a rare talent. And she is a beautiful woman too."

"Mmm," Lucius mumbled.

"What a wonderful evening it has been," Amy said with a sigh of contentment as Lucius handed her down onto the pavement. "And to-morrow I will be Grandpapa's hostess for tea. Are you not looking forward to Miss Allard's visit of all things, Luce?"

"Of all things," he said curtly.

He could not blame her for being there at the Reynolds soiree tonight, of course, though he had been inclined at first to do just that—schoolteachers ought to remain inside the walls of their schools so that castoff lovers did not have to run the risk of running headlong into them when they least expected it.

But he *could* blame her for accepting the invitation to tea. She had had a clear choice. She could have said yes or she could have said no.

She had said yes, damn her eyes.

He was feeling almost dangerously out of sorts. Yet he could not even retreat to White's or some other gentlemen's haunt in London to drown out his sulks in noise and action and alcohol.

10

"You are home safe and sound, then, miss," Keeble observed with almost paternal solicitude when he let Frances into the school so soon after her knock that she suspected he must have been standing in the hallway waiting for her. "I worry when any of you ladies are out after dark. Miss Martin has invited you to join her in her sitting room."

"Thank you," Frances said, following him up the stairs so that he could open the door for her and even announce her as if she were visiting royalty.

She had suspected that her friends would be awaiting her return, but even so her heart sank. She so wanted to creep off to her room to lick her wounds in private. Was it only last night she had made the bold and liberating decision never to spare another thought for Lucius Marshall, Viscount Sinclair? But how could she have known that by some bizarre twist of fate she would meet him again tonight? She *never* attended parties in Bath. She had not sung in public outside the school since coming here.

It was not just bizarre. It was *cruel.* When her eyes had alighted on him, she . . .

"Well?" Susanna jumped to her feet as soon as Frances stepped into the sitting room, and regarded her with eager face and sparkling eyes. "Need we ask if you were a resounding success? How could you not have been?"

"Were you as well received as you deserve to be?" Anne asked, smiling warmly at her. "Did everyone make much of you?"

"Come and tell us all about your performance," Miss Martin said. "And pour yourself a cup of tea before you sit down."

"I'll do that for her," Susanna said. "Sit, Frances, sit, and allow me to wait on Bath's newest celebrity. After tonight I daresay you will be a star and invited everywhere."

"And neglect my duties here?" Frances said, sinking into the nearest chair and taking a cup of tea from Susanna's hand. "I think not. Tonight was wonderful, but I am very happy being a schoolteacher. I was a little worried about my choice of song, but it was well received. I believe everyone was pleased. Mrs. Reynolds did not appear to be disappointed in me."

"Disappointed?" Anne laughed. "I should hope not. I expect she is congratulating herself upon having discovered you before anyone else did. I should love to have heard you, Frances. We should all have loved it. We have been thinking about you all evening."

"And Mr. Blake was the perfect escort, I hope?" Miss Martin asked.

"Absolutely," Frances said. "He did not leave my side all evening and was very obliging. He waited outside his carriage just now until Mr. Keeble had let me in at the door."

"He looked very dashing this evening, I must say," Susanna said, her eyes twinkling. "Anne and I peeped out from her window as you were leaving—just like a couple of schoolgirls."

"And how was the rest of the soiree?" Anne asked. "Do tell us about it, Frances."

"Betsy Reynolds played well," Frances told them. "She was first on the program and was very nervous, poor girl, but she did not play any wrong notes or slow down noticeably as she went along as she usually does. It was a good concert, and there was supper afterward. Everyone was most amiable."

"Were there many guests?" Susanna asked. She stole a mischievous look at Claudia Martin and winked at the others. "Were there any dukes there? I shall expire of envy if there were."

"No dukes." Frances hesitated. "Only an earl. He was very kind. He has invited me to take tea with him tomorrow."

"Has he?" Claudia Martin said sharply. "In a public place, I hope, Frances?"

"An earl." Susanna laughed. "I hope he is ravishingly handsome."

"How splendid for you," Anne said. "But you do deserve the attention, Frances."

"On Brock Street," Frances said to Claudia, "with his *grandson* and *granddaughter* in attendance, Susanna."

"I am delighted to hear it," Claudia said, "provided the grandchildren are not infants."

"Well." Susanna pulled a face. "There goes my notion of high romance, though even grandfathers can be handsome—and amorous, I suppose."

"They are not infants," Frances said. "Miss Marshall is a pretty young lady, not much older than some of our senior girls—or perhaps not any older at all. The viscount is to bring a carriage to take me to Brock Street."

The very thought was enough to set her hand to trembling, and some of her tea sloshed over into the saucer.

"I suppose with a title like that Viscount Sinclair must be his grandfather's heir," Susanna said. "Perhaps my dream may be resurrected after all. Is *he* ravishingly handsome, Frances?"

"Gracious," Frances said, forcing the corners of her mouth up into a smile, "I did not notice."

"Did not *notice*?" Susanna rolled her eyes at the ceiling. "Where did you leave your eyes when you went out tonight? But I daresay he is. And I daresay he will conceive a grand passion for you, Frances, unless he has already done so, and will sweep you off your feet, and you will end up one day as the countess of . . . where?"

"I have no idea." Frances surged to her feet and set her cup and wet saucer down on the table beside her. "I cannot remember. I am sorry. It has been a busy evening, and now I am so tired I cannot think straight. And I cannot afford the time to go out to tea tomorrow. I have a whole set of essays coming in during the morning, and I am on homework supervision duty tomorrow evening. I have a French exam-ination to set for the senior class. And there is choir practice. Perhaps I will send a refusal, excusing myself."

"But you agreed to go?" Anne asked.

Frances looked helplessly at her.

"I did," she said. "But it would not be too rude to send an excuse if it is genuine, would it? I do not know which house on Brock Street to send it to, though."

That realization sent panic waves galloping and somersaulting through her, and she sat down abruptly again and spread her hands over her face. She fought hysteria.

"Frances," Susanna said, aghast, "I did not mean to offend. I was merely teasing. Do forgive me."

"I am sorry," Frances said, lowering her hands. "I am not an-noyed with you, Susanna. I am just tired."

"You can mark essays and set the exam while you are on home-work supervision," Anne said. "Better yet, I will take the homework duty for you, since Mr. Upton has promised to come in tomorrow just to give David an art lesson. Then you will have time to go for tea *and* keep up with your work. I am sure Claudia will not object to your missing one choir practice."

"I will not," Claudia said. "But there is more to this than weari-ness and a potentially busy day ahead. You find the invitation over-whelming, Frances? Is there any particular reason?" She leaned across the space between their chairs and laid a sympathetic hand on Frances's arm.

It was that touch that did it. A whole flood of emotion spilled forth from Frances, translating itself into words as it came.

"I have met Viscount Sinclair before," she said in a rush, "and would far rather not have met him again." The rawness of the distress she had been forced to hold deep within herself for the past hour and a half lodged itself in her throat and chest.

"Oh, poor Frances," Anne said. "He is someone from your past? How unfortunate that he should come to Bath. I suppose he did not know you were here."

"It was not very long ago," Frances said. "Do you remember the snowfall after Christmas that delayed my return to school? I did not remain with my great-aunts as I let you all believe at the time. I had already started back here when the snow began. My carriage ended up buried in a snowbank when Viscount Sinclair overtook it and then stopped suddenly because there was a snowdrift ahead of him. He took me on to the closest inn, and we spent the following day in company with each other. He brought me back here as soon as the road was clear. He knew that I lived in Bath, you see."

But he had come back here anyway. He had not called on her here, though—*of course* he had not. This evening's meeting had been quite by chance. His manner, both when she first saw him standing in the drawing room doorway—ghastly moment!—and when he had approached her with the earl, had been stiff and unsmiling. He had been quite displeased, in fact.

He had no *business* being displeased. He knew she lived in Bath.

"I am sorry," she said again. "Both for not telling you all then and for telling you now. It was a slight incident at the time, so slight that it did not seem worthy of mention. I was just a little shaken to see him again tonight so unexpectedly, that is all. I *am* sorry. Did you all have a pleasant evening?"

But they were all looking at her quite solemnly, and she knew that she had not deceived them for a moment. What a foolish thing to say, after all, that about the incident's having been so slight that she had not even thought it worth mentioning.

"It would have been very quiet," Anne said, "except that Miriam Fitch and Annabelle Hancock got into a fight again just before bedtime and Matron was obliged to send for Claudia."

"But no blood was shed," Miss Martin added, patting Frances briskly on the arm and removing her hand. "So we must not complain. Now, Frances, do you need me to find some task for you that simply must be performed after school tomorrow? Do you wish me to absolutely refuse to reprieve you in order that you might take tea with the earl and his grandchildren? I can be a marvelous tyrant when I wish to be, as you very well know."

"No." Frances sighed. "I said I would go, and it would be unfair of me now to expect you to get me out of it, Claudia. I will go. It is really no big thing at all."

She got to her feet again and bade them all good night. She really did feel mortally tired, though she doubted she would be able to sleep. And now she felt bad at having unburdened herself—or half unburdened herself anyway—to her friends, who must think her a complete ninnyhammer.

An added irritant to her already troubled mind was the fact that Mr. Blake had misinterpreted her insistence upon sitting with him at supper—as well he might. He had caught hold of her hand in the carriage on the way back to the school and raised it to his lips. He had told her that he was proud and gratified to have been her chosen escort for the evening. Fortunately he had not said—or done!—anything more ardent than that, but even that much had seriously discomposed her.

She had never been a tease, but this evening she had come close to being just that, albeit unwittingly.

Anne caught up to her on the stairs and took her arm and squeezed it.

"Poor Frances," she said. "I can see that you have had a nasty shock this evening. And of course the very fact that you suppressed the truth after Christmas suggests that Viscount Sinclair meant more to you than you care to admit. You do not have to admit it now either. We are your friends to share your secrets when you need to divulge them, and to leave you in peace with those you would prefer to guard. We all have and need secrets. But perhaps tomorrow will help you put some ghosts to rest."

"Perhaps," Frances agreed. "Thank you, Anne. One would think I would have learned my lesson more than three years ago—I have not even told you the full story of what happened before I came here, have I? But it seems I did not learn. Why do women tumble so foolishly into love?"

"Because we have so much love to give," Anne said. "Because it is our nature to love. How could we nurture children if we were not so prone to tumbling headlong into love with even the scrawniest mites to whom we might give birth? Falling in love with men is only a symptom of our general condition, you know. We are sorry creatures, but I do not believe I would be different even if I could. Would you?"

Had Anne loved David's father? Frances wondered briefly. Was there some terrible tragedy in Anne's past that she knew nothing about? She supposed there must be.

"Oh, I don't know," she said, laughing in spite of herself. "I have never had a son on whom to lavish my affections as you have, Anne. Sometimes life seems—empty. And how ungrateful that sounds when I have this home and this profession and you and Susanna and Claudia."

"And Mr. Blake," Anne said.

"And Mr. Blake."

They both laughed softly and took their leave of each other for the night.

Frances leaned her head back against the closed door when she was finally inside her room. She closed her eyes, but she could not stop a few hot tears from escaping and rolling down her cheeks.

She had actually been feeling happy—not just contented or gratified or pleased, but *happy*. Mr. Blake had been attentive but not cloyingly so all evening. He had been an amiable, interesting companion. She had considered him quite seriously as a possible beau and had decided that she really would be foolish to discourage him. It felt good to be in company with a man again and to feel herself liked and even admired. Her decision had pleased her. It meant that she had finally put behind her that slight incident after Christmas as well as everything from years ago. It meant that she was looking to a brighter future.

And she had been singing again. That was what had caused the active happiness. She did not care that perhaps she had chosen the wrong song. The point was that she had chosen what *she* wanted to sing, and though she had been absorbed in the singing of it, as she always was when she performed, she had also been aware that in fact it had not been the wrong song after all. She had sensed the favorable reaction of her listeners, and she had felt that almost-forgotten excitement of forging with them the strong, joyful, invisible bond that could sometimes unite artist and audience. When she had finished singing and heard the momentary hush that followed the final bars of the music, she had known—ah, yes, that was when she had known happiness.

And then she had opened her eyes and smiled about at her audience and . . .

And had found herself gazing at Lucius Marshall.

At first there had been simple, mindless shock. And then the plunge from happiness to wretchedness had been total. And now she felt mortally weary.

He was back in Bath when she no longer wanted him to be there. Only now would she admit to herself that for days, even weeks, after his departure she had hoped and hoped that he would come back.

How foolish and unreasonable of her!

Now he had come back, but he had made no attempt to call upon her. He would no doubt have left again without her ever knowing he had been here if there had not been the accident of tonight's meeting.

It hurt that he had made no attempt to see her.

There was no such thing as common sense, it seemed, in affairs of the heart.

When Lucius knocked on the door of Miss Martin's school the following afternoon he was admitted by an elderly, stoop-shouldered porter, who wore a black coat shiny with age, boots that squeaked with every step he took, and a shrewd squint that said as clearly as words that every man who stepped over the threshold was to be considered an enemy to be watched closely.

Lucius cocked an eloquent eyebrow at the man as he was shown into a not-quite-shabby visitors' parlor and shut firmly inside while the porter went to inform Miss Allard of his lordship's arrival. But it was not she who was first to come. It was another lady—of medium height and ramrod-straight posture and severe demeanor. Even before she introduced herself, Lucius realized that this must be Miss Martin herself, despite the fact that she was younger than he might have expected, surely no more than a year or two older than himself.

"Miss Allard will be another five minutes yet," she explained after introducing herself. "She is conducting a practice with the senior choir."

"Is she indeed, ma'am?" he said briskly. "You are fortunate to have such an accomplished musician as a teacher here."

It had bothered him—or his pride anyway—for a whole month before he put her from his mind that Frances had chosen to teach at a girls' school rather than go away with him. But since last evening he had found himself even more bothered that anyone with such a truly glorious voice could have chosen a teaching career when an illustrious career as a singer could have been hers with the mere snap of her fingers. It made no sense to him. *She* made no sense to him. And the fact that he did not know her, did not understand her, had kept him awake and irritable through much of the night. He scarcely knew her at all, he realized, and yet he was allowing her to haunt him again as no other woman had come close to doing.

"And no one is more sensible of that fact than I, Lord Sinclair," Miss Martin said, folding her hands at her waist. "It is gratifying to have her talent recognized by no less a person than the earl, your grandfather, and I am pleased that he has seen fit to invite her to take tea with him. However, Miss Allard has duties at this school and will need to be back here by half past five."

By the time this headmistress grew into an old battle-ax, Lucius thought, she would have had much practice. No doubt her girls—and her teachers—were all terrified of her. Good lord, it was almost a quarter to four now.

"I shall return her here not even one second past the half hour, ma'am," he said, raising his eyebrows and regarding her with cool hauteur. But if she felt in any way intimidated, she did not show it.

"I wish I could spare a maid to accompany her," she said, "but I cannot."

Good Lord!

"You must trust to my gentleman's honor, then, ma'am," he told her curtly.

She did not like him—or trust him. That was perfectly clear. The reason was less so. Did she know about that episode after Christmas? Or did she just distrust all men? He would wager that it was the latter.

And *this* was what Frances had chosen over him? It was enough to make a man turn to some serious drinking. But then this was what she must have chosen over a singing career too.

And then the door opened and Frances herself stepped into the room. She was dressed as she had been up on the Royal Crescent, in a fawn-colored dress with a short brown spencer over it and an unadorned brown bonnet. She also wore a tight, set expression on her face, as if she had steeled herself for a dreadful ordeal. She looked, in fact, remarkably like the prunish shrew whom he had hauled out of an overset carriage just after Christmas and dumped on a snowy road—except that her nose was not red-tipped today or her mouth spewing fire and brimstone.

He would have left her there knee deep in snow to fend for herself if he had known half the trouble she was going to cause him.

"Miss Allard?" He swept her his most elegant bow.

"Lord Sinclair." She curtsied, her eyes as cool and indifferent as if he had been a fly on the wall.

"I have informed Viscount Sinclair," Miss Martin said, "that he is to have you back here at precisely half past five, Frances."

Her eyes flickered, perhaps with surprise.

"I will not be late," she promised, and turned to leave the room without waiting to see if Lucius was ready to follow her.

A minute or two later they were seated side by side in his carriage, and it was turning onto Sutton Street before swinging around in a great arc onto Great Pulteney Street. She was clinging to the leather strap above her head, presumably so that she would not sway sideways and inadvertently brush against his arm.

He was deeply irritated.

"I have taken to devouring lady teachers when I cannot wait for my tea," he said.

She turned an uncomprehending face toward him.

"And what," she asked, "is that supposed to mean?"

"You cannot sit much farther away from me," he said, "without putting a dent in the side of the carriage, and I warn you I would be somewhat displeased if that were to happen. If I should decide to attack, though, you may scream and Peters will come running to your rescue even if only to stop you from murdering his eardrums."

She let go of the strap, though she turned her face away and looked out through the window on her side.

"Of all the places in England where you might have gone to enjoy yourself," she said, "why did you have to choose Bath?"

"I did not," he said. "My grandfather chose it for his health. He is a very sick man and fancies that the waters agree with him. I came to keep an eye on him. Did you think I had come deliberately to see you, Frances? To renew my addresses, perhaps? To stand beneath your bedchamber window and serenade you with lovelorn ballads? You flatter yourself."

"You make very free with my name," she said.

"With your—? You might at least *try* not to be ridiculous— *ma'am,*" he retorted.

He watched her profile—or what he could see of it around the brim of her bonnet—as they proceeded along the long, straight stretch of Great Pulteney Street, and wondered why she was angry. She surely could not seriously believe that he had come to Bath to torment her. He was not even the one who had invited her to tea this afternoon—or the one who had accepted the invitation. He was not the one who had abandoned her after Christmas either. It had been the other way around.

Like Miss Martin's, her posture was stiff and straight as any ramrod. She continued to gaze out the window like a queen looking for subjects on whom to confer a royal wave.

"Why are you angry?" he asked her.

"Angry?" She turned to look at him again, her nostrils flared, her eyes flashing. "I am not angry. Why should I be? You are a mere courier, are you not, Lord Sinclair, sent to bring me to the Earl of Edgecombe's house? It was kind of him to invite me and I am pleased to come."

She sounded it!

"Despite all the women I have known," he said, "I have never yet come close to fathoming the female mind. You were given the chance to prolong and advance our relationship three months ago, but you rejected it—quite emphatically, if memory serves me correctly. And yet now, Frances, your whole demeanor tells me that you think you have a grievance against me. Is it possible that I somehow *hurt* you?"

Color flamed in her cheeks and light flashed from her dark eyes—and she grabbed for the strap again as the carriage passed through the diamond-shaped Laura Place and circled the fountain in the middle of the road.

"What absurdity is this?" she cried. "How could you possibly have hurt me?"

"I do believe men and women sometimes react differently to the sort of . . . liaison in which you and I became involved," he said. "Men are able to enjoy the moment and let it go, while women are more inclined to find their hearts engaged. It was certainly never my intention to hurt you."

But, devil take it, he thought irritably, he had not exactly let the moment go, had he?

"And you most certainly did *not*," she said with hot indignation as the carriage rumbled onto the shop-lined Pulteney Bridge to cross the river. "How presumptuous of you, Lord Sinclair! How . . . *arrogant* of you to imagine that you broke my heart!"

"Frances," he said, "we shared a bed and a great deal more for one whole night. You make yourself ridiculous when you call me *Lord Sinclair* in that prim schoolteacher's voice as if I were some distant stranger."

"With the exception of that one night, which ought not to have happened and which I have regretted ever since," she said, "I *am* prim.

And I *am* a schoolteacher and proud of it. It is what I choose to be—for the rest of my life."

She turned her head sharply away again.

"That balding gentleman who would have relinquished you to my grandfather and me without a fight last evening is not your betrothed, then?" he asked.

He heard her draw in a sharp, indignant breath.

"What Mr. Blake is—or is not—to me is absolutely none of your business, my lord," she said.

He glowered at the back of her bonnet. She really was prim and shrewish and prickly and a mass of contradictions. He did not know why the devil she had stuck in his memory and in his emotions the way she had. The sooner he removed her from both the happier he would be.

Perhaps if he tried very hard he could contrive to fall in love with Portia Hunt this spring. But, good Lord, even if it were possible—and he very much doubted it was—Portia would be horrified!

"Why the devil do you choose to be a teacher when you ought to be singing professionally?" he asked abruptly. Because he had arrived in the drawing room doorway only as she was finishing her song last evening, it was still difficult to believe that Frances and that singer could be one and the same person.

"I would ask you to watch your language, Lord Sinclair," she said.

He surprised himself—and her, it seemed—by emitting a short bark of laughter.

"I believe," he said, "you may have just provided the answer to my question. You did not tell me after Christmas that you could sing like that."

"Why would I have told you such a thing?" she asked, looking around at him. "Ought I to have said, 'Oh, by the way, Mr. Marshall, I sing in a way that might just impress you a little.' Or ought I to have woken you up one morning with a particularly strident aria?"

He chuckled at the mental image of her waking him thus on the second morning, as she lay tucked up in his arms in her bed.

He did not know if she was having the same thought, but however it was, her eyes suddenly lit with merriment, her lips twitched, and she could not prevent a gurgle of laughter from escaping them.

"I wonder," he said, "if I would have found it arousing."

The prim schoolteacher made an instant reappearance, and she sat back on her seat and directed her eyes forward.

For a moment—damnation!—he had been entranced by her all over again.

"My grandfather has been very much looking forward to meeting you again," he said after a few moments of silence. "And my sister is beside herself with excitement. She is not yet out, you see, and does not often have a chance to entertain and even play hostess."

"Then she may play it for me," she said. "I am accustomed to young ladies and their uncertainties and exuberances. I will be a very undemanding guest."

Conversation lapsed between them then as the carriage began its slow climb uphill.

She set her hand in his when he offered it to help her alight from the carriage after it had stopped on Brock Street—their first touch since he had pressed his card into her palm outside the school three months ago. He felt again the slenderness of her hand, the long, slim artist's fingers. Even through her glove and his own he felt the shock of familiarity.

She preceded him inside the house while his grandfather's butler held the door open.

Lucius glowered at her back and went after her.

11

The carriage ride had been a horrible ordeal for Frances, bringing to mind as it did the last time she had ridden in the same vehicle with Lucius Marshall, Viscount Sinclair. He had held her hand then. For a large part of the journey he had had his arms right about her. They had kissed. They had dozed in each other's arms.

Today she had been horribly aware of him physically. She had been very careful not to touch him—until she could no longer avoid doing so when he offered a hand to help her alight outside the house on Brock Street.

As they entered the house and were preceded upstairs by the butler after he had taken her bonnet and gloves and spencer, she felt bruised and humiliated.

Is it possible that I somehow hurt you?

She still seethed at the arrogance of it.

Men are able to enjoy the moment and let it go, while women are more inclined to find their hearts engaged.

How mortifyingly true that seemed to be! His whole manner and conversation had demonstrated that he had not suffered one iota as a result of what had happened between them.

He had enjoyed the moment and let it go.

She had been battling a bruised heart ever since.

Despite all the women I have known . . .

Of which number she was one insignificant unit. If she had gone with him to London when he had asked, how soon would he have tired of her? Long before now, she was sure.

But, she thought, her coming here this afternoon had nothing whatsoever to do with him. She squared her shoulders and donned her best social manner as she was ushered into a cozy sitting room at the front of the house. The Earl of Edgecombe was rising from a chair by the fire, a welcoming smile on his thin, rather wan face, and Miss Marshall was hurrying toward her, both hands outstretched, her cheeks flushed, her face eagerly smiling.

"Miss Allard," she said when Frances set her hands in hers, "I am so delighted that you were able to come. Do take the seat beside Grandpapa if you will. The tea tray will be sent up immediately."

"Thank you." Frances smiled warmly at the girl, who was clearly on her best behavior and half elated, half anxious lest she make some mistake. She was pretty, with her brother's brown hair and hazel eyes, though her face was heart-shaped, with rounded cheeks and a pointed little chin.

The earl smiled kindly at Frances and reached out his right hand for hers as she approached. He carried it to his lips.

"Miss Allard," he said, "you do us a great honor. I hope I have not taken you away from anything very important at your school."

"I am sure," she said, taking the chair next to his, "that the junior choir was quite delighted to discover that there was to be no practice this afternoon, my lord."

"And so," he said, "you conduct a choir and you teach music, including pianoforte lessons. But how much do you sing, Miss Allard?"

"Last evening," she told him as he took his seat again and Viscount Sinclair took another chair and Miss Marshall fluttered about while the tea things were brought in by a maid and the butler, "was the first time I have performed outside a school setting in several years. It was a good thing for my nerves that the audience was not larger."

"And it was a tragedy for the musical world," he said, "that the audience was so small. You do not only have a good voice, Miss Allard, or even a superior voice. You have a *great* voice, definitely one of the loveliest I have ever heard in almost eighty years of listening. No—not *one of*. It *is* the loveliest."

Frances would not have been human if she had not felt a glow of pleasure at such lavish and apparently sincere praise.

"Thank you, my lord." She could feel herself flushing.

A plate of dainty sandwiches was set on a table close to where Miss Marshall sat behind the tea tray, together with scones spread with clotted cream and strawberry jam. There was also a plate of fancy cakes. The girl poured the tea into exquisitely fine china cups and brought one to each of them before offering the sandwiches.

"But you must have been told all this before," the earl said. "Many times, I suppose."

Yes. Sometimes by people whose opinion she could respect. Ultimately, after her father's death, by people who had promised fame and fortune while caring not one iota for her artist's soul. But—for a variety of reasons of which youthful vanity was not the least—she had believed them and allowed them to act for her and almost ruined herself in the process. And then she had lost Charles because of her singing and finally had behaved very badly. Much really had been ruined—all her girlhood dreams, for example. Sometimes, even though only three years had passed since she had seen the advertisement for the teaching position at Miss Martin's and applied for it and been sent to Bath by Mr. Hatchard for an interview with Claudia—sometimes it was hard to believe that all those things had happened to her and not someone else. Until last night she had not sung in public for three long years.

"People have always been kind," she said.

"Kind." He laughed gruffly as he took one small sandwich from the plate. "It is not kindness to be in the presence of greatness and pay homage to it, Miss Allard. I wish we were in London. I would invite the *ton* to spend an evening at my home and have you sing to them. I am not a renowned patron of the arts, but I would not need to be. Your talent would speak for itself, and your career as a singer would be assured. I am convinced of it. You could travel the world and enthrall audiences wherever you went."

Frances licked her lips and toyed with the food on her plate.

"But we are not in London, sir," Viscount Sinclair said, "and Miss Allard appears to be quite contented with her life as it is. Am I not right, ma'am?"

She lifted her eyes to his and realized how like his grandfather he was. He had the same square-jawed face, though the earl's had slackened with age and was characterized by a smiling kindliness, whereas the viscount's looked arrogant and stubborn and even harsh. He was gazing at her with intense eyes and one raised eyebrow. And his tone of voice had been clipped, though perhaps she was the only one who noticed.

"I like to sing for my own pleasure," she said, "and for the pleasure of others. But I do not crave fame. When one is a teacher, one owes good service, of course, to one's employer and to the parents of one's pupils as well as to the pupils themselves, but one nevertheless has a great deal of professional freedom. I am not sure the same could be said of a singer—or any other type of performer, for that matter. One would need a manager, to whom one would be no more than a marketable commodity. All that would be important would be money and fame and image and exposure to the right people and . . . Well, I believe it would be hard to hang on to one's integrity and one's own vision of what art is under such circumstances."

She spoke from bitter experience.

They were both looking attentively at her, Viscount Sinclair with mockery in every line of his body.

He had called her prim. It was foolish to allow such a description to hurt. She *was* prim. It was nothing to be ashamed of. It was something she had deliberately cultivated. His hand, she noticed, was playing with the edge of his plate—that strong, capable-looking hand that had chopped wood and peeled potatoes and sculpted a snowman's head and rested against the small of her back as they waltzed and caressed her body . . .

Miss Marshall got up to offer the scones.

"Not, surely," the earl said, "if one had a manager who shared one's artistic vision, Miss Allard. But what of your family? Did they never encourage you? Who are they, if I might be permitted to ask? I have never heard of any Allards."

"My father was French," she said. "He escaped the Reign of Terror when I was still a baby and brought me to England. My mother was already deceased. He died five years ago."

"I am sorry to hear that," he replied. "You must have been very young to be left alone. Did you have other family here in England?"

"Only my two great-aunts have ever had anything to do with me," she said. "They are my grandmother's sisters, daughters of a former Baron Clifton."

"Of Wimford Grange?" He raised his eyebrows. "And one of these ladies is Mrs. Melford, is she? She was once a particular friend of my late wife's. They made their come-out together. And so you are her great-niece. Wimford Grange is no farther than twenty miles from my home at Barclay Court. Both are in Somerset."

And that fact, of course, would explain why she and Lucius Marshall had been traveling the same road after Christmas. She did not look at him, and he made no comment.

"I have not seen Mrs. Melford for a few years," the earl said. "But I wonder why the present Clifton has not helped you to a career in singing."

"He is really quite a distant cousin, my lord," Frances said. She had not even set eyes on him last Christmas.

"I suppose so," he agreed. "But I probably embarrass you with all this talk of your family and your talent. Let us talk of something different. The concept of a school for girls is an interesting one when most people would have us believe that education is wasted on the female half of our population or that the little education girls require can best be learned from private governesses. You would disagree with both opinions, I assume?"

His eyes were twinkling beneath his white brows. He was effectively changing the subject and choosing one that was sure to provoke some response in her. It did, of course, and they had a lively discussion of the merits of sending girls away from home to be educated, and of instructing them in such subjects as mathematics and history. It was a topic too in which Miss Marshall was pleased to participate. She had always thought it would be great fun to go to school, she told Frances, but she had inherited her sisters' governess and remained at home instead.

"Not that I did not have a good education from her, Miss Allard," she said, "but I *do* think it would have been marvelous to have had pianoforte lessons from you and to have sung in one of your choirs. The girls at your school are very fortunate."

Frances could almost feel mockery emanating from the direction of Viscount Sinclair's chair even though she kept her eyes away from him and he did not participate a great deal in the conversation.

"Well, thank you," Frances said, smiling at the girl. "But they are fortunate in their other teachers too. Miss Martin makes a point of choosing only the best. Though I suppose I aggrandize myself by saying that, do I not?"

"I would have liked it," Miss Marshall said, "and to have had friends among girls my own age."

The conversation came back to music eventually but no longer concerned Frances personally. They compared favorite composers and pieces of music and favorite solo instruments. The earl told them of performances by famed musicians he had heard years ago, in Vienna and Paris and Rome.

"The Continent was still open to young bucks making the Grand Tour in my day," he said. "And, ah, we had a time of it, Miss Allard. The French, and particularly Napoléon Bonaparte, have much to answer for. Lucius was deprived of that treat, as was his father before him."

"You need to get my grandfather onto this topic when you have an hour or three to spare, Miss Allard," Viscount Sinclair said. They were mocking words, and yet it seemed to her that they were affectionately spoken. Perhaps he had *some* finer feelings.

"You saw Paris?" she asked the earl. "What was it like?"

The Earl of Edgecombe was indeed only too ready to talk about the past. He entertained them so well with stories of his travels and the places and people he had seen that Frances looked up in surprise when

Viscount Sinclair got to his feet and announced that it was time to re-turn Miss Allard to the school.

At some time during the past hour she had relaxed and started ac-tively to enjoy herself. Perhaps Anne had been right last evening. Perhaps she *was* setting to rest a few ghosts today. She had seen the other side of Viscount Sinclair's nature today—the arrogant, mocking, less pleasant side that she had seen when she first met him and had largely forgotten the next day and the next. It was as well to be re-minded of what exactly she had walked away from.

She could not have been happy with such a man. Though he was also, of course, a man who had come to Bath in order to care for his grandfather and who had brought his young sister with him.

Ah, life was confusing sometimes. People would be so much easier to like or dislike if there were only one facet to their natures.

The earl and Miss Marshall rose with her. The earl took her hand in his and raised it to his lips once more.

"This has been an honor and a pleasure, Miss Allard," he said. "I do hope I have the chance of hearing you sing again before I die. I be-lieve it will become one of my dearest wishes, in fact."

"Thank you. You are very kind." She smiled at him with some-thing bordering on affection.

Miss Marshall actually hugged her.

"This has been such *fun,*" she said, revealing all her youthfulness in the exuberance of her farewell.

"It has indeed." Frances smiled warmly at her. "And I have been treated royally by my hostess. Thank you for entertaining me so well."

But the girl turned impulsively to her brother just as Frances would have stepped out of the room ahead of him.

"Luce," she said, "you have been saying that if I am to be allowed to go with you and Grandpapa to the assembly in the Upper Rooms three evenings from tonight, we must find an older lady to accompany me. May we invite Miss Allard. Oh, please, *may* we?"

As Frances looked at her in dismay, the girl gazed at her brother, her eyes imploring, her hands clasped to her bosom.

How dreadfully gauche of the girl to ask in her hearing!

"Older?" Viscount Sinclair cocked one eyebrow.

"Well, she *is*," the girl said. "I did not say *old*, Luce, only *older*. And she is a *teacher*."

"It is a splendid suggestion, Amy," the earl said. "I wish I had thought of it for myself. Miss Allard, *will* you so honor us? Though perhaps since you live in Bath, attending one of the assemblies will be no great treat for you."

"Oh, but I have never attended one," she said.

"What? Never? Then do please agree to attend this one as our special guest," the earl said.

"Please, please do, Miss Allard," Miss Marshall cried. "Caroline and Emily—my sisters—will expire of envy if I write and tell them I am to go after all."

Frances was terribly aware of the silent figure of Viscount Sinclair standing beside her. She turned and glanced up at him, her teeth sinking into her lower lip. How could she refuse without hurting Miss Marshall, who obviously was desperate to be allowed to attend an assembly before she was officially out?

He did not help her. But how could he without appearing churlish in front of his relatives?

"I wish you would, Miss Allard," he said curtly. "You would oblige all of us."

The trouble was that she had always thought it would be wonderful to actually dance in the Upper Rooms, which she had seen, but only with a party of girls one day when she took them sightseeing. She had once attended balls in London and had always enjoyed them exceedingly.

But how could she go to this one?

How could she not, though? Now the invitation had been extended by all three of them.

"Thank you," she said. "That would be delightful."

Miss Marshall clapped her hands, the earl bowed, and Viscount Sinclair ushered her out of the room without another word, one of his hands firm against the small of her back and feeling as if it burned a hole there.

They rode side by side in the carriage back to the school without exchanging a word. It was most disconcerting. At one moment Frances almost asked him if he really minded her going to the assembly, but of course he minded—as did she. She thought of asking him if he wished her to send back a refusal with him after all. But why should she? She had been properly invited, even if it had been impulsive of Miss Marshall to speak out as she had without consulting her brother privately first.

Besides, if he minded or if he wished for her to change her mind, he had a tongue in his head just as she did. Let *him* be the first to speak.

And yet her heart, she realized, was in a very fragile condition, and she would certainly do it no good by seeing him again after today. Even now she would suffer some sleepless hours in the nights to come, she did not doubt. Good heavens, she had actually made love with this silent man beside her. She could recall every detail of that night of intimacy with great clarity.

And of their wretched parting the next day.

The carriage drew to a halt outside the school at precisely half past five. Peters opened the carriage door and set down the steps, and Viscount Sinclair descended and handed Frances down onto the pavement. He escorted her to the door of the school, which Keeble was already holding open.

"I shall come to escort you to the Upper Assembly Rooms three evenings from tonight, then," Viscount Sinclair said.

"Yes," she said. "Thank you."

"Perhaps," he said, and it seemed to her that his eyes burned into hers, "we will get to dance together again, Miss Allard."

"Yes." She turned and hurried inside and up to her room, where she hoped to be able to gather her scattered thoughts sufficiently to get a few of her essays marked before dinner.

I shall come to escort you. . . .

Perhaps we will get to dance together again . . .

Life was so terribly unfair. Just last evening she had been feeling happy again. And now . . .

Now it seemed that everything about her—every part of her body, her head, her emotions—was in a seething turmoil.

She read attentively through one four-page essay before realizing that she had not absorbed a single word.

It would be well, she told herself severely, to remember that she was a teacher. It was her primary and only really important role in life.

She was a *teacher*.

She started to read from the beginning again.

Lucius frowned at his image in the looking glass a few mo-ments after he had dismissed his valet. He always took pains to look his best. It was, after all, part of being a gentleman always to look fashionable and well groomed, especially when one was known as something of a Corinthian. But why the devil had he made poor Jeffreys discard three perfectly respectably tied neckcloths before he had been satisfied with the fourth?

Was he turning into some sort of dandy?

He was going to an assembly in *Bath,* for the love of God, not to a ball at Carlton House! He would be fortunate if there were a dozen people below the age of fifty there. It was very probably going to be one long snore of an evening. And yet here he was, going to more than usual trouble over his appearance.

He could hardly believe that he, Lucius Marshall, Viscount Sinclair, was actually going to attend such an insipid gathering. He rarely attended balls or routs even in London, though he would have to do so this spring, of course. He could treat this evening as something in the nature of a rehearsal for things to come.

His frown became a grimace, and he turned away from the glass.

Amy was already dressed and pacing the sitting room floor, he found when he went downstairs, even though she and their grandfather were not scheduled to walk across to the Upper Rooms for half an hour yet. She had been in a fever of excitement all day, quite unable to settle to anything.

"Well, you look remarkably pretty this evening," he said after she had caught up the sides of her skirt and pirouetted before him and he had looked her over critically from head to toe. He approved of her pale blue muslin dress—he had helped pick it out two days ago—and her carefully curled and coifed hair. Her maid had had the good sense not to try to make her look older than her years. Although she did not have either Caroline's height and elegance or Emily's dimples and natural curls, she might yet turn out to be the prettiest of the three, he thought. Margaret, of course, had been a beauty in her day and was still handsome now that she was in her thirties and the mother of three.

"Will I do, then?" Amy looked at him, flushed and bright-eyed.

"Very well indeed," he said. "If you are mobbed by all the gentlemen tonight, I shall have to beat them off with my quizzing glass."

"Oh, Luce." She laughed in obvious delight. "I hope you will not look quite so fierce when you stand beside me or no one will muster the courage to ask me to dance at all. You do look splendid, though."

"Thank you, ma'am." He made her a mock bow. "You *will* walk slowly when you leave the house with Grandpapa, Amy? You will not gallop along in your excitement and force him to keep up with you?"

She sobered instantly. "Of course I will not," she said. "I think the waters really must be doing him some good, do not you, Luce? He has looked quite well lately."

"He has," he agreed, though they both knew that he would never actually *be* well again.

"I just can't wait to go," she said, clasping her hands to her bosom, "or to see Miss Allard again. She is exceedingly amiable and treats me like a grown-up. And she is lovely too, even though she does not dress in the first stare of fashion. I admire her lovely dark hair and eyes. Oh, *when* will Grandpapa be ready?"

"At exactly the time he said he would be," Lucius told her, striding over to the window. "You know how punctual he always is. And if *I* am to be punctual, I must be on my way. I see Peters has the carriage outside."

A couple of minutes later he was on his way to Miss Martin's school again.

There had been letters from his mother and Caroline this morning. Prominent in the news they had both been eager to impart was the fact that the Marquess of Godsworthy had arrived in town for the Season with Lord and Lady Balderston—and with Portia, of course. His mother had called upon the two ladies with Caroline and Emily. Miss Hunt was in good looks, they had reported. Lady Balderston had asked about him and said she looked forward to seeing him in the near future.

Portia Hunt was always in good looks, and so that was no news. He could not remember ever seeing her with the proverbial hair out of place—not even when she was a child.

The carriage drew to a halt outside the school doors, and Lucius descended to the pavement, feeling rather as if he were up to something clandestine—he was about to escort another woman to a ball.

A strange scene met his eyes when the porter answered the door to his knock. Frances Allard was standing in the middle of the hallway, wearing a dress of silver-shot gray muslin with a silver silk sash beneath her bosom and two rows of the same silk ribbon about the hem. Another lady was kneeling on the floor beside her, a needle and thread in her hand while she stitched up a part of the ribbon that must have pulled loose from the dress. A third lady was bending toward the second, a few pins cupped in the open palm of her hand. Miss Martin was draping a paisley shawl about Frances's shoulders and smoothing it into place.

The two seamstresses turned identically flushed and laughing faces his way as he stepped inside. Frances bit into her lower lip, looking faintly embarrassed, but then she laughed too.

"Oh, dear," she said.

The vivid loveliness of her merry expression smote him like a fist to the abdomen and fairly robbed him of breath for a moment.

"*Another* gentleman who chooses to arrive five minutes before his appointed time," Miss Martin said severely.

"I do beg your pardon." Lucius raised his eyebrows. "Should I perhaps go back outside and wait on the pavement until the five minutes have expired?"

They all dissolved into laughter again—even Miss Martin smirked.

"No, no, I am ready," Frances said as the thread was snapped free and the ribbon about her hem pulled into place. "You have met Miss Martin, Lord Sinclair. May I present my fellow teachers, Miss Jewell and Miss Osbourne?"

She indicated the two seamstresses, both of whom were young and pretty. They were both looking at him with frank interest.

"Miss Jewell?" He bowed to the fair-haired, blue-eyed teacher. "Miss Osbourne?" He bowed to the auburn-haired little beauty.

They both curtsied in return.

A night out for one of their number, he suddenly realized, must be a momentous occasion for all of them. He felt that he was being given an unwilling glimpse into another, alien world, in which life for women was not a constant and idle round of parties and balls and routs. Yet these teachers were all young and all personable. Even the stiff-mannered, dour Miss Martin was not an antidote.

But why the devil had Frances chosen to be one of them? She did not need to be.

The porter, silent and glowering, as if he resented the intrusion of any male except himself into this hallowed female domain, held the door open, and Lucius followed Frances out onto the pavement and handed her into the carriage.

"The weather has stayed fine for the occasion," she said brightly as the carriage rocked into motion.

"Would you have canceled if it had rained, then?" he asked.

"No, of course not." She clung with both hands to the ends of her shawl.

"You were, then," he said, "merely making polite conversation?"

"I am sorry if I bore you," she said, an edge of annoyance in her voice. "Perhaps I ought to have remained silent. I shall do so for the rest of the journey."

"What do you usually do for entertainment?" he asked her after she had suited action—or rather inaction—to words for a minute or so. "You and those other teachers? You live in Bath yet you have never been to an assembly. Do you put the girls to bed each night and then sit together conversing over the clacking of your knitting needles?"

"If we do, Lord Sinclair," she said, "you need not concern yourself about us. We are quite happy."

"You said that once before," he told her. "And then you changed the word to *contented*. Is contentment enough, then, Frances?"

He thought she was not going to answer him. He watched her in the faint light of dusk. She was not wearing a bonnet tonight. Her dark hair was sleek over her head and dressed in curls at the back of her neck. They were not elaborate curls, but they were certainly more becoming than the usual knot. She looked elegant and lovely. She was going to make every other woman in the Upper Rooms look overfussy.

"Yes, it is," she said. "Happiness must always find its balance in unhappiness and excitement in depression. Contentment is more easily maintained and brings with it tranquillity of mind and peace of soul."

"Good Lord!" he said. "Could anything be more of a complete bore? I think you are a coward, Frances."

She turned wide, indignant eyes on him.

"A coward?" she said. "I suppose it was cowardly of me not to throw away my career, my security, my future, and my friends and go off to London with you."

"*Very* cowardly," he said.

"If cowardliness means being sane," she said, "then, yes, by your definition I am a coward, Lord Sinclair, and make no apology for the fact."

"You might have been happy," he said. "You might have taken a chance on life. And I would soon enough have discovered your talent, you know. You might have sung for larger audiences than you will ever find here. You cannot tell me that with your voice you have never dreamed of fame."

"And fortune," she said sharply. "The two inevitably go together, I believe, Lord Sinclair. I suppose *you* would have made me happy. I suppose *you* would have sponsored my singing career and have made sure that I met all the right people."

"Why not?" he asked. "I would not have chosen to keep your talent all to myself."

"And so," she said, her voice trembling with some emotion that he thought must be anger, "a woman is quite incapable of knowing her own mind and finding the contentment, even happiness, she wants of life without the aid and intervention of some *man*. Is that what you are saying, Lord Sinclair?"

"I was unaware," he said, "that we were speaking of men and women in general. I was speaking of you. And I know you quite well enough to understand that you were not made for contentment. How absurd of you to believe that you were. You are fairly bursting at the seams with passion, Frances—not all of it sexual, I might add."

"How dare you!" she cried. "You do not know me at all."

"I beg your pardon," he said. "I certainly know you in the biblical sense—and one night was quite enough for me to draw certain conclusions about your capacity for sexual passion. I have spoken with you—and quarreled with you—on several occasions, this evening included. I have laughed and played with you. And, perhaps most significant of all, I have heard you sing. I know you quite well."

"Singing has nothing to do with—"

"Ah, but it does," he said. "Anyone who uses an extraordinary talent to the full, forgetting very self in the process, has no choice but to pour out himself or herself. There is no hiding on such occasions, whether the product is a painting or a poem or a song. When you sang at the Reynolds soiree, you revealed far more than just a lovely voice, Frances. You revealed yourself, and only a dolt would have failed to see you for the deeply passionate woman that you are."

It was strange. He had not consciously thought these things before. But he knew that he spoke the truth.

"I am quite contented as I am," she said stubbornly, setting her hands palm down on her lap and staring down at her spread fingers.

"Ah, yes," he said, "very much the coward, Frances. You give up the discussion and fall back upon platitudes because your case is unarguable. And you lie through your teeth."

"You become offensive," she said. "I have given you no permission to speak so freely to me, Lord Sinclair."

"Perhaps that is so," he said. "You have given me only your body."

She inhaled sharply. But she let the breath out slowly again and refrained from answering him.

He had not noticed the passing landmarks of the journey. He realized suddenly, though, that they were approaching the Upper Assembly Rooms. It was just as well. Good Lord, he had not intended to quarrel with her. He might not have done so if she had not irritated him by opening the conversation with her bright, inane comment on the weather.

As if they were no more than polite strangers.

The sooner he left Bath and got back to the serious business of getting himself married, the better it would be for everyone. And Portia Hunt was in London waiting for him. So were her mama and his and all their family members.

Bath, London. London, Bath . . . Devil take it, it was like the choice between the devil and the deep blue sea!

Where had the familiar life gone that had given him perfect contentment for the past ten years or so?

But as he descended from the carriage and turned to hand Frances down, he did catch himself out.

Contentment?

He had been *contented* for the past ten years?

Contented?

A dozen times during the past three days Frances had been on the brink of writing to Miss Amy Marshall with some excuse not to attend the assembly. There was too much schoolwork to be done—classes to prepare and papers to mark—and there were extra music lessons with individual girls to be fitted in, and practices with the junior and senior choirs and the madrigal group.

Her life as a teacher occupied most of her waking hours.

But her friends, who ought to have supported such a responsible attitude, had not cooperated on this occasion.

"You must go and enjoy yourself for Miss Marshall's sake," Claudia had said. "You said she needed a female chaperone, and it may be too late to find another. And you must go for the Earl of Edgecombe's sake too. He sounds like a courtly gentleman even if he *is* an aristocrat."

"And you must go and enjoy yourself for *our* sakes," Anne had said with a sigh. "You are actually going to attend one of the assemblies at the Upper Rooms, Frances—as the invited guest of an earl and a viscount. We will want to enjoy it vicariously through you. We will want to hear every single detail the morning after."

"And perhaps," Susanna had added, the usual twinkle of mischief in her eyes, "Viscount Sinclair will realize that he ought not to have let you go after Christmas, Frances, and will begin a determined courtship of you. Perhaps he will sweep you off your feet and put poor Mr. Blake to rout." But she had also rushed up to hug Frances, all teasing at an end. "Do enjoy yourself. Just *enjoy* yourself."

Anne had come to Frances's room, though, while she was getting ready for the evening and asked her if it really was going to be painful for her to be in company with Viscount Sinclair for a whole evening.

"Perhaps," she had said, "I ought not to have said that about your going to enjoy the evening for our sakes. How selfish of me!"

But by then it had been too late to avoid going, and Frances had assured her that going to tea at Brock Street really had cured her of any foolish infatuation she may have felt for the man after Christmas.

That had been just before Susanna and Claudia had also come to her room and just before Viscount Sinclair was due to arrive, and they had all gone downstairs with her to wait in the visitors' sitting room. And then, of course, Anne had noticed that part of the ribbon at her hem had come unstitched and Susanna had dashed upstairs for needle and thread and pins, and all had been laughing panic while Anne had stitched.

It had not occurred to any of them to move from the hallway into the sitting room or to Mr. Keeble not to open the door when the viscount had knocked on it.

It had all been rather embarrassing and rather funny. And then he had offered to go back outside to wait and the situation had seemed funnier still. And, of course, it really was rather exciting to be going to an assembly. Perhaps even to dance there.

Perhaps with him.

He had mentioned their dancing together when he had brought her home after tea that afternoon.

But she was no longer feeling so cheerful as she descended from the carriage outside the Upper Rooms. Gracious heavens, he had called her a coward. And a passionate woman.

You are fairly bursting at the seams with passion, Frances—not all of it sexual, I might add.

He had referred openly to the night they had spent together. He had reminded her that he knew her in the biblical sense.

He had accused her of hiding behind her contentment, too cowardly to reach for happiness.

It was not cowardice. It was a hard-won good sense.

If only, she thought as she stepped ahead of him through the doors into the Upper Rooms, he did not look so devastatingly handsome tonight in his black tailed evening coat and pantaloons with a silver embroidered waistcoat and white linen and expertly tied neckcloth. Or so suffocatingly male with his square-jawed, handsome face and intense hazel eyes.

And then she forgot some of her agitation at the realization that she was actually here. She was attending a ball at the Upper Assembly Rooms. At least part of her reason for deciding to come after all, she realized, was her desire to be part of such a gathering again. She had missed society. She had not been actively unhappy without it, but she *had* missed it. Fellow guests moved about the high-ceilinged entry hall and she felt an unexpected welling of excitement.

Viscount Sinclair set a hand at the small of her back in order to move her forward. But before she could feel more than a shiver of awareness at his touch, Miss Marshall came hurrying toward them—she must have been watching for them from the ballroom doorway. She looked fresh and pretty and youthful and quite exuberant.

"Miss Allard," she said, stretching out both hands, as she had done on Brock Street, clasping Frances's, and kissing her cheek, "how very prompt you are. Grandpapa and I arrived barely five minutes ago—and yes, Luce, we fairly crawled here, I swear. How lovely you look in silver, Miss Allard. Your gown perfectly complements Luce's colors." She laughed lightly.

Oh, gracious, what an unfortunate remark! Frances moved away from his hand and smiled brightly as the girl took her arm and they moved off in the direction of the ballroom. Lord Sinclair came along behind.

"Oh, my!" Frances said when they paused in the doorway. "I have only ever seen the room in daylight. It looks very much more splendid with all the candles lit, does it not?"

There were several chandeliers overhead, each filled with lit candles. The orchestra members on the dais were tuning their instruments. A number of people stood or sat in conversational groups or promenaded about the perimeter of the dance floor.

She must notice every single detail, she thought, so that she could give a faithful account of it all to her friends tomorrow.

"This is the first assembly you have attended in a while, is it, Miss Allard?" Viscount Sinclair asked.

She had told him and his grandfather at tea the other day that she had never attended an assembly here. But she understood his meaning in a flash. And when she turned to look at him, she found the expected almost satanic gleam in his eye.

"Yes," she said. "It is."

"It looks as if it will be well enough attended," he said, "though we are only in Bath and cannot therefore expect a great squeeze. An assembly can, of course, be perfectly enjoyable with very few guests. Even two are enough, provided one is a man and the other a woman so that they can dance together. Even an orchestra is not indispensable."

"How absurd, Luce!" His sister laughed merrily.

But Viscount Sinclair kept his eyes on Frances and his eyebrows raised.

"Would you not agree with *me*, Miss Allard?" he asked.

She would not blush, she thought. She would *not*.

"But then it would not really be an assembly, would it?" she said.

"And the man and woman concerned," he added, "might soon tire of dancing and look for some other diversion. You are quite right. I suppose we should be thankful that there is a tolerable crowd here this evening."

Why was he doing this? Frances wondered. He had not seemed pleased to see her at any of their three meetings since his return to Bath.

Fortunately, the Earl of Edgecombe came up to them at that moment. He had remained in the ballroom with his granddaughter while she was alone, he explained after greeting Frances and bowing over her hand, but now he would remove to the card room if they would all excuse him.

"I have danced at a few informal assemblies at home," Miss Marshall confided to Frances while Viscount Sinclair took his grandfather through into the other room, "but never at anything this grand. Caroline and Emily will be envious when I write and tell them about it tomorrow."

There were not a great many young people present, Frances noticed. And though she had been dazzled at first glance by the finery of the guests, she could see on closer inspection that very few were dressed in quite the style one would expect to see at a *ton* ball. She was glad of it, though. She had been afraid that she would feel conspicuous in her less than fashionable gown.

"It is rather grand," she said. "But next year, Miss Marshall, when you make your come-out, you will be delighted to find that there is something even grander than this to experience."

"Oh, you must call me Amy, please," the girl said. And then her expression brightened further and she raised her fan to wave to someone across the dance floor. "There is Rose Abbotsford with her mama. And that must be the brother she spoke of. He is exceedingly handsome, is he not?" She unfurled her fan as her brother came up to them again.

"Before you set your cap at all the young blades in the room, Amy," he said, "do remember that you are to dance the opening set with me. As it is, Mama will probably have my head for allowing you to come here at all."

And then a gentleman was bowing before Frances, and she saw that he was Mr. Blake.

"Miss Allard," he said. "I did not dare hope to see you here this evening. But I am, of course, delighted to do so."

He glanced at her two companions as she curtsied to him, and she introduced him to them, though he had of course seen them at the Reynolds soiree.

"It was exceedingly kind of you, my lord," he said to Viscount Sinclair, "to invite Miss Allard here as your guest."

"Oh," Frances said, embarrassed, "I am here more in the nature of a chaperone than a guest, Mr. Blake."

"No, indeed, you are not," Amy cried, tapping Frances sharply on the arm with her fan. "The very idea!"

"Thank you, sir," Viscount Sinclair said in such a stiff, haughty voice that Frances looked sharply at him. He held a quizzing glass almost but not quite to his eye. "But Miss Allard is the personal guest of the Earl of Edgecombe."

Mr. Blake bowed, and looking at him, Frances was not sure he had understood that he had just been dealt a frosty setdown. She felt indignant on his behalf. Did Viscount Sinclair feel that he had been imposed upon by having a mere physician presented to him? Good heavens, *she* was a schoolteacher.

"Is it now too much to hope," Mr. Blake asked her, "that you are free to dance the second set with me, Miss Allard? I had already spoken for the opening set with Miss Jones before I saw you."

"Miss Allard is to dance the second set with me," Viscount Sinclair said.

Frances had a brief moment in which to decide whether she would brawl openly with him or let the matter go. She glanced at him and saw that one of his eyebrows was cocked. Perhaps, she thought during that one moment, he would be quite happy if she took the first course. There was an open challenge in that eyebrow.

"Yes." She smiled into his eyes. "Lord Sinclair most particularly asked for it while escorting me here in the carriage."

"Ah," Mr. Blake said. "The third set, then, perhaps, Miss Allard?"

"I shall look forward to it," she told him.

The first set was being announced, she realized then, by the Master of Ceremonies, and the orchestra sat poised to play. All annoyance, all embarrassment, fled as she turned her attention to the dance floor. She was excited even though she did not expect to dance much herself. She would at least be dancing the second and third sets, and that was more than she had expected.

But she was not to miss the opening set of vigorous country dances after all. Mr. Blake had gone to claim his partner and Viscount Sinclair had led his sister onto the floor and Frances had found a vacant seat. But Mr. Gillray, Mr. Huckerby's brother-in-law, to whom she had been introduced after the Christmas concert at school, came and asked her if she would dance with him, and so she had all the pleasure of participating in the ball right from the first moment.

And a very definite pleasure it was too. She found herself smiling and then laughing through some of the more intricate turns and twirls, the steps fresh in her memory as she was always the one who partnered Mr. Huckerby when he taught the girls. Amy Marshall, farther down the line, was openly enjoying herself too. Viscount Sinclair watched her with an indulgent smile on his face though he once caught Frances's eye and held it for a long moment.

And she was to dance the next set with him. She did not know whether to be glad or sorry. He was easily the most handsome and distinguished gentleman present, and just the thought of dancing with him again made her want to swoon. But the farther she stayed away from him, the better for her peace of mind, she knew. Her precious peace.

Her *contentment*.

But, heaven help her, that old magic was weaving its web about her again with every passing moment.

She did want to dance with him again—she desperately wanted it. Just one more time.

13

Mr. Algernon Abbotsford was presented to Amy after the first set was over, and he very properly asked Lucius's permission to lead her out into the second set. Having granted that permission, Lucius was free to turn his attention to his own partner, who was conversing with a lady he did not know.

Truth to tell, his attention had not been far from her ever since their arrival. And if he had ever deceived himself into thinking that he had not been looking forward to this evening with almost as much eagerness as Amy and that he had not taken pains with his appearance because he was to see Frances Allard again, then he was finally being forced into facing the rather lowering truth.

Damnation!

And if *she* truly believed that she was a woman made for placid contentment, then she was even more given to self-deceit than he. A woman less designed to dwindle into old age as a spinster school-teacher he could not imagine. Her cheeks, her eyes, her whole demeanor, glowed with a passionate enjoyment of the occasion even though this was a mere Bath assembly.

He knew, as no one else did, how easily and totally her love of dancing could be converted to sexual passion.

Not that he intended to effect quite that conversion tonight!

"Ma'am?" he said now, bowing before her. "This is my dance, I believe?"

Her eyes swept up to meet his, and he knew she remembered that they were the exact words he had used in that cold, dingy Assembly Room at the inn before they waltzed and then made love.

He was not really sure why he felt compelled tonight to remind her of that occasion. Sheer devilry, perhaps? Or perhaps he felt the need to confront her, to force her out into the open, to . . . Well, he did not know what it was he was up to. He rarely thought about the motives for what he did and said. He had always been a man of impulse and action.

"I believe it is, my lord," she said, setting her hand in his. "Thank you."

"It is not, alas, a waltz," he told her as he led her onto the floor. "There are to be none tonight. I have inquired."

"I have heard," she said, "that the waltz is not often danced in Bath."

"It is a damnable crime of omission," he said. "But if it *were* to be danced here, Frances, we would dance it together."

"Yes," she agreed, and turned her head to look into his eyes.

Something fleeting and wordless passed between them at that moment. Desire, yearning, knowledge—he was not sure which. Perhaps all three. Certainly there was full carnal awareness there.

They were a severe annoyance to each other, he and Frances Allard. They were as much inclined to quarrel as to be civil with each other. But there was a spark of something, which had been ignited during the day preceding their waltz three months ago and fanned to full flame during and after their waltz. That spark had still not quite been extinguished even three months later.

And, by Jove, he would no longer pretend to himself that he regretted having seen her again, that he ought to have avoided her, that he wished her to the devil. He was not good at this game of self-deception, even if she was.

He was deuced happy to be with her once more.

This was to be another country dance, but it was slower and more stately than the first. He escorted her to the long line of ladies and took his place opposite her in the line of gentlemen. She looked startlingly foreign in comparison with the other ladies, he thought—dark and vivid and lovely. A rose among thorns. No—unfair. More like a rare orchid among roses.

And roses suddenly seemed bland.

He could not remember the last time he had danced two sets in a row at any ball. Even one set was often more than he could stomach. Whoever had decreed that dancing was to be a favored mode of enjoyment for an evening ought to have been deported to the colonies as a mortal threat to the sanity of the male of the species, he had always thought. If he wanted to get close to a woman—and he frequently did—there were far more direct ways of going about it than cavorting with her about a ballroom floor in company with a large gathering of other persons similarly inclined.

But waltzing with Frances Allard after Christmas had been a sexual experience in itself. More than that, it had been exciting and exhilarating. And now he was to dance with her again, and everything in his being was focused upon her, tall and very slender in her silver muslin, her sleek, dark hair gleaming in the light of the candles overhead, her eyes glowing with the anticipation of pleasure.

Tomorrow or the next day or the next he was going to have to get back to London and turn his mind to duty, he supposed—perish the thought. But first there was tonight, and by God he was going to enjoy every passing moment for what it was worth.

The music began, the gentlemen bowed, and the ladies curtsied. The lines advanced toward each other, each gentleman clasped his partner's right hand just above the level of their heads, and turned once about with her before the lines returned to their places.

The orchestra played on, and the dancers tramped out the stately measures of the set, their dancing shoes beating out a rhythmic tattoo on the polished floor. They moved about each other, Lucius and Frances, sometimes face-to-face, sometimes back-to-back. They clasped hands, advanced down the room and back with the lines, wove in and out about other couples, came together again, twirled down between the lines from the head of the set to its foot when their turn came, their arms linked, their hands joined between them.

They did it all without exchanging another word with each other, though there were frequent opportunities for snatches of conversation. Yet he scarcely removed his eyes from hers the whole time, and he held her gaze with the power of his will. His senses were raw with his awareness of her—the sheen of silver ribbon and dark hair as they caught the light, the whisper of muslin as she moved, the slender warmth of her hand in his, the familiar fragrance of her that must come from soap rather than a heavier perfume, he believed.

But one thing more than any other became blazingly clear to him as they danced. She might have rejected him three months ago, but it was not because of indifference, by Jove. He supposed he had known it even at the time, but he was certain of it now.

Frances Allard was nothing short of a coward.

And if there was one thing he was determined to accomplish before the school door closed behind her tonight, it was to force her out of her complacency, to force her to understand that she had lost more than she had gained by choosing the old comfortable security over him. To force her to admit her mistake.

He totally forgot that he had already admitted to himself that it had not been a mistake at all.

The air between them fairly crackled.

By the time the set came to an end the sheen of perspiration on her face and bosom made her lovelier yet—and even more desirable. So did the slight heaving of her bosom, caused by her exertions. Her lips were parted, her eyes shining.

"Thank you," she said as he held out his right arm to take her hand on his sleeve. "That was very pleasant."

"That word again." He speared her with a hard glance. "Sometimes I could shake you, Frances."

"I *beg* your pardon?" She looked back at him in some surprise.

"I hope," he said, "you never praise your choirs or your musicians by telling them their performances were pleasant. It would be enough to make them renounce music forever. If I had my way, I would have the word banished from the English language."

"I wonder you danced with me at all, Lord Sinclair," she said. "You appear not to like me a great deal."

"Sometimes," he said, "it seems that liking has little to do with what is between us, Frances."

"There is *nothing* between us," she told him.

"Even animosity is *something*," he said. "But there is more than just that."

He directed her toward where Amy was standing with the Abbotsfords, looking even more animated than she had when they arrived, if that were possible.

"You will join Amy and my grandfather and me for tea in the tea-room after the next set," he told Frances. He had suddenly remembered that she was to dance next with Blake, the physician, who clearly had designs on her, though he must be proceeding at the devil of a snail's pace if he had not contrived some way of inviting her to attend the assembly with him this evening. The man was not going to bear her off for tea as he had done at the Reynolds soiree, though.

"Is that a request, Lord Sinclair?" she asked. "Or a command?"

"I will go down on bended knee if you wish," he said. "But I warn you that my doing so will occasion considerable gossip."

She laughed.

His heart never failed to beat faster when she did so. Laughter transformed her even when she was already flushed and glowing. She must surely have been created for laughter. It made her real—whatever the devil he meant by that.

"I will come quietly, then," she promised.

Her swain came for her soon after and led her away, his half-bald head shining in the light of the candles. The Master of Ceremonies brought an earnest, bespectacled young man to introduce to Amy, and the youth bore her off to dance the quadrille.

Lucius slipped into the card room before the Master of Ceremonies could take it into his head to present *him* with another partner too. His grandfather, he could see, was absorbed in play.

He felt out of sorts and irritable again—rather familiar feelings these days and not likely to go away during the coming weeks and months, he supposed. He tried to remember what life had been like before he went down to Barclay Court just before Christmas. Surely he was not normally surly and irritable but the most placid and genial of souls.

Surely he was not normally inclined to being besotted with lady schoolteachers either.

Why the devil could his grandfather not live forever?

Or why could he not have had a dozen brothers—all older than himself?

The quadrille seemed to go on forever. He was ready for tea.

Tea, for God's sake!

Mr. Blake was a tolerably accomplished dancer. He was also an amiable partner and complimented Frances on both her appearance and her dancing skills. He expressed again his pleasure at seeing her at the assembly.

"If I had known you were able to attend such events, Miss Allard," he said, "I would have invited you myself, since I have come with my sister and brother-in-law. Perhaps you would care to join us at the theater one evening?"

"That would be very agreeable, sir." She smiled. "If I can be excused from my evening duties at the school as I have been this evening, that is. It is kind of you to think of me."

"It is certainly no hard task to *think* of you, Miss Allard," he assured her, bending his head a little closer to hers. "Indeed, I find myself doing so rather frequently these days."

She was glad the figures of the dance separated them at that moment. All sorts of emotions were still churning around inside her after the last set, and she felt quite inadequate to the task of dealing with an ardor she was not yet ready to entertain. She concentrated instead upon enjoying the quadrille that they danced together. She tried briefly to recapture the pleasure she had felt in Mr. Blake's interest just a week ago but just could not seem to do it. Viscount Sinclair was right, she realized suddenly—the words *pleasant* and *pleasure* really were rather bland.

She noticed the viscount's absence from the ballroom far more than she noticed Mr. Blake's presence—not a promising sign at all. The whole atmosphere of the ball had suddenly fallen flat.

Why could one's heart not be commanded as easily as one's head? she wondered. Why could one not choose which man to love—though *love* was not quite the appropriate word for the emotions that churned about inside her head and her body. But whatever the right word *was,* one ought to be able to choose which man would stir one's blood and quicken one's heartbeat and fill one's world with the power of his presence.

She was going to have to try harder after this evening was over, she decided—after she had seen Viscount Sinclair for the last time.

She so *wished* to form an attachment to Mr. Blake. His interest in her really ought to be a blessing in her life.

"I am sorry," she said when the set ended and he asked her if she would do him the honor of taking refreshments with him and his relatives, "but I have already agreed to join the Earl of Edgecombe's party for tea. He really did invite me here tonight because he felt Miss Marshall needed an older lady as a chaperone—or companion, if you like."

"Oh, but not very much older, Miss Allard," he said gallantly, bowing over her hand. "I understand perfectly, though, and honor you for putting a perceived obligation before what might be your personal inclination. I shall do myself the honor of calling upon you at Miss Martin's school one day soon, then, if I may."

"Thank you." She smiled at him again. And yet for some unfathomable reason she felt she had been dishonest with him—or maybe it was not so unfathomable. She was going to have to be very careful not simply to use him in the coming days in order to hide from her bruised heart.

How *foolish* beyond words that she was allowing her heart to be bruised again!

She enjoyed the half hour spent in the tearoom. It was because the

Earl of Edgecombe and Amy Marshall again treated her as a favored guest, she told herself, and because the conversation was lively and full of laughter and her surroundings were a feast for the senses. She was going to have much with which to regale her friends tomorrow. And she would, she knew, always remember tonight.

But deep down she knew that she would not have felt half the exhilaration she did feel if Lucius Marshall, Viscount Sinclair, had not been there at the table too. He might be horribly annoying at times, and he had a habit of saying things deliberately to discompose her—or of remaining silent with the same motive—but he was always exciting company, and being in his presence again brought back memories of an episode in her life that she had tried hard to forget but now admitted she would not have missed for all the consideration in the world.

Those days had brought her vividly alive.

And she felt vividly alive again this evening.

She was going to suffer again after tonight was over, she knew, perhaps almost as much as she had suffered back then, but there was nothing she could do to prevent that now, was there? Life just had a habit of doing such things to people. There was no hiding from suffering, no matter how hard one tried to cultivate a tranquil life in which the highs and lows of emotion were leveled off.

The highs would insist upon forcing their way into one's life when one least expected them. Who, after all, could have predicted such a severe snowstorm on just the day she had chosen for travel? Who could have predicted its glorious aftermath?

And who could have predicted that her seemingly innocent decision to accept the invitation to sing at the Reynolds soiree three evenings ago would lead her to meet Lucius again, and that doing so would bring her to this moment?

And because the highs insisted upon invading one's life, then so did the lows. It was inevitable—the two were inextricably bound together.

There was no point in anticipating the latter, though, since they were inevitable anyway. And so she allowed herself openly to enjoy what remained of the evening and anticipated the pleasure she would have in telling Claudia, Anne, and Susanna all about it tomorrow—though the pain would be with her by then.

She danced every remaining set after tea, including one more country dance—the last of the evening—with Viscount Sinclair. She was sorry when the assembly ended, but all good things did end. There was no holding back time.

The low to follow the high began far sooner than she had expected, though.

The Earl of Edgecombe did not need a carriage to take him back home as his house on Brock Street was very close. And since there was such a press of carriages about the Upper Rooms, Viscount Sinclair had directed his own to wait outside the house. Frances strolled back there with Amy, the girl's arm linked through her own, while the two gentlemen came some distance behind.

"I have never had a more wonderful time in my life," Amy said with a heartfelt sigh as they walked down onto the Circus. "Have you, Miss Allard?"

"Indeed," Frances said, "I do not believe I have."

"Everyone wanted to dance with me," the girl said naively. "And with you too. You did not miss a single set, did you? I was delighted to see Luce dancing with you a second time. He drives Mama to distraction because he *never* dances."

"Then I must consider myself honored," Frances said.

"Of course," Amy continued, "he will have to dance any number of times this Season, I daresay. He promised Grandpapa at Christmas that he would take a bride this year, and I suppose she will be Miss Hunt, who has been waiting for him forever. She is in town already with her mama and papa and the Marquess of Godsworthy, her grandfather, a particular friend of my grandpapa. But *I* will not be able to dance again until next year, when I am to make my come-out. It is most provoking."

Frances's heart was hammering against her ribs. She had very sensibly sent him on his way after Christmas, and she certainly had not been foolish enough during the last few days to expect any renewal of his attentions. She did not *want* their renewal. But of course knowing that he was about to marry, that he had already chosen his bride, in fact, did hurt. Quite unreasonably so. But then reason had nothing to say to affairs of the heart. She had once spent the night with him. He was the only man with whom she had had sexual relations. It was understandable, then, that she should feel hurt—or if not hurt, then . . . depressed.

"Having to wait for something one desires greatly *is* provoking," Frances said. "But your come-out will be glorious when the time finally comes, and it will be even more so because you have waited so long. But those are sensible words you have doubtless heard a dozen times. In your place, I would be very inclined to throw a noisy tantrum."

Amy laughed with delight and squeezed her arm.

"Oh, I *do* like you," she said. "And when I return to Bath— though I do not know when that will be—I shall write and tell you so and come to the school to see you. I wish we did not have to leave Bath so soon as I feel just like a grown-up here, away from my sisters. But Luce says we must return to London tomorrow or the next day."

Ah! Another blow. Though in reality it was no such thing, of course. She must not make any grand tragedy out of the events of the past four days. She had not expected to see any of them after tonight—at least, with her intellect she had not expected it.

"I shall look forward to seeing you again at some time in the future, then," Frances said as they came to a stop outside the house on Brock Street. Viscount Sinclair's carriage waited there, Peters up on the box. She wondered if she could suggest riding alone back to the school, but she knew it would not be allowed. Besides . . .

Well, besides, she could not deprive herself of the last few minutes of agony in his company, could she?

Agony?

What sentimental drivel!

She drew her borrowed shawl more tightly about her shoulders. It was still only springtime and the air was cool.

Amy hugged her as the gentlemen came up to them. The earl held out his right hand and, when Frances set her own in it, covered it with his other hand.

"Miss Allard," he said, "I thank you most sincerely for coming with us tonight. Your company has meant a great deal to Amy, I know. I will be going to London with my grandchildren within the next day or two. But when I return, I shall invite you to sing for me. I hope you will agree to do it."

"I would be delighted, my lord," she said.

"Lucius will take you home now," he said. "Good night, Miss Allard."

"Good night, my lord," she said. "Good night, Amy."

She was back inside the carriage with Viscount Sinclair again a minute later, and it was proceeding on its way. The journey would take ten minutes, she estimated. She had ten minutes left.

How foolish to feel panic at the thought.

"Tell me you enjoyed yourself tonight," he said abruptly after the first minute or so had passed in silence.

"Oh, I did," she assured him. "It was very—"

"If you say *pleasant,*" he said, "I shall throttle you, Frances."

"—delightful," she said, and smiled in the darkness.

"Tell me you found it *delightful* because I was there," he said. "Tell me you would not have enjoyed it nearly as much if I had not been."

The inside of the carriage was very dark. She could not see his face when she turned her head to look at him.

"I will tell you no such thing," she said indignantly. "The very idea! The arrogance of it! Of course I would have enjoyed the evening just as much—better!—if you had not been there."

"Liar!" he said softly.

"You appear to be under the delusion, Lord Sinclair," she said, "that you are God's gift to women."

"A cliché unworthy of you," he said. "Tell me you have regretted rejecting me after Christmas."

"I have not!" she cried.

"Not even one tiny little bit?" he asked.

"Not even half that much," she said.

"A quarter, then?" He laughed softly. "You are a terrible liar, Frances."

"And you," she said, "are more conceited than any man I have ever met in my life."

"Is it conceited of me," he asked her, "to have met someone and felt an overwhelming attraction to her, to have felt her equal attraction to me, to have consummated that attraction, and then to believe that she must have felt some twinge of regret at saying good-bye to me, especially when she did not need to do so?"

"It was better to suffer that little twinge," she said tartly, "than to become your mistress."

"Aha!" he said. "So you do admit to some twinge, do you?"

She bit her lip but did not answer him.

"I never did say that making you my mistress was my intention," he said.

"But you would not say that your intention was marriage either," she said. "Pardon me, Lord Sinclair, but I am unaware of any other relationship that would have been possible between us if I had gone away with you."

"Courtship?" he suggested. "We needed more time together, Frances. We were not nearly finished with each other."

"You speak from the perspective of the idle rich," she said. "I need to work for my living. And my work is here."

"I offered to stay here," he reminded her, "but you would have none of it. And I offered to take you to London with me and find you somewhere to live and some decent female to stay with you for respectability."

"And you would have paid all the expenses, I suppose," she said.

"Yes, of course." She knew from the tone of his voice that his eyebrows had arched arrogantly above his eyes.

"I would have been a *kept* woman," she cried. "Can you not see that? I would have been your *mistress* no matter what other name you might have attempted to put upon our connection."

"Lord!" he exclaimed. "You would argue that black is white, Frances, if I dared to suggest otherwise. But arguing gives me a headache, and I avoid headaches at all costs. There is no discussing any matter sensibly with you, is there? You must always have the last word."

She turned toward him again to make some retort, but *he* turned to *her* first, set one arm about her shoulders, held her chin firm with the other hand, and kissed her hard on the mouth.

The shock of it caused her mind to shatter into incoherence.

"Mmm." Her hand came up to his shoulder to push him away.

"Don't fight me," he murmured fiercely against her lips. "Don't fight me, Frances."

And because his very touch had destroyed all rational thought processes for the moment, she gave up her instinctive resistance to his embrace. She slid her fingers up into his hair instead and kissed him back with all the ardor she had been suppressing for three long months.

He parted her lips with his own, and his tongue came deep into her mouth, filling her with warmth and longing and raw need. For a while she gave in to pure sensation and turned in order to set both arms about him and press her bosom to his chest.

Ah, it had been so long.

It had been forever.

She had missed him so much.

His hands roamed over her and then strained her to him.

But powerful as physical passion could be, it could not entirely obliterate thought for longer than a few moments. She was not free to give in to his ardor as she had been after Christmas because she knew that *he* was not free. He had promised to marry, and he was going to London tomorrow or the next day to do just that. Actually, he had made that promise even before he met her in the snowstorm.

That realization caused her stomach to somersault.

She lowered her hand and pushed against his shoulder.

"No!" she said against his lips.

"Damn it, Frances," he said, lifting his head a few inches from hers. "Goddamn it all to hell!"

She did not reprove him for the shockingly blasphemous language. She bit her lip instead and blinked her eyes in the darkness so that she would not openly weep.

He tried to renew the interrupted embrace, but she turned her face sharply away.

"Miss Hunt might not approve," she said.

"Miss—? Who the devil told you about Portia?" he asked.

Ah, so she was *Portia* to him, was she?

"Amy, I suppose." He answered his own question.

"Yes, Amy," she admitted. "I wish you joy, Lord Sinclair."

"If you *Lord Sinclair* me one more time," he said, "I might well have to do violence to your person, Frances. I am not yet betrothed to Portia Hunt."

"Not *yet*," she said. "But you soon will be. Take your arm from about my shoulders if you please."

He obeyed abruptly, leaving her feeling so bereft that even dragging air into her lungs seemed like a physical effort almost beyond her power to perform.

They rode side by side in silence for the rest of the way. When the carriage made its big turn from Great Pulteney Street onto Sydney Place and then Sutton Road, they both reached for the leather straps over their heads so that they would not touch each other. When the carriage rocked to a halt outside the school, there was suddenly total silence except for the snorting and stamping of the horses.

The door opened and the steps were set down.

Viscount Sinclair sat where he was. So did Frances.

"Some people," Peters muttered from outside on the pavement, "would like to get to their beds sometime tonight."

"Damn your impudence!" Viscount Sinclair exploded with what sounded like genuine wrath and was out of the carriage in a flash. "If I choose to keep you up past your bedtime, Peters, you may choose at any time to quit my service and good riddance."

"Right you are, guv," the coachman said, sounding quite uncowed. "I'll let you know when that time comes."

Viscount Sinclair turned to hand Frances down. He led her to the door of the school, which opened as they approached it. Keeble stood peering out like a suspicious parent, a frown on his face.

"Well, Frances," Viscount Sinclair said, his hands clasped at his back. "It would seem that this is good-bye—again."

"Yes." She fought panic.

They gazed at each other for a long moment in the faint light of the lamp burning in the hall. He looked very grim and square-jawed. Then he nodded his head twice, turned abruptly, and strode away back to his carriage.

Frances stepped inside the hall without looking back, and the door closed behind her.

It was over.

Again.

But it was over.

14

It was an enormous relief to Frances to find the school in darkness apart from the single lamp burning in the hall and a candle at the top of the stairs. She had half expected to find her friends waiting for her in the hallway as they had been when she left for the assembly.

Keeble made some comment to the effect that he had been just about to lock up for the night and go to bed. But instead of laughing at his little joke, as she normally would have done, she dashed past him with no more than a hasty thank-you and good night and hurried upstairs before he could say anything more.

She was almost safely past Miss Martin's sitting room on the way to her own room before the door opened.

"Not now, Claudia," she said. "I hope I have not kept you up. Good night."

As soon as she was in her room, she cast herself across the narrow bed, facedown, and covered her head with both arms as if she could thereby shut out everything that threatened her, even thought.

He promised Grandpapa at Christmas that he would take a bride this year, and I suppose she will be Miss Hunt, who has been waiting for him forever.

How foolish—how utterly *ridiculous* of her to have been so upset by those words.

I am not yet betrothed to Portia Hunt.

Not yet.

And between the two—between hearing of his impending engagement and marriage from Amy and his own admission of it in the carriage, she had let him kiss her. She had even kissed him back.

Though a *kiss* was a very mild way of describing their hot embrace.

She half heard the tap on her door and ignored it. But a few moments later she was aware that someone had come into the room and was sitting quietly on the chair beside her bed. Someone touched her arm, rubbed it lightly, patted it.

"I suppose," Frances said, removing her arms from over her head though she did not turn her face, "if I said I had a wonderful time and am now so tired that I am too weary even to undress for bed, you would not believe me."

"Not for a single moment," Claudia said.

"I did not think so." Frances turned her head without lifting it. Claudia was sitting very upright, her hands folded in her lap, looking her usual composed, rather severe self. "I did have a wonderful time. I danced every set, including one with Mr. Blake and one with Mr. Huckerby's brother-in-law. And then I made an idiot of myself when Viscount Sinclair brought me back here. I allowed him to kiss me in the carriage—indeed I did somewhat more than just allow it. But I already knew that he is about to be betrothed, that soon he will be married."

Claudia looked at her tight-lipped.

"It was as much my fault as his," Frances said. "I allowed the kiss. I wanted it. I was eager for it."

"But you," Claudia said, "are not about to be betrothed, Frances. And I suppose he initiated the embrace. It *was* his fault."

Yes, it was. If it was true that Miss Portia Hunt was waiting for him in London, that he was to marry her this year—and it *was* true—then he ought not to have spoken to her as he had in the carriage. And he ought not to have kissed her.

"What is it about me, Claudia?" she asked wearily. "Why do I always attract the wrong men? And why is it that when I do attract the right man I cannot fall in love with him? Is there something wrong with me?"

"Sometimes," Claudia said, "particularly when I hear you sing, Frances, I understand that you are a deeply passionate woman with a romantic heart. It is a dangerous combination for a woman, all the more so perhaps because women are expected to be nothing else but a bundle of tender sensibilities and there are plenty of men who are quite ready to take advantage of the fact. Life can be a tragic thing for us. It is safer, I have come to believe, for a woman to make a person of herself, to be proud of who or what she is and to grow comfortable with herself, regardless of what others say of her or expect of her— particularly the male world. If she is very fortunate—though admittedly it is rare—a woman can live independently of men and draw contentment from the world she has created for herself."

She got to her feet and crossed the room to the window, where she stood looking out into darkness, her spine very straight.

"That is what I did three years ago," Frances said wearily, "when I came here. And I have been happy, Claudia. I thought nothing could shake me from that contentment, until I ran into a snowstorm while I was returning here after Christmas."

"I suppose," Claudia said, her voice soft and pensive, "there is no such thing in this life as perfect happiness, Frances. We can only do the best we are able to make our lives tolerable. I sometimes think there must be more to being a woman than this, but *this* is what I have chosen for myself, and I would rather my life as it is than as it might be if I were the possession of some man, or else dependent upon the males of my own family."

"And when one falls," Frances said, pulling herself up into a sitting position at the edge of the bed, "one must simply pick oneself up and start all over again. The most simple of adages are often the wisest."

"Except that in your case," Claudia said, turning her head and half smiling, "you do not have to start right from the beginning again. Your classes await you tomorrow and your choirs and music pupils— and they all adore you, Frances. And your friends will be waiting eagerly at the breakfast table to hear all about the splendor of an assembly at the Upper Rooms. They so much want and even need to hear that you enjoyed yourself."

Frances smiled wanly. "I will not disappoint them," she said. "And then I will be ready to administer a French oral examination to the middle class, and to smile and praise my music pupils so that they will be inspired to reach greater heights. I will not let you down, Claudia."

"I am absolutely certain you will not," Claudia said. "We all learn to bury a broken heart beneath layers of dignity, Frances. You have done it for more than three years, and you will do it again. Good night."

After she had gone, Frances heard the echo of Claudia's words and frowned at the closed door—*We all learn to bury a broken heart . . .*

Had Claudia ever done that?

Had she?

I am not yet betrothed to Portia Hunt.

Not yet. But you soon will be.

She got wearily to her feet and began to undress.

Although the Earl of Edgecombe rose early the following morning for his usual visit to the Pump Room to drink the waters, it was obvious to Lucius that he was weary from his exertions of the night before. He was certainly in no state to travel all the way to London. Yet he still insisted that when his grandchildren returned there, he would go with them rather than go home to Barclay Court. He wanted to see his friend Godsworthy again. He wanted to witness the progress of the courtship between Lucius and Portia Hunt—though he did not mention her by name.

He wanted, Lucius knew, though he did not say as much, to be part of the excitement that would surround their betrothal and planned wedding.

Lucius was desperate to leave Bath even though only London and Portia and marriage awaited him. He had behaved badly after the assembly—and even during it, by Jove. He had gone out of his way to remind her of the first time they had danced together and to arouse her out of her controlled enjoyment of the evening. And then, in the carriage, when as her escort he was supposed to be protecting her from harm . . .

Well, he had been unable to deny himself the indulgence of that one last kiss. That was the trouble with him—he was not accustomed to exercising self-control, to *thinking* before he acted. Heaven knew where that embrace would have led if she had not put a firm stop to it.

And yet the very fact that she was always so sensible and controlled when he *knew* that passion throbbed just behind the facade and occasionally burst through for tantalizingly brief moments—that very fact irritated him almost beyond endurance.

They did not leave Bath the day after the assembly, then. Neither did they leave the next day since Amy, who had gone shopping with Mrs. Abbotsford and her daughter the day before, had been invited to join them and young Algernon Abbotsford on an excursion to some village not far from Bristol and begged permission to be allowed to go with such tragic certainty that she would be denied the treat that Lucius could not resist giving in to her.

One day longer was neither here nor there, he supposed.

His grandfather too went off to visit a friend during the afternoon, leaving Lucius with altogether too much time on his hands and too many unwelcome thoughts to weigh on his mind.

Dash it all, *when* had the promise he had made his grandfather come to be seen as a definite commitment to marry Portia Hunt? Had he ever stated aloud to anyone that she was going to be the one? But then, if not Portia, who? He *had* committed himself to choosing a bride—an *eligible* bride.

There could be no less appealing prospect.

The perfect and perfectly eligible bride!

The word *perfect* and all its derivatives should be stricken from the English language together with the word *pleasant*. The world would be a better place without them.

He sat with a book and brooded and fumed and schemed and despaired and cursed his lot in life for a whole hour before snapping the book shut—he had not read a single page—and striding out of the sitting room. He set out on a brisk walk down into the center of the city, along by the river, over the Pulteney Bridge, and along Great Pulteney Street. By the time he reached the end of it, he had stopped even pretending to himself that he had come walking for the benefit of his health, that his direction had been random, but that since he had come this way he might as well take a solitary turn about Sydney Gardens.

He was not a man much given to aimless or solitary walking. He favored far more vigorous exercise for his health. Besides, it was not a day that invited a pleasure stroll. It was gray and blustery and chilly. He might have spared a pitying thought for Amy, who had set out on the excursion with such exuberant hopes, except that he was quite sure the presence of young Algernon in the party would render her totally oblivious to inclement weather.

No, he was not out for a pleasure stroll. Here he was turning onto Sutton Street instead of crossing the road to Sydney Gardens, eyeing the school on the corner with Daniel Street, and remembering that it was Saturday and there would be no classes today—a fact that did not necessarily mean that she would be free, of course. It was a boarding school. Someone had to look after the girls and entertain them even at the weekends.

What the *devil* was he doing here?

He stood for a moment frowning at the front door, wondering if it would be more cowardly to knock or to turn tail and flee. He was not by nature a ditherer—or a coward. Or a thinker, for that matter.

He stepped up to the door, raised the brass door knocker, and let it fall against the door.

All of two minutes must have passed without any response, leading Lucius to the conclusion that the porter did not actually live in the hall, within one foot of the front door, but only occupied it when he was expecting someone. But it was he who eventually opened the door and peered out. His expression immediately turned both sour and suspicious.

"Ask Miss Allard if she will grant me a few minutes of her time," Lucius said briskly, stepping over the threshold without an invitation.

"She is giving a lesson in the music room," the porter told him.

"And?" Lucius raised his eyebrows.

The man turned and walked away, his boot heels squeaking on the hard floor.

"You had better go and wait in there," he said ungraciously, nodding his head in the direction of the visitors' sitting room.

When he was alone inside the room, Lucius stood at the window looking out on the meadows beyond Daniel Street and wishing he were anywhere else on earth but where he actually was. He was not in the habit of pursuing unwilling females, especially when the world was so full of willing ones. But it was too late to run away now.

He could hear the distant sounds of girlish laughter and a pianoforte playing—and then not playing. Across the meadow a group of girls, presumably from the school, was playing some organized game. The teacher supervising them looked like the auburn-haired one—Miss Osbourne. He had not noticed them when he arrived—which said something about his preoccupation. They were probably all shrieking their heads off.

When the door opened behind him, he half expected to turn and see Miss Martin again. But it was Frances herself, looking white to the very lips, who stepped inside. She closed the door behind her back.

"What are you doing here?" Her voice was actually shaking, but whether from shock or anger or some other emotion it was hard to say.

He knew something at that moment with ghastly clarity.

He was not going to be able to let her go this time.

It was that simple.

"I came to see you," he said.

"Why?" Two spots of color had appeared in her cheeks. Her eyes had turned hard.

"Because there is something still to be said between us," he said, "and I do not like to leave things unsaid when they should be spoken."

"There is nothing else to be said between us, Lord Sinclair," she said. "Nothing whatsoever."

"There you are wrong, Frances," he said. "Come out with me. Come walking in Sydney Gardens."

"I am in the middle of giving a music lesson," she told him.

"Dismiss the girl early," he said. "She will be ecstatic. Do you have other lessons to follow this one?"

She compressed her lips for a moment before answering. "No," she admitted.

"Then come walking with me," he said.

"Have you noticed the weather today?" she asked him. "It is going to rain."

"But it is not raining yet," he said. "It may not rain all day—just as it did not snow all over Christmas. Bring an umbrella. You cannot claim to be English, Frances, and yet fear stepping outdoors lest it rain. You would be housebound all your life."

"I do not want anything more to do with you," she told him.

"If I thought you truly meant that," he said, "I would be gone in a flash. But I think you lie. Or if you do not do so quite consciously, then I believe you deceive yourself."

"You are a betrothed man," she said. "Miss Portia Hunt—"

"I am not betrothed *yet*," he told her.

"But you soon will be."

"The future," he said, "is just a theory, Frances. It is not fact. How can any of us know what we will be doing *soon*? Now, at this precise moment, I am not a betrothed man. And you and I have unfinished business."

"We do not—"

"You are such a coward, Frances." He was beginning to feel frustrated, angry. Was she really going to refuse to come? And why the devil was he pressing her when she was so clearly reluctant to have any more dealings with him?

But he knew—he *knew* beyond any doubt—that her attraction to him was just as powerful as his to her.

"It is not cowardly," she said, "to avoid inevitable and pointless pain."

"I cause you pain, then?" His incipient anger disappeared in a moment. She had finally admitted to more than just a twinge.

But she would not answer him. She clasped her hands at her waist and looked composed and pale again. She gazed very steadily into his eyes.

"Give me one more hour of your life," he said. "It is not a great deal to ask, is it?"

There was an almost imperceptible slumping of her shoulders and he knew that she would not deny him.

"One hour, then," she said. "I will go and dismiss Rhiannon Jones and let Miss Martin know that I am going out for a while."

He stared broodingly at the door after she had left the room. He ought, he supposed, to have stopped to think, to *consider,* before coming here. But, devil take it, it was his life, and there must be a way of living it to his own satisfaction and doing his duty by his family and position at the same time.

But how could he have thought or considered? When he had left the house on Brock Street, he had not known where he was going.

He had certainly not known why.

Or had he?

He gazed out the window with unseeing eyes, looking back wistfully on the time, not too long ago, when his life had been uncomplicated and perfectly satisfactory.

Well, it would be satisfactory again, dash it all.

It *would.*

He had promised to find the perfect bride.

But there was more than one kind of perfection.

He paid their way into Sydney Gardens, just on the other side of the road at Sydney Place, and they walked along beside a bowling green until the path wound upward, twisting and turning as it did so between lawns and among trees whose branches swayed and tossed in the wind.

It was not by any means an ideal day for strolling in any park. There was not another soul in sight apart from the two of them.

Frances shivered even though she was dressed warmly—in the exact cloak and bonnet and half-boots she had been wearing the first time she met him, in fact, she realized suddenly. She felt chilled to the bone, but not so much from the buffeting of the weather as from the fact that she was actually walking here beside him again, one day after she thought he had returned to London, two days after they had said good-bye forever—again.

She had already lived through a day of pain so intense that it had seemed like stark despair. Was she to have to endure the same all over again later today and tomorrow?

Would he never go away and stay away?

Would she never have the resolve to send him away and mean it?

She had received a card with the morning post from Mrs. Lund, Mr. Blake's sister, inviting her to join Mr. Lund and herself at the theater next week. Mr. Blake was to be of the party too, she had added. Although Frances had hesitated, she had written back to accept. Life had to continue, she had reasoned. And perhaps now she would finally be able to put the past behind her and concentrate her attention upon the man who seemed eager to be her beau. It was not as if she had to make any final decision about him yet. She did not even have to tell him everything about herself yet. It was merely an evening at the theater to which she had been invited.

She had congratulated herself—again—upon her good sense. But here she was, just a few hours later, walking in Sydney Gardens with Lucius Marshall—who was soon to marry a Miss Portia Hunt.

"For someone who had something important to say," she said, breaking a lengthy silence, "and who was granted merely one hour of my time, you are remarkably silent, Lord Sinclair."

They walked onto a brightly painted and exquisitely carved Chinese bridge and paused for a few moments to gaze down into the slate-gray waters of the canal below. Under different circumstances, she was half aware, she would be feasting her senses on all the beauty that surrounded them, inclement weather notwithstanding.

"Do you believe in fate, Frances?" he asked her.

She considered her answer. Did she?

"I do believe in coincidence," she said. "I believe that some unexpected things happen to catch our attention, and that what we do with those moments might affect or change the whole course of our life. But I do not believe we are blown about helplessly by a fate over which we have no control. There would be no point in free will if that were so. We all have the power to decide, to say yes or no, to do something or not to do it, to go in this direction or that."

"Do you believe," he asked her, "that the whole course of your life brought you to that snow-clogged road when it did, and that the whole course of my life brought me to the same place at the same time? And do you believe that coincidence as you call it willed it so? Or that in some quite unconscious way *we* did ourselves? Was it perhaps not simple, random accident that it was you who were there and not some other woman, or that it was me and not some other man?"

The strange, unlikely possibility made her feel breathless. Could life really be that . . . deliberate?

"You were warned that it would snow," she said. "You might have chosen not to travel that day. I had seen all the signs of an approaching storm for days. I might have waited to see what would happen."

"Precisely," he said. "Either one of us or both could have heeded the warnings and warning signs, which appear to have deterred every other intended traveler in that area. But neither of us did. Has it struck you as curious that we met no one else on that road? That no one else stopped at that inn?"

No, it had not. She had never thought of it. But she thought of it now. She had wanted to set out earlier that morning, but her great-aunts had persuaded her to sit an extra hour with them over breakfast. If she had left when she had intended, she would very probably never have met him.

How she *wished* she had set out earlier!

Or did she?

What was he trying to say, anyway?

He set out along the path again, and she fell into step beside him. He did not offer his arm. He had not done so since they left the school, in fact. She was thankful for it. But she did not need to touch him in order to feel him with every fiber of her being.

Was it possible, she wondered, that it was not just the fact that she had lain with him that drew her so powerfully to him, that had made it impossible to forget him, that had made her life an agony during the past few days? She had loved before. Surely she had loved Charles. But she had never felt quite like this.

They walked onward in silence again. They still had not encountered anyone else since entering Sydney Gardens. Everyone else in Bath had more sense than they, it seemed.

When they reached the top of the hill, they paused again to look down on trees and lawns and winding paths. A roofed pavilion was in view to the left. So was the famed labyrinth a little lower down. Maps of the maze were available from the Sydney Hotel beside the entrance to the Gardens, Frances had heard, for use by those too afraid of getting lost for an indeterminate length of time before finding their way out again. Behind them was a row of swings, one of them creaking in the wind.

There were all the signs of the fact that these were *pleasure* gardens, not least among them the sheer beauty of nature. Yet she felt the very antithesis of joy as she looked on them all. Where was this hour leading them? It was leading absolutely nowhere at all.

His silence unnerved her, though she had sworn to herself that she would not break it again. But when she looked across at him, she found him looking back, an unfathomable expression in his eyes.

His words took her totally by surprise.

"Do those swings beckon you as strongly as they do me?" he asked her.

What? For a moment her mind was catapulted back to the inn kitchen on the first morning they spent there, when they were eating breakfast and he had suddenly challenged her to a snowman-building contest. That, she realized then—yes, just *that*—had been the real start of everything between them. If she had refused . . .

She turned her head to look at the swings. The broad wooden seats were suspended from tree branches overhead on long, plaited ropes. Because they were set in a grove of trees, they looked as if they were sheltered from the wind. Only the one swing at the far end swayed and creaked.

"Even more strongly," she said, and she turned, catching up the hems of her dress and cloak as she did so, and strode toward the nearest swing.

The need to break the terrible tension between them was overwhelming. What more sure way than to frolic on a child's swing?

"Do you need a push?" he asked as she seated herself.

"Of course not," she said, pushing off with both feet and then stretching out her legs and bending them back under the seat to set her swing in motion and propel herself higher and higher. "And I bet I'll be first to kick the sky."

"Ah, a challenge," he said, taking the swing next to hers. "Did no one ever teach you that it is unladylike to make wagers?"

"That is a rule imposed by men because they are afraid of losing to women," she said.

"Ha!"

They swung higher and higher until the ropes of their swings creaked in protest and the wind whipped at her skirts and the brim of her bonnet and fairly took her breath away on the forward descent and ascent. With every upward swing Frances could see more and more of the gardens below. With every downward swoop she was aware of tree branches rushing by only a few feet away.

"Wheeee!" she cried on one descent.

"The exact word I was searching for," he called, passing her in the opposite direction.

They were both laughing then and swinging and whooping like a pair of exuberant children until by unspoken assent they gradually slowed and then sat side by side, their swings gently swaying.

"One problem," he said. "There was no sky to kick."

"What?" She turned to him, wide-eyed. "You did not *feel* it? That means you did not swing high enough to touch it. I did and I win."

"You, Frances Allard," he said, "are lying through your teeth."

He had said those exact words before, and the occasion rushed to her mind with startling clarity. They had been lying in bed, and she had just told him she was not cold and he had replied that it was a pity as he might have offered to warm her up.

I am frozen, she had said then.

You lie through your teeth, ma'am, he had answered her, *but I like your spirit. Now, I suppose I need to think of some way of warming you . . .*

What was she doing here? she wondered suddenly. Why was she doing this again—frolicking with him, wagering against him, laughing with him?

Just a few minutes ago, it seemed, she had been trying to get Rhiannon Jones to feel the melody with her right hand and allow the passion of it to rise above the accompaniment with the left.

"Frances—" he began.

But at that exact moment a large drop of moisture splattered against one of her cheeks and she saw a few more darken the fabric of her cloak. He held out a hand, palm up, and they both looked up.

"Damnation!" he exclaimed. "We are about to get rained upon, and you did not bring an umbrella even though I advised you to do so. We are going to have to make a dash for the pavilion."

He took her by the hand without a by-your-leave, and a moment later they were running toward the pavilion a short distance away down the hill while the heavens gave every indication that they were about to open in earnest at any moment. By the time they reached shelter, they were both breathless and laughing again.

The pavilion had been built more as a sun shelter than as a refuge from the rain. It was walled on three sides, with a roof that jutted out in front a couple of feet beyond the side walls. Fortunately for them, the wind was blowing from behind and the inside of the shelter remained dry. They sat on the wide bench against the inside wall and watched as the expected deluge arrived. It came down in sheets, drumming against the thin roof, forming a curtain across the front opening, almost obliterating the view of lawns and trees beyond. It felt like sitting behind a massive waterfall.

"One can only hope," she said, "that this is not about to set in for the day."

But their laughter had faded, and their solitude seemed far more pronounced here than it had out in the deserted gardens.

He took one of her hands in his and held it in both his own while she looked away and tried not to react to the warmth of his touch.

"Frances," he said, "I think you had better come to London with me."

She tried to remove her hand then, but he held it in a firm clasp.

"That *was* fate," he said. "And it was speaking loudly and clearly. It was so insistent a fate that it threw us together again this week when we had missed the chance it presented to us after Christmas. Forgive me for saying this, but I have known many women, Frances, and I have not mourned the departure of a single one of them from my life. Until you, that is. I have never before known one for only two days and still been obsessed with her three months later."

"I suppose," she said bitterly, "it is because I said no to you and you are not accustomed to women who deny you what you want."

"I have considered that as a distinct possibility," he admitted.

"But injured pride, if that was all that was involved, would actually have sent me dashing off in the opposite direction to find another woman to bolster my sagging confidence in my own charms. I could never grovel before any woman simply because she had thwarted my will. I would be off in pursuit of more easy prey instead."

"Of which there is doubtless plenty," she said tartly.

"Quite so," he said. "I am young, you see, Frances, and have all my hair and all my teeth, tolerably white. I am also wealthy and titled, with the prospect of vastly more in the future. It is an irresistible combination for many women. But all that is beside the point under present circumstances. I *am* groveling before you, you see."

"Nonsense!" Her heart was hammering against her ribs. She would have been able to hear it, she was sure, if the sound of the rain against the roof had not been almost deafening. "You want to get me into bed, that is all."

Her cheeks grew hot at the bold vulgarity of her own words.

"If that were all it was," he said, "I would have been satisfied long ago, Frances. I have *had* you in bed. One bedding is often enough to satisfy simple lust. Yet I am not satisfied."

She grew hotter. But she could hardly reprove him for his very direct words. She had led the way.

"You need to be in London," he said. "Bath becomes suffocating after a week or two."

"You find it so only because you are idle here," she said. "I am not."

"Even apart from the fact that you could be with *me* if you were in London," he said, "you need to be there for your *singing*, Frances. You are wasting your talent by teaching music when you should be performing it. If you were in London, I could introduce you to the right people and you would acquire the exposure you need and the audience you deserve."

She snatched her hand from his and stood up abruptly, suddenly panic-stricken. He wanted to prostitute her talent, then, just as George Ralston had done? And be his mistress on the side, no doubt? Even though he was about to marry someone else? She felt suddenly bilious.

What had she *expected*? She took one step closer to the outdoors and then stopped. There had been no easing of the cloudburst yet.

"I *hated* London when I lived there," she said, "and vowed that I would never go back there. And I do not need *anyone* to introduce me to the *right people*. I am happy as I am. Can you not understand that?"

"Contented," he said. "You have admitted before, Frances, that you are *contented*. And I say again that you are not a woman made for contentment. You were made for glorious, passionate happiness. Oh, and for unhappiness too, of course. The challenge of living is to reach for the one and learn from the other, if only the strength to endure. Come with me."

"I will not," she said. "Oh, I absolutely will *not*. You think that happiness and sexual passion are one and the same, Lord Sinclair, and that the latter is something to be indulged at all costs. There is more to life than physical gratification."

"For once we are in total agreement," he said. "You still believe I am trying to persuade you to be my mistress, Frances, do you not?"

"I do," she said, turning to look down at him. "And if you say otherwise you lie—or you deceive yourself. I am an independent woman here. I am not wealthy, but I am beholden to no one. I have a freedom many women can only dream of. I will not give that up to become your toy until you tire of me."

"My *toy*?" he said. "Are you not *listening*? I want to help you share your talent with the world and be happy and fulfilled as a result. Rid yourself of the notion that I am a simple, unprincipled rake. I want you in bed, yes. Of course I do. But more than that, I want *you*."

She shook her head slowly. She wanted the issue to remain simple. She wanted nothing that would tempt her, as she had been tempted for a few moments back in December. She wanted nothing to shake her resolve to be *sensible*.

"Do you not understand even now?" he asked her. "I am asking you to be my wife, Frances."

Her mouth opened to reply even before he had finished speaking. She stared at him and closed it again with a clacking of teeth.

"What?" she said.

"I have discovered," he said, "that I do not want to live without you. I happen to be currently in need of a wife. My grandfather is dying, I am his heir, and I have promised to do my duty and take a bride while he is still living, it is to be hoped. Only today has it occurred to me that you are perfectly eligible, Frances. Your father presumably had some connection with the French court, and you have family ties with Baron Clifton. There will be some who will feel, of course, that I ought to ally myself with someone of more obviously equal or superior rank and fortune to my own, but I have never paid too much heed to what others think, especially where my own comfort and happiness are concerned. And my grandfather, whose contrary opinion is the only one that does matter to me, is inordinately fond of you—and he honors and respects your talent. He will be won over in a moment when it becomes clear to him that I will have no one but you. And my mother and sisters will be won over—they love me and want my happiness when all is said and done. Marry me, Frances. I do not much like the look of this stone floor, but I will go down on one knee before you if you wish. It is something you will be able to boast of to our grandchildren."

He flashed a grin at her.

She could not seem to draw sufficient air into her lungs. It was not that there was not enough inside the pavilion. There seemed to be far too much of it, in fact. Her legs were shaking, but if she had tried to return to her seat on the bench, she would have staggered and fallen, she was sure. She stood where she was.

He wanted to *marry* her?

"You are to marry Miss Hunt," she said.

He made an impatient gesture with one hand.

"That is the general expectation," he admitted. "We saw a fair amount of each other while we were growing up, as her family often visited my grandparents and we often visited them. And, of course, our families embarrassed us horribly—or me, anyway—by referring openly to their hopes that we would make a match of it one day and by teasing us mercilessly if we so much as exchanged a glance. And my mother holds firmly to the notion that Portia has been waiting for me to the advanced age of three-and-twenty. But I have never spoken a word to her of any intention to marry her, nor she to me. I am under no obligation whatsoever to offer for her."

"Perhaps," she said, "she would disagree with you."

"She has no grounds for doing so," he said. "I have made my own choice and it is you. Marry me, Frances."

She closed her eyes. They were words the romantic, unrealistic part of her had dreamed for three months of hearing. She had even enacted scenes similar to this in her imagination. But if she could ever have expected to hear them in reality, she would have dreaded them. Her heart, she thought, would finally break in all earnest.

When she opened her eyes she was feeling dizzy and somehow staggered back to her seat. He took first one and then both of her hands in his own—they were warm and large enough to encompass her own. He lowered his head and held both of them against his lips.

"I cannot go back to London," she said.

"Then we will live at Cleve Abbey," he said. "We will raise a large, riotous family there, Frances, and live happily ever after. You may sing for all our neighbors."

"You know you could not live in the country indefinitely," she told him. "You will have to take your place in the House of Lords when you inherit the earldom. I cannot go back to London or polite society."

"Cannot?" he asked. "Or will not?"

"Both," she said. "There is nothing in the life you offer me that attracts me."

"Not even my person?" he asked her, lowering her hands.

She shook her head.

"I do not believe you," he said.

She looked up at him with a flash of anger.

"That is the trouble with you," she said. "You really cannot take no for an answer, can you, Lord Sinclair? You cannot believe that any woman in her right mind would prefer the sort of life I lead here to the sort of life you offer me, or that she would prefer relative solitude here to a life in the beau monde with you."

Both his eyebrows arched upward. But he looked rather as if she had struck him across the face.

"No!" He frowned. "This is not good enough, Frances. What is so abhorrent about life in London or life as the Viscountess Sinclair that you would reject me in order to avoid them? I cannot believe you are so averse to me personally. I have seen you, I have felt you, I have *known* you when your guard is down, and that woman responds to me with a warmth and a passion that match my own. What *is* it?"

"I am not eligible," she said. "Not to be the Viscountess Sinclair. Not to be acceptable to your grandfather or your mother or the *ton*. And I am not going to say any more about it."

There was no point in saying more—in pouring out the whole sorry story of her life. He was an impulsive man, she knew. She doubted he had really thought out all the implications of what he was doing this morning. He liked to get what he wanted, and for some reason he wanted her. He would not listen if she told him all. He would brush everything aside and try to insist anyway that she marry him.

It simply could not happen—for her sake and for his.

And for the sake of his grandfather, whom she liked and respected.

Good sense must rule the day as it had ruled the last three years of her life—with a few notable exceptions.

And so she lost her chance for joy. Fate had singled her out quite markedly, both after Christmas and this week—he was quite right about that—and she rejected fate, setting against it the power of her own free will. What else, after all, was free will for?

She would *not* destroy her hard-won new life and his into the bargain.

"I do not *like* society," she said as if that were explanation enough for refusing an offer that was hugely advantageous to herself and that he knew was emotionally appealing to her. "It is artificial and vicious and not what I would choose as the environment in which to live the rest of my life. It is what I deliberately left behind me more than three years ago in order to come here."

"If I had been there then," he said fiercely, his eyes blazing into hers, "and if you had known me then, if I had asked you then what I have asked you now, would you have made the same choice, Frances?"

"Hypothetical questions are like the future you spoke of earlier," she said. "They are a meaningless figment of the imagination. They have no reality. I did *not* meet you then."

"*No* is your final answer, then," he said. It was not really a question.

"Yes," she said, "it is."

"Good God!" He released her hands. "One of us must be mad, Frances, and I fear it may be me. Can you look me in the eye, then, and swear to me that you have no feelings for me?"

"Nothing is ever as simple as that," she said. "But I will not swear either way. I do not have to. I have said no. That is all that needs saying."

"By Jove, you are right." It was he who got to his feet this time. "I beg your pardon, ma'am, for causing you such distress."

His voice was tight with hostility.

She suddenly realized that they were surrounded by silence again except for the sounds of water dripping off the roof onto the soaked ground. The rain had stopped as suddenly as it had begun.

"But there is still a part of me, Frances," he added, "that could cheerfully throttle you."

She closed her eyes and set a hand over her mouth as if to stop the outpouring of words she would regret. She was assailed with such a yearning to hurl herself into his arms and throw good sense to the winds that she felt physically sick again.

Thoughts whirled through her head in a chaotic jumble.

Perhaps she should be more like him and simply *act* instead of always thinking.

But she would not do it. She *could* not.

She got to her feet, stepped past him, and looked up at the sky. It still looked full of rain, and indeed there was still a fine drizzle falling.

"The hour is at an end, Lord Sinclair," she said. "I am going back to the school now. You need not accompany me."

"Damn you, Frances," he said softly.

They were the last words he said to her—the last words of his she would ever hear, she thought as she hurried down the path, heedless of the fact that it was very wet and muddy and even slippery in places.

He had wanted her to *marry* him.

And she had said no.

Because, for a whole host of reasons, a marriage between them simply could not work.

And because love was simply not enough.

She was mad, she thought. She was mad, mad, mad.

He had asked her to *marry* him.

No, it was not madness. It was sanity—cold, comfortless, merciless sanity.

She was half running by the time she came to the gates and emerged from the gardens onto Sydney Place. And she was half sobbing too, though she tried to tell herself that it was only because she was out of breath from hurrying to get back to school before the rain came down heavily once more.

Lucius had wanted to marry her, and she had been forced to say no.

Actually participating in all the busy rituals of the spring
Season—attending balls and routs and Venetian breakfasts and concerts and theater performances, riding in Hyde Park during the morning and tooling a curricle about it during the fashionable hour of the
afternoon, being drawn into a thousand and one other frivolous activities—actually participating in it all did help to distract one's thoughts
from past humiliations and one's spirits from taking up permanent
residence in the soles of one's boots, Lucius found over the coming
month, especially when one also spent a large portion of one's nights
at White's or one of the other gentlemen's clubs and one's mornings at
Jackson's boxing saloon or Tattersall's horse auction or one of the
other places where gentlemen tended to congregate in significant num-
bers and one could forget about being on one's best social behavior.

Of course, it was all very different from the life he was accustomed
to, and he was forced to endure the wincing sympathies and rowdy
teasing of a number of his acquaintances, who could not fail to notice
that he was living at Marshall House instead of in his usual bachelor
rooms and that he was participating in the activities of the marriage
mart and who, if the truth were told, were only too glad that it was
not their turn to be thus occupied.

He danced with Emily at her come-out ball and with Caroline at
her betrothal ball two weeks later. He took both sisters—and even
Amy once or twice—shopping and walking and driving. He took his

mother visiting and shopping and browsing at the library. He escorted them all to the theater and the opera. He even, for the love of God, escorted them to Almack's one evening, that insipid bastion of upperclass exclusivity, where there was nothing to do *but* dance and eat stale bread and butter and drink weak lemonade and make himself agreeable to a veritable host of young female hopefuls and their mamas.

But their hopes, raised no doubt by the sight of someone so eligible in unaccustomed attendance at *ton* revelries, were entirely misplaced and no doubt they soon realized it. For even before he arrived back in London from Bath a dinner at the Marquess of Godsworthy's town house on Berkeley Square, at which his family members were the guests of honor—and indeed the *only* guests, he was soon to discover—had already been arranged, as had a similar dinner and small soiree at Marshall House a few evenings later. And soon after his return—the very day after, in fact, when he paid a courtesy call on the Balderstons with his mother and sisters—arrangements were made for the two families to sit together in the Earl of Edgecombe's box at the theater one evening within the week.

On each occasion—during both dinners, during the courtesy call, and at the theater—Lucius found himself seated beside Portia Hunt. They could not have seemed more like an established couple if they had already been betrothed.

She was indeed in good looks—*very* good looks. She had the sort of beauty that only improved with age. Her blond curls and blue eyes and perfect features and English rose complexion had made her merely exceedingly lovely as a girl. Now she was nothing short of beautiful—and added to that beauty were a poise and dignity that proclaimed her to be a lady of perfect breeding.

Everything about her was perfect, in fact. There was not a pimple or a mole or a squint or a fatal flaw in sight. And she was the sort of woman to whom duty was so instinctive that she would doubtless present her husband with an heir and a spare within two years of the nuptials before she even *thought* of the possibility of bearing daughters.

She would be the perfect wife, the perfect hostess, the perfect mother, the perfect viscountess, the perfect countess.

The word *perfect* definitely needed to be stricken from the English language.

Lucius bore it all with determinedly gritted teeth and stiff upper lip. He had made the fatal—and quite unexpected—mistake of falling in love, and the woman had snubbed and rejected him. On the whole it was a good thing. Although his grandfather had admired Frances Allard as a singer, he might have taken a dimmer view of accepting her as a candidate for the role of future Countess of Edgecombe—even though she was a lady with impeccable connections on her father's side, at least.

From the moment he had left Bath—and a rather ghastly moment it had been too—Lucius had set the whole experience of falling in love and blurting out an impulsive marriage proposal behind him with a grim firmness of purpose.

He had made a promise at Christmas time, and by God he would keep it. And since he could not have the woman he had wanted, he would have Portia instead. He could not do better, after all—a thought he entertained with a slight grimace.

His mother was a fond parent and liked to see all of her children enjoy their particular moment in the sun. For the first two weeks after Lucius's return to town that moment belonged to Emily as she pre-pared for her presentation to the queen and then her come-out ball. And for the next two weeks the moment was Caroline's as Sir Henry Cobham finally came to the point and talked marriage settlements with Lucius and then made his offer to Caroline herself. And of course the occasion necessitated another ball at Marshall House in celebra-tion of their betrothal.

Had Lucius offered for Portia Hunt within that month, he would have unfairly taken the focus of attention away from one of his sisters and his mother would have been upset.

At least, that was what he told himself—he was trying hard to give more of his time and attention and affection to his family than he had been in the habit of doing through the heedless years of his young manhood.

But to procrastinate indefinitely was not an option for him this spring. He had made his promise to his grandfather, and nothing remained but to make his formal offer and be done with it.

He would do it, he decided, the morning after Caroline's ball. There was no further excuse for delay. Already his mother was making pointed remarks, and his grandfather was regarding him with twinkling eyes every time Portia's name was mentioned—and it was mentioned with ominous frequency.

He dressed with care under Jeffreys's expert ministrations and took himself off on foot to Berkeley Square—only to find after steeling himself to the ordeal that Lord Balderston was not at home. The ladies were, however, the butler informed him. Did Lord Sinclair wish to wait upon them?

Lord Sinclair did, he supposed, though he thought longingly of his male friends now fencing or sparring or looking over horseflesh at all the usual haunts—and not a one of them with a care in the world.

When he was shown into the morning room, however, he found that Portia was in there alone.

"Mama is still in her own apartments after the late night at Caroline's ball," she explained after he had made his bow to her.

It was understandable. It was somewhat surprising, in fact, that Portia herself was up and so neatly dressed and coifed that she was able to receive guests on a moment's notice. There had not been a mother or sister in sight when he had left Marshall House.

Did she add early rising to her other virtues?

"Do you wish to send for her?" he asked, looking about the empty room. "Or for your maid?"

"Do not be foolish, Lucius," she said with cool poise, indicating a chair while she seated herself gracefully and picked up her embroidery frame. "I am no green girl to be needing a chaperone in my own home while entertaining a longtime friend."

They were on a first-name basis, having known each other for many years. Were they also friends?

"Lady Sinclair must be very gratified," she said, "with one daughter married and another betrothed and Emily taking so well with the *ton*. And Amy will surely do as well next year if she can learn to curb her natural exuberance."

Her needle flashed in and out of the cloth, producing a perfect peach-colored rose.

"I hope," he said, "she will never learn that lesson, Portia. I like her well enough as she is."

She looked up at him fleetingly.

"It was unfortunate," she said, "that you took her walking in the park so late the afternoon before last. She ought not to have been seen by the fashionable crowd. And she ought not to have laughed with such unconsidered delight at something you said to her and so made herself conspicuous. Lord Rumford ogled her through his quizzing glass, and we all know *his* reputation."

"When my sister is on my arm," he said, "she is quite safe from the impertinences of rakes, Portia. And girls who are not yet out need fresh air and exercise just as desperately as young ladies who are."

He was feeling irritated again, he thought. Dash it all, irritation was becoming almost habitual with him. Doubtless ninety-nine out of every one hundred ladies in London would agree with Portia.

Would Frances? He ruthlessly quelled the thought.

"Your fondness for your sisters is commendable," Portia said. "But I am sure you would not wish to hurt Amy's chances of taking well next year after her presentation."

He stared at her blond curls and wondered if the years ahead were to be filled with such gentle reproofs for his every opinion and action. He would be willing to wager a fortune that they were. He would escape, he supposed, as most husbands did, by tramping about his lands, gun in hand and dog at heel, when in the country and by retreating to his clubs when in town.

"It was remarkably kind of you," she continued, "to take her with you when you went to Bath. Her youthful presence must have been a great comfort to Lord Edgecombe."

"I believe it was," he said. "And I enjoyed it too."

"But was it wise," she asked him, "to allow her to attend a soiree?"

He raised his eyebrows, but she did not look up from her work.

"And an assembly at the Upper Rooms?" she continued. "Mama was shocked beyond words when Emily told us that, I do not mind telling you, Lucius."

Her hair was parted neatly down the middle, he saw, though the parting extended for only a few inches above her brow before disappearing under her carefully arranged curls.

Not like someone else's that he knew . . .

"At least," she said, "you had the good sense to hire a schoolteacher to accompany her, but the woman really ought to have stopped her from dancing, Lucius."

His eyes narrowed with fury, and he silently contemplated the pleasure it would give him to flatten even one of those perfect curls and throw the whole coiffure out of balance.

"Miss Allard was my grandfather's particular guest," he said. "Amy danced with my permission."

"One can only hope," she said, "that you have not done her irreparable harm, Lucius. I shall look forward to offering her guidance and countenance next year."

As his wife and Amy's sister-in-law, no doubt.

"Will you?" he said.

She looked up, and her needle remained suspended over her work.

"I have offended you," she said. "You need not trouble yourself, Lucius. Ladies know better than gentlemen what is what and are quite prepared to restore and keep the proprieties while men go freely about their own business."

"Of raking?" he said.

He looked for two spots of color in her cheeks, but he realized suddenly that Portia never blushed—or needed to, he supposed.

"I think we might maintain a silence on that subject, Lucius," she said. "What gentlemen do in their own time is their business and of no concern whatsoever to well-bred ladies."

Good Lord! Devil take it! Would her calm not be ruffled if he went raking through life from their wedding day to the day of his death? The answer, he suspected, was that indeed it would not.

"You came here this morning to call upon Papa?" she asked him.

"I did," he admitted. "I will come back some other time."

"Of course you will," she said, looking steadily at him.

Did she have any feelings for him? he wondered. Any *warm* feelings? Did she really *want* to marry him? *Him*, that was, as opposed to just Viscount Sinclair, the future Earl of Edgecombe?

"Portia," he said as she resumed stitching, "do you have the feeling that we are being thrown together at every turn this spring, whether we wish it or not?"

Her needle paused, but she did not look up.

"Of course," she said. "But why should we not wish for it?"

His heart sank.

"You wish for a connection with me, then?" he said.

A *connection*—what a clanger of a euphemism!

"Of course," she said.

"Of course?" He raised his eyebrows as she looked up.

"Men are so foolish." For a moment the look she bent on him seemed almost maternal. "They avoid reality at every turn. But it cannot be avoided indefinitely, Lucius."

"You *wish* to marry me, then?"

There—the word was out, and he could not recall it or pretend that they were talking of something else.

"Of course," she said.

His heart had no farther to sink. It attempted the impossible anyway.

"Why?" he asked her.

"Why?" It was her turn to raise her eyebrows. She rested the hand holding the needle on top of her work and seemed to forget it for the moment. "I have to marry *someone*, Lucius, and you are my most eligible choice. *You* have to marry someone, and I am *your* most eligible choice."

"Is it a good enough reason?" He frowned at her.

"Lucius," she said, "it is the *only* reason."

"Do you love me?" he asked her.

She looked almost shocked.

"What a foolish question," she said. "People like you and me do not marry for such a vulgar reason as love, Lucius. We marry for position and fortune and superior bloodlines."

"It all sounds horribly unromantic," he said.

"You are the last person I would expect to speak of romance," she said.

"Why?" he asked again.

"Forgive me," she said, "but your reputation is not entirely unknown to me, sheltered though I have always been from vulgarity. You will no doubt wish to continue that life, which I very much doubt you would call romantic. And therefore you will not expect or even wish for romance with your wife. You need not worry. I neither expect nor wish for it either."

"Why?" he asked.

"Because romance is very foolish," she said. "Because it is ungenteel. Because it is entirely imaginary. Because it is wishful thinking, usually on the woman's part. Men are wiser and do not even believe in it. Neither do I."

Until a few months ago, he thought, he would have agreed with her. Perhaps he still did. Romance had not really done him any good in the last few months, had it, beyond making him eternally irritated?

"What about passion?" he asked her. "Would you not expect that in your marriage?"

"I most certainly would not!" she said, openly shocked now. "The very idea, Lucius!"

He gazed gloomily at her as she returned her attention once more to her embroidery, her hand as steady as if they had been discussing the weather.

"Have I ever said or done anything to lead you to expect that I would offer for you?" he asked her.

He had, of course—very recently. He had just admitted to coming here this morning to call on her father.

"You have not needed to," she said. "Lucius, I understand that you are reluctant and procrastinating. I understand that all men are the same way under similar circumstances. I understand too that eventually they all do what they must do, as will you. And the consequences will not be so very dreadful. There will be a home and a wife and a family where there were none before, and they are necessary components of a comfortable, genteel life. But in the main the man's life does not change a great deal and does not need to. All the fear of leg shackles and parson's mousetrap and those other foolish clichés men use are really quite without foundation."

He wondered briefly if she was really cold to the very heart or if she was just unbelievably sheltered and innocent. Was there some man somewhere who could spark passion in her? He doubted it.

"You are determined to have me, then, are you, Portia?" he asked her. "There is nothing that would deter you?"

"I cannot imagine anything that would," she said, "unless Mama and Papa withdrew their consent, of course. That is most unlikely, though."

Heaven help him, he thought, he was a goner—as if he had not realized that before. He was here, for God's sake, was he not?

Damn Frances. Damn her all to hell. She could have rescued him from this. He had asked her to marry him and told himself afterward that he would not have done so if he had stopped to think. But if she had taken a chance as he had and said yes, he would not have needed to think. He would have been too busy feeling—elation, passion, triumph.

Love.

But she had said no and so here he was, facing a life sentence as surely as his name was Lucius Marshall. Without having done anything more than pay a morning call on a man who was not even at home, he had gone too far with Portia, it seemed, to withdraw.

But before the conversation could resume, the door opened to admit her mother, who was looking very smug indeed though she expressed chagrin that Lord Balderston had chosen that very morning to go early to his club when he *always* remained home until well after breakfast.

They conversed, the three of them, on a few inane topics that included the obligatory remarks on the weather and one another's health until Lucius felt enough time had passed that he could decently make his escape.

What the devil was he about to get himself into? he asked himself as he strode off in the direction of Jackson's, where he hoped to don the gloves and pound the stuffing out of someone or, better yet, have someone pound the stuffing out of him. Though there was nothing future about his predicament.

She was beautiful and refined and accomplished and perfect. She was also a woman he had never quite been able to bring himself to like—and their conversation this morning had done nothing to change that.

And yet he was as surely leg-shackled to her as if the banns had already been called. He had gone to see Balderston this morning, and both Lady Balderston and Portia knew it. There could be only one reason for such a visit. And he had promised to call again. Portia fully expected it of him.

I will come back some other time.

Of course you will.

And then he felt fury again.

At least you had the good sense to hire a schoolteacher to accompany her, but the woman really ought to have stopped her from dancing.

To hire a schoolteacher!

The woman!

Frances!

He clamped his teeth together and lengthened his stride. He could never quite decide whether the longing to throttle her was stronger than the hurt and humiliation of her rejection. Or the pain of knowing he would never see her again.

Or the niggling suspicion that she had shown more good sense than he and had saved him from himself. He had had *no idea* when he set out from Brock Street that day that he was about to offer her marriage. He had not even known he was going to the school to see her, for God's sake.

But calm good sense had never been his forte. He had always forged his way into the future with impulsive, reckless abandon.

He did it again not much more than twenty-four hours after his visit to Berkeley Square.

And again it was over Frances Allard.

17

"Mrs. Melford is in town, I have heard," the Earl of Edge-combe said at breakfast. It was one of his better days healthwise, and he had got up to take the meal with his family.

For once there had been no ball or late party the night before, with the result that they were all gathered at the table with the exception of Caroline, who had joined a party at Vauxhall with Sir Henry last evening and had not returned home until after the fireworks.

"Is she?" Lady Sinclair asked politely, looking up briefly from the letter she was reading.

"With her sister," the earl added. "They scarcely ever come to town. I do not know when I last saw them."

"Oh?" His mother sounded quite uninterested, Lucius thought as he cut into his beefsteak. She was busy reading her letter again.

"They are great-aunts of the present Baron Clifton of Wimford Grange," the earl explained. "Mrs. Melford made her come-out with my Rebecca, and they remained the best of friends all their lives until Rebecca's passing. What pretty girls they both were!"

"Ah," the viscountess said, looking up from her letter again, a little more interested now that she understood her father-in-law was talking about ladies who were virtually their neighbors in Somersetshire.

Lucius suddenly remembered why the name of Mrs. Melford was familiar to him.

So did Amy.

"Oh, but Mrs. Melford and her sister are Miss Allard's great-aunts too," she said. "Are they indeed in town, Grandpapa?"

"Whoever is Miss Allard?" Emily asked. "Do please pass the sugar, Amy."

"She is a lady who has the most glorious soprano voice in Christendom," the earl told Emily, pushing the sugar bowl across the table to her himself. "I do not exaggerate. We heard her sing when we were in Bath."

"Oh," Emily said, stirring a spoonful of sugar into her coffee, "the teacher. I remember now."

"It is not going to rain, is it?" the viscountess asked of no one in particular, her eyes going to the window. "It will be most provoking if it does. I have my heart set upon walking to the shops today."

"I believe I shall go and pay my respects to the ladies this afternoon," the earl said. He chuckled suddenly. "It will be a pleasure to talk with people almost as ancient as I."

"I shall accompany you if I may, sir," Lucius said.

"*You*, Luce?" Emily looked at him in some surprise and then laughed. "You will go with Grandpapa to visit a couple of old women when Mama always says that pulling teeth would be easier than dragging you off to pay courtesy calls?"

"*Elderly*, Emily," their mother said with sharp reproof. "Elderly *ladies*."

"I will go too," Amy said, brightening noticeably. "May I, Luce? May I, Grandpapa?"

"Well, *I* am not going," Emily declared. "I am going shopping with Mama."

"Nobody asked you, Em," Amy pointed out. "Besides, Mrs. Melford and her sister are the great-aunts of *my* friend, and I particularly want to meet them."

Lucius was left to wonder, as he got ready for the visit later in the day, why *he* wanted to meet them. Emily had, after all, spoken nothing but the truth when she had mentioned his aversion to paying social calls. And the two ladies must indeed be elderly. Doubtless the conversation would consist of lengthy health reports and even more lengthy reminiscences about the dim distant past and he would have to pinch himself to keep awake after the first few minutes.

Was he going simply because they were related to Frances? It would be the damnedest of poor reasons if that were so.

But what other reason could there possibly be?

In the event he was not bored at all. Mrs. Melford, a small, round lady, whose good-humored countenance still bore evidence of the prettiness his grandfather had spoken of, was delighted to see the husband of her old friend and exclaimed with delight over the fact that his grandchildren had chosen to accompany him. The two of them did indeed talk about the past, but they did so with such wit and humor that they kept both Lucius and Amy laughing and eager to hear more.

"But there is nothing more calculated to alienate young persons," Mrs. Melford said at last, "than to have two old people prosing on about a past so distant that even to me it seems like something from another lifetime. Tell me about yourself, child." She smiled kindly at Amy.

Amy immediately launched into a description of her newest triumph, her visit to Bath, where she had been allowed to attend a soiree and had heard Miss Allard sing, and where she had played hostess when Miss Allard came to tea and attended an assembly in the Upper Rooms with Miss Allard as her grandpapa's special guest and her companion.

"I liked her exceedingly well, ma'am," she said, beaming at her elderly hostess. "She treated me just as if I were a grown-up."

"Well, and so you are, child," Mrs. Melford said, "even if you have not yet made your come-out. You have that all to look forward to. How fortunate you are! You have the look of your grandmama, you know, especially about the mouth and chin, and all the world fell in love with her, as your grandfather will tell you. He did too."

"I did indeed," the earl confessed. "I rushed her off to the altar within six weeks of meeting her lest she see someone else she preferred."

"She had eyes for no one else but you, as you very well know," Mrs. Melford assured him as they all laughed. "But did you really meet our dear Frances when you were in Bath? And was she indeed singing again? I so wish we had been there to hear her."

She spoke with obvious affection for her great-niece.

This was one of the ladies she had left behind the morning of that snowstorm, Lucius thought. It was in their ancient carriage, driven by their ancient coachman, that Frances had been traveling when he overtook her.

"It amazes me," the earl said, "that no one discovered Miss Allard's talent when she lived in London."

"We understood that someone had," Mrs. Melford said. "Her father always saw to it that she had voice lessons with the best teachers, you know. It was both his dream and hers that she would be a great singer one day. But then he died suddenly, poor man, and Frances went to live with Lady Lyle for a couple of years even though we offered her a home with us. We heard that someone had agreed to sponsor her and that she was indeed singing. We expected to hear any day that she had become famous, but one day she wrote quite suddenly from Bath to inform us that she had taken a teaching position at Miss Martin's school there. We have been concerned for her happiness ever since, but when she spent this past Christmas with us in the country, it seemed to us that she was indeed quite contented with her chosen career."

Lady Lyle? Lucius raised his eyebrows but made no comment.

"She assured me that she was quite happy with what she was doing with her life when I was impertinent enough to ask her why she was not enthralling the world with her singing," the earl said.

"Both Gertrude and I think of her almost as a daughter," Mrs. Melford told them. "I was never blessed with children of my own, and Gertrude never did marry. We both fairly dote upon Frances."

The earl inquired politely about Miss Driscoll, who had not appeared to greet the visitors. She was in bed, her sister explained, quite unable to shake off the chill she had taken during the journey up to town. She suffered from a perennially weak chest, it seemed, and was a source of endless worry to her sister.

"Though one consolation is that at least we have access to the best physicians here in town," she added.

"She doubtless needs a good tonic," the earl said. "Something to cheer her up. You must ask your physician to prescribe something suitable, ma'am. I would recommend a course of the waters at Bath, but perhaps you feel that your sister is too weak to make the journey."

"Indeed I do," Mrs. Melford said, "though I will keep the recommendation in mind."

That was the point at which Lucius abandoned common sense and spoke impulsively again without giving himself any chance to think first.

"Perhaps, ma'am," he suggested, "Miss Driscoll would benefit most from seeing Miss Allard again."

Mrs. Melford sighed. "I am quite sure you are right, Lord Sinclair," she said. "How wonderful that would be for both of us. But Gertrude will have to improve considerably in health before we can travel down to see her."

"I meant, ma'am," he said, "that perhaps *she* can come *here*."

Now what was he meddling in? his brain asked him. He paid it no heed.

"Oh, but she will be busy with her teaching duties until well on into the summer," Mrs. Melford said. "I am sure she cannot be spared."

"Not even for the sake of a beloved aunt?" Lucius asked. "If she knew that Miss Driscoll was in poor health and not making a rapid recovery even though she has been attended by a London physician, surely she would ask to be released from her duties for a week or two on compassionate grounds, and surely Miss Martin would not detain her."

"Do you think so?" Mrs. Melford looked quite eager at the prospect. "It is kind of you to show such concern, Lord Sinclair. And really I cannot imagine why I did not think of it for myself. A visit from Frances would be just the thing to lift Gertrude's spirits. Our niece always brings such a draft of fresh air into our lives."

"Oh," Amy cried, clasping her hands to her bosom, "I do hope you send for her, Mrs. Melford, and I do hope she comes. Then I will be able to see her again. I will have Luce bring me here. I would like it of all things."

"And perhaps," the earl said, chuckling, "she will sing for Miss Driscoll, and I will wangle an invitation to hear her again too. I cannot imagine a better tonic."

"I shall do it," Mrs. Melford said with firm decision, clapping her hands together. "I daresay she may not be able to get away in the middle of a school term, but I will not know if I do not ask, will I? I can think of nothing I would like better than to see Frances again, and I am convinced that a visit from her will do Gertrude the world of good."

"Perhaps, ma'am," Lucius said, smiling his most charming smile, "you should say in your letter that the idea was all yours."

"And was it not?" Her eyes twinkled at him.

And what the deuce had *that* been all about? Lucius wondered during what remained of the visit and after they had taken their leave. Why would he have pounced upon a slim opportunity of enticing Frances to London?

Did he really *want* to see her again?

But for what purpose? Had she not made herself clear enough the last time he saw her? Had he not suffered enough rejection and humiliation at her hands?

What the deuce was he hoping to accomplish?

Just yesterday he had gone to Berkeley Square to talk marriage settlements with Balderston—and found him from home.

He had not returned this morning.

Would he go back there tomorrow?

Very probably Frances would not even come.

And if she did, so what? She would be coming to see her ailing great-aunt, not him.

But if she *did* come, he thought, clamping his teeth together as Amy prattled away to their grandfather beside her on the carriage seat and presumably to him too, he would certainly make it a point to see her.

No one had yet written *the end* beneath their story. It was not finished.

Deuce take it, it was not finished.

Not in his mind, anyway.

That is the trouble with you. You really cannot take no for an answer, can you, Lord Sinclair?

Yes, of course he could. He did it all the time. But how could he accept a no when he had never been quite convinced that she had not desperately wanted to say yes?

Then why the devil had she not?

The outskirts of London were not attractive in the best of circumstances. They looked downright ugly in the rain and with a swirling wind blowing rubbish across open spaces and into soggy piles against the curbs next to the pavements.

Frances ached in every limb, having made the journey from Bath all in one day in the dubious comfort and at the very plodding speed of her great-aunts' carriage, with Thomas up on the box. She had a bit of a headache. She felt slightly damp even though all the windows were firmly shut. She was also chilly.

But really she was not thinking much about either the view beyond the windows or her physical discomforts—or even about being back in London. She was not coming here either to enjoy herself or to mingle with society, after all. No one would even know she had been here.

She was coming because Great-Aunt Gertrude was dying. Not that Great-Aunt Martha had announced the fact in such stark words, it was true, but the conclusion was inescapable. She had begged Frances to come if she possibly could even though she knew it was the middle of a school term. And though she had added that she was sure dear Frances would not be able to get away before the end of term and that she must not distress herself if she really could not, she had sent an inescapable sign that her great-niece's presence in London was an urgent necessity. Instead of sending the letter by post, she had sent it with Thomas and the ancient private carriage—"for your comfort if you should be able to get away," she had added in a postscript.

Claudia had granted her leave of absence before Frances had even formed the words to ask for something so inconvenient, assuring her that she would find a temporary replacement to carry on with her teaching duties. Anne had hugged her wordlessly. Susanna had helped pack her bags. Mr. Huckerby had offered to conduct her choir practices while she was gone. Each of her classes urged her to hurry back.

Frances had actually dissolved into tears after sharing the contents of the letter with her friends.

"They are just *great*-aunts," she had said. "I have not seen a great deal of them during my life and I write to them only once a month. But now that it seems likely that I may lose one of them, I realize what an anchor they have always been to my existence and how much I rely on their love and support. With my father gone, they are all I have of my very own. And I do love them."

It was of them she had thought with most distress after Lady Fontbridge had made her threat more than three years ago. It was largely because of them that she had made the promise to leave London and never return. She could not have borne it if they had been told. So much of their world would have been destroyed.

"Of course you do," Claudia had said briskly. "Stay as long as you need to, Frances. We will all miss you, of course, including the girls, but no one in this life is quite indispensable. It can sometimes be a humbling realization."

And so here she was, in London again and sick with anxiety. Great-Aunt Gertrude had never enjoyed robust health, and she tended to coddle herself by staying too far away from fresh air and too close to the nearest fire. But Frances had never thought of actually losing her.

When the carriage finally rocked to a halt outside a respectable-looking house on Portman Street, she waited impatiently for Thomas to open the door and set down the steps and then hurried up to the house door, which opened even before she reached it, and into a tiled hall, where she fell into Great-Aunt Martha's open arms.

"Frances, my love," her aunt cried, beaming with happiness, "you *did* come! I hardly dared hope you would be able to get away. And how lovely you look, as usual!"

"Aunt Martha!" Frances hugged her back. "How is Aunt Gertrude?" She was almost afraid to ask. But the first thing she had noticed—with enormous relief—was that her great-aunt was not wearing black.

"A little better today despite the damp weather," Aunt Martha said. "She has even got up from her bed and come down to the sitting room. What a delightful surprise *this* is going to be for her. I have not breathed a word about your coming. And indeed, I can scarcely believe that you have come only because I asked. I do hope Miss Martin has not dismissed you permanently?"

"She has granted me a leave of absence," Frances said. "Aunt Gertrude is actually getting better, then? She is not—"

"Oh, my poor love," Aunt Martha said, taking her arm and leading her in the direction of the staircase. "You did not imagine the worst, did you? She never was dangerously ill, but she has been dragged down by a chill she has been unable to shake off, and she has been in dreadfully low spirits as a result. We both have. It seemed to me—very selfishly, my love—that seeing you would be just the tonic we both needed."

Great-Aunt Gertrude was not on her deathbed, then? It was the best of good news. At the same time Frances thought ruefully of all the trouble she had put Claudia to by leaving the school so abruptly for a few weeks in the middle of a term—and of all the disruption to her classes and choirs and music pupils.

It was enormously touching, though, to know that her presence meant so much to her aunts. She would never take them for granted again, she vowed. And it really was lovely to see Great-Aunt Martha again. Frances felt a rush of tears to her eyes and blinked them away.

There was great jubilation when she appeared in the sitting room, which was hot and stuffy with a fire roaring in the hearth. Great-Aunt

Gertrude sat huddled close to it, a heavy woolen shawl about her shoulders and a lap robe over her knees, but both were cast aside the moment she set eyes upon her great-niece, and she got to her feet with surprising alacrity and came hurrying toward her. They met and hugged tightly in the middle of the room while Great-Aunt Martha fluttered about them, telling excitedly of the secret she had kept to herself for all of four days lest dear Frances not be able to come and Gertrude be plunged into even deeper gloom with disappointment.

Later, as she sat with a cup of tea in her hand and a plate of cakes—Aunt Martha had put three on it though she had asked for only one—on her knee, Frances felt warm and happy and pleasantly tired. It was obvious that Aunt Gertrude was not in the best of health, but neither was she dangerously ill. Frances even felt a twinge of guilt about having come here, but she had not come under false pretenses, and it seemed that she really had been a tonic for her aunts' spirits. They were chattering merrily and seemed not even to have noticed that the fire had died down considerably.

She would spend a week or so with them and enjoy herself without guilt, Frances thought rather sleepily, and then she would go back to school and work doubly hard until the end of the term. There would be all the extra work of preparing for the year-end prize-giving and concert.

Perhaps she would try to visit her aunts in the country for another week during the summer. They needed her, she had just realized—and really she needed them too.

"Some friends of yours came calling on me a few days ago, Frances," Great-Aunt Martha said, beaming at her. "Poor Gertrude was still in bed that day and did not meet them, but we will certainly invite them back."

"Oh?" Frances looked inquiringly at her, a little flutter of alarm in the pit of her stomach. Someone who knew her was already aware that she was returning to London?

"The Earl of Edgecombe called on me," Aunt Martha said. "His late wife and I used to be bosom bows when we were girls, you know, and I always did like him exceedingly. It was most obliging of him to call."

Frances felt as if her stomach performed a complete somersault. Ah, yes, of course. She remembered then that he had said he once knew Great-Aunt Martha. She had not even *thought* of the possibility . . .

But her aunt had spoken of *friends* calling on her.

Plural.

"And he brought his grandson and one of his granddaughters with him," Aunt Martha continued. "Viscount Sinclair and Miss Amy Marshall. They are delightful young people. And they were all full of praises for your singing, Frances, after hearing you in Bath. I do not wonder at it, of course."

"I only wonder that you have not done more of it and become famous," Great-Aunt Gertrude said.

Frances's heart had plunged and lodged somewhere in the soles of her shoes. This was the stuff of her worst nightmares. She must somehow dissuade her aunts from inviting them all back here. She could not bear to see them again.

She could not bear to see *him*.

Gracious heaven, why had he come here? Just because his grandfather had wished to?

"And you accompanied them to an assembly at the Upper Rooms," Aunt Martha continued, looking at her niece with a beaming smile. "It did my heart good, my love, to hear that you have started enjoying yourself again. We have always thought that you are too young and lovely to bury yourself inside a school and have no chance to meet suitable beaux."

"Oh," Frances said with a forced smile, finishing off her tea and setting the cup and saucer down on a table beside her, "I am really quite happy as I am, Aunt Martha. And I am not entirely without beaux."

She had been to the theater with Mr. Blake and his sister and brother-in-law one evening during the past month and to dine with them on another. She had been to two services at Bath Abbey with Mr. Blake alone, and both times they had strolled back to the school by a long, circuitous route. What was between them could not exactly be called a courtship, she supposed, but she was very thankful that it could not. She far preferred a mild friendship that might—or might not—blossom into something warmer with time.

"What I would like to know," Aunt Martha said, leaning forward in her chair, her eyes still twinkling, "is whether you danced with Viscount Sinclair, Frances."

Annoyingly, Frances could feel herself blushing.

"Yes, I did," she said. "He was very obliging. The earl had invited me to accompany them to the assembly at Miss Marshall's urging, and the viscount was kind enough to dance with me after he had first led his sister out."

"You did not tell me, Martha," Aunt Gertrude said, "and I did not think to ask—is Viscount Sinclair both young and handsome, by any chance?"

"And charming too," Aunt Martha said, and the elderly ladies exchanged a knowing smirk. "Now, was it one set or two you danced together, Frances, my love?"

"Two," Frances said, horrified by the turn the conversation was taking. "But—"

"*Two.*" Aunt Martha clapped her hands together and looked enraptured. "I *knew* it. I knew as surely as I know my own name that he admired you."

"Frances! How splendid!" Aunt Gertrude leaned forward and forgot about her shawl again. It slipped unheeded from her shoulders to the cushion behind her. The lap robe was already pooled at her feet. "Viscountess Sinclair! I *like* it."

They were teasing her, of course. They were both chuckling merrily.

"Alas, I am afraid you are quite mistaken," Frances said, trying to keep her tone light and the smile on her face. "Viscount Sinclair is to marry Miss Portia Hunt."

"Balderston's girl?" Aunt Martha said. "What a shame! Though I suppose it is no such thing for the lady herself. He is *very* handsome, Gertrude. But all may not be lost. No mention was made of any betrothal while they were here, and I have not seen any announcement in the papers since we came here, though I read them all quite conscientiously each morning. And he was pointedly interested in you, Frances, though he did not say so openly, of course. Without him I doubt I would have thought of inviting you here as a tonic for Gertrude's spirits."

"What?" Frances stared at her, aghast.

"It was he who suggested it." Aunt Martha smiled smugly. "And though it was exceedingly kind of him to show such solicitude for two old ladies, something told me at the time that there was a young man with an ulterior motive. He wished to see you again himself, Frances."

"This was all Viscount Sinclair's idea?" Aunt Gertrude asked, looking quite charmed. "I like him already, Martha, though I have never yet clapped eyes on him. He sounds like a young man who knows what he wants and how to get it. We must invite him here to dine one evening—with his sister and the Earl of Edgecombe, of course. We came to London to see something of society after so long, did we not, yet after almost three weeks we have seen nobody—at least, *I* have not. But it is time I did. I already feel worlds better than I felt even an hour ago. Oh, Frances, dearest, I am only just realizing that you are actually *here*."

Frances stared mutely at them.

This was *his* doing?

He was the one who had suggested luring her here?

Why?

He was not betrothed yet?

"But here we are rattling on," Aunt Martha said, getting to her feet, "and you are so tired from your journey, Frances, that you are really looking quite pale. Come, my love. I will take you to your room, where you must rest until dinnertime. We will talk again this evening."

Frances bent to kiss Aunt Gertrude's cheek and allowed herself to be led from the room and up to a pleasant bedchamber on the floor above, which had obviously been prepared for her in the hope that she would come.

She lay down on the bed when she was alone, and stared up at the canopy over her head.

He had been here, in this very house.

He had suggested that she be sent for. Perhaps he had even suggested that Great-Aunt Gertrude's condition be exaggerated so that she would be more sure to leave her duties behind. It would be just like him to do something so devious and high-handed.

How dared he!

Could he not take no for an answer? Could he not leave well enough alone?

Was it possible that he still wished to marry her? But when he had offered her marriage there in Sydney Gardens, he had done so entirely from impulse. That had been perfectly obvious to her. Surely when he had thought about it afterward he would have admitted to himself that he had had a narrow escape from doing something quite indiscreet.

After a whole month she was still raw with the pain of having seen him again, danced with him again, touched him, kissed him, talked with him, quarreled with him—and refused a marriage offer from him!

She was still deeply, hopelessly, in love with him.

She had been since just after Christmas, of course, and the feeling stubbornly refused to go away.

Perhaps because *he* stubbornly refused to go away.

And now he had contrived to see her again, using her great-aunts in a despicably devious plot to lure her to London.

Why?

He was the most irritating, provoking, overbearing man she had ever known. She deliberately set her mind to thinking of all she most disliked about him. She tried to visualize him as he had been on the road that first day when she had bristled with hostility toward him—and he had returned the compliment.

But instead she saw him turning suddenly to hurl a snowball at her and then engaging in a high-spirited, laughter-filled fight before bearing her backward into the snow, his hands on her wrists . . .

Frances sighed deeply and despite herself drifted off to sleep.

18

Lord Balderston had borne his lady and daughter off to the country for a few days to help celebrate the birthday of some distant relative. It was with some sense of temporary reprieve, then, that Lucius went riding in the park early one morning in the thoroughly congenial company of three male friends. The fact that a fine rain was drizzling down from a gray sky did not in any way dampen his spirits. Indeed, it added the advantage of an almost deserted Rotten Row so that they could gallop their horses along it without endangering other, more sober-minded riders. As he returned home to change for breakfast, he did not even have to hold the usual inner debate with himself about what he ought to do after he had eaten. He could not go to the house on Berkeley Square even if he wished to do so.

Only his grandfather and Amy were up, the others being still in bed after a late night at some ball he had not even felt constrained to attend. He rubbed his hands together with satisfaction and viewed the array of hot foods set out on the sideboard. He was ravenous.

But Amy was clearly bursting to tell him something and could not wait until he had made his selection and taken his place at the table.

"Luce," she said, "guess what?"

"Give me a clue," he said. "No, let me guess. You have had ten hours of sleep and are now overflowing with energy and ideas on how to use it—with me as your slave."

"No, silly!" she said. "Grandpapa has just had an invitation to dine at Mrs. Melford's tomorrow evening, and I am invited too. Mama will not say no, will she? You simply must speak up for me— you and Grandpapa both."

"I don't suppose she will," he said guardedly, "provided it is a private dinner."

"Oh, and you are invited too," she said.

That was what he had been afraid of. One visit had been amusing, but . . .

"Miss Allard has come up from Bath," she said.

Ah!

Well!

"She has, has she?" he asked briskly. "And I am expected to give up an evening to dine with Mrs. Melford and her sister merely because Miss Allard is there too?"

Merely!

"It would be the courteous thing to do, Lucius," his grandfather said, "since you are the one who suggested she be summoned."

"And so I did," Lucius admitted. "I hope her arrival has had the desired effect."

"Mrs. Melford declares that Miss Driscoll made something of a miraculous recovery within an hour of the arrival of their great-niece," his grandfather told him. "It was an inspired suggestion of yours, Lucius. May I send back an acceptance for you as well as for Amy and myself?"

Lucius stood with a still-empty plate in his hand and an appetite that seemed somehow to have fled. When he had watched Frances run away from the pavilion in Sydney Gardens after refusing to marry him or give him a thoroughly satisfying reason for doing so, he had thought that if he never saw her again it would be rather too soon.

Yet he had undeniably maneuvered matters so that she would come to London to see her great-aunts.

And was he now going to stay away from her?

"Yes, please do, sir," he said with as much carelessness as he could summon.

"I shall look forward to it of all things," Amy said, turning her attention back to her own breakfast. "Will not you, Luce?"

"Of all things," he said dryly as he scooped fried potatoes onto his plate and moved on to the sausages.

He would probably do something asinine like count down the hours until he would see her again. Like a love-struck mooncalf.

But would Frances? Look forward to it of all things, that was?

Frances was beginning to think—and hope—that her great-aunts had forgotten about their plan to invite the Earl of Edgecombe to come to dinner with Viscount Sinclair and Amy Marshall. Two days passed and nothing more was said about it.

She enjoyed those days. Her aunts—not only Great-Aunt Gertrude, but Great-Aunt Martha too—visibly improved in both health and spirits during that time. And so did she, she felt. It was good to be with them again, to be fussed over, to be the apple of their eye, to have the feeling of being part of a family. She really had been very depressed during the last month, and indeed she had not been in the best of spirits since Christmas.

She would stay for a week, she had decided. And she would not worry about being back in London. She was not planning to go out anywhere, after all, and the world was unlikely to come calling.

She was mistaken about the plan for dinner, though, as she discovered late in the afternoon of that second day, only a few hours before the guests were due to arrive. Her aunts had kept it a secret until the last moment, they explained, thinking to delight her with the surprise when they finally informed her.

They also begged her, with identical beams of sheer delight, to put on her prettiest gown and to allow Hattie, their own personal maid, to dress her hair suitably for evening.

It was bad enough to know that Lucius was going to be here within a couple of hours, Frances thought as she scurried upstairs to get ready. But far worse was the fact that her great-aunts seemed determined to play *matchmaker*. How excruciatingly embarrassing if he or any of the others should notice!

She had brought her cream silk to London with her. Not that she had expected to have occasion to wear it. But any lady must go prepared for a variety of circumstances when she traveled. She wore it for dinner, and she did not have the heart to send Hattie away and disappoint her aunts. And so by the time she descended to the sitting room a mere ten minutes before the guests were due to arrive, she was wearing her hair in a mass of soft curls at the back, with an elaborate arrangement of fine braids crisscrossing the smoothly brushed hair over the crown of her head.

She looked very fine, she had admitted to Hattie when the coiffure was complete. But that very fact embarrassed her. What if he thought she had done it for him? What if his grandfather and Amy thought it?

They came one minute early—Frances had, of course, been watching the clock on the mantel in the sitting room.

Amy came into the room first, all youthful high spirits as she curtsied first to Aunt Martha and then to Aunt Gertrude and smiled warmly at each of them. She stretched out both hands to Frances and looked as delighted to see her as if they were long-lost sisters—alarming thought.

"Miss Allard!" she exclaimed. "I am *so* glad to see you again. And you have made Miss Driscoll all better, as Luce predicted you would."

The Earl of Edgecombe came next, all bent frailty and twinkling eyes as he made his bow to the older ladies and then reached out his right hand to Frances.

"By fair means or foul, ma'am," he said, beaming genially at her, "I mean to hear you sing again before I die."

"I hope, my lord," she said, setting her hand in his and watching him carry it to his lips, "you are not planning to do that anytime soon."

He chuckled and patted her hand before releasing it.

And then came Lucius, bringing up the rear, looking quite impossibly handsome in his black evening clothes with dull gold embroidered waistcoat and white linen and lace. He was smiling charmingly at the aunts and then turning to make a formal bow to Frances.

She curtsied.

The aunts smirked and looked charmed.

"Miss Allard?" he said.

"Lord Sinclair."

Drawing air into her lungs was taking a conscious effort.

Everyone seemed remarkably pleased with everyone else despite the fact that they were an ill-assorted group. They proceeded in to dinner almost immediately, the earl with a great-aunt on each arm and Viscount Sinclair with Frances on his right arm and Amy on his left. And the conversation remained lively throughout the meal and in the sitting room afterward.

Soon, Frances thought, the evening would be over and her ordeal at an end. The courtesies would have been observed and in five days' time she could retreat to Bath and her normal life.

It was a strangely dreary prospect, considering the fact that she really did like teaching—and that she loved all her pupils and had genuine friends at the school.

"I daresay Miss Marshall could entertain us at the pianoforte if only there were one in this house," Great-Aunt Martha said. "And I know that Frances could with her voice. But I will not suggest that she sing unaccompanied, much as I know she would acquit herself well if she did."

"She has always had perfect pitch," Great-Aunt Gertrude explained.

"I am very thankful there *is* no instrument," Amy said, laughing merrily. "And I daresay Grandpapa and Luce are glad of it too. Anyone who ever says I play competently is being excessively kind to me."

"I will not pretend that I am not disappointed to be unable to hear Miss Allard sing again," the earl said, "but all things happen for a purpose, I firmly believe. There *is* a pianoforte at Marshall House, you see, and a superior one too. It will be my greatest pleasure to entertain you three ladies to dinner one evening later in the week. And afterward, Miss Allard, you may sing for your supper." His eyes twinkled kindly at her from beneath his white eyebrows. "If you will, that is. It will not be a condition of your coming to dine. But *will* you sing for me there?"

As had happened in Bath, then, this encounter was to be prolonged, was it? She was to see them all yet again?

Frances glanced at her great-aunts. They were beaming back at her, both of them looking utterly happy. How could she say no and deny them a little more pleasure? And really, deep down, did she even want to say no?

"Very well, then," she said. "I will come and sing, my lord, just for you and my aunts. Thank you. It will be my pleasure."

"Splendid!" He rubbed his hands together. "Caroline will accompany you. I shall ask her tomorrow morning. You must come one afternoon and discuss your choice of music with her and practice a little."

"Thank you," she said. "That would be a good idea."

"Will you grant one more request?" he asked. "Whatever else you choose to sing, will you also sing what you did in Bath? I have longed to hear it again."

"And I love to sing it, my lord." She smiled warmly at him.

She was sitting at some remove from the fireplace, since Great-Aunt Gertrude always liked to keep the fire built high. The earl turned his attention to Great-Aunt Martha, who sat close to him, and Great-Aunt Gertrude invited Amy to sit on the stool by her feet and tell her all about her exciting experiences in Bath and what she had done in London since then. Viscount Sinclair, who had been standing behind his grandfather's chair, one arm leaning on the back of it, came to sit on the sofa beside Frances.

"You are in good looks tonight," he said.

"Thank you." She had tried her best all evening to ignore him—rather akin, she thought ruefully, to trying to ignore the incoming tide when one was seated on the beach in its direct path.

"I trust," he said, "Miss Martin's school was not left in a state of chaos and incipient collapse when you came here."

"It is no thanks to you that it was not," she said sharply.

"Ah."

It was all he said in acknowledgment of the fact that she knew his role in bringing her here.

"I trust," she said, "Miss Hunt is in good health. *And* good looks."

"I really do not give a tinker's damn," he said softly, prompting her to look fully at him for the first time. Fortunately, he had spoken quietly enough that she was the only one to have heard his shocking words.

"Why did you do this?" she asked him. "Why did you persuade my great-aunt to send for me?"

"She needed you, Frances," he said. "So did your other aunt, who was actually bedridden the last time I was here."

"I am being asked to believe, then," she said, "that your motive was purely altruistic?"

"What do *you* think?" He smiled at her, a rather wolfish smile that had her insides turning over.

"And why did you come here the first time anyway?" she asked. "Just to visit two elderly ladies out of the kindness of your heart?"

"You are angry with me," he said instead of answering. And instead of smiling now, he was looking at her with intense eyes and compressed lips and hard, square jaw.

"Yes, I am angry," she admitted. "I do not like being manipulated, Lord Sinclair. I do not like having someone else thinking he knows better than I what makes me happy."

"Contented," he said.

"Contented, then," she conceded.

"I *do* know better than you what will make you *happy*," he said.

"I think not, Lord Sinclair."

"I could accomplish it," he said, "within a month. Less. I could bring you professional happiness. And personal happiness in such abundance that your cup would run over with it, Frances."

She felt a yearning so profound that she had to break eye contact with him and look down hastily at her hands.

"My chances for either kind of happiness were ruined more than three years ago, Lord Sinclair," she said.

"Were they?" he said as softly as before. "Three years?"

She ignored the question.

"I have cultivated contentment since then," she said. "And incredibly I have found it and discovered that it is superior to anything else I have ever experienced. Don't ruin that too for me."

There was a lengthy silence while the earl and Great-Aunt Martha laughed together over something one of them had said, and Amy's voice prattled on happily to Great-Aunt Gertrude.

"I believe I already have," Viscount Sinclair said at last. "Or shaken it, anyway. Because I do not believe it ever was contentment, Frances, but only a sort of deadness from which you awakened when I hauled you out of that fossil of a carriage, spitting fire and brimstone at me."

She looked up at him, very aware that they were not alone together in the room, that her great-aunts were only a few feet away and were very probably observing them surreptitiously and with great interest. She was quite unable therefore to allow any of the emotions she felt to show on her face.

"You are to be married," she said.

"I am," he agreed. "But one important question remains unanswered. Who is to be the bride?"

She drew breath to say something else, but her attention was drawn to the fact that the earl was getting to his feet with the obvious intention of bringing the visit to an end.

Viscount Sinclair rose too without another word and proceeded to thank the aunts for their hospitality. Amy hugged Frances and assured her that she would somehow persuade her mama to allow her to come downstairs when Mrs. Melford and Miss Driscoll and Miss Allard came for dinner.

"After all," she said naively, "you are *my* special friend. Besides, I would not miss hearing you sing again for worlds. I may not perform music with any great flair, Miss Allard, but I can recognize when someone else does."

The earl bowed over Frances's hand again.

"Prepare more than one song, if you will," he said. "After listening to you once, I know that I will long for an encore."

"Very well, my lord," she promised.

Viscount Sinclair bowed to her with his hands clasped behind his back.

"Miss Allard," he said.

"Lord Sinclair."

It was an austere enough farewell, but it did not deter Frances's aunts from going into raptures after their guests had left.

"The Earl of Edgecombe is quite as charming as he was as a young man," Aunt Martha said. "And almost as handsome too. And Miss Amy Marshall is a delight. But Viscount Sinclair—"

"—is handsome enough and charming enough to make any woman wish she were young again to set her cap at him," Aunt Gertrude said. "But it is a good thing we are not young hopefuls, Martha. He had eyes for no one but Frances tonight."

"He was very charming to us," Aunt Martha said, "but every time he looked at Frances, his eyes fairly devoured her and he forgot our very existence. Did you notice how he went to sit beside her, Gertrude, the moment we drew the attention of Lord Edgecombe and Miss Marshall away from them?"

"Well, of course I noticed," Great-Aunt Gertrude said. "I would have been severely disappointed if our ruse had not worked, Martha."

"Oh, goodness," Frances protested. "You must not see romance where there simply is none. Or try to promote it."

"You, my love," Aunt Martha said, "are going to be the Viscountess Sinclair before the summer is out unless I am much mistaken. Poor Miss Hunt is just going to have to find someone else."

Frances held both hands to her cheeks, laughing despite herself.

"I absolutely agree with Martha," Aunt Gertrude said. "And you cannot tell us that you are indifferent to him, Frances. We would not believe you, would we, Martha?"

Frances bade them a hasty good night and fled to her room.

They did not understand.

Neither did he.

Was there such a thing as fate?

But if there were, why was it such a cruel thing? For what it had set in her path three separate times now since Christmas was quite, quite unattainable.

Did *fate* not understand?

But one important question remains unanswered. Who is to be the bride?

Did he still want to marry her, then? Had it not been mere rash impulse that had prompted him to offer for her in Sydney Gardens while the rain poured down all around them?

Did he love her?

Did he?

Frances had agreed to sing at Marshall House, though she had imposed a sort of condition.

Very well, then. I will come and sing, my lord, just for you and my aunts.

They were words that echoed in Lucius's head during the coming days while he schemed ruthlessly to thwart her modest will. She had not meant those words literally, he told himself.

At least, she probably *had,* he conceded, since there was something very strange, almost unnatural, about Frances's attitude to her own talent. But she *ought* not to have meant them. Anyone with her voice ought to be eager to sing for an audience of a million if that many persons could only be packed within one room. It would be a criminal waste to allow her to sing just for his grandfather and her great-aunts—and presumably for his mother and sisters and him too.

Frances Allard had shuttered herself—body, mind, and soul—behind the walls of Miss Martin's School for Girls for far too long, and it was time she came out and faced reality. And if she would not do it voluntarily, then by God he would take the initiative and drag her out. Perhaps she would never give him the chance to make her happy in any personal sense—though even on that matter he had not yet conceded final defeat. But he would force her to see that a glorious future as a singer awaited her. He would do everything in his power to help her to that future.

Frances had not been born to teach. Not that he had ever been present in one of her classrooms to discover that she was not up to the task, it was true. She very probably was, in fact. But she had so clearly been born to make music and to share it with the world that any other occupation was simply a waste of her God-given talent.

He was going to bring her out into the light. He was going to help her—force her, if necessary—to be all she had been born to be.

And so he ignored the words she had spoken to his grandfather— *I will come and sing, my lord, just for you and my aunts.*

He knew someone. The man was a friend of his and had only recently married. He was a renowned connoisseur of the arts, notably music, and was particularly well known for the concert he gave at his own home each year, at which he entertained a select gathering of guests with prominent musicians from all over the Continent and with new discoveries of his own. Just this past Christmas his star performer had been a young boy soprano whom he had discovered among a group of inferior church carolers out on Bond Street. He had married the boy's mother in January.

It was strange to think of Baron Heath as a married man with two young stepchildren. But it seemed to happen to all of them eventually, Lucius thought gloomily—marriage, that was. At least Heath had had the satisfaction of choosing his own bride and marrying for love.

Lucius invited him to attend a concert at Marshall House and promised him a musical treat that would make his hair stand on end.

"She has an extraordinarily lovely voice," he explained, "but has had no one to bring her to the attention of people who can do something to sponsor her career."

"And I will soon be clamoring to be that sponsor, I suppose," Lord Heath said. "I hear this with tedious frequency, Sinclair. But I do trust your taste—provided we are talking of taste in voices, that is, and not in women."

Lucius felt a touch of anger, but he quelled it.

"Come," he said, "and bring Lady Heath. You may listen and judge for yourself whether her singing voice does not equal her beauty."

But a singer needed an audience, Lucius believed. How could Frances sing as she had in Bath with only his family and hers and the Heaths looking on? Yet even in Bath the audience had been modest in size.

The music room in Marshall House would seat thirty people in some comfort. If the panels between it and the ballroom were removed, there would be room for many more, and the size of the combined rooms would give range for the power of a great voice.

And a concert needed more than one performer . . .

His schemes became more grandiose by the hour.

"I am thinking of inviting a few people to join us in the music room after dinner on the evening Miss Allard comes here with her great-aunts to dine, sir," he told his grandfather at tea three days before the said dinner. "Including Baron Heath and his wife."

"Ah, a good idea, Lucius," the earl said. "I should have thought of it for myself—and of Heath. He can do something for her. I do not imagine Miss Allard will have any objection."

She well might, Lucius suspected. He knew her better than his grandfather did. But he held his peace.

"I have the distinct impression," the viscountess said, "that it is this Miss Allard rather than Mrs. Melford and Miss Driscoll who is to be the guest of honor at our table. It is extraordinary when one remembers that she is a schoolteacher."

"You will see, Louisa," the earl told her, "that it is *she* who is extraordinary."

Caroline meanwhile had uttered a muffled shriek at Lucius's words.

"And I am expected to accompany Miss Allard before an audience that includes *Baron Heath*?" she said. "When is she coming here to practice, Luce?"

"The afternoon after tomorrow," he said. "You had better not mention Lord Heath to her, though, Caroline, or any other guests. You will only make her nervous."

"Make *her* nervous!" Her voice had risen almost to a squeak. "How about *me?*"

"When she begins to sing," Amy said kindly, "no one will even notice your playing, Caroline."

"Well, thank you for that," Caroline said before laughing suddenly.

Amy laughed with her. "I did not mean it quite the way it sounded," she said. "Your playing is quite superior—far better than mine."

"Which is not much of a compliment, Amy, when one really thinks about it," Emily said dryly.

"And *you,* Father," the viscountess said firmly, "are looking tired. Lucius will help you to your room, and you will lie down until dinnertime."

"Yes, ma'am," the earl said with a twinkle in his eye—and a slight gray tinge to his complexion.

No one had voiced any objection to the idea of making the musical part of the evening into a full-blown concert, though, Lucius thought as he climbed the stairs slowly, his grandfather leaning heavily on his arm. Not that he had used those words exactly, of course, to describe his plans. But any small—or large—gathering of people for the purpose of listening to a few musical performances could be loosely defined as a concert.

He had three days during which to gather a respectably sized audience to do Frances Allard's talent justice—at the height of the Season, when every day brought a flood of invitations to every *ton* household. But it could be done, by Jove, and he would do it. Her feet were going to be set firmly on the road to success and fame that evening. He had no doubt of it.

And it would be all his doing.

That might prove small comfort in the years ahead, of course.

But all was not yet lost on the personal front. He was not married yet, or even betrothed—not officially anyway. The Balderstons were back in town, but he had contrived to avoid them for all of twenty-four hours.

He had never been a man to give up lightly on what he badly wanted. And new leaf or no new leaf, he had not changed in that particular.

He desperately wanted Frances Allard.

19

Marshall House was a grand mansion on Cavendish Square in the heart of Mayfair, Frances discovered on the afternoon of the day before she was to dine there. She might have expected as much, of course, since it was the town house of the Earl of Edgecombe. But she felt apprehensive and strangely conspicuous as she bowed her head and hurried inside after Thomas had handed her down from the ancient carriage outside the doors.

She was very aware that she really was back in London.

She saw no one within, though, except for a few servants and the young lady who awaited her in the room to which she was shown and introduced herself as Miss Caroline Marshall. She was tall and poised and pretty and bore little resemblance to her brother.

Of him there was no sign.

The room was massive and gorgeously decorated, with its high ceiling painted with a scene from mythology and gilded friezes and crystal chandeliers and mirrored walls and a gleaming wood floor. It fairly took Frances's breath away. *This* was where she was to sing for the earl and her aunts tomorrow evening?

It was very clearly not the family drawing room.

Miss Marshall offered an explanation that partly reassured her, though.

"The pianoforte in here is superior to the one in the drawing room," she explained, "and my grandfather insists that nothing but the best is good enough for you, Miss Allard. I cannot understand why the panels have been removed, though. This is the music room and the ballroom combined. Tomorrow evening they will have been replaced, I do not doubt, and your voice will not have to fill such a vast space. But really this is not good enough. You ought to be able to practice in the space you will be singing in."

How glorious it would be, though, Frances thought wistfully as her eyes feasted upon the opulent splendor of the double chamber, to rise to the challenge of singing to an audience that filled this vast space. She had once dreamed of singing in just such a place.

As she warmed up her voice with scales and exercises she had learned as a girl, she fit her voice to the room, well aware though she was that tomorrow evening she would have to make an adjustment to a smaller space.

"Oh, goodness," Miss Marshall said even before they began to practice either of the pieces they had chosen for the occasion, "the combined room is not too big for you after all, is it? How extraordinary!"

They practiced in earnest then, and Frances reveled in the chance just to sing. She did sing at school, of course, but not often or at great length—or to the full power of her voice. The purpose of the school and her role as teacher there, after all, was to draw music out of her pupils, not to indulge her desire to create music of her own. It was a noble purpose, she had always thought. It was a joy to help young people realize their full potential.

She still did think so, but, oh, it felt good to indulge in a whole selfish hour of singing.

"Now I know what Amy meant," Miss Marshall said when they were finished and she was folding the sheets of music neatly on the stand, "when she assured me that no one would notice my accompaniment once you had started to sing. I have never heard a lovelier voice, Miss Allard."

"Well, thank you." Frances smiled warmly at her. "But you are a very accomplished pianist, you know, and need never fear an audience. You have no cause to feel nervous about tomorrow evening, though, do you, when there will be only your family and my great-aunts to hear us. My aunts are quite unthreatening, I do assure you."

She drew on her bonnet and tied the ribbons beneath her chin, taking one last awed look about the ballroom, which would be hidden from view behind panels tomorrow evening. But when Miss Marshall spoke next, it was not to her, she realized.

"How long have *you* been standing there?" she asked. "I thought you were escorting Miss Hunt to Muriel Hemmings's garden party."

She was speaking, of course, to Viscount Sinclair, who was lounging in the doorway of the music room as if he had been there for some time.

"Some cousins arrived from the country," he said, "and the garden party had to be abandoned in favor of entertaining them."

"Well, you might have made your presence known, Luce," his sister said crossly. "Were you *listening*?"

"I was," he admitted. "But if you hit one wrong note, Caroline, I did not hear it. I am certain that Miss Allard did not."

"You must give the order for the panels to be put back between the rooms," she said. "It has been most inconvenient to practice in this space. Miss Allard's voice is more than up to it, though, I might add."

"Yes," he said, pushing himself away from the doorjamb in order to stand upright, "I noticed that too."

Frances did not quite look at him.

"I must go," she said. "I have been here ten minutes longer than I intended to be. Poor Thomas will be tired of waiting for me."

"Poor Thomas is probably sipping his ale by now," Viscount Sinclair said, "if he is capable of driving that carriage at a pace faster than a sedate crawl, that is. I sent him away."

"You did what?" She raised her eyes to his and glared indignantly at him. "Now I will have to *walk* home."

He clucked his tongue. "It is *such* a long way," he said, "especially on a sunny, warm day like this."

He did not understand. She might be *seen* if she wandered the streets of fashionable Mayfair.

"Luce," his sister said severely, "Miss Allard did not bring a maid with her."

"I will escort her," he said.

"I do not need a maid," Frances said. "I am not a girl. And I would not put you to such trouble, Lord Sinclair."

"It will be no trouble at all," he said. "I need the exercise."

What else could she say with Miss Marshall present? He knew very well that she would not make a scene. There was a gleam in his eyes that was beginning to look familiar.

For someone whom she had twice rejected—she, a mere school-teacher—he was being remarkably persistent. But she had known from the start that he was a determined, sometimes belligerent man. And she had learned since that he was impulsive and reckless and not easily persuaded to give up what he had set his mind on.

For some reason he had set his mind on getting her to agree to some sort of relationship with him. Whether it was still marriage she did not know. But it did not matter anyway. She had said no once, and she must continue to say it.

She walked silently beside him down the long, curving stairway to the great hall and the front doors. She must just hope that the streets between Cavendish Square and Portman Street would be deserted this late in the afternoon.

Lucius had been invited to take tea at Berkeley Square with the Balderstons and Portia and the Balderston cousins. But though he might have felt honor bound to attend the garden party since he had said long ago that he would, he felt no such compunction after the plans were changed. He sent a polite excuse and remained at home.

He had been pacing the hallway outside the ballroom—and occasionally standing stock still—since a few minutes after Frances's arrival, which he had observed from an upper window. He could hardly believe what he had heard. He had thought her magnificent at the Reynolds' soiree, but what he had not realized there was that her voice had been on a leash because of the relatively small size of the drawing room.

This afternoon it had been unleashed, though she had kept perfect control over it nevertheless.

Heath's hair was going to do more than stand on end. He would be fortunate indeed if it did not fly right off his head.

But Lucius had not arranged to walk her back to Portman Street only to talk about her singing or quarrel with her. Devil take it, he was in love with the woman and yet he knew so little about her. Not knowing a woman had never seemed important to him before. Women were strange, contrary, irrational, oversensitive people anyway, and he had always been contented to keep his distance from his mother and sisters and never even to try to know or understand the women he bedded. It had never really occurred to him until he thought about it now that he did not know Portia either, although he had been acquainted with her most of his life. It had not seemed to matter—and still did not.

It mattered with Frances.

"This is not the way back to Portman Street," she said as he drew her hand through his arm and set out from Cavendish Square with her.

"There are any number of ways of getting there," he said, "some faster and more direct than others. You are not going to tell me, are you, Frances, that you have so little physical stamina that we must take the shortest route."

"It has nothing to do with stamina," she said. "My great-aunts are expecting me back for tea."

"No, they are not," he said. "I sent back a message with Thomas, informing them that I was taking you for a walk in the park before bringing you home. They will be charmed. They like me."

"You *what*?" She turned an indignant face on him and drew her hand free before he could clamp it to his side. "You had no business sending any message at all, Lord Sinclair. You had no business sending my carriage away. I have no wish to walk in the park. And how conceited of you to believe that my aunts like you. How do you *know* they do?"

"You look lovely when you are angry," he said. "You lose the cool, classical madonna look and become the passionate Italian beauty that you are deep down."

"I am *English*," she said curtly. "And I do not *wish* to go to the park."

"Because it is I who am escorting you?" he asked. "Or because you are not—forgive me—dressed in the first stare of fashion?"

"I care nothing for fashion," she said.

"Then you are very different from any other lady I have ever known," he said. "Or any gentleman, for that matter. We will not take the paths that will be frequented by the fashionable multitude at this hour, Frances. I am too selfish to share you. We will take some shady path and talk. And if you were dressed in rags you would still look more beautiful to me than any other woman I have ever known."

"You mock me, Lord Sinclair," she said, but she fell into step beside him again, her hands clasped firmly at her back. "I do not believe you take life very seriously at all."

"Sometimes it is more amusing not to," he said. "But there are certain things I take very seriously, Frances. I am serious at the moment. I have a hankering to know exactly what it is that I have lost since you will not have me."

That silenced her. She looked up at him with uncomprehending eyes and then dipped her head sharply as two people approached them and then passed with murmured greetings.

"I know a number of facts about you," he said. "I know that your mother was Italian and your father some sort of French nobleman. I know that you are related to Baron Clifton. I know you grew up in London and left it two years after your father's death in order to teach music and French and writing at Miss Martin's school in Bath. I know that you are a very good cook. I know you have one of the loveliest soprano voices—perhaps even *the* loveliest—of our generation. I know other things about your character. I know that you are devoted to duty and can be stubborn and sometimes downright belligerent and also amiable and affectionate to those you love. I know you are sexually passionate. I even know you biblically. But I do not really *know* you at all, do I?"

"You do not need to," she said firmly as they reached a side gate into Hyde Park and entered it and turned onto a narrow, shaded path that ran parallel to the street outside though thick trees hid it from view. "No one can be a totally open book to another person even if there is the intimacy of a close relationship between them."

"And there is no such intimacy between us?" he asked.

"No. Absolutely not."

He wondered how much of a fool he was making of himself. He tried to imagine their roles reversed. What if she had pursued him and twice he had told her quite clearly that he did not want her? How would he feel if she came after him again anyway, maneuvered matters so that she could get him alone, and then demanded to know who he was?

It was an uncomfortable picture.

But what if the signs he had given her were mixed? What if, while his lips had said no, his whole being had said yes?

"Tell me about your childhood," he said.

Good Lord, had he taken leave of his senses? He had never been interested in anyone's *childhood*!

She sighed aloud and for a few moments he thought she was going to keep silent.

"Why not?" she said eventually, as if to herself. "We are taking a very long way home and might as well have *something* to talk about."

He looked down at her. She was dressed in cream-colored muslin, with a plain straw bonnet. She looked quite unfashionable. Yet she looked neat and pretty and adorable. Bars of sunlight and shade danced over her as they walked.

"That is the spirit," he said.

For the first time a smile played about her lips as she glanced up at him.

"It would serve you right," she said, "if I talked for the next several hours without pausing for breath about every single detail I can remember of my childhood."

"It would," he agreed. "But the thing is, Frances, that I doubt I would be bored."

She shook her head.

"It was a happy, secure childhood," she said. "I never knew my mother and so did not miss her. My father was all in all to me, though I was surrounded with nurses and governesses and other servants. I had everything money could buy. But unlike many privileged children, I was not emotionally neglected. My father played with me, read to me, took me about with him, spent hours of every day with me. He encouraged me to read and learn and make music and do and be all I was capable of doing and being. He taught me to reach for the stars and settle for nothing less."

He could have asked her why she had forgotten that particular lesson, but he did not want to argue with her again or cause her to turn silent again.

"You lived in London?" he asked her.

"Most of the time," she said. "I loved it here. There was always somewhere new to go, some other church to admire or museum or art gallery to wander about or market to explore. There was so much history to absorb and so many people to observe. And there were always shops and libraries and tearooms and parks to be taken to. And the river to sail on."

And yet now she shunned London. After Christmas he had been unable to lure her back here even though he had offered her an abundance of luxuries to replace those she seemed to have lost since childhood.

What a comedown it must have been for her to have to remove to Bath to teach—and to wear clothes that were either several years old, like the two evening gowns he had seen her wear, or else inexpensively made like today's muslin.

"But I did go into the country too," she said. "My great-aunts sometimes had me to stay with them. They would have taken me to live when I arrived in England—Great-Aunt Martha was already widowed then. I suppose they thought that a gentleman could not raise a daughter alone, especially in a country that was foreign to him. But though I love them dearly and have always been grateful for the affection they have lavished on me, I am glad my father would not give me up."

"He had ambitions for you as a singer?" he asked, noting again that she dipped her head sharply downward when an elderly couple he did not know strolled past them on the same deserted path as the one he had chosen.

"Dreams more than ambitions," she said. "He would not even hire a singing master for me until I was thirteen, and he would not allow me to sing at any auditions or public concerts even when my singing master said I was ready. It was to wait until I was eighteen, my father said, when my voice would have matured, and even then only if it was what I really wanted for myself. He was very adamant in his belief that a child ought not to be exploited even if she was talented."

"But did he not expect that you would be thinking of marriage at the age of eighteen?" he asked.

"He recognized it as a possibility," she said. "And indeed when Lady Lyle agreed to sponsor my come-out when I was eighteen, he insisted that we postpone doing anything about my music until after the summer was over. By then he was dead of a sudden heart seizure. But he had dreamed for me because he knew I had dreams. He would not have pushed me into anything against my will. That was what my mother's father—my grandfather—had done to her when she was very young."

"Your mother was a singer?" he asked.

"Yes," she said. "In Italy. She was a very good one too, according to my father. He fell in love with her and married her there."

"But did you allow your dream and your ambition to die with your father?" he asked her. "Did you make no attempt to sing at any auditions or to attract any sponsor?" Had not her aunts said that she had had a sponsor and even done some singing in public? "You went to live with Lady Lyle, did you not? Did she not offer you any help?"

"She did." There was a change in her voice. It was tighter, more emotionless. "And I did sing a few times to small audiences. I did not like it. When I saw the advertisement for a teacher at Miss Martin's school in Bath, I applied for it and was offered the position. I have not regretted the decision I made to take it. I have been happy there—oh, *contented,* if you will. But there is nothing wrong with contentment, Lord Sinclair."

Ah. For a while he had felt drawn into her life. She had seemed to enjoy telling her story—there had been a glow in her face, a smile in her eyes, animation in her voice. But she had shut him out again. A lovely young lady who had been brought out under the sponsorship of a baroness must surely have had marriage prospects even if, as Lucius guessed, her father had left her without a penny. But even if there had been no particular beau in her life, there had been the dazzling prospect of an illustrious career as a singer stretching before her. It had been her father's dream and her own for most of her life. Lady Lyle had been prepared to help her.

Yet she had given it all up at the advanced age of twenty?

Something was missing in her story. Something quite momentous, Lucius suspected. Something that was quite possibly the key to the mystery that was Frances Allard.

But she was not going to tell him.

And why should she? She had rejected him at every turn. She owed him nothing.

But someone should have done more for her at the time.

It was not too late, though, for her dream to be reborn.

He taught me to reach for the stars and settle for nothing less.

Tomorrow evening she would touch those stars and even grasp them.

He may have to say good-bye to her again and abide by it this time, but first he would, by Jove, restore her dream to her.

She looked up at him with a half-smile.

"I did not suspect, Lord Sinclair," she said, "that you could be such a good listener."

"That is because you know me as little as I know you, Frances," he said. "There are many things about me that you do not suspect."

"I do not think I dare ask for examples," she said, and actually laughed.

"Because you are afraid that you might grow to like me after all?" he asked her.

She sobered instantly. "I do not dislike you," she said.

"Do you not?" he said. "But you will not marry me?"

"There is no connection between the two," she said. "We cannot marry everyone we like. We would live in a very bigamous society if we did."

"But if two people like each other enough," he said, "a marriage between them stands a better chance of succeeding than if they do not like each other at all. Would you not agree?"

"That," she said, "is rather an absurd question. Will Miss Hunt not have you? Does she not like you?"

"I might have guessed that you would bring the conversation around to Portia," he said, taking her by the elbow and leading her out through the gate at the end of the path they had taken and back out onto the street. He took the most direct route to Portman Street from there. "I take it very unkindly in you, Frances, to have refused me. I have to marry *someone* this year after all, as Portia herself has pointed out to me, and if you will not have me then I suppose I will have to have her. And before you pour scorn upon my head and sympathies upon hers, let me add that she told me with the same breath that she also must marry someone and he might as well be me. There is no sentiment involved on either side, you see, and very little liking either. There is no danger that you would be breaking another woman's heart if you made off with me yourself. Would you care to put the matter to the test?"

"No," she said, "I would not."

"Would you care to explain exactly why, then?" he asked.

It was an ill-mannered question to ask and invited a sharp set-down that could only wound him. However, the question was out and he awaited her answer. It was brief.

"No," she said, "I would not."

"It is not that you do not care for me?" he asked her, taking her elbow again and hurrying her across a road before tossing a coin into
the outstretched hand of a crossing sweeper who had cleared a path
for them.

"I do not wish to answer any more questions," she said. But a few
moments later she spoke again. "Lucius?"

He looked down into her upturned face, jolted as he always was
on the rare occasion when she used his given name.

"Yes?" he said.

"I will come to dinner at Marshall House tomorrow evening," she
said, "and I will sing in the music room afterward for your grandfather and my great-aunts. I will even take pleasure in doing so. But that
must be the end. I shall be returning to Bath within the next two or
three days. It *must* be the end, Lucius. You may not believe that you
will be better off marrying Miss Hunt, but I assure you that you will.
She is of your world, and she has the approval of your family and hers,
I daresay. Affection and even love will grow between you if you try
hard. You must forget about your obsession with me. That is all it is,
you know. You do not *really* love me."

He was furiously angry even before she had finished speaking.
Had they still been in the park he would have lashed out at her. But the
street on which they walked, though not busy, was in constant use.
And who knew how many people lurked within sight or hearing behind the windows of the houses lining the street?

"Thank you," he said curtly. "It is kind of you, Frances, to point
out to me whom I love and whom I will grow to love. It is reassuring
to know that what I feel for you is only an obsession. Knowing that, I
shall recover in a trice. Ha! It is already done. There is your great-
aunts' house just up ahead, ma'am. It has been my pleasure to escort
you home even if the course we took *was* rather too circuitous for
your taste. I shall look forward to seeing you tomorrow evening.
Good day to you."

"Lucius—" She was looking up at him with stricken eyes.

"On the whole, ma'am," he said, "I believe I prefer *Lord Sinclair*.
The other suggests an intimacy between us that I no longer cultivate."

"Oh," she said. "Oh."

He rapped on the door knocker for her and executed an elegant bow when it opened almost immediately. He did not watch her step inside. He turned and strode down the street.

He felt thunderous.

He felt murderous.

You must forget about your obsession with me.

He ground his teeth.

That is all it is, you know. You do not really love me.

Would to God she were right!

But sometimes, he thought, love could feel remarkably like hatred.

This was one of those times.

20

Mrs. Melford and Miss Driscoll arrived promptly at Marshall House the following evening with their great-niece and were received graciously in the drawing room by Viscountess Sinclair, to whom the Earl of Edgecombe presented them.

"I have, I believe, met you before, Mrs. Melford," she said, "and you too, Miss Driscoll. It was many years ago, though, when my husband was still alive. And you are Miss Allard." She smiled at Frances. "We have heard much about you and are greatly looking forward to hearing you sing after dinner. And I must thank you for being so kind to Amy when she was in Bath. It irks her to be the youngest in the family and to have to wait another year for her come-out."

"She entertained me most graciously when I took tea at Brock Street, ma'am," Frances assured her. "I was made to feel quite at home."

There were nine people gathered in the drawing room, she had noted—rather more than she had expected. That made twelve altogether. But that fact surely could not account for the nervousness she felt. Or perhaps *nervousness* was the wrong word. She had not slept well last night or been able to settle to any activity today. The anger with which Viscount Sinclair had parted from her after escorting her home had bothered her ever since. For the first time she had been forced to consider the possibility that he really did have deep feelings for her, that his pursuit of her was not motivated merely by lust or thwarted will or impulse.

She could not escape the conclusion that he had been *hurt* yesterday.

And she was sorry then that she had not simply told him the whole story of her life. It could not matter now, could it? And it would have finally deterred him, shown him that a marriage between them was quite impossible.

The viscountess presented everyone to the new arrivals. The pretty, fair-haired young lady with the dimple in her left cheek when she smiled was Miss Emily Marshall. The earnest young gentleman with spectacles pinching the bridge of his nose was Sir Henry Cobham, Caroline Marshall's betrothed. The other couple were Lord and Lady Tait. From her resemblance to Emily Marshall, Frances guessed that Lady Tait was an older sister.

The evening proceeded well enough after the introductions had been made. Frances avoided Viscount Sinclair, a task made somewhat easier by the fact that he seemed equally intent upon avoiding her. She sat between Mr. Cobham and Lord Tait at dinner and found them both easy conversationalists. Her great-aunts were both in good spirits and clearly enjoying themselves.

All that remained to do, Frances thought as the meal drew to an end and she watched for Lady Sinclair to give the signal for the ladies to withdraw and leave the gentlemen to their port—all that remained to do was sing for the pleasure of the earl and her aunts, and then they could take their leave and the whole ordeal would be over.

Tomorrow, or more probably the next day, she would return to Bath. And this time she was going to immerse herself fully in her life there and her work as a teacher. She was going to forget about Mr. Blake—it was unfair to try to force herself into welcoming his interest when she felt no regard for him beyond a mild gratitude. She was going to forget about beaux altogether.

Most of all, she was going to forget about Lucius Marshall, Viscount Sinclair.

She thought about the music she would sing and tried to get her mind prepared. Her only wish was that she could sing in the drawing room rather than in the music room. The latter seemed just a little too magnificently formal for a relatively small family entertainment. However, she supposed it would look different with the panels shutting it off from the vaster ballroom.

"Miss Allard," the earl said suddenly, addressing her along the length of the table, "it has seemed in the last few days that it would be just too selfish to keep your performance all to ourselves. And so Lucius has invited some friends to join us after dinner in order to listen to you. We considered that the surprise would please you. I hope it does."

Some friends.

Frances froze.

She did indeed mind. She minded very much.

This was London.

"How splendid!" Great-Aunt Martha exclaimed. "And how very thoughtful of you both." She beamed first at the earl and then at the viscount. "*Of course* Frances does not mind. Do you, my love?"

How many were *some*? Frances wondered. And who *were* they?

But her aunts, she could see, were fair to bursting with pride and happiness. And the earl could not have looked more pleased with himself if he had been holding out to her the gift of a diamond necklace on a velvet cushion.

"I will be honored, my lord," she said.

Perhaps *some* meant only two or three. Perhaps they would all be strangers. Surely they would, in fact. She had not been here in three years.

"I knew you would be pleased," the earl said, rubbing his hands together with satisfaction. "But the honor is all ours, I assure you, ma'am. Now. You will not wish to be fussed with having to be sociable to other guests for the next little while. You will wish to relax quietly before you sing. Lucius will escort you to the drawing room while the rest of us proceed to the music room. Lucius?"

"Certainly, sir." Viscount Sinclair got up from his place farther along the table and extended an arm as Frances rose from her place. "We will join you in half an hour?"

Frances set a hand on his sleeve.

The dining room and drawing room were not on the same floor as the music room. No particularly noticeable sounds were coming up from below. Nevertheless, Frances had an uneasy feeling that there *would* be sounds—of people—if only they were to descend the staircase.

"How many people are some friends?" she asked.

"Already, Frances," he said, opening the door into the drawing room and ushering her inside, "you are sounding annoyed."

"Already?" she said, turning to face him. "I will be even more so, then, when I know the answer?"

"There are people with a quarter of your talent who would kill for the sort of opportunity with which you are to be presented tonight," he said.

Her eyes widened.

"Then give the opportunity to *them*," she said, "and save them from having to commit murder."

He cocked one eyebrow.

"And *what* sort of opportunity?" she demanded to know.

"I daresay you have not heard of Lord Heath," he said.

She stared mutely. Everyone had heard of Lord Heath—everyone who was musically inclined, anyway.

"He is a renowned connoisseur and patron of music," he explained. "He can promote your career as no one else in London can, Frances."

That was what her father had once said. He had been planning to bring her to the baron's attention, though he had said that it would be very difficult to do since everyone with even a modicum of musical talent was forever pestering him to listen.

"I *have* a career," she said, "and you have taken me away from it in the middle of a term under largely false pretenses. I will be returning to it within the next day or two. I need no patron. I have an *employer*— Miss Martin."

"Sit down and relax," he told her. "If you work yourself into a fit of the vapors, you will not be able to sing your best."

"How many, Lord Sinclair?" she asked him.

"I am not sure I can give you an exact number," he said, "without going along to the music room and doing a head count."

"How *many*? *Approximately* how many?"

He shrugged. "You should be glad," he said. "This is the chance for which you have waited too long. You admitted to me yesterday that this was both your dream and your father's."

"Leave my father out of this!" She suddenly felt cold about the heart and sat down abruptly on the closest chair. She had had a ghastly thought. "The panels that divide the music room from the ballroom had been removed yesterday. Your sister drew your attention to the fact and reminded you to have them put back in place. Has it been done?"

"Actually no," he said. He strolled to the fireplace and stood with his back to it, watching her.

"*Why* not?"

Dear God, the combined rooms would make a sizable concert hall. Surely that was not—

"You are going to be magnificent tonight, Frances," he told her. His hands were clasped at his back. He was looking at her with an intensity that might have disconcerted her under other circumstances.

Yes, that *was* the intention, she realized. The panels between the two rooms had been removed deliberately because the audience was expected to be too large for the music room alone. And they had done it—*he* had done it—without consulting her.

Just as he had brought her to London by trickery, without consulting her wishes.

"I ought to walk out of here right now," she said. "I *would* if doing so would not make my great-aunts appear foolish."

"And if it would not disappoint my grandfather," he said.

"Yes."

She glared at him. He stared back, tight-jawed.

"Frances," he said after a few moments of hostile silence, "what are you afraid of? Failing? It will not happen, I promise you."

"You are nothing but a meddler," she said bitterly. "An arrogant meddler, who is forever convinced that only he knows what I ought to be doing with my life. You *knew* I did not wish to return to London, yet you maneuvered matters so that I would come anyway. You *knew* I did not want to sing before any large audience, especially here, but you have gathered a large audience anyway and made it next to impossible for me to refuse to sing before it. You *knew* I did not wish to see you again, but you totally ignored my wishes. I think you really do imagine that you care for me, but you are wrong. You do not manipulate someone you care for or go out of your way to make her miserable. You care for no one but yourself. You are a tyrant, Lord Sinclair—the worst type of bully."

He had, she thought, turned pale while she spoke. Certainly his expression had grown hard and shuttered. He turned abruptly to stare down into the unlit coals in the fireplace.

"And you, Frances," he said after long moments of uncomfortable silence, "do not know the meaning of the word *trust*. I have no quarrel with your choosing to teach rather than sing. Why should I? You are free to choose your own course in life. But I do need to understand your reason for doing so—and there *is* a reason beyond simple preference or even simple poverty. I have no real quarrel with your refusal to come to London with me after Christmas or to marry me when I asked you a little over a month ago. I do *not* consider myself God's gift to women, and I do not expect every woman to fall head over ears in love with me—even those who have bedded with me. But I need to understand the reason for your refusal, since I do not believe it is aversion or even indifference. You will not trust me with your reasons. You will not trust me with *yourself*."

She was too angry to feel renewed regret that she had not been more open with him yesterday.

"I do not *have* to," she cried. "I am under no compulsion to confide in you or any man. Why should I? You are nothing to me. And I am certain of only one thing in this life, and that is that I may trust myself. I will not let *myself* down."

He turned to look at her, all signs of humor and mockery wiped from his face.

"Are you sure of that?" he asked her. "Are you sure you have not already done so?"

She understood suddenly—she supposed she had known it all along—why she had been able to contemplate a future with Mr. Blake but not with Lucius Marshall. Beyond a full confession about her past, including what had happened just after Christmas, she would not have had to share anything of her deepest self with Mr. Blake—not ever. Some instinct told her that. Courtesy and gentility and certain shared interests and friends would have taken them through life together quite contentedly. With Lucius she would have to share her very soul—and he his. Nothing else would ever do between them—she had been wrong yesterday about open books. As a very young woman she might have risked opening up to him—indeed she would have welcomed such a prospect. Young people tended to dream of the sort of love and passion that would burn hot and bright throughout a lifetime and even beyond the grave.

Although she was only twenty-three she shrank from the prospect of such a relationship now—and yearned toward it too.

She remembered their night together with sudden, unbidden clarity and closed her eyes.

"I will come to escort you to the music room in twenty minutes' time," he said. "It is a concert I have arranged for you, Frances. There will be other performers, but you will be last, as is only fitting. No one would wish to have to follow you. I will leave you alone to compose yourself."

He crossed the room with long strides, not looking at her. But he paused with his hand on the doorknob.

"If you ask it of me when I return," he said, "or even now, I will take you home to Portman Street. I will find some excuse to make to the guests in the music room. I am endlessly inventive when I need to be."

He waited, as if for her answer, but she made none. He let himself quietly out of the room and closed the door behind him.

It was a miracle beyond hoping for, Frances supposed, that there would be no one in the music room and ballroom who would recognize her. Strangely, the realization made her feel almost calm—resigned to her fate. There was nothing she could do about it now. She could leave the house, of course—she could do it without even waiting for Lucius's return. But she knew she would not do that.

The Earl of Edgecombe would be disappointed.

Her great-aunts would be upset and humiliated.

And somewhere deep within her there was a more selfish reason for staying.

A lifelong dream was being painfully reborn.

He had not answered her question about the size of the audience. But he had not needed to. She knew that it must be large. Why else would the panels between the music room and the ballroom have been removed? Even the music room itself was a fair-sized room and must be capable of seating a few dozen people. But it was not large enough for tonight's audience.

And one member of that large audience was to be Lord Heath. How proud her father would be if he could know that!

The artist in her, the performer who had grown up dreaming of singing in public, yearned to sing tonight regardless of the consequences.

A painter, after all, did not paint a canvas and then cover it with a sheet so that no one would see it. A writer did not write a book and set it on a shelf beneath other books so that no one would ever read it. A householder, as the biblical story would have it, did not light a lamp and set it beneath a basket so that it would give no light to those within the house.

She had not even realized fully during her years of teaching how much she had repressed her natural instinct to sing so that others would hear.

He taught me to reach for the stars and settle for nothing less.
Papa!

Well, tonight she would sing, both for him and for herself.

And tomorrow she would make arrangements to return to Bath.

* * *

Lucius's intention when he left the music room was to creep off to his own room to sulk in private for twenty minutes—or to storm at the four walls in righteous fury. But he had the niggling suspicion that his thoughts would be more than a little disturbing if he went somewhere where he would have nothing else to do but allow them to rattle about in his head and clamor accusingly at him.

A meddler.

A tyrant.

A bully.

You do not manipulate someone you care for or go out of your way to make her miserable.

Damnation!

His next instinct was to stalk off to the music room and shoo everyone out of the house. There must be a dozen and one other entertainments for them to take themselves off to, after all—there always were during the Season. But though he was frequently impulsive and even reckless, he was almost never bad-mannered—not on such a colossal scale, anyway. Besides, this was not his house. And his grandfather had looked forward so much to this evening.

What he actually ended up doing was going to the music room to see who had come and to make himself agreeable. And it looked, he thought as soon as he walked into the room, as if everyone he had asked had come—and that was actually a vast number of people. The music room was crowded. So was the ballroom, though admittedly many people had not yet taken their seats but were milling about making a great deal of noise.

He greeted Baron Heath and his wife and showed them to the seats in the front row that had been reserved for them. He exchanged pleasantries with a number of friends and acquaintances. He made a point of welcoming Lady Lyle and assured her that she was going to particularly enjoy the concert. When she looked slightly mystified, he smiled at her and told her that she would see what he meant soon enough.

He made his way toward Portia Hunt and the Balderstons and realized with something of a grimace that this was the first time he had given them a thought all evening. The Marquess of Godsworthy, he noticed, was in conversation with his grandfather.

"This is very pleasant," Lady Balderston said. "A concert at Marshall House is an unusual treat."

"It will be the *best* treat, ma'am," Lucius assured her.

"Caroline told me that the schoolteacher from Bath is to sing," Portia said. "Is it wise, Lucius? The audience here is likely to be far superior in taste to what she is accustomed to."

"Miss Allard was not *born* a schoolteacher, Portia," he told her. "Nor was she born in Bath. She grew up here in London as a matter of fact and had the best of singing masters."

"One can only hope," she said, "that those seated at the back will be able to hear her. Forgive me, Lucius, but your mama is busy with the guests. Is she aware that Amy is here?"

"There is not much concerning her daughters of which my mother is unaware," he said. "Amy is a member of this family, and this is a family evening that has been opened up to our friends."

He nodded amiably and walked away before he could start feeling irritable again. He already felt a number of negative things without adding irritability to the list.

The other entertainers had already arrived, and more and more of the members of the audience were taking their seats. There was nothing worse than concerts that started late. It was time to fetch Frances.

She would have his head on a platter when she saw the size of the audience, he thought as he made his way back up to the drawing room. For some reason that escaped his understanding she had given up her dream three years ago and was more than reluctant to take it up again.

A meddler. A tyrant. A bully.

Well, he was guilty as charged, he supposed. Better to be a meddler than a milksop. He had always met life head-on. He was not likely to change at this late date.

She was standing by the window, her back to the room, looking out into the heavy dusk. She looked very straight-backed, but when she turned at the sound of the door, he could see that her face and general demeanor were calm and composed.

He was, he realized, in the presence of the consummate professional. She had been taken by surprise and she had not liked it one bit, but she was now ready to sing.

"Shall we go?" he asked.

She crossed the room without a word and took his offered arm.

It was perhaps, he thought, the last time he would walk anywhere with Frances Allard. She did not want him—or rather she would not have him. And it was time he gave up the pursuit. After tonight she would have a clear choice—he was convinced of that. She could return to Bath or she could put herself into Heath's hands and forge a new and glorious career.

At least he had arranged matters so that she would have that choice. But he would meddle no more.

If proving his love for her meant letting her go, then he would do it.

It would be the hardest thing he had ever done, though. Passivity did not come naturally to him.

Frances paused when they reached the doorway into the music room and her hand tightened slightly on his sleeve.

"Ah," she said softly, "so this is what *some friends* look like."

There was no question in her words. He did not offer any answer but led her to the empty seat between her great-aunts in the front row.

"Is this not a delightful surprise, dearest?" Miss Driscoll asked her as she seated herself.

"You are not too dreadfully nervous, my love?" Mrs. Melford asked.

Lucius moved away to take his own place on the other side of the center aisle. But everyone was seated, he had seen. And a near hush had fallen at his appearance. He stood again, welcomed everyone, and introduced the first performer of the evening, a violinist of his acquaintance who had been enjoying some success in Vienna and other parts of the Continent during the past year.

His performance was flawless and well received by the audience.

So was that of the pianist who followed him and that of the harpist who followed her. But it was hard for Lucius to concentrate. Frances's turn was next.

Had he made a dreadful error in judgment?

He did not doubt that she would acquit herself well, but . . . Would she ever forgive him?

But, devil take it, *someone* had to shake her out of her torpor.

He got to his feet to introduce her.

"My grandfather and my youngest sister and I attended a soiree in Bath several weeks ago," he said, "at which there was musical entertainment. It was there, as part of that entertainment, that we heard for the first time a voice my grandfather still describes as the most glorious soprano voice he has heard in almost eighty years of listening. It was a voice we felt both honored and privileged to hear. Tonight we will hear it again, as will you. Ladies and gentlemen, Miss Frances Allard."

There was polite applause as Frances got to her feet and Caroline took her place at the pianoforte and spread out sheets of music on the stand.

Frances looked slightly pale but as composed as she had been in the drawing room. She looked calmly at the audience and then lowered her head and even closed her eyes for a few moments. She was, Lucius could see while a hush fell in the combined rooms, filling her lungs slowly with air and then releasing it.

Then she opened her eyes and nodded to Caroline.

She had chosen "Let the Bright Seraphim" from Handel's *Sampson,* an ambitious piece for trumpet and soprano. There was no trumpet, of course, only the pianoforte and her voice.

And so her voice became the trumpet, soaring through the intricate runs and trills of the music, filling both rooms with pure sound, which was never shrill, which never overpowered the space or overwhelmed the listeners. Voice, music, space—all were one glorious, perfect blend.

"Let the bright Seraphim in burning row, their loud, uplifted angel trumpets blow."

She looked at the audience as she sang. She sang to them and for them, involving them all in the triumph of the lyrics and the brilliance of the music. And yet it was clear that this was no mere performance to her. This time—and for the first time—Lucius could *see* her as she sang, and it was clear to him that she was deep in the world of the music, creating it anew with every note she sang.

He was in that world with her.

So immersed was he, in fact, that he started with surprise when a loud and prolonged applause followed the song. Belatedly he joined in, his throat and chest constricted with what could only be unshed tears.

To say that he was proud of her would be an imposition. He had no *right* to claim any such feelings. What he felt was . . . joy. Joy in the music, joy for her, joy for himself that he was part of the experience.

And then, even more belatedly, he realized that he should have stood and made some comment and asked for another song. But it was unnecessary to do so. The applause had died away, to be succeeded by a few shushing noises as Caroline spread out another sheet of music and awaited the signal to begin playing.

Frances sang "I Know That My Redeemer Liveth."

What had been pure brilliance in the first piece became sheer raw emotion in the second. Before she had finished Lucius was blinking back tears, totally unaware of the ignominy of weeping in public at a mere musical performance. She sang it better than she had the last time, if that was possible. But the last time, of course, he had had to fight distractions in order to hear her.

He was on his feet even before the final note had died away, though he did not immediately applaud. He watched her, tall and regal and beautiful, stay in the world of the music until the last echo of sound had died away.

During the timeless moment between the last bar of music and the first sounds of applause, Lucius knew beyond all doubt that Frances Allard was the woman he would love deep in his soul for the rest of his life even if he never saw her again after tonight. And, despite everything, despite all she had accused him of earlier in the drawing room, he was not sorry for what he had done.

By God, he was not sorry. He would do it all again.

And *she* would never be sorry. She could surely never *ever* regret tonight.

Finally she smiled and turned to indicate Caroline, who really had done a superb job at the pianoforte. Both of them bowed, and Lucius stood beaming at both, happier than he could ever remember feeling in his life.

It was impossible in that moment not to believe in happy endings.

21

Frances was happy. Consciously, gloriously happy.

She was where she belonged—she knew that. And she was doing what she knew she had been born to do.

She was filled to the brim and overflowing with happiness.

And instinctively, without thought, she turned as the applause gradually died down to smile at Lucius, standing in the front row, beaming back at her with what she could not avoid seeing was pride and an answering happiness.

And surely more than that.

How foolish she had been! From almost the first moment of their acquaintance she had been given the chance to reach for the stars, to risk all for the vividness of life—for passion and for love itself. And then for music too.

She had chosen not to take the risk.

And so he had taken it for her.

She felt a rush of love so intense that it fairly robbed her of breath.

But the Earl of Edgecombe was making his way toward her. He took her right hand there in front of everyone, bowed over it, and raised it to his lips.

"Miss Frances Allard," he said, addressing the audience. "Remember the name, my friends. One day soon you will boast of having heard her here before she became famous."

The concert was over then, and there was the buzz of conversation as some people rose from their places and a line of footmen appeared at the ballroom doors, bearing trays of food and drink to set on the white-clothed tables at the back.

But Frances was not left unattended even though the earl turned away to speak with her great-aunts. Viscount Sinclair stepped up to take his place. He was looking wary again.

"There are no words, Frances," he said. "There simply are no words."

She wanted to weep then. But his mother had come forward too, and she actually hugged Frances.

"Miss Allard," she said. "I have been to heaven and back this evening. My father-in-law and Lucius and Amy did not exaggerate when they spoke so glowingly of your talent. Thank you for coming here to sing to us."

Lord Tait bowed and Lady Tait beamed and said she could not agree more with her mama. Emily Marshall linked an arm through Caroline's and then smiled at Frances.

"I heard you, Caroline," she said, "and you did superlatively well. But Grandpapa was right. One day I will be able to boast that *my sister* accompanied Miss Allard during her first concert in London."

Amy, sparkling with enthusiasm, hugged Frances too.

"And *I* shall be able to boast to everyone I know that you were my special friend before I was even out," she said.

Frances laughed. It did not escape her notice that she was surrounded by Lucius's family, and that they were all looking on her with approval. It was a precious moment that she knew she would look back upon with pleasure.

And then they all stepped aside as another lady and gentleman came forward. Lord Sinclair performed the introductions. But Frances had seen the gentleman before. He was Lord Heath. She curtsied to him and Lady Heath.

"Miss Allard," he said, "I hold one concert each year around Christmas time, as perhaps you know, at which I gather together for the delight of my friends and carefully chosen guests the very best musical talent I can attract from all over England and the Continent. I wish you will allow me to make an exception to my usual rule and arrange an additional musical evening now, during the Season, with you as the sole performer. I do assure you that everyone who has heard you tonight will wish to do so again. And word will spread like the proverbial wildfire. There will not be enough room in my house for those who will wish to attend."

"Perhaps, then, Roderick," Lady Heath said, laying a hand on his sleeve and looking at Frances with smiling eyes, "you should consider hiring a concert hall for the occasion."

"Brilliant, Fanny!" he said. "It shall be done. Miss Allard, I need only your word of agreement. I can make you great in no time at all. No, let me correct that ridiculous assertion. You do not need me for that—you already *are* great. But I can make you the most sought-after soprano in Europe, I make bold to claim, if you will put yourself into my hands. I must enjoy this feeling of slight power while I may, though. It will not last long. Very soon you will not need either my patronage or anyone else's."

His words served up with them a healthy dose of reality.

It was too much to bear. Too much light had come flooding into her life in too short a time. She felt a desperate need to take a step back, to hold up a staying hand, to *think*. She would have given anything at that moment, she felt, to have seen the calm, sensible face of Claudia Martin in the crowd nearby. She longed for Anne and Susanna.

She was aware at the same time of Viscount Sinclair beside her, silent and tense, his eyes burning into her.

"Thank you, Lord Heath," she said. "I am deeply honored. But I am a teacher. I teach music among other subjects at a girls' school in Bath. It is my chosen career, and even now I long to get back to my pupils, who need me, and to my fellow teachers, who are my dearest friends. I love singing for my own satisfaction. Occasionally I enjoy singing for an audience, even one as large as this. But I do not wish to make a career of it."

There was certainly truth in what she said. Not the whole truth, perhaps, but . . .

"I am sorry to hear it, ma'am," Lord Heath said. "*Very* sorry indeed. I am afraid I misunderstood, though. When Sinclair invited me here tonight, I thought it was at your request. I thought you wished to be promoted. If you do not, I understand. I have a stepson with an extraordinarily sweet voice, but my wife keeps a very firm rein on my ambitions for him. Quite rightly so—he is a child. I respect your decision, but if you should ever change your mind, you may call upon me at any time. I have been exceedingly well blessed to have heard the purest of boy soprano voices and now the most glorious of female soprano voices all within five months."

Frances looked up at Lord Sinclair after they had moved away.

"I may yet find myself shaking you until your teeth rattle, Frances," he said.

"Because I do not share your ambitions for me?" she asked him.

"Because you *do*," he retorted. "But I am not going to argue with you anymore. I am not going to manipulate or bully you ever again, you will be delighted to know. After tonight you will be free of me."

She would have reached out and set a hand on his sleeve then, though with what motive she did not know, but other people crowded about, wishing to talk with her, congratulate her, and praise her performance. Frances smiled and tried to give herself up to the mere pleasure of the moment.

And there *was* pleasure. There was no point in denying it. There was something warm and wonderful about knowing that what one did, what one *loved* doing, had entertained other people and more than entertained them in a number of cases. Several people told her that her singing had moved them, even to tears.

And then some of her pleasure was dashed as Viscount Sinclair presented her to Lord and Lady Balderston and the young lady with them.

"Miss Portia Hunt," he said.

Ah.

She was exquisitely lovely, with the perfect type of English rose beauty that Frances had always envied when she was growing up until she realized that she could never be like it herself. And in addition to her loveliness, Miss Hunt displayed an excellent taste in clothing and a perfect poise and dignity of manner.

How could any man look at her and not love her?

How could *Lucius* . . .

Miss Hunt's smile was gracious and refined.

"That was a very commendable performance, Miss Allard," she said. "The headmistress and teachers at your school must be proud indeed of you. Your pupils are fortunate to have you as their teacher."

She spoke with well-mannered condescension—that latter fact was immediately apparent.

"Thank you," Frances said. "I am honored to have the opportunity to shape the minds and talents of the young."

"Lucius," Miss Hunt said, turning to him, "I shall take the liberty of accompanying Amy upstairs to her room now that the concert has ended."

Lucius. She called him *Lucius*. And clearly she was familiar with the family and with Marshall House. She was going to *marry* him, after all. He might deny it, clinging to the strict truth of the fact that he was not betrothed to her yet, but here was reality right before Frances's eyes.

And did it matter?

"You must not trouble yourself, Portia," he told her. "My mother will send her to bed when she thinks the time appropriate."

Miss Hunt smiled again before turning away to join her parents, who were now talking with Lady Sinclair. But the smile, Frances noticed, did not quite reach her eyes.

Frances turned to Lord Sinclair to find him looking back at her with one eyebrow cocked.

"One of those excruciating moments sprung to life from one's worst nightmare," he said. "But behold me still alive and standing at the end of it."

He was speaking, she supposed, of the fact that she and Miss Hunt had come face-to-face.

"She is lovely," she said.

"She is *perfect*." His other eyebrow rose to join the first. "But the trouble is, Frances, that I am not and have never wanted to be. Perfection is an infernal thing. *You* are far from perfect."

She laughed despite herself and would have turned away then to join her great-aunts, but two more people were approaching, and she turned to them, still smiling.

Ah!

The gentleman, who was ahead of the lady, still looked boyishly handsome with his baby-blond hair and blue eyes and rather round face. He also looked somewhat pale, his eyes slightly wounded.

"Françoise," he said with eyes only for her. "Françoise Halard."

She had known before she entered the music room on Lord Sinclair's arm that something like this might happen. She even remembered thinking that it would be a minor miracle if it did not. But from the moment she had started singing until now she had forgotten her fears—and her knowledge that she ought not to be here.

But here was the very person she had most wished to avoid seeing—unless that honor fell to the woman behind him.

"Charles," she said and extended one hand to him. He took it and bowed over it, but he did not carry it to his lips or retain it in his own.

"You know the Earl of Fontbridge, then?" Lord Sinclair asked as Frances felt that she was looking down a long, dark tunnel at the man she had once loved and come close to marrying over three years ago. "And the countess, his mother?"

She turned her eyes on the woman standing behind him. The Countess of Fontbridge was as large and as formidable as ever, almost dwarfing her son, though more by her girth and the force of her presence than by her height.

"Lady Fontbridge," she said.

"Mademoiselle Halard." The countess did not even try to hide the hostility from her face or the harshness from her voice. "I see you have returned to London. When you decide to give a concert in future, Sinclair, you may wish to divulge the identity of those persons who are to perform for your guests so that they may make an informed decision about whether it is worth attending or not. Though on this occasion it is altogether possible that my son and I would not have understood that Miss Frances Allard was the same person as the Mademoiselle Françoise Halard with whom we once had an unfortunate acquaintance."

"Françoise," the earl said, gazing at her as if he had not even heard what his mother had just said, "where have you *been*? Did your disappearance have something to do with—"

But his mother had laid a firm hand on his arm. "Come, Charles," she said. "We are expected elsewhere. Good evening to you, Sinclair."

She pointedly ignored Frances.

Charles bent one lingering, wounded look upon Frances before submitting to being led away by the countess, whose hair plumes nodded indignantly above her head as she swept from the room without looking to left or right.

"Your own excruciating little moment sprung to life from nightmare, Frances?" Viscount Sinclair asked. "Or should I say *Françoise*? I take it Fontbridge is a discarded lover from your past?"

"I had better leave," she said. "I daresay my aunts are ready to go. It has been a busy evening for them."

"Ah, yes, run away," he said. "It is what you do best, Frances. But first perhaps I can cheer you up a little. Let me take you to Lady Lyle."

"*She* is here?" Frances actually found herself laughing. All she needed to complete the disaster of the evening now was to find that George Ralston was here too.

"I thought that she would like to hear you," he said. "And that you would like to see her once more. I invited her to come."

"Did you?" She smiled up at him. "Did you really? Do you not suppose I would have called upon Lady Lyle before now if I had wished for a tender reunion with her?"

He sighed out loud.

"I remember," he said, "that on a certain snowy road several months ago I informed you that you were going to have to ride up with me in my carriage and you gave me a flat refusal. At that moment, Frances, I made the greatest mistake of my life. I gave in to a chivalrous impulse, albeit grudgingly, and stayed to argue. I ought to have driven away and left you to your fate."

"Yes," she said, "you ought. And I ought to have stuck with my first decision."

"We have been the plague of each other's lives ever since," he said.

"*You* have been the plague of *mine*," she said.

"And you have been nothing but sweetness and light to me, I suppose," he said.

"I have never wanted to be anything at all to you," she told him. "I have always been firm on that."

"Except on one memorable night," he said, "when you joined your body with mine three separate times, Frances. I do not believe it was ravishment."

Oh, goodness, she thought, they were quarreling in full sight of a whole ballroomful of people. And she had just spotted Lady Lyle, sitting slightly apart from everyone else just inside the ballroom. She was looking as elegant as ever, her distinctive silver hair piled high and decorated with plumes. She was also looking slightly amused, her eyes fixed upon Frances.

"I have no wish to speak with Lady Lyle," Frances said. "And I have no wish to remain here any longer. I am going to join my great-aunts now. Thank you for what you tried to do for me this evening, Lord Sinclair. I realize that you thought it would please me, and for a while it really did. But I am going to go back to Bath within the next few days. This is good-bye."

"Again?" One of his eyebrows lifted once more and he smiled. But for all that, she thought, there was a certain bleakness in his eyes—a bleakness that was echoed in her heart. "Does this not become a little tedious, Frances?"

She could have reminded him that it would not have been necessary this time if he had left well enough alone and not suggested that Great-Aunt Martha summon her to London, supposedly to Great-Aunt Gertrude's deathbed.

"Good-bye," she said, and realized only when the word was out that she had whispered it.

He nodded his head a few times and then turned abruptly to stride away into the ballroom.

Frances watched him go and wondered if this now finally was the end.

But how could it *not* be?

The Countess of Fontbridge knew that she had come back to London.

So did Charles.

And so did Lady Lyle.

It would not take long for George Ralston to discover it too.

All she was left to hope for was that Bath would still be a safe enough refuge.

22

Lucius fully intended to honor his vow to let Frances go this time. He had made his feelings and intentions clear to her, he had done his utmost to get her to admit that she was not indifferent to him, he had even tried to be selfless and further the singing career that ought to have been hers a long time ago even if he could not at the same time further any romance between them.

But she had remained stubborn.

He had no choice but to let her go—unless he was prepared to make even more of an ass of himself than he already had.

He was simply going to have to keep himself busy with wedding plans.

His own, perish the thought.

When he sat through an afternoon visit with Portia and her mama, however, the very day after the concert, he found himself feeling trapped rather than joyful or even resigned. He had just brought Amy home from a visit to the Tower of London and had poked his head around the door of the drawing room to inform his mother that he did not expect to be home for dinner.

A moment later he cursed himself for not checking with the servants to see if anyone was with her. But curses, even silent ones, were now pointless. There they all were—his mother, Margaret, Caroline, and Emily, with Lady Balderston and Portia. If Tait had not been there too, looking hopefully toward the door as if for rescue, Lucius might have withdrawn after a brief exchange of pleasantries. But he did not have the heart to abandon his brother-in-law to his lonely fate.

And so two minutes later he was sitting on a sofa beside Portia, a cup of tea in his hands.

It seemed that he had interrupted a lengthy discussion on bonnets. He exchanged an almost imperceptible grimace with Tait as it resumed.

But Portia turned to him after everything that could possibly be said on the subject had been said.

"Mama has explained to Lady Sinclair that it really was a mistake to allow Amy to attend the concert here last evening," she said.

"Indeed?" Instant irritation set in.

"The whole thing was a mistake, in fact," she continued, "and will doubtless be an embarrassment to you for the next few days. But I daresay you did not know, and that must be your defense. It will be my defense on your behalf. Mistakes need not be quite disastrous, though, unless we refuse to learn from them. I am assured that you will learn caution, Lucius, especially when you have someone with a more level head to advise you."

He was looking at her with both eyebrows raised. What the deuce was she talking about? And was she offering her level head as his future adviser? But of course she was. She was not offering, though—she was *assuming*.

"In future you must choose the musical talent at your concerts with greater care," she said kindly. "You ought to have checked Miss Allard's credentials more carefully, Lucius, though one really ought to be able to assume that a schoolteacher is respectable. Mama and Papa and I certainly made that assumption when we condescended to seek an introduction to her."

Everyone was listening, of course. But they seemed to be content to allow Portia to do the talking.

Lucius's eyes narrowed. Irritation was no longer an option. He had moved beyond it to something more dangerous. But he kept his feelings leashed.

"And what exactly is it, Portia," he asked, "that makes Miss Allard *un*respectable? What sort of gossip have you been listening to?"

"I really do not believe, Lord Sinclair," Lady Balderston said, her voice stiff with suppressed indignation, "we can ever be accused of being vulgar enough to listen to *gossip*. We heard it from Lady Lyle's own lips last evening, and Lady Lyle was once kind and misguided enough to give a home to that French girl, who is now trying to pass herself off as an Englishwoman."

"And *this*," Lucius said, raising his eyebrows, "is Miss Allard's sin, ma'am? That some people pronounce her name *Halard*? That she had a French father—and an Italian mother? She was planted here as a baby, perhaps, so that she might grow into a French spy? How exciting that would be! Perhaps we should dash off to capture her and drag her in chains to the Tower of London to await her fate."

Tait turned a snort of laughter into a throat-clearing exercise.

"Lucius," his mother said, "this is hardly the time for levity."

"Did someone say it was, then?" he asked, turning his eyes on her and noticing that Emily beyond her was regarding him with dancing eyes and her dimple in full view.

"I like the French pronunciation of her name," Caroline said, "and wonder that she changed it."

"The truth is, Lucius," Portia said, "that Lady Lyle was compelled to turn Miss Allard out of her home because she was consorting with the wrong people and singing at private parties no respectable lady should even *know* about, let alone attend, and building a scandalous reputation. Who knows what else she was involved in."

"Portia, my love," her mother said, "it is better not to talk of such things."

"It is painful to do so, Mama," Portia admitted. "But it is necessary that Lucius know how perilously close he brought Lady Sinclair and his sisters to scandal last evening. The truth must be broken very gently to Lord Edgecombe, who is resting in his bed this afternoon. We will rely upon the discretion of Lady Lyle to tell no one else what she told us. And *we* will certainly not spread the word. She swore us to secrecy, but we would not dream of saying anything to anyone anyway."

"She swore you to secrecy." Lucius's eyes had narrowed again.

"She would not wish anyone to know how she was once deceived by her charge, would she?" Portia asked. "But she felt that Mama and Papa should know. And that I should know."

"Why?" Lucius asked.

For once Portia looked almost nonplussed. But she recovered quickly.

"She knows, I suppose," she said, "of the close connection between our families, Lucius."

"I wonder," he said, "that she did not simply speak to me."

"What *I* believe," Margaret said, "is that Lady Lyle was chagrined that she could not claim any of the glory for Miss Allard's performance last evening and contrived a way of introducing some spiteful gossip into our family circle so that we would drop our acquaintance with her. I believe it is all a pile of nonsense."

"So do I, Marg," Emily said. "Who cares what Miss Allard once did?"

"I would be honored to accompany her again anytime," Caroline said. "I wonder that you would want to repeat such silliness, Portia."

"Oh, but we must thank Lady Balderston and Portia for bringing what they heard to our attention," Lady Sinclair said, ever the diplomat. "Better that than discover it was being whispered behind our backs. Miss Allard appears to have corrected any faults there were in her nature when she stayed with Lady Lyle, though, and that does her credit. And I will be forever glad that I did not miss the opportunity of hearing her glorious voice last evening. Perhaps, Emily, someone would like another cup of tea."

Lucius got abruptly to his feet.

"You are leaving, Lucius?" his mother asked.

"I am," he said curtly. "I have just remembered that I must call upon Miss Allard."

"To thank her in person for last evening?" his mother asked. "I do think that is a good idea, Lucius. Perhaps your grandfather will wish to accompany you if he is up from his afternoon rest. Even Amy—"

"I will go alone," Lucius said. "I thanked her last evening. I have another mission today."

He did pause, but it was too late not to complete what he had begun to say—they were all, without exception, looking expectantly at him.

"I am going to ask her to marry me," he said.

Although the drawing room floor was covered from wall to wall with a thick carpet, a pin might nevertheless have been heard to drop as he strode from the room.

And *now* what the devil had he gone and done? he asked himself as he took the stairs two at a time up to his room.

He had opened his mouth and rammed his foot in it, boot and all, that was what.

But the thing was, he was not even sorry.

Frances spent a busy morning. She had not expected to do so after the excitement and upsets and general turmoil of the evening before. And she had had an almost sleepless night to boot.

But her great-aunts remained in bed late, and so she was alone in the breakfast room when the letter from Charles was delivered into her hand.

He begged to see her again. He had never understood why she had run away without a word. It was true that they had quarreled during their final meeting, but they had always made up their disagreements before that. He was no longer angry with her, if that was what she feared. He could see that she had redeemed herself since leaving. He understood that she had been teaching quietly and respectably in Bath ever since she left London.

She folded the letter and set it beside her plate. But her appetite was gone.

She had met the Earl of Fontbridge early in her come-out Season, and they had quickly fallen in love. He had wanted to marry her—but it would take some time to bring his mother around to accepting the daughter of a French émigré as his wife. And then her father had died. And then his mother would have to be reconciled to the fact that she had no fortune. And then he did not think that his future wife ought to be known as a singer who actually sang for her living. As Frances had wondered if he would *ever* consider the time and circumstances just right for them to marry, she had also started to fall out of love with him. And then they had had a bitter quarrel after he had heard of one particular party at which she had sung. She had defended her right to do as she wished since they were not even officially betrothed, and then she had told him that that was the end, that she never wanted to see him again.

And indeed she had not done so—not until last evening. And in the meantime she had *promised* never to see him again. She had done worse than that . . .

She was honor bound, then, not to answer the letter.

She was developing a nasty history, she thought, of not offering the explanations that ought to be made. And besides that, the two years following her father's death had been fraught with errors and misjudgments on her part—the result of having been the pampered, adored daughter of a man who had sheltered her and guided her and made most of her decisions for her.

She closed her eyes and pushed her plate away. She had made it a practice not to think of those two years. She had done well since. She had taken charge of her own life, and she was proud of what she had made of it. But of course it was impossible to put something entirely from mind simply by the power of one's will—especially when that something was as prominent as two misspent years of one's life. She had often wished she could go back and do things differently at the end. She still wished it.

Well, she thought, opening her eyes and staring down at the white tablecloth, she *was* back. And it was too late to creep out of London as she had crept in, unseen. All the people she had particularly wanted to avoid—Charles, the Countess of Fontbridge, Lady Lyle—had actually seen her. She did not doubt that George Ralston knew by now too that she was here.

If it was too late to creep away unseen, then perhaps she should stop even stepping lightly.

Perhaps she could do things differently after all, even if her actions were belated.

An hour later she was on her way alone and on foot to call upon the Countess of Fontbridge. It was not the fashionable time to make social calls, but then this was no social occasion.

When she was admitted to the earl's house on Grosvenor Square, she asked if the countess was at home and entrusted to the butler's care a short letter she had written to Charles, with the instructions that it was to be placed into his own hands. She was left standing in the tiled hall, but she did not really expect that the countess would refuse to admit her. A few minutes later she was shown into a small sitting room on the floor above.

No greetings were exchanged. The countess was standing before a small desk, her head at an arrogant tilt, her hands clasped at her waist. She did not offer her visitor a chair.

"So you have seen fit to break your word, Mademoiselle Halard," she said. "I suppose you have come here this morning with some explanation. None is acceptable. It is to be hoped that when you decided to return to London, you also came prepared to take the consequences."

"I came because one of my great-aunts was ill, ma'am," Frances said. "When I agreed to sing at Marshall House last evening at the request of the Earl of Edgecombe, I was quite unaware that other guests were being invited to listen to me. My great-aunt is better and the concert is over. I will be returning to Bath without further delay. But I did not come here to offer an excuse. I ought not to have made the agreement I did with you more than three years ago. I did so because I was angry on Charles's behalf that you controlled his life so ruthlessly that you thought you could buy off the woman he wished to marry. I did so with bitter cynicism. By that time I had no intention of marrying him. I had even told him so."

"There were to be consequences of your breaking our agreement," the countess reminded her.

"Yes, there were." They still greatly troubled Frances, but she would not be ruled by fear any longer. Perhaps Lord Sinclair had done her a favor after all in bringing her here under false pretenses. Perhaps all this had needed to happen. "And you may proceed to implement them if you choose, ma'am. I am in no position to stop you, am I? But I do wonder why you would bother. I made a promise to you three years ago that I fully intended to keep. But forever is too long a time for any agreement. Your purpose was to separate me from your son. That it was accomplished even before you paid me such a handsome sum is neither here nor there. My purpose was to pay off some troublesome debts. It was done and is forgotten about. I will be returning to Bath soon and remaining there to teach. But I will not promise never to come back here. I will no longer give you or anyone else that hold over me."

The Countess of Fontbridge bent a hard, narrow-eyed gaze on her, but before she could say more—if she intended doing so—Frances turned and left the room.

She felt slightly dizzy as she descended the stairs and stepped out onto the pavement and into the fresh air—and vastly relieved that Charles had not made an appearance. He must be from home.

For a moment she was tempted to turn her steps homeward. She had lived through more emotional turmoil during the past twenty-four hours—less!—than she had experienced in the three years before this past Christmas, she was sure. But there was no point in stopping now.

A short while later she was being ushered into a far more opulent sitting room than the one she had just left. And Lady Lyle was not standing with an unwelcoming pose to receive her. Rather, she was reclining on a sofa, petting a small dog in her lap with one hand and looking somewhat amused.

"Well, Françoise," she said by way of greeting, in the low, velvet voice that sounded so familiar, "you find yourself unable to ignore me after all, do you? Am I to feel honored, child? You are in reasonable good looks, though those clothes are shockingly provincial and your gown last evening was no better. And your hair! It is enough to make one weep."

"I am a schoolteacher, ma'am," Frances reminded her.

Lady Lyle shushed the lapdog, which had been yapping at the advent of a stranger into its territory.

"So it is said, Françoise," Lady Lyle said. "How amusing that you have been in Bath all this time and as a *teacher*. What an excruciatingly boring life it must have been."

"I enjoy teaching," Frances said. "I like everything about it."

Lady Lyle laughed again and made a dismissive gesture with one hand.

"George Ralston will be interested to know that you are back," she said. "He will forgive you and restore you to favor, Françoise, though it was very naughty of you to disappear without a word. I have already written to him and interceded on your behalf."

"I am going back to Bath," Frances told her.

"Nonsense, child," Lady Lyle said. "Oh, do sit down. It gives me a stiff neck to have to look up at you. You have no intention whatsoever of leaving. You have been doing some careful scheming and have won the favor of the Earl of Edgecombe and Viscount Sinclair, who were in Bath recently, I understand. *And* you have secured the interest of Lord Heath through their sponsorship. I give you full credit. It has taken you a few years but you have done it. And I must say that your voice has actually improved. That was an impressive performance last night. But your schemes will get you no farther, you know. Even apart from the fact that you are not free to accept the patronage of Baron Heath, there is the fact that you are about to lose your influential friends, Françoise. One word in the ear of a certain young lady who is about to be affianced to Sinclair and in those of her mama and papa, and your only recourse is to look elsewhere for the furtherance of your career. Oh, and by the way, child, that word was dropped into those ears last evening. Nothing too, too damning, I assure you, but it does not need to be with that young lady. She is *very* proper, and she has *very* firm control over poor Sinclair."

Even just yesterday Frances might have cringed. But something had snapped in her this morning, and she felt as if she were alive again after a long, deathlike sleep. She had thought herself free in the new life she had built for herself, but she had not been free at all. Her past needed to be dealt with before she could call herself free.

She had not sat down.

"I am not in your debt, Lady Lyle," she said, "though I have a feeling that you are about to claim that I am so that you can have the old hold over me. I never was in debt to you except perhaps for my board while I lived here—at your insistence after Papa died. But I paid that debt many times over. I am not bound to George Ralston either, though I am sure he would soon be assuring me that I am his slave for life if I were to stay in London long enough to hear him."

"Slave!" Lady Lyle looked amused again. "Poor George! And after all he did for you, Françoise. You were well on your way to being famous."

"I believe *notorious* would be a more appropriate word," Frances said. "You may say whatever you wish to Miss Hunt or to Lord Sinclair and even to Lord Heath. It does not matter to me. I am going back to Bath—by choice. It is where my home is and my profession and my friends."

"Oh, poor Françoise," Lady Lyle said, pushing the dog to the floor and moving into an upright sitting position before patting the sofa cushion beside her. "Have you not punished yourself enough? Come and sit here and let us be done with this foolish wrangling with each other. We were always fond of each other, were we not? And I adored your papa. You still desperately want your career in singing. There is no point in denying it. It was perfectly evident last evening. Well, you can *have* it back, you silly child. You never needed to throw it away and then scheme to get it back by your own efforts. We will have a word with Ralston and—"

"I am leaving now," Frances said. "I have other things to do this morning."

"Ah," Lady Lyle said, "you sound just like your papa. He was stubborn too and so very proud. But handsome and charming and quite, quite irresistible."

Frances turned to leave.

"Ralston will not be pleased, Françoise," Lady Lyle said. "Neither am I. And I *do* know where to find you now. I daresay it will be no trouble at all to discover the name and direction of the school at which you teach and the identity of the head of the board of governors or the headmistress or whoever it is who employs you. Bath is not a large place, and I daresay there are not many girls' schools there."

For a moment Frances felt as if icy fingers had reached out to grasp her. But she was no longer the girl she had been three years ago to cringe beneath every threat.

"Miss Martin's school is on Daniel Street," she said curtly without turning. "Good day to you, ma'am."

She held her poise until she was back out on the street, but then her shoulders sagged. It was all very well to have hurled defiance in the teeth of both the Countess of Fontbridge and Lady Lyle this morning, but the euphoria of doing so had given her a false sense of security. In reality her world was threatening to come crashing down about her ears. The Countess of Fontbridge now knew where she lived and worked. So did Lady Lyle. Both ladies, she knew, were very capable of spite. If either one of them chose to make life difficult for her there, she would have to leave. Not that she had kept any secrets from Claudia. But it was imperative that the teachers at a respectable girls' school be above reproach. She would not be able to stay if any breath of scandal concerning her got to the ears of the parents of her pupils—or to those of Claudia's unknown benefactor.

And it was all Viscount Sinclair's fault! Without his interference she would not have come to London and all this would not have happened.

No, that was unfair.

She did think about calling at Marshall House, but to what purpose? It would be most improper to go there and ask to speak to Viscount Sinclair.

It would be better to write to him. He had been a nuisance and a bother to her for some time, but he did deserve, perhaps, to be given a full, truthful explanation for her refusal to marry him.

Besides, she was dreadfully in love with him. She needed to make him understand.

She would not write to him from here in London, though, she decided as she walked home. As like as not he would rush impulsively over to Portman Street again and try to persuade her into doing what he would know deep down was not possible.

Anyway, it had been very evident last evening that his betrothal to Miss Hunt was imminent.

She would wait until she was back in Bath and then write to him.

A last good-bye.

She smiled wanly at the thought.

That left only her great-aunts to consider.

It had not been just cynicism that had led her into making Lady Fontbridge the promise to go away without another word to Charles and to stay away forever. It had also been fear—not so much for herself as for her great-aunts. She could not bear to think of them being hurt—they had often told her that she was like a daughter to each of them, that she was the person they loved most of all in the world besides each other.

The countess might yet decide to be spiteful.

Her great-aunts were both up, she discovered when she arrived home. They were sitting out in the little summer house in the back garden, enjoying the fine weather.

Frances made a decision as she went to join them there.

A little less than three hours later she was on her way back to Bath. It was already afternoon. It would certainly have been wiser to wait until morning, as her aunts had tried to convince her, but once the decision had been made she had been almost desperate to be back in Bath, back to the sane, busy routine of school life, back with her friends.

It was almost certain that she would have to stop somewhere on the road for the night, but she was not penniless. She could afford one night at an inn.

It was not just a desperation to be in Bath that drove her to such an abrupt departure, though. It was also a desperation to leave London, to leave *him* before he could come with more excuses to speak with her—and she very much feared that he *would* come despite his protestations to the contrary last evening.

She could not *bear* to see him again.

She wanted her heart to have a chance to begin mending.

Her great-aunts had been disappointed, of course. What about Baron Heath? they asked her. What about her singing career? What about Lord Sinclair? He was surely in love with their dear Frances. They had both come to that conclusion last evening.

But finally they had accepted her decision and assured her they felt well blessed that she had come all the way to London just to see them and had stayed for almost a whole week.

They had insisted upon sending her back in their traveling carriage.

And finally, after lengthy, tearful farewells and tight hugs Frances was on her way.

This was a little like the way it had all begun after Christmas, she thought as the London streets gradually gave place to countryside and she tried to find a comfortable position in the carriage—she felt weary right through to the marrow of her bones. It was fitting perhaps that this was how it would all end.

But this time there was no snow.

And this time there was no Lucius Marshall coming along behind her in a faster carriage.

She shed a very few tears of self-pity and grief and then dried them firmly with her handkerchief and blew her nose.

If he had many more dealings with Frances Allard, Lucius decided, he might well find that he had ground his teeth down to stumps.

He had arrived at the house on Portman Street, all prepared to shake the living daylights out of her, only to find that she had flown from there a scant half hour before. He had then had to spend all of ten minutes with her rather tearful great-aunts, who declared that he ought to have come sooner and persuaded their dear Frances to stay longer. But she had decided that she had been away from her classes long enough and must return to them immediately even though she could not possibly expect to reach Bath today.

"You sent her in your carriage, then, ma'am?" he had asked, addressing Mrs. Melford.

"Of course," she had told him. "We certainly would not allow her to travel in the discomfort of a stagecoach, Lord Sinclair. She is our *niece*—and our heir."

He had taken his leave soon after. And that, of course, ought to have been that.

End of story.

Good-bye.

The end.

But he had left the drawing room at Marshall House with such a flourish of high drama—totally unplanned and unrehearsed—that it would seem anticlimactic now to creep back there with the announcement that he had abandoned his plan to offer Frances Allard marriage because she had left town.

Offer her marriage indeed after she had refused him once and shown no sign of changing her mind since!

He really did appear to be suffering from an incurable case of insanity.

After walking back to Marshall House, he took the stairs two at a time up to his room—at least, that was his intention. But he met a veritable wall of people at the top of the first flight—they must have been watching for him at the drawing room window and had come to intercept him.

He half expected to see Portia among them, but neither she nor Lady Balderston was there. All the rest of them were, though, except his grandfather—even Amy.

"Well, Luce?" that young lady called out when he was still six stairs below them. "Did she say yes? *Did* she?"

"Amy," their mother said sharply, "hold your tongue. Lucius, whatever have you *done*?"

"I have been out on a wild-goose chase," he said. "She was not there. She is on her way back to Bath."

"I have never been more mortified in my life," his mother said. "Portia will not have you now, you know. Lady Balderston will not allow it, and neither will Lord Balderston, I daresay, when he hears what has happened. And even if *they* would, I do not believe *she* will. She behaved with great dignity after you had left and even advised Emily on the gown she ought to wear to the Lawson ball tomorrow evening. But you humiliated her in front of most of your family."

"Did I, Mama?" He came up to the top stair and Tait stepped to one side to give him room. He also managed to favor his brother-in-law with a private smirk. "How? By suggesting that she is a gossip? I ought to have been more tactful, perhaps, but I spoke nothing but the truth."

"I quite agree," Emily said. "As if I am not perfectly capable of choosing my own gown!"

"I have never liked Lady Lyle," Margaret added. "She always has a half-smile on her face. I do not trust it."

"Oh, do be quiet," the viscountess said. "You are being quite deliberately obtuse, Lucius. You know very well that Portia has been expecting a marriage offer from you every day for the past month and more. We have *all* expected it."

"Then you have all been wrong," he said. "I promised to choose a *bride* this spring, not Portia Hunt."

Amy clapped her hands.

"I am glad, Luce," Caroline said. "I have not liked Portia's attitude this spring. I have not liked *her*."

"And you believe Miss Allard is a suitable choice?" his mother asked, frowning.

"I cannot see why not," he said, "except that she has refused me more than once."

"*What?*" That was Emily.

"Is she *mad*?" That was Margaret.

Tait grimaced.

"Oh, no, Luce," Amy said. "No! She would not do that."

"Oh, do be quiet, all of you," Lady Sinclair said. "You will be waking your grandfather."

"He is still sleeping?" Lucius asked.

"He has overtaxed his strength, I am afraid," his mother said. "He is not at all the thing today. And now this. He will be very upset, Lucius. He has had his heart set on your marrying Portia. Are you sure you did not act with more than usual impulsiveness this afternoon? Perhaps if you were to call at Berkeley Square and apologize—"

"I'll not do it," Lucius said. "And while I am standing here talking, I am wasting valuable time. Pardon me, but I have to change my clothes. My curricle should be at the door within half an hour."

"Where are you going?" His mother looked pained.

"After Frances, of course," he said, heading for the next flight of stairs. "Where else?"

Amy, he could hear, whooped with delight before being shushed by their mother.

* * *

Frances was aching in every limb. It was impossible to find a comfortable position on the hard seat of the carriage. And whenever she did think that perhaps she had found one, the vehicle was sure to bounce over a hard rut or else jar through a pothole and she was reminded that if the carriage had ever been well sprung it was no longer so.

Even so she found herself near to dozing as evening approached. Soon it would be dusk and they would be forced to stop, she knew. She had refused her great-aunts' offer of a maid to accompany her for respectability. She did not mind being alone. They would not stop at a busy or fashionable posting inn, and her serviceable clothes would prevent her hosts and fellow guests from being too scandalized.

Tomorrow she would be back at the school. There would be little rest, of course. She would have to find out exactly what the temporary teacher had been doing with her classes and she would have to prepare to take over the next day. It would not be easy. She had never before taken even as much as a day off work. But she welcomed the thought of being busy again.

And every passing day would push the glorious wonder of last evening's concert and the terrible moment of saying a final good-bye to Lucius farther and farther back in memory until finally a whole day would pass when she would not think of either the height or the depth of emotion the last week had brought her.

She was dreaming of being inside a block of snow hiding from Charles. She was dreaming that she was singing and holding a high note when a snowball collided with her mouth and she saw Lucius grinning broadly and applauding with enthusiasm. She was dreaming that the senior madrigal choir was singing for Lord Heath but everyone was flat and singing at a different tempo while she flapped her arms in an ineffectual attempt to restore order.

She dreamed a dozen other meaningless, disjointed, vivid dreams before starting awake as the carriage swayed and tipped, seemingly out of control.

Frances grabbed for the worn leather strap above her head and waited for disaster to strike. There were the sounds of thundering hooves and yelling voices, and then horses came into view—traveling in the same direction as her own carriage was taking. They were pulling a gentleman's curricle, Frances could see, her eyes widening in indignation. A *curricle* on the road to Bath? And traveling at such a breakneck speed? It was thundering past on what seemed to be a particularly narrow stretch of road. What if there was something coming the other way?

She pressed her face to the window and peered up at the driver on his high perch. He was very smartly clad in a long buff riding coat with several capes and a tall hat set at a slight angle.

Frances, eyes wide as saucers, was not *quite* sure she recognized him. He was up high and almost past her line of vision. But the groom up behind him was neither. He was looking utterly contemptuous and yelling something, presumably at Thomas, that she mercifully could not hear. Just the expression on his face told her that it was not complimentary, though.

She had not been mistaken, then. If the man was Peters, the driver was certain to be Viscount Sinclair.

Why was she somehow not surprised?

She leaned back in her seat after the light vehicle was past. She closed her eyes, caught between fury and a totally inappropriate hilarity.

He talked about banishing the word *pleasant* from the English language. But it seemed that he had already totally obliterated the word *good-bye* from his own personal vocabulary.

She did not relinquish her hold on the strap. When Thomas pulled the carriage to an abrupt halt she was ready for the resulting jars and jolts that might have catapulted her across to the seat opposite and flattened her nose against its backrest had she been unprepared.

She looked out the window and ahead along the road. But the scene was very much what she had expected. The curricle, now in the care of Peters alone, was stationary and positioned right across the road. Viscount Sinclair was striding toward the carriage, his long coattails flapping against his glossy boots, his riding whip tapping against both. He was looking decidedly grim.

"If you would only choose to travel the king's highway in a carriage instead of an apology for an old boat, Frances," he said after yanking the door open, "you might have been to Bath and back by now. Move over."

Frances gazed helplessly at him and moved.

It offended Lucius's Corinthian soul to have to ride in the old fossil. But there was no avoiding such a fate—the carriage would offer more privacy than his curricle, especially with Peters—and, more important, Peters's ears—riding up behind. He very much hoped that none of his friends was tooling along the road to Bath to see the vehicle in which he traveled, though. He would never recover from the ignominy.

"Thanks to you I have lost a perfectly perfect bride today," he said, slamming the door and taking the seat beside Frances—he remained firmly on the surface of it instead of sinking comfortably into it, he noticed. "And I want recompense, Frances."

Understandably she sat across the corner to which she had retreated and stared at him with hostile eyes.

There was a good deal of bad-tempered shouting going on outside, presumably while Peters and Thomas exchanged genealogies again, and then Peters must have driven the curricle onward, as instructed. A posting chaise rumbled past in the opposite direction, its coachman's face purple with rage, and then the carriage in which Lucius sat with Frances creaked and jarred into slow motion and proceeded on its way.

"Miss Hunt actually refused you?" she asked at last. "I am surprised, I must confess. But in what sense am I responsible, pray?"

"She did not refuse me," he said. "She was not given a chance. I announced in her hearing and her mama's that I was off to Portman Street to offer you my compliments and my hand. By the time I discovered you gone and crept home again, both ladies had left Marshall House in high dudgeon, and in my mother's considered opinion Portia would no longer have me if I crawled toward her on my hands and knees, eating dirt as I went, or humble pie—whichever happened to be available."

"And would you do it if you were given the opportunity?" she asked.

"Crawl on my hands and knees?" he asked. "Good Lord, no. My valet would resign on the spot, and I am partial to the way he ties a neckcloth. Besides which, Frances, I have no wish to marry Portia Hunt—never have had and never will. I believe I would rather be dead."

"She is very lovely," she said.

"Exceedingly," he agreed. "But we had this conversation last evening, Frances. I would rather talk about you."

He was babbling, he knew—making a joke of things that were not really funny at all. Truth to tell, he had no business being where he was. But he was not about to admit that.

"There is nothing to say about me," she said. "I think you had better summon your curricle and go back to London, Lord Sinclair."

"On the contrary," he said, "there is a great deal to talk about. The fact that you are a Frenchwoman masquerading as an English-woman, for example. How is one to know that you are not a spy?"

She clucked her tongue.

"You knew that I was French," she said. "Does it matter whether I choose to be known as Françoise Halard or Frances Allard? Somehow people expect a Frenchwoman to be flamboyant, to talk with her hands, to flutter with emotion. They expect her to be *foreign*. I grew up in England. I am an Englishwoman in every way that matters."

If he had to travel very far in this carriage, he thought, his spine would surely suffer permanent damage—not to mention his hind-quarters.

"I will release you from suspicion as a spy, then," he said. "But what about the fact that you were singing at orgies before you became a teacher, Frances? You must have some interesting anecdotes to relate about that."

Suddenly he felt grim again. And she looked tight-lipped.

"Orgies," she said softly.

"Lady Lyle did not use that exact word," he said. "She was speaking to Portia and so would have felt obliged to temper her language. But that is what she meant."

She turned her head to look out the window. She was not wearing a bonnet—it was lying on the seat opposite. Her profile, he could see, looked as if it were carved out of marble. It was about that color too.

"I do not have to justify myself to you, Lord Sinclair, when you take that tone with me," she said. "Or even when you do not, for that matter. You may get out of my aunts' carriage and go back to town."

He heaved an audible sigh of exasperation.

"I cannot do it, though, you see," he told her. "I cannot simply go away, Frances. Not until our story has been ended. I remember reading a book as a boy—an ancient tome from my grandfather's library. I became totally immersed in the story and let two perfectly decent summer days go by outdoors while I remained indoors and lapped up its contents. And then the story came to an abrupt halt—the last who-knows-how-many pages were missing. I was left feeling as if I were hanging over the edge of a cliff by my fingernails with no hope of rescue. And no one I questioned had ever read the infernal thing. When I hurled the book across the library, it sailed through a window, taking a large pane of glass with it, and I lost my allowance for at least the next six months. But I have never forgotten my wrath and frustration. They have been rekindled lately. I like stories to have neat endings."

"We are not living within the pages of a book," she said.

"And therefore the story can end however we wish it to end," he said. "I no longer demand a happily-ever-after, Frances. It takes two to make a happy marriage, and so far we seem to have a total of one willing partner. But I do need to know *why*—why you have spurned me, why you rejected an opportunity last evening with Heath that many musicians with half your talent would kill for. Deuce take it, what *happened* in your past? What skeleton are you hiding in your wardrobe?"

She almost noticeably slumped into her corner.

"You are right," she said. "You deserve an explanation. Perhaps I would have offered it in Sydney Gardens if I had realized that you were really serious in your offer and not merely acting from romantic impulse. I ought to have told you when you took me walking in Hyde Park—but I did not. I intended to write to you from Bath. But now I will have to say it in person."

"From Bath?" he said. "Why not from London?"

"Because," she said with a sigh, "I was afraid you would come to confront me after reading the letter. I was afraid that you would not see sense."

She looked up at him, and he held her gaze. A smile tugged at the corners of her lips.

"Do you never see sense?" she asked him.

"There is a fine line between sense and nonsense," he said. "I have not yet worked out exactly where you belong on the line, Frances. Tell me about the skeleton in the wardrobe."

"Oh," she said, "there are enough to fill a whole mansionful of wardrobes. It is not one single thing, but a whole host of things. I made a mess of my life after my father died, that is all. But I was fortunate enough to be able to break free and build a new life for myself. It is what I am going back to now. It is a life that cannot include you."

"Because I am a viscount, I suppose," he said irritably, "and heir to an earldom. Because I live much of my life in London and mingle with the *ton*."

"Yes," she said. "Precisely."

"I am also Lucius Marshall," he said, and had the satisfaction of seeing her eyes brighten with tears before she looked down at her hands.

The carriage had lumbered around a bend in the road, and the evening sunlight slanted through the window beside him to shine on her hair.

"Tell me about Lady Lyle," he said. "You lived with her for a couple of years but almost bit my head off when I told you last evening that I had invited her to hear you sing. Then she dropped a word in Portia's fertile ear. She could only have meant mischief."

"She was very fond of my father," she said. "I believe she was in love with him. Perhaps—no, probably—she was his mistress. She sponsored my come-out and was attentive to me in other ways too. When he died, she invited me to live with her and it seemed natural to me to go there. I do not believe she meant me harm. But he left enormous debts behind him, some of them to her. I was quite destitute, though I did have hopes of making an advantageous marriage."

"To Fontbridge," he said.

She nodded.

Fontbridge was something of a milksop, a mother's boy. It was hard to picture Frances in love with him. But then it was notoriously difficult to understand anything she did. Besides, that had been several years ago. And Fontbridge was good-looking in the sort of way that might bring out the maternal instinct in some women.

"I was uncomfortable about being totally dependent upon Lady Lyle," she said. "I was very grateful and very happy when she brought me to the attention of a man who was willing to sponsor and manage my singing career. And he was very complimentary and very sure that he could bring me fame and fortune. I signed a contract with him. It seemed like a dream come true. I could have my singing career, I could pay off all my father's debts, and I could marry Charles and live happily ever after. I was a very naive girl, you must understand. I had lived a very sheltered life."

"Who?" he asked. "Who was this sponsor?"

"George Ralston," she said.

"Dash it all, Frances!" he exclaimed. "The man makes a career of preying upon helpless, foolish women. Did you know no better? But of course you did not. Did *Lady Lyle* know no better?"

"She had told me," she said, "that singing would enable me to pay off my father's debts to her and my own for the expenses I had incurred while living with her. I felt honor bound—though that was only later. At first I was so ecstatic just at the thought of finally singing as I had always dreamed of doing that the money and the debts were quite secondary considerations."

"And so," he said, "you sang at orgies."

"At *parties*," she said. "I was soon disappointed. I could not choose either the places at which I sang or the songs or even the clothes I wore—my contract stated that George Ralston had total control over such matters. And the audiences were almost exclusively men. If the parties were also orgies I did not know, though I daresay they were. I received a few offers through my agent—none of them marriage offers, you will understand—and he tried to persuade me that they came from wealthy and influential men who could further my career even faster than he could. Soon, he kept telling me, I would be singing at large concert halls and would have the artistic freedom to sing whatever I wished to sing."

"Good Lord, Frances." He made a grab for one of her hands and held it tightly when she would have withdrawn it. "Is *this* the terrible past you have been keeping from me? What an idiot you are, my love."

"I still moved in society," she said. "I still went to *ton* parties. But word was beginning to leak out. Charles heard of where I was singing and for whom. He confronted me with it and commanded me to stop and we had a terrible quarrel. But even before that I had decided I could never marry him. He could not break away from beneath his mother's thumb, and I knew his character was essentially weak. And he told me that it would be out of the question for me to sing in public after I had become his countess."

"What an ass," Lucius said.

"But it would be no different with you," she said, looking sharply up at him and squinting a moment before the carriage moved around another bend and set her face in shadow again. "If it had been possible for me to take up Lord Heath's offer—if I were not still under contract with George Ralston, that is—and if he could have arranged for me to sing at prestigious concerts in England and on the Continent, you would not still have wanted me as your wife. A viscountess does not do such things."

"Devil take it, Frances."

But he was too exasperated to be able to think of words to speak. He caught her up in his arms instead, pressed his mouth to hers, and held her tight until she relaxed and kissed him back.

"You always presume to know me so well," he said when he finally lifted his head. "I am frequently an impulsive, ramshackle fellow, Frances, but I would have to be a raving lunatic to be asking you to marry me and then arranging for Heath to hear you sing if I thought having the singing career you *ought* to have and marriage to me were mutually exclusive activities. Damn it, you have made a great deal out of nothing."

"It never did feel like nothing," she said bitterly, pulling away from him and retreating to her corner again. "My father's debts were larger than I thought, I had signed a contract I could never get out of, and Lady Lyle became less pleasant when I started to complain."

"A contract," Lucius said. "How old were you, Frances?"

"Nineteen," she said. "Does that fact make a difference?"

"*Of course* it does," he said. "It is not worth the paper it is written on. You were a *minor*."

"Oh," she said. "I did not realize that mattered." She pressed both hands to her face for a moment and shook her head. "Things kept going from bad to worse. And then the worst thing of all happened. After I had quarreled with Charles, the Countess of Fontbridge came to see me. She had not heard of the quarrel, but she was determined to separate us. She offered me money—a large sum—if I would agree to leave London without another word to Charles and never come back again."

"And you took the money?" He looked at her incredulously—and also with something of a grin.

"I did," she said. "I was so angry. But I also had no choice but to promise—at least, I *thought* I had no choice. And then I thought—why not? Why not take her money even though I had no intention of marrying her son anyway? So I did. I needed money to set myself free, and so I rationalized my decision. I gave it all to Lady Lyle, and then I packed a valise and left the house while she was at an evening party. I had no plans, but the next day I saw the advertisement for the teaching job at Miss Martin's, and the day after that her London agent agreed to send me down to Bath for an interview. I needed to leave, Lucius, and I did leave. There was nothing for me in London. I thought I was tied to a contract that I found quite abhorrent, scandal was about to break around me, and either Lady Lyle or Lady Fontbridge could have unleashed it in a moment. I left, hoping almost against hope that I would have a chance to start again, to build a better life for myself. And incredibly it worked. I have been happy ever since. Until I met you."

"Ah, my love." He took her hand again, but this time she succeeded in pulling it away.

"No, you do not understand," she said just as the carriage made a sharp turn into the cobbled stable yard of a small country inn, where Peters was already standing beside the curricle. "You do not understand why I had to give my promise to the Countess of Fontbridge. She knew something that Lady Lyle had told her, something I did not even know myself. Lady Lyle wanted to make sure that I did not marry Charles, I suppose, and stop singing and paying her large sums of money for debts she had quite possibly fabricated. But my only thought was that my great-aunts must never discover the truth. It would have hurt them unbearably, I believed."

She seemed not to have noticed that the carriage had stopped. With one raised hand Lucius stopped Peters from opening the door.

"I am not who you think I am," she said.

"Neither Françoise Halard nor Frances Allard?" he asked softly.

"I am not French at all or English either," she said. "My mother was Italian, and so was my father as far as I know. I do not, in fact, know who he was—or is."

He stared at her profile as she spread her hands across her lap and looked down at them.

"She was a singer," she told him. "My father fell in love with her and married her even though she was already with child by someone else. After she died, a year after my birth, he brought me back to England with him and brought me up as his daughter. He never breathed a word of the truth to me—I heard it for the first time just over three years ago."

"Are you sure, then," he asked, "that it is true?"

She smiled at her hands. "I suppose part of me always wondered if perhaps it was a malicious invention," she said. "But my great-aunts confirmed it just today. I told them the truth before I left, only to discover that my father had done so when he first arrived in England with me. They have always known."

She was weeping, he realized when a spot of moisture fell onto her lap and darkened the fabric of her dress. He handed her a handkerchief, and she took it and pressed it to her eyes.

"So you see," she said, "I cannot marry anyone of high rank. I cannot marry you. And before you rush in to contradict me, Lucius, stop and *think*. You have made a promise to your grandfather and indeed to your whole family. I have met them, and I have seen you with them. I know you are fond of them. More than that, I know you *love* them. And I know that your impetuosity is more often than not motivated by love. You are a far more precious person than I think you realize. For your family's sake you cannot marry me."

And then—absurdly—*he* wanted to weep. Was it true? Was he perhaps not quite the wastrel he sometimes believed himself to be?

I know that your impetuosity is more often than not motivated by love.

"It is almost dark," he said, "and if this inn does not offer a decent beef pie for dinner I am going to be mightily out of sorts. I suppose you are ready for a cup of tea?"

She blew her nose then and looked about her as if realizing for the first time that they were not still rattling along the highway.

"Oh, Lucius." She laughed shakily. "Two cups would be better."

"Just one thing," he said before giving Peters the signal to open the door and let down the steps. "For tonight we are Mr. and Mrs. Marshall. We will not scandalize our host by arriving in the same carriage and announcing ourselves as Viscount Sinclair and Miss Allard."

He did not give her a chance to reply. He jumped out of the carriage and turned to hand her down.

"I was beginning to think, guv," Peters said, "that I was going to be up until the wee hours of the morning waiting to attract old Thomas's attention so that he would turn in here rather than crawling on past."

Lucius ignored the witticism.

24

"It does matter," she said. "It really does, Lucius."

"It most certainly does not." He looked at her in obvious exasperation. "Good Lord, Frances, if only you had told me all this when we were in Sydney Gardens, marooned by the rain, we could have been married by now and proceeding to live happily ever after."

"We could *not*." But all was pain about her heart. "You never stop to *think*, Lucius."

They could not immediately continue the discussion. They were in the public dining room, there being no private parlors at the inn. There was only one other group there, and they were at the far side of the room, deep in conversation. But the landlord had arrived with their food—roast beef and vegetables. Frances wished she had ordered only bread and butter and tea.

Lucius was looking handsome and elegant. He had changed for dinner, and he was freshly shaved. That latter activity had been performed in her full view while she sat on the large bed in their shared room, her arms clasped about her knees. He had been shirtless.

The scene had felt almost suffocatingly domestic. And she had been able to see all the rippling muscles of his arms and shoulders and back. He really did have a splendid physique. Not that her perusal of him had been entirely scientific. She had been terribly aware of him sexually.

She had been very aware too of the fact that they would be

spending the night together in that room—and in that bed. It had not occurred to her to be in any way horrified.

"It matters to you," Lucius asked, picking up his knife and fork and cutting into his beef, "that Allard—or Halard, I suppose—was not your real father?"

"It mattered very much at first," she said, "and I was inclined not to believe it. But it did not seem to me the sort of thing Lady Lyle would have invented. She was greedy and occasionally spiteful, but I did not believe her to be wicked. Eventually, once I had recovered from the first shock, I realized that the love he had always lavished upon me was even more precious than I had always thought it since I was not even his flesh and blood. But it mattered in other ways. I was an imposter in society. I could not have married Charles even if I had still loved him. And this is not even all in the past tense. I cannot marry *you*."

She put a forkful of food into her mouth and then found the effort of chewing it almost beyond her powers.

"Are you really so naive, Frances?" he asked. "Numerous members of the *ton* do not have the parents they profess to have. Have you not heard it said that once a woman has presented her husband with an heir and a spare she can proceed to enjoy life in any manner she chooses provided she is discreet? There are many women of good *ton* who do so with great enthusiasm and present their husbands with an array of hopeful offspring that he did nothing to beget. What did your great-aunts have to say on the matter?"

"They told me," she said, "that I was a tiny, big-eyed child when they first saw me and they fell in love with me on sight. They told me that when my father told them the truth about me, it simply made no difference to them. My father was their beloved nephew, and he acknowledged me as his own. And so it never occurred to them not to acknowledge me as their great-niece. They told me I was the apple of their eye."

"When I called there this afternoon," he said, "they also told me that you are their heir."

"Oh," she said, setting down her knife and fork with something of a clatter and giving up even the pretense of eating.

"You are not going to weep again, are you, Frances?" he asked her. "If I had known, I would have brought a dozen clean handkerchiefs with me, but I did not know. Don't cry, my love."

"Oh, I am *not*," she said. "But three years ago when the Countess of Fontbridge came to me with her threats, it was of them I thought. I could not bear to have them know how they had been deceived all those years. And I suppose I could not bear the thought of losing their love. But when I went out to the summer house today to tell them the truth, they looked at me in dismay because *I* knew. And then they hugged me and kissed me and called me a goose for having doubted them for one moment."

"You see?" he said, his plate already almost empty. "They agree with me, Frances—about your being a goose. It never pays to give in to threats and blackmail. I'll go and find Lady Fontbridge and plant her a facer, if you wish—or I would if it were not ungentlemanly to do such violence to a lady."

"Oh, Lucius." She laughed. "I called on her this morning and told her that though I was leaving for Bath I would no longer consider myself bound by the promise I made more than three years ago—except the one not to marry Charles because I had not intended to marry him anyway. And I called on Lady Lyle and told her that I no longer considered myself in her debt or under obligation to George Ralston. When she threatened to pursue me to Bath with her vicious gossip, I told her the name of the school and where to find it."

His fork remained suspended halfway to his mouth. He grinned at her and made her heart turn right over in her bosom, she was sure.

"Bravo, my love!" he said.

She sighed. "Lucius," she said, "that is the third or fourth time you have called me that in the last hour or so. You must stop. You really must. You need to set your mind to fulfilling the promise you made your grandfather. If Miss Hunt is no longer a candidate, you will need to find someone else."

"I have found her," he said.

She sighed again. "Your bride must be someone acceptable to your family," she said. "You know she must. You made the promise as soon as you knew the Earl of Edgecombe was failing in health. Do you know why you made that promise? Because it was the dutiful thing to? Yes. I believe duty means much to you. Because you *love* him, and your mother and your sisters too? *Yes*. You bound yourself to marrying and settling down and having a family of your own, Lucius, because you *love* the family that nurtured you and felt that you owed them that stability in your life."

"You are very ready to assign all sorts of sentimental motives to me today," he said. His plate was empty. He set down his knife and fork and picked up his glass of wine. "But if there is some truth in what you say, Frances, there is truth in this too. I will marry for *love*. I have decided that, and that puts you in an awkward position. For I love you. And so I cannot settle for anyone else. And yet I have a certain promise to keep before the summer is out."

The landlord arrived to clear away their plates. A maid behind him carried in two dishes of steaming pudding. Frances waved hers away and asked for tea.

"Your father acknowledged you from the moment of your birth, did he not?" Lucius asked as soon as they were alone again. "He was married to your mother? He gave you his name?"

"Yes," she said, "of course."

"Then you are legitimate," he said. "In the eyes of the church and the law you are Frances Allard—or perhaps Françoise Halard."

"But no high stickler, knowing the truth, would want to marry me," she said.

"Good Lord, Frances," he said, "why would you want to marry a high stickler? It sounds like a dreadfully dreary fate. Marry me instead."

"We are arguing in circles," she said.

He looked up from his pudding to smile at her.

"It has only now struck me," he said, "that you never did make suet pudding and custard to follow the beef pie, Frances. But I will say this. That pie was so satisfying that the pudding would surely have gone to waste if you had made it."

She loved him so very, very much, she thought, gazing across the table at him. She must have fallen in love with him—

"I believe," he said, "I fell in love with you after tasting the first mouthful of that pie, Frances. Or perhaps it was when I walked into the kitchen and found you rolling out the pastry and you slapped at my hand when I stole a piece. Or perhaps it was when I lifted you out of your carriage and deposited you on the road and you gave it as your opinion that I ought to be boiled in oil. Yes, I think it must have been then. No woman had ever spoken such endearing words to me before."

She continued to gaze at him.

"I must know something, Frances," he said. "Please, I must know. Do you love me?"

"That has nothing to do with anything," she said, shaking her head slowly.

"On the contrary," he said, "it has everything to do with everything."

"Of course I love you," she said. "Of *course* I do. But I cannot marry you."

He sat back in his chair, his pudding only half eaten, and beamed at her in that intense-eyed, tight-lipped, square-jawed way in which he had looked at her before. It could hardly be called a smile, and yet . . .

"Tomorrow," he said, "you will continue on your way to Bath in the old boat, Frances. You have teaching duties there, and I know they are important to you. I will return to London in my curricle. I have duties awaiting me there, and they are important to me. Tonight we will make love."

She licked dry lips and saw his eyes dip to follow the movement of her tongue.

He had given up the argument, then.

Her heart broke just a little more.

But there was tonight.

"Yes," she said.

* * *

He could not believe what a difference loving her made—consciously loving her, not just bedding an attractive body for which he had conceived a strong sexual desire.

He had, he supposed, fallen in love with her early, as he had told her at dinner. Why else would he have pleaded with her to go to London with him when he had no real plan and when there was every reason *not* to take her? Why else would he have found it impossible to forget her in the three months after she had rejected him even though he had convinced himself that he had? Why else would he have made her such an impulsive marriage offer in Bath? And why else would he have pursued her so relentlessly ever since?

But somewhere along the way—and it was impossible to know exactly when or why it had happened—his feelings for her had shifted and deepened so that he was no longer just *in* love with her. He *loved* her. The beauty of her person and of her soul, the strong, sometimes misguided, almost always irritating sense of duty and honor by which she lived her life, the way she had of tipping her head slightly to one side and regarding him with a look of exasperation and unconscious tenderness, the way her face had of lighting up with joy when she forgot herself, her ability to give herself up to fun and frolicking and laughter—ah, there were a hundred and one things about her that had brought him to love her, and a hundred and one other intangibles that made her into the only woman he had ever loved—or would ever love.

When they came together, naked, in the middle of the wide bed in their inn room, he wrapped both arms about her slender, warm body and drew it against his and found that he was almost trembling. The thought that he might yet lose her threatened to overwhelm him, and he set his lips, parted, over hers and concentrated upon the moment.

Now, at this precise moment, she was naked and eager in his arms, and now was all that mattered.

Now they were together.

And she had admitted that she loved him. He had known it—in his heart he had known. But she had spoken the words.

Of course I love you. Of course I do.

"Lucius," she said against his mouth, "make love to me."

"I thought that was what I was doing." He drew back his head to grin down at her in the faint light being cast through the window by the lamps burning in the stable yard below. "Am I not doing well enough?"

Her whole body trembled with her laughter. He *loved* it when she did that.

"Of course," he said, turning her onto her back and looming over her, one arm beneath her head, one knee pressed between her thighs, "you are rather hot to handle, Frances. Red hot. I might burn myself with touching you. You are not coming down with some fever by any chance, are you?"

She laughed again and reached for the back of his head. She drew his mouth down to hers once more and thrust her breasts up against his chest.

"I think I am," she said. "And I think it is going to get worse before it gets better. But there is only one cure I can think of. Make me better, Lucius."

She spoke in a low, throaty voice that raised goose bumps along his arms and down his spine.

"My pleasure, ma'am," he said, his lips feathering kisses down over her chin and throat. "Shall we dispense with the foreplay this time?"

"This time?" she said, twining her fingers in his hair. "Is there to be another time, then?"

"How many hours are left in the night?" he asked.

"Eight?" she suggested.

"Then there will be other times," he said. "One hour for play, one for rest between times. Three other times, then? Perhaps four since this is likely to be brief."

"Then let us dispense with the foreplay this time," she said, and laughed softly again.

He came down on top of her, slid his hands beneath her, positioned himself between her thighs, and thrust hard and deep into her wet heat.

He had known almost from the start that she was a passionate woman. But tonight she had abandoned all her inhibitions to it. He had not lied when he had told her that she was almost too hot to handle. What followed his mount was pure, mindless, glorious carnality. She met him thrust for thrust, and they mated with vigor and panting breath and mingled heat and sweat—and ultimately with a shared and shattering climax.

Aware at the last possible moment that they were at a public inn and the walls might not be as thick and soundproof as they ought, he opened his mouth over hers to absorb her final cry.

Then he turned his head to one side, relaxed his weight down onto her, and sighed.

"The secret when one intends to spend a whole night at play," he said, "is to save some energy, to conduct the first bout in a restrained manner and build to a lusty climax with the final bout sometime after dawn."

"But that is exactly what we are doing, is it not?" she said softly, her breath warm against his ear. "Wait until that final bout, Lucius. It will shatter the globe, and we will find ourselves shooting through space."

"Heaven help me," he said. "And heaven help the world."

And he promptly fell asleep without first bothering to move off her.

Was it possible, Frances wondered during one of the drowsy times in the course of that night when she was not either making love or dozing, that some people lived life this vividly day after day, week after week, even year after year? Giving joy and taking it with reckless disregard for the consequences or the future or anything, in fact, except the precious moment as it was being lived.

The cautious part of her mind told her she was being foolish, even immoral. But something in her soul knew that if she never reached for joy she would never find it and at the end of her life she would know that she had deliberately turned away from the most precious opportunities her life had offered as a gift.

She could not marry Lucius. Or rather she *would* not because she knew that without his family's blessing he would never be quite happy. And how could they give that blessing if his bride was the daughter of an Italian singer and some unknown Italian man?

She could not marry him, but she could love him now tonight.

And so she did, giving herself up to all the passion she felt for him. They made love over and over again, sometimes with swift vigor as they had done at the start of the night, sometimes with prolonged, tantalizing, almost agonizing foreplay and long, rhythmic couplings, which were so excruciatingly sensual and beautiful that they both, by unspoken consent, held back from the moment when excitement would be unleashed to hurl them over a precipice into satiety and peace and sleep.

His hands, his body, his powerful legs and arms, his mouth, his hair, his smell—all became as familiar to her in the course of the night as her own body. And as dear. She came to understand the idea that man and woman could become one flesh. When he was inside her, it was hard to know where she ended and he began. Their bodies seemed made to fit together, to mate together, to relax together.

"Happy?" he murmured against her ear when dawn was graying the room. He had one arm beneath her neck, his fingers twined with hers, while his other hand described lazy circles over her stomach and one of his legs was draped over both of hers.

"Mmm," she said.

But daylight inevitably followed dawn, she knew.

"You will be glad to get back to work?" he asked.

"Mmm," she said again. But really she would. She had always been happy at the school, and the work there had always brought her satisfaction. Her fellow teachers were the closest friends she had ever had. She loved them—it was as simple as that.

"The rest of the school year will be busy?" he asked. He took her earlobe between his teeth and rubbed his tongue over the tip, causing her toes to curl up.

"There will be final examinations to set and mark," she said. "There will be farewell teas for the senior girls who are leaving, and placements to arrange for the charity girls in positions for which their education and personal inclinations qualify them. There will be the selection of new girls for next year—Claudia always involves all her teachers in those decisions. And there is the end-of-year prize-giving evening and concert for parents and friends. Several of my music pupils will be performing and all my choirs. There will be daily practices from now until that evening comes. Yes, I will be too busy to think of anything else."

"Will you be thankful for that?" he asked.

She kept her eyes closed and did not answer him for a while.

"Yes," she said.

He turned her head with their interlaced hands and kissed her on the lips.

"And you will be busy," she said, "attending all the balls and parties for the rest of the Season."

"My mother and the girls do seem to enjoy dragging me about," he said.

"And you will be wanting to meet someone new," she said. "Perhaps—"

He kissed her again.

"Don't talk nonsense, love," he said. "In fact, don't talk at all. I feel another energy attack coming along."

He took her free hand in his and brought it against him. She could feel him harden into arousal again and wrapped her hand about him.

"But I am too lazy to come over on top of you," he said, "or to lift you on top of me. Shall we see if there is a lazy way to love?"

He turned her onto her side against him, lifted one of her legs over his hip, pressed himself against her and wriggled into a better position, and pushed inside her. She pivoted her hips in order to give him deeper access.

And they loved slowly and lazily, their warm, almost relaxed climax coming several minutes later.

He lifted her leg back off his hip, and they drifted off to sleep for a while, still joined.

The sun was up and shining in her eyes when she next awoke.

Tomorrow you will continue on your way to Bath . . . I will re-turn to London. . . .

Tomorrow had indisputably arrived.

She should be coming back to London with him. She should be going back to stay with her great-aunts, allowing them to fuss over her as she prepared for her betrothal celebrations and then her wedding before summer was out.

She should be going back to speak with Heath, to make arrangements with him for the concert he wanted to plan for her. She should be practicing her singing and preparing for the career that was just waiting for her to reach out and grasp.

But there was something far more important that she should be doing.

She should be going back to Bath, back to Miss Martin's, back to her pupils and her teaching duties and all that had made her life rich and meaningful during the past three and a half years.

She might have crumbled all that time ago, caught as she was between the ultimatum the Countess of Fontbridge had given her and the ruthless exploitation of her talent that Ralston and Lady Lyle had engaged in for two years.

But she had not crumbled despite a sheltered upbringing. Rather, she had had the strength of character and purpose to turn her back on a rather disastrous start to her adulthood and to make a new life for herself.

He had been wrong to call her a coward, Lucius had come to realize, to accuse her of settling for contentment when she could be reaching for happiness with him—and with her singing.

She had not run away from her old life.

She had run *to* a new one.

It was wrong to expect her to give it up simply because she loved him and he wanted her to marry him. It was wrong to expect her to give it up for the prospect of a singing career even though she had dreamed all her life of such a career.

She *had* a life and she *had* a career, and she owed both of them her presence and her commitment at least until the end of the school year in July.

The hardest thing Lucius had done in a long while was to allow her to go on her way without trying to persuade her to go back to London with him—and even without begging her to allow him to come for her in July.

For she was right. Even though he knew now that he could not possibly marry any woman for whom he did not care, he also knew that the blessing of his family—his mother's and his sisters' as well as his grandfather's—was important to him.

Whether his love for Frances would outweigh their disapproval if it should come to that he did not know, though he rather thought it might. But he did know that he must do all in his power to win their approval.

It would be easier to do that if he returned alone, if they were not simply confronted with a fait accompli.

And so after a breakfast they might as well not have ordered for the amount either of them ate, they took their leave of each other in the stable yard, he and Frances Allard.

Thomas was already seated up on the box of her carriage, the docile-looking pair of horses hitched to it awaiting the signal to start. Peters, meanwhile, stood at the head of a more frisky pair hitched to the curricle and looked eager to be on his way, though he had looked disappointed when informed this morning that he was not going to be driving the vehicle himself.

Lucius took both of Frances's hands in his outside the open door of the carriage. He squeezed them tightly, raised one to his lips, and held it there, his eyes closed, for a few moments.

"Au revoir, my love," he said. "Have a safe journey. Try not to work too hard."

Her dark eyes, wide and expressive, gazed back into his own as if she would drink in the sight of him in order to slake her thirst for the rest of the day.

"Good-bye, Lucius," she said. She swallowed awkwardly. "Good-bye, my dearest."

And she snatched her hands away and scrambled into the carriage without assistance. She busied herself with organizing her belongings while he closed the door, and she kept her head down while he nodded to Thomas and the old carriage lurched into motion.

She kept her head down until the moment when the carriage was turning onto the road and out of sight. Then she looked up hastily and almost too late, raising one hand in farewell.

And she was gone.

But not forever, by Jove.

This was not good-bye.

He was never going to say good-bye to her again.

Even so, he thought as he strode over to the curricle, swung up to the high seat, and took the ribbons from Peters's hand, it *felt* like good-bye.

He was damnably close to tears.

"You had better hang on tightly," he warned as Peters clambered up behind. "As soon as we turn onto the road I am going to spring them."

"I would think so too, guv," Peters said. "Some people who aren't too keen on eating country breakfasts would like to eat their midday meal in London."

Lucius sprang the horses.

25

When no betrothal announcement concerning Viscount Sinclair had appeared in any of the London papers within two weeks of his startling announcement in the drawing room at Marshall House, Lady Balderston made it clear to Lady Sinclair in a series of hints and roundaboutations that if Viscount Sinclair would care to make an abject apology, he would be received with forgiveness and understanding. It was said, after all, that half the gentlemen who had attended the concert had fallen in love with Miss Allard—and it was a well-known fact that Viscount Sinclair frequently spoke and behaved impulsively.

When no such abject apology—or any apology at all, for that matter—had been made after another two weeks, Lady Portia Hunt suddenly became the *on dit* in fashionable London drawing rooms as word spread that she had dismissed the suit of Viscount Sinclair in favor of the advances of no less a personage than the Marquess of Attingsborough, son and heir of the Duke of Anburey, was making toward her. And suddenly, as proof that the gossips did not lie, the two were to be seen everywhere together—driving in Hyde Park, seated side by side in a box at the theater, dancing at various balls.

Lucius meanwhile had not been idle even though he was far less active than he usually was. He spent hours at a time sitting in his grandfather's apartments, either beside the bed or else in the private sitting room when the elderly gentleman was feeling well enough to get up.

He had, the physician said, suffered another minor heart seizure.

Lucius sat at his bedside the afternoon of his return to London and chafed one of his cold, limp hands between both his own.

"Grandpapa," he said, "I am sorry I was not here sooner. I have been halfway to Bath and back."

His grandfather smiled sleepily at him.

"When I called on Mrs. Melford and Miss Driscoll yesterday afternoon," Lucius explained, "I found that Frances had just left to return to Bath. I went after her."

"She does not want to sing after all, then," the earl asked, "even though Heath was so impressed with her?"

"She does," Lucius told him. "But she is a teacher, and the school and her pupils and fellow teachers are more important to her than anything else at the moment. She does not wish to be away from them any longer."

His grandfather's eyes were on his face.

"And she does not want you either, Lucius?" he asked.

Lucius rubbed more warmth into his hand.

"She does," he said. "She wants me as badly as I want her. But she does not believe she is worthy of me."

"And you could not persuade her otherwise?" The old man chuckled. "You must be losing your touch, my boy."

"No, I could not, sir," Lucius said, "because I did not have the authority to convince her. She will not marry me unless I have the full blessing of my family."

His grandfather closed his eyes.

"She knows," Lucius said, "just as well as I do that you have your heart set upon my marrying Portia."

Those keen eyes opened again.

"It is something Godsworthy and I have talked about over the years as a desirable outcome," he said. "But you must cast your mind back to Christmas time, Lucius, when I told you that your choice of bride must be your own. Marriage is an intimate relationship—of body and mind and even spirit. It can bring much joy if the partners are committed to friendship and affection and love—and much suffering if they are not."

"You will not be upset if I do not marry Portia, then?" Lucius asked. "And really, Grandpapa, I cannot. She is perfect in every way, but I am not."

His grandfather chuckled softly again.

"If I were a young man," he said, "and if I had not yet met your grandmother, Lucius, I do believe I would have fallen in love with Miss Allard myself. I have been aware of your growing regard for her."

"She had a sheltered upbringing," Lucius explained, "but there was no money left after her father died. She fell into the hands of Lady Lyle and George Ralston, of all people. He got her to sign a contract to manage her singing career. You can imagine if you will, sir, the kind of singing engagements he found for her. They were very much less than respectable. He and Lady Lyle raked in the money for a while—supposedly to pay off debts. Fontbridge was courting Frances, but the countess is too high a stickler to look kindly upon his wedding the daughter of a French émigré. Then Lady Lyle took a hand in breaking off the connection—Fontbridge had told Frances she would not be able to sing after their marriage, and doubtless Lady Lyle feared the loss of income. She dropped poison in Lady Fontbridge's ear. But her plan succeeded too well. Not only did the countess frighten Frances away from Fontbridge, but she also caused her to break away entirely from the life she had been living. She went to Bath without a word to any of them and has been teaching there ever since."

"My admiration for her has grown," the earl said. "And the fact that she has returned there now, Lucius, rather than allow herself to be swept away on Heath's enthusiasm and ours, shows steadiness and strength of character. I like her more and more."

"It is the poison dropped in the countess's ear that is of most concern to Frances, though," Lucius said. "It is that which she sees as disqualifying her most to be my bride. It seems that she was not Allard's daughter even though he married her mother before she was born—and knew when he married her that she was with child by another man. Frances does not know her real father's identity but assumes he was Italian, like her mother. Allard acknowledged her at birth and brought her up as his daughter and never breathed a word of the truth to her. But he *did* tell Mrs. Melford and Miss Driscoll—and Lady Lyle, who I gather was his mistress. By law, then, Frances is legitimate."

His grandfather lay with closed eyes for a long time. Lucius even thought that he might have drifted off to sleep. There was a slight gray tinge to his skin, and it looked parchment thin. Lucius felt rather like weeping—for the second time in one day. He stroked the hand he still held between his own.

"Lucius, my boy," his grandfather said at last, his eyes still closed, "your marriage to Miss Allard has my blessing. You may tell her so."

"Perhaps you can do that yourself, sir," Lucius said. "There is a prize-giving and concert at the school at the end of the school year. All of her choirs will be singing, and some of her individual music pupils will be performing too. I thought we might attend."

"We'll do it," his grandfather said. "But now I will rest, Lucius."

He was snoring lightly even before Lucius could tuck his hand beneath the blankets.

Lady Sinclair and her daughters were surprisingly easy to persuade.

Lucius's mother was so pleased to have him living at Marshall House and behaving responsibly—most of the time—and showing concern and kindness for his grandfather and a willingness to escort his sisters on various outings that she was sure she would be delighted with any bride he chose since she had quite reconciled herself to the idea that he might never be finished sowing his wild oats. And if Miss Allard's birth was of questionable legitimacy—well, so was that of a large segment of the *ton*. Genteel people simply did not talk of such matters.

A week later Lucius learned that she had made a point of speaking with the Countess of Fontbridge at Almack's the evening before when she had taken Emily there. She had deliberately brought the conversation around to Frances Allard and had talked quite openly about her birth and connections but had also given it as her opinion that a young lady of such modesty and gentility and astonishing talent could only be a desirable friend to cultivate and perhaps—who could know for sure?—even more than a friend to the family in time.

Oh, and did Lady Fontbridge know that Miss Allard was heir to both Mrs. Melford and Miss Driscoll, great-aunts of Baron Clifton? With both of whom ladies, by the way, she had such a close and loving relationship that there were *no* secrets between them whatsoever?

"I have never heard Mama talk like it before," Emily said proudly. "She quite outdid any of the tabbies in sweetness and venom, Luce. One could tell from the stiff, haughty look on the countess's face that she understood very well indeed."

"Emily," their mother said sharply, "do watch your tongue. Your mother a tabby, indeed!"

But everyone gathered about the breakfast table only laughed.

Margaret, who at Christmas time had been volubly in favor of Portia as her brother's bride, had married Tait for love and now gave it as her opinion that if Miss Allard was the woman Lucius loved, then *she* was not going to say anything to dissuade him. Besides, Tait had warned her long ago that Lucius would slit his throat rather than marry Portia when the time came.

Caroline, who was still living with her head in the clouds following her betrothal, could only applaud her brother's choice of someone with whom he was so obviously enamored. Besides, she still felt somewhat awed by Miss Allard's singing talent and thought that she would like very much to have her as a sister-in-law.

Emily had been severely disillusioned with Portia since seeing more of her than usual this spring. She did not think Portia at all right for Luce. Miss Allard, on the other hand, was perfect, as witness the fact that she had had the backbone to return to Bath to teach even though Luce had gone after her to try to persuade her to come back to London.

Amy was simply ecstatic.

A week or so after her meeting with the Countess of Fontbridge at

Almack's, the viscountess ran into Lady Lyle at a garden party to which she had taken both Caroline and Emily, and had a very similar sort of conversation with her about Frances—if conversation was the word, since Lady Sinclair did most of the talking and Lady Lyle listened with her habitual half-smile playing about her lips.

"But she *was* listening," Caroline reported afterward.

Lucius was not allowing his mother to fight all his battles, however. He encountered George Ralston at Jackson's boxing saloon one morning. Normally the two would have ignored each other, not because of any particular hostility between them but because they moved in totally different crowds. But on this particular morning Lucius took exception to the fall of Ralston's cravat and told him so—to the mystified surprise of his friends. And then, quizzing glass to his eye, Lucius noticed a splash of mud on one of Ralston's top boots and wondered audibly that anyone could keep such a slovenly valet unless he were basically slovenly himself.

He then, as if the thought had just struck him, invited Ralston to spar with him.

By now his friends' reaction had progressed from surprise to amazement.

It was not a friendly sparring bout. Ralston was incensed at the insults to which he had been subjected by one of society's most respected Corinthians, and Lucius was more than ready to give him satisfaction.

By the time Gentleman Jackson himself put a stop to the bout after six rounds of a planned ten, Lucius had shiny cheekbones and shinier knuckles and ribs that would remind him of the bout for several days to come, while Ralston had one eye reduced to a puffy slit, a cut over the other eye, a nose that glowed red and looked suspiciously as if it might be broken, and bruises about his arms and torso that would turn blacker by day's end and keep their owner awake and stiff for many days and nights to come.

"Thank you," Lucius said at the end of it all. "This has been a pleasure, Ralston. I must remember to tell Miss Frances Allard the next time I talk with her that I ran into you and spent a pleasant hour, ah, *conversing* with you. But perhaps you remember her as Mademoiselle

Françoise Allard. Lord Heath is eager to sponsor her singing career—had you heard? She may well take him up on the offer since she is quite free to do so. You met her, I believe, when she was still a minor? A long time ago. Perhaps you do not even remember her after all. Ah, you have a tooth loose, do you? If I were you, I would not wiggle it, old chap. It might settle back into place if you leave it alone. Good day to you."

"And what the devil was *that* all about?" one of the more obtuse of his friends asked him when they were out of earshot of Ralston.

"So *that* is the way the wind blows, is it, Sinclair?" a more astute friend asked with a grin.

It was indeed.

The two months until the end-of-year concert at Miss Martin's school in Bath seemed interminable. And of course they were fraught with anxiety for Lucius since there was no assurance that Frances would be pleased to see him again or that she would have him even though he would be arriving armed with the blessing of every single member of his family.

One never knew with Frances.

In fact, just *thinking* about her stubbornness could arouse severe irritation in him.

He was just going to have to kidnap her and elope with her if she said no again. It was as simple as that.

Or go down on his knees and plead.

Or sink into a romantic decline.

But he would not think of failing. His grandfather, who was ready to try the Bath waters again, and Amy, who was mortally tired of London, were going with him. So were Tait and Margaret, who would not miss the action for worlds, they said. At least *Tait* said that. Margaret was far more genteel and declared her eagerness to see Bath again, since she had not been there in five years.

And Mrs. Melford and Miss Driscoll were going, since Bath was not far off their route home and they were eager to see their dear Frances in the setting of her school. And they had always wanted to meet her friends there, including Miss Martin, and to hear her choirs.

Lucius strongly suspected that they had decided to go there after hearing that *he* was going. They wanted him to marry their great-niece.

And he, heaven help him, was more than willing to oblige.

The last month of the school year was always frantically busy. This year was no exception. There were examinations to set and mark, oral French examinations to administer, report cards to make out, prizewinners to select—and the final concert to prepare for.

That last was what consumed everyone's energies through every spare moment that was not taken up with academics and eating and sleeping—and even those last two activities had to be curtailed during the final week.

Frances was perhaps the busiest, since all the musical items with the exception of the country dancing were hers to prepare and perfect. But all the teachers had a part to play. Claudia was to be the mistress of ceremonies, and she had her own final speech to prepare. Susanna had written, cast, produced, and stage-managed a skit on school life and rehearsed with her girls for long hours and in great secrecy—and with much laughter, judging by the sounds that drifted down from her classroom. Mr. Upton had designed the stage sets for the whole concert, and Anne had a group of girls—plus David—producing them in the art room every afternoon and evening when they could escape from study and homework.

Frances had given Claudia notice effective the end of the year. She had *not* been running away when she came here more than three years ago. She had come to make her life better and to find herself, and she was proud of the success she had achieved at both. But if she stayed, she had decided after several sleepless nights and several frank talks with her friends, then she *would* be hiding from reality.

For reality and dreams had finally coincided, and if she turned away this time she would be denying fate and might never again have the chance to fulfill her destiny.

She was going to find Lord Heath. She was going to put herself in his hands and discover where her singing voice could take her.

She was going to follow her dream.

Anne and Susanna had both shed tears over her, though both vehemently declared that she was doing the right thing. But they would miss her dreadfully. Their life at the school would not be the same without her.

But they would never *speak* to her again, Susanna told her, if she did not go.

And they would hear of her progress and her fame, Anne told her, and burst with pride over her.

She was simply not going to accept the notice, Claudia declared. She would hire a replacement teacher until Christmas. If by then Frances wished to return, her position would be open for her. If not, then a permanent replacement would be made.

"You will not fail whatever happens, Frances," she said. "If you go on to sing as a career, then it will be what you were born to do. If you find that after all the life does not suit you, then you will return to what you do superbly well, as numerous girls who have been at this school during the past three years will testify for the rest of their lives."

And so the day of the concert dawned and progressed in the usual pattern, with every possible disaster threatening and being averted at the last possible moment—dancers could not find their dancing slippers and singers could not find their music and no one could find Martha Wright, the youngest pupil at the school, who was to be first on the stage to welcome the guests and who was finally found shut inside a broom closet, reciting her lines with tightly closed eyes and fingers pressed into her ears.

Susanna was peeping around the stage curtain shortly before the program was to begin to see if anyone had come—always the final anxiety of such evenings.

"Oh, my," she said over her shoulder to Frances, who was arranging her music on a music stand, "the hall is full."

It always was, of course.

"Oh, and look!" Susanna continued just when she had seemed about to drop the curtain back in place. "Come and *look,* Frances. Six rows back, left-hand side."

Frances always resisted the temptation to peep. She was too afraid that someone in the audience would catch her at it. But she could hardly refuse when Susanna looked at her with such saucer eyes and flushed cheeks—and then impish grin.

Frances looked.

Strangely, though they were more to the middle than the left, it was her great-aunts she saw first. But before she could react to the joy that welled up in her, she realized that Susanna had never met them and would not therefore recognize them. Her eyes moved left.

The Earl of Edgecombe sat next to Great-Aunt Martha, and then Lady Tait and Lord Tait and then Amy and then . . .

Frances drew a slow, long breath and allowed the curtain to fall into place.

"Frances." Susanna caught her up in a hug despite the curious glances of a few of the girls who were busy in the wings. There were tears in her eyes. "Oh, Frances, you are going to be *happy.* One of us is going to be happy. I am so . . . *happy.*"

Frances was too numb to feel anything except bewilderment.

But there was no time for feelings. It was seven o'clock, and Claudia always insisted that school functions begin promptly.

Anne appeared with Martha Wright, squeezed her thin shoulders and even kissed her cheek, and sent her out onto the stage.

The dress rehearsal during the afternoon had proceeded as badly as it possibly could. But Miss Martin had cheerfully assured girls and teachers alike that that was always a good sign and boded well for the real performance during the evening.

She was proved quite right.

The choirs sang in perfect pitch and harmony, the dancers were light on their feet and did not get tangled up in their ribbons even once, the choral speaking group recited with great verve and dramatic expression as if they were one voice, Elaine Rundel and young David

Jewell sang their solos to perfection, Hannah Swan and Veronica Lane played their duet on the old pianoforte without hitting a wrong key, though it must have been clear even to the least musical ear in the audience that the instrument had had its day and was not likely to have many more, and the skit Susanna's group performed, depicting teachers and girls preparing for a concert, drew laughter from the audience and applause even before it was finished.

The evening ended with a speech by Miss Martin, outlining some of the more significant achievements of the year, and then the presentation of prizes.

Frances never afterward knew how she had got through it all. Every time she was on stage conducting a choir and turned to acknowledge the applause of the audience, she saw either her great-aunts beaming up at her or the earl and Amy. She never once glanced at Lucius. She dared not.

But she knew he was smiling at her with that gleam in his eyes and that tight-lipped, square-jawed expression that demonstrated pride and affection and desire.

And love.

She no longer doubted that he loved her.

Or that she loved him.

The only thing she had doubted was the possibility that there could ever be any future for them.

But the Earl of Edgecombe was with him. So were Amy and Lord and Lady Tait. So were her great-aunts.

What could it mean?

She did not dare answer her own question.

She tried not even to ask it. She tried to concentrate on the concert, to give the girls the attention they deserved. Unwittingly, she gave them even more than usual, and they performed for her even better than they usually did.

But finally the last prize had been presented and the last applause had died away, and there was nothing left to do but go out into the hall with the girls and the other teachers to mingle with the guests while trays of biscuits and lemonade were handed around.

Great-Aunt Martha and Great-Aunt Gertrude were there waiting to hug Frances and exclaim over the loveliness of all the music. Amy was right behind them. Lord Tait bowed to her and Lady Tait smiled with something more than just graciousness in her manner. The Earl of Edgecombe, looking a little more stooped than usual, took both her hands in his, squeezed them, and told her that she appeared to be just as good a teacher as she was a singer—and *that* was saying something.

Lucius remained in the background and was in no hurry to come forward, it seemed. But Frances, glancing at him, felt as if her knees might buckle under her. His eyes were positively devouring her.

"Frances," he said at last, reaching for her hand and carrying it to his lips when she offered it, "I have said good-bye to you for the last time. I positively refuse to say it ever again. If you try to insist, I shall go off on my own without a word to sulk."

She could feel the color rising in her cheeks. Her great-aunts were listening. So were his grandfather and sisters and brother-in-law. So were Anne and David, who had come up behind her.

"Lucius!" she said softly.

He would not let her hand go. His eyes were definitely smiling now.

"The final impediment has been removed," he said as Susanna approached from behind him. "We have the blessing of every member of my family. I have not asked your great-aunts, but I would wager we have their blessing too."

"Lucius!"

She was beginning to feel horribly embarrassed. People were beginning to *look*. A number of the girls were beginning to nudge one another and titter. There was their teacher, Miss Allard, in the middle of the hall, her hand held close to the heart of a handsome, fashionable gentleman who was laughing down into her face, the expression on his own suggesting that it was more than just amusement he was feeling.

Claudia had noticed and was coming their way.

Frances looked at him in mute appeal.

And then her daring, impulsive, annoying, wonderful Lucius did surely the most reckless thing he had ever done in his life. He risked everything.

"Frances," he said without even trying to lower his voice or make the moment in any way private, "my dearest love, will you do me the great honor of marrying me?"

There were gasps and squeals and shushing noises and sighs. Someone sniveled—either Amy or one of the aunts.

It was the sort of marriage proposal, a distant part of Frances's brain thought, that no woman would ever even *dream* of receiving. It was the sort of marriage proposal every woman deserved.

She bit her lip.

And then smiled radiantly.

"Oh, yes, Lucius," she said. "Yes, of course I will."

She had been wrong. The last applause of the evening had not yet died away. Her cheeks flamed as everyone within hearing distance clapped again.

Viscount Sinclair, lowering his head as if to kiss the back of Miss Allard's hand, kissed her briefly and hard on the lips instead.

And then they were claimed by family and friends and squealing girls.

"And now," Claudia said at last with a sigh that was belied by warmly smiling eyes, "I suppose I am going to *have* to accept your resignation after all, Frances. But I always did say I would be prepared to do so in a good cause, did I not?"

26

The wedding of Miss Frances Allard and Viscount Sinclair was solemnized at Bath Abbey one month after the very public marriage proposal and acceptance.

The viscountess—soon to become the *dowager* viscountess—had wanted the nuptials to take place in London at St. George's on Hanover Square. Mrs. Melford had wanted them to be held in the village church at Mickledean in Somersetshire.

But much as her great-aunts were Frances's family, her friends at the school were at least as dear to her. And though Anne was planning to spend part of the summer in Cornwall, neither Susanna nor Claudia could leave Bath, as there were nine charity girls to care for at the school.

It was inconceivable to Frances that all three of her closest friends should not attend her wedding.

And Lucius put up no argument.

"Provided *you* are there, my love," he said, "I would be quite happy to marry in a barn on the farthest Hebridean island."

And so Frances was able to dress for her wedding in her own familiar room at the school—the very last day it would be hers—and say her own private farewells to her fellow teachers before they left for the church and she descended to the visitors' sitting room where Baron Clifton, her cousin of some remove, was waiting to escort her to the church and give her away.

"Frances," Susanna said, looking at her smart new pale blue dress and flower-trimmed bonnet, "you look so very beautiful. And you are going to be a *viscountess* today. All I can say is that it is a good thing Lord Sinclair is not a duke. I would fight you for him."

She laughed merrily at her own joke, but there were tears in her eyes too.

"I will leave your duke for you," Frances said, hugging her. "He will come along one of these days, Susanna, and sweep you off your feet."

"But how will he ever find me," the girl asked, "when I live and teach within the walls of a school?"

The question was lightly asked, but Frances could guess that Susanna, young and lovely though she was, probably despaired of ever making a marriage of her own or even of having a beau.

"He will find you," Frances assured her. "Lucius found me, did he not?"

"And kept finding you and finding you." Susanna laughed again and made way for Anne.

"Ah, you do look lovely, Frances," she said. "The dress and bonnet are handsome, but it is your glow of happiness that makes you beautiful. *Be* happy! But I know you will. It is a love match, and you are marrying an extraordinary man, who is going to allow you a career in singing—who is encouraging you to pursue it, in fact."

"You will be happy too, Anne," Frances said as they hugged. "I know you will."

"Oh," Anne said, "I *am* happy. I have David and I have this life. It is far preferable to what I had before, Frances. Here I belong."

She was smiling and very obviously delighted for her friend. But Frances always sensed a touch of sadness behind Anne's warm smiles.

But Claudia had appeared in the doorway of her room.

"Oh, Frances," she said, "*how* we are going to miss you, my dear. But it is not a day for self-pity. I am truly, truly happy for you."

Claudia Martin was not the type to do a great deal of hugging. Neither was she the type to weep for any reason. She did both now—

or if she did not actually weep, two tears definitely trickled down her cheeks.

"Thank you," Frances said while Claudia's arms were still about her. "Thank you for taking a chance on me when I was desperate. Thank you for making me feel like a professional teacher and a friend—and even a sister. Claudia, I want you to be this happy one day too. I *do* want it."

But then it was time for them to leave.

And soon after that it was time for Frances to go to her own wedding at the Abbey.

The congregation was not very large. Even so, a surprising number of people had come down from London for the occasion, including Baron Heath and his wife and stepchildren.

Most important, Lucius saw as he waited at the front of the Abbey for his bride to appear, all her family and friends, including the charity girls from the school, wearing their Sunday best, and all his family were in attendance.

Just a year ago he would have cringed at the thought of wanting all his family about him.

Just a year ago he would have cringed at the thought of marrying.

He certainly would not have believed that today—or any day—he would be marrying for love.

Ah, but *love* was not nearly a powerful enough word.

He *adored* Frances. He liked her and admired her in addition to all the romantic and lustful feelings he had for her.

And then there she was, stepping into the nave and approaching on Clifton's arm, slender and elegant and darkly beautiful.

He remembered his first sight of her—a fleeting glimpse as his carriage passed hers in the middle of a snowstorm. And he remembered his second sight of her as he hauled her out of her submerged carriage—a bedraggled virago, breathing fire and brimstone.

He remembered her making beef pie and bread.

He remembered her carving a smiling mouth on her snowman and stepping back to regard it with pleased satisfaction, her head tipped slightly to one side.

He remembered her waltzing with him and humming the tune.

He remembered stepping into the doorway of the Reynolds drawing room and discovering that the singer who had so captivated his soul was Frances Allard.

He remembered . . .

But today he did not have to rely upon memory from which to draw pleasure. Today they were here before their family and friends to pledge themselves to a lifetime together.

She was here at his side, her very dark eyes luminous with the wonder of the moment.

It was a moment he would live to the full now while it was happening—and a moment he would hold in memory for the rest of his life.

He smiled at her, and she smiled back.

"Dearly beloved . . ." the clergyman began.

The morning had been cloudy with the threat of possible rain. But when Viscount Sinclair stepped out into the Abbey Yard with his new viscountess on his arm, the sun was shining down from a sky of pure blue.

"We have gone through some extremes of weather together, my love," he said, looking down on her. "But now we have sunshine. Do you suppose it is a good omen?"

"It is nothing," she said, "but a lovely day. We do not need omens, Lucius, only our own will to grasp our destiny and live it."

He took her hand and they dashed across the yard, past the small crowd of interested spectators who had stepped out of the Pump Room, and beneath the arches to the carriage that awaited them with Peters up on the box. It would take them back to the school, where a wedding breakfast awaited them and their guests.

"The hall has been forbidden to me for the past two days," Frances explained. "But Claudia and Anne and Susanna have been in there for long hours at a time with the girls. I think they have been decorating the room."

Lucius laced his fingers with hers.

"It will doubtless be a work of art," he said. "We will admire it, Frances, and greet our guests and be happy with them. Today I have kept a promise, and my grandfather has lived to see it. And today we have made two elderly sisters, your great-aunts, very happy. But now, this moment, is ours alone. I do not intend to waste it. Ah, *this* is convenient."

The carriage was making a sharp turn onto the Pulteney Bridge and had thrown them together.

"Very." Frances looked across at him with bright, laughing eyes.

He wrapped one arm about her shoulders, lowered his head, and kissed her long and thoroughly.

Neither of them seemed the slightest bit concerned that there were no curtains to cover the windows.

The world was welcome to share their happiness if it so chose.

Coming soon from Piatkus Books

Simply Love

Mary Balogh

Anne Jewell is a teacher at Miss Martin's School for Girls, a genteel academy in Regency England. Now she must confront the disturbing tragedy that gave her a beautiful son but locked her heart away many years ago.

While on a summer holiday in Wales, Anne meets Sydnam Butler, a taciturn hero of the Peninsula Wars. Gentle yet courageous, he is unlike any man Anne has ever encountered. But he too carries scars of the past. When Anne returns to St Martin's, she makes a surprising discovery and has no choice but to test Sydnam's love. Their passion becomes a showdown between long-buried fears and grand dreams . . .

Simply Love is the second book in a dazzling quartet of Regency novels. Set in a select academy for young ladies, Mary Balogh invites us into a special world – a world of innocence and temptation . . .